From Here
to
Fourteenth Street

by

Diana Rubino

The New York Saga, Book One

From Here to Fourteenth Street

Cover Art by *Debbie Taylor*

The Wild Rose Press, Inc.
PO Box 708
Adams Basin, NY 14410-0708
Visit us at www.thewildrosepress.com

Publishing History: previously published by Domhan Books, 2000, as *I Love You Because*
First American Rose Edition, 2015
Print ISBN 978-1-5092-0402-1
Digital ISBN 978-1-5092-0403-8

The New York Saga, Book One
Published in the United States of America

Dedication

To my ancestors who came to America for a better life:
God bless you and God bless America.

"My father told me, 'You see that boy? When he come here, you give him a little bit more, no charge him, he no got no father.' "

—*Angela Rosati, daughter of an Italian immigrant grocer in Queens, New York*

"Another policeman. Theodore something, I think he said."

No. There can't be anything wrong. "Thanks," she whispered, gently nudging Madame Branchard aside. She descended the steps, gripping the banister to support her wobbly legs. *Stay calm!* she warned herself. But of course it was no use; staying calm just wasn't her nature.

"Theodore something" stood before the closed parlor door. *He's a policeman?* Curious, she looked him up and down. Tall and hefty, a bold pink shirt peeking out of a buttoned waistcoat and fitted jacket, he looked way out of place against the dainty patterned wallpaper.

He removed his hat. "Miss Caputo." He strained to keep his voice soft as he held out a piece of paper.

"Yes?" Her voice shook.

"I'm Theodore Roosevelt. I have a summons for you, Miss Caputo." He held it out to her. But she stood rooted to that spot.

He stepped closer and she took it from him, unfolding it with icy fingers. Why would she be served with a summons? Was someone arresting her now for something she didn't do?

A shot of anger tore through her at this system, at everything she wanted to change. It eclipsed her fear, made her blood boil. She flipped it open and saw the word "Summons" in fancy script at the top. Her eyes widened with each sentence as she read. "I can't believe what I'm seeing."

Praise for Diana Rubino

Winner of the Romantic Times Top Award for
The Wild Rose Press urban fantasy *FAKIN' IT*

~*~

"FROM HERE TO FOURTEENTH STREET by Diana
Rubino is all that and then some. Everything about this
book is what writing should be—original and
wonderfully executed. Bravo!"

~*Karen L. Williams, Rhapsody Magazine*

~*~

"Vita and Tom face economic problems, prejudice, and
cultural differences. Ms. Rubino's research is obvious."

~*Kathe Robin, Romantic Times*

~*~

"A masterful job of researching the life of Italian and
Irish immigrants in turn-of-the-century New York, its
society and politics and crime. She paints a vivid
picture of the degradation immigrants of Italian descent
suffered, particularly at the hands of the earlier Irish
immigrants they succeeded. …If you like vivid
characters and a book that carries you effortlessly back
to an earlier time, *FROM HERE TO FOURTEENTH
STREET* is a good choice."

~*Elizabeth Burton,*
Book Nook Romance Reviews

~*~

Other books in the New York Saga
at The Wild Rose Press, Inc.
The End of Camelot (Book Three)
Bootleg Broadway (Book Two)

Chapter One

Mott Street, New York City's Lower East Side
August 1894

Vita crushed a cockroach with her shoe and bundled her hand-stitched blouses in her arms. Stepping into her tenement hallway, she held her breath and dashed past the shared toilet. The stench sickened her. She rushed down the stairs and into the sticky morning. Pushcart peddlers jammed the street. The pungent odors of raw fish, horse dung, and sweat hit her all at once.

Crossing the street, she saw an urchin lift a cop's billfold from his back pocket. Trying to fix a broken wheel, the cop didn't turn around.

"Hey! Gimme that, you!" Vita snatched the billfold from the guttersnipe's hand. He kicked her in the shin.

"Ow!" She grasped her leg. Her blouses scattered on the ground. He darted into the crowd and vanished.

Straightening up, she met a pair of sharp green eyes. The cop thrust his hand out, palm up.

She gave him the wallet. "I didn't take this! A street kid slid it from your pocket and I saved it!"

His eyes narrowed. "So where is this kid?"

An ear-shattering gunshot ripped through the air. Heads turned. Mr. Violino, the tailor, staggered out of his shop and collapsed.

Oh, poor Mr. Violino! How could anyone want to

hurt such a sweet old man? Poverty turned everybody against one another, even Italians.

"Don't you dare move, miss," the cop ordered. "I need to get to that shooting, so stay where you are. Or else." He pushed through the mob to the crime scene.

Or else what? She wasn't afraid of cops. But her boss—he decided whether she ate or starved. She turned and ran the other way.

Dodging heaps of trash, she swerved to avoid a dead horse lying in the street. Three half-starved urchins in filthy clothes jumped and played on the rotting carcass.

At Canal Street, she entered the smoke-belching factory. Stark and ugly in muddy brick, it mocked her as she leaned on the wooden door. Climbing the dark stairwell to the sweltering third floor, she braced herself against the wave of body odor. "No leatherhead cop is gonna keep me from my job," she vowed through clenched teeth. Her vision of his green eyes faded as she bent over her sewing machine to suffer another day of drudgery.

Toiling over the mind-numbing work, she conjured up her favorite daydream: an elegant brownstone with lacy iron gates, bay windows, polished floors, marble fireplaces. No trash flung down air shafts, no shared toilets, no backyard privies...

...above Fourteenth Street.

****

Tom McGlory strode down Mott Street, her image in his mind. He held her dropped blouses, filthy and beyond repair. He must've scared the bejeezus out of her that morning. No wonder she didn't wait around like he'd ordered.

He approached the Broome Shirtwaist Factory. It looked like a jailhouse—bars on the windows, stark and dreary. As he entered, the walls closed in on him. He gasped for air. He could hardly breathe in here. Man alive, what a tomb! The steady rat-a-tat of sewing machines rattled his teeth. Thank God his job took him outdoors.

Tom walked down the narrow aisle. Hunched over their machines, not one woman dared look up at him. He stopped at a beat-up metal desk. The boss chomped on a cigar, his shirt straining at the buttons.

"Yeah?" he croaked, tipping his head back to meet Tom's gaze. "Whadda you want—officer?"

"A girl who works here dropped these." Tom placed the blouses on the desk. "She's got red hair, about yay high"—he indicated Vita's height—"and blue-gray eyes, slender, wearing a green skirt and white blouse—"

"Nah, never seen 'er." He cut Tom off, snatched the blouses, and waved him away like a fly.

"You sure? They have the factory mark on them."

"Over a hunnerd gals work here. I ain't never seen one looks like that." He shooed Tom away again and spat onto the floorboards.

She's worth the wait. With an about-face, Tom exited the factory, bought some grapes from a vendor, and waited for her to come out at quitting time. He glanced at his pocket watch. Should be about twenty more minutes. In the stream of the "hunnerd gals" in all shapes and sizes, he'd find her.

****

Vita hunched over her piecework, imprisoned in the numbing toil. A hairy hand clamped down on her shoulder. She looked up at Mr. Strozzoni—Wrench Neck they called him, because of the way he strained his neck, a nervous tic or something. Sweat stained his celluloid collar. "Hey. A copper come lookin' for you," he rasped in his cigar-gruffed voice. "He wait for you outside."

"What copper?"

He yanked her up by the elbow and dragged her to the door like he couldn't get rid of her fast enough. Twenty rows of eyeballs rolled, and their gaze followed her out of the workroom. She stumbled, dizzy with fright. Oh, no, Butchie got run in again? Her brother couldn't stay out of trouble.

Wrench Neck shoved her out into the stairwell. "Don' you come back here no more. You're a thief. We don' wan' no thiefs here."

Thief? She'd never stolen a spool of thread. Then it hit her—the blouses she'd dropped in the street. Someone must've turned them in—but who knew *she'd* dropped them?

It didn't matter now. She was out of a job. Still in shock, she couldn't think straight.

Her shoes clanged down the metal stairs. She went outside and squinted in the sun.

An imposing figure startled her. Those green eyes. It couldn't be…it was the cop from this morning.

He stood before her, arms folded across his chest.

She turned, ready to bolt, but a silent command told her to stay put.

"You dropped some blouses on the street this morning." His voice was gentler than it had been earlier. So he'd found the blouses! "They had the factory label," he went on. "I described you to the boss man. He told me he'd never seen you. But I could tell he was lying." His arms unfolded. His posture relaxed. "I had to wait for you. Why are you out before everybody else?"

She stepped back. Her bottom smacked into the brick wall. "Why do you think? He just fired me. But I didn't take your wallet. A street arab took it."

He nodded. "I believe you. I'm not accusing you of anything."

"Then why are you waiting for me?" She tilted her head, really curious now.

"I just wanted to find you." He took a step forward. "Look, let me help you get another job. I feel responsible—"

She gaped up at him. The sun formed a halo of light about him. His jawline curved nicely, not too square. "No, you done enough already." She turned away but needed one last glimpse of those green eyes. As she turned, she tripped over her own feet.

He grabbed her arm to steady her. "I'm just clumsy," she stammered.

"It's quite all right," he said.

No one ever said *quite*, not around here. A smile frolicked on his lips, as if he knew she'd been staring. Crescent laugh lines cut into his cheeks.

"I really want to help you." His voice softened with apology.

Shaking her head, she started to leave, but he walked beside her. She sneaked sideways glances at him. The planes of his face weren't weatherbeaten like those of the railroad yard laborers. Black hair crowned his head in glossy waves. It reminded her of long-ago nights in Italy, the sky bejeweled with stars. A trimmed mustache rimmed his upper lip. Muscles bulged beneath his blue jacket. His gravity seemed to mask some deeper emotion. She sensed sadness in those eyes that held a spark of streetwise spirit.

Neighbors halted in their tracks and stared with narrowed eyes. Vita Caputo in trouble with the law now? She pictured them saying, *Eh, the whole tribe's a bunch of rowdies,* over their purple wine tonight, Mott Street buzzing with gossip louder than the organ grinders. Head held high, she matched them cocked brow for cocked brow. But inside she went on praying—*I need another job, I need another job!*

"Will you tell me your name? Please?" He drew her from her thoughts. A shiver of alarm coursed through her. *Should I tell him my real name or give him a fake one?*

"It would be an offense to withhold your identity from a policeman." He ended that with a smile that sent strange tingles through her belly.

"Miss Caputo. Now goodbye." She didn't want him calling her Vita.

His lashes blinked like bats' wings. "Your father wouldn't be Lorenzo Caputo, would he?"

"What if he is?" she shot back.

"Then your brothers are Bruno and Vincente."

He knew her family, all right, but not as friends, since they were just Larry, Butchie, and Vinny around here. But cops weren't on her family's list of friends, either. To them, cops rated lower than parish priests.

"Does that have anything to do with me?" She steadied her voice.

"No, but they've been booked for minor offenses before, and assaulting a policeman twice—my cousin

6

Mike McGlory." The stern tone returned as he swung his nightstick.

"I know what they did, and I ain't proud of it," she admitted. "But here I am, obeying the law, and I get kicked outta my job."

Her family's offenses ranged from starting a brawl at a cousin's wedding to robbing geraniums to assaulting a cop. To them, the first two were none of the law's business. The fight at the wedding was over whose wine was better. The flower-robbing, in Vinny's eyes, was legit—"God put them here, so why should I pay for 'em?" was his reasoning. Simple Italian logic.

She looked up at the cop, almost hoping she'd trip again so he'd catch her. But he was still the leatherhead who put her out on the streets.

"I'm Tom McGlory, and I want to help you find another job. Where are you headed, Miss Caputo?" His question sounded innocent enough, but his butting in riled her. She took a deep breath to calm down.

She set her eyes straight ahead at the horse and cart parked by the grocer's. "It's none a your business where I'm headed," she snapped. She didn't trust cops. Maybe he wanted to use her for something. Cops bamboozled immigrants into doing their dirty work. She wasn't falling for none of his lowdown schemes.

"Since your visit cost me my job, the only place I can go is looking for another one so I can eat tonight." Why not sling some guilt his way? Maybe, if he was half human, he'd appreciate what she'd just gone through.

"I'm sorry for the trouble all this has caused you." Again, his tone gentled. "I can talk to your boss. He should take you back. I'll head back there right this minute and explain that you stopped a robbery and that's how you dropped the blouses."

"Don't do me no favors, Officer." She held up her hand. "You don't owe me nothin'." She glanced around for a clock so she could figure how much money she'd lost already. She wasn't about to ask him for the time of day. She had to find another job before she lost a whole day's pay. Forget a kitchen curtain—that got shoved onto the luxury list. They might have to give up eggs and eat stale bread for a while.

"Then may I escort you somewhere?" he pushed on, his voice casual, yet his eyes sparkled.

She knew hers didn't, so she avoided his stare.

He gave her *agita* in her stomach. But he seemed so kind. She'd seen strong-arms in action, and he wasn't one of them. Still, she didn't need his help. "No, I need to get myself into another wage-paying job. Nobody's paying me to make chit-chat with a cop." They halted at the corner as a streetcar rumbled past. "But I have one question first."

"What is it?" His eyes lit up.

"Why would you wanna help me? I ain't even Irish."

She didn't wait for an answer because she didn't care. She just wanted him to think about it. She turned and walked away, hoping to lose him.

She wished she had a pocket full of rocks, to feast on a sausage sandwich and enjoy this rare stint of freedom. But forget it. Leisure—and big lunches—were luxuries she'd have to wait many more years to afford. Now she had to skip lunch until she found a job.

Walking toward the nearest factory, self-scolding comments fell from her lips: "You're a fool, letting thoughts of this cop amuse you!" This fantasy was no different from her daydreams at the sewing machine to fight the deadening boredom. But at that rattling machine, she made her lofty plans. In her quest to get ahead, she attended neighborhood meetings for tenement reform with her cousin Baldo, the "mayor" of Mott Street. All the streets down here had unofficial mayors, businessmen on the lookout for the neighborhoods. Baldo, a barber, got along great with everybody. He and Vita badgered the ward heeler, the district boss, and sometimes even a sympathetic reporter, demanding decent living conditions. But she had to do more.

She saw how bosses treated her family, how cops and judges took payoffs from politicians and let criminals off, and how slumlords made their tenants live six families to a flat. But hers was one of the blessed families on Mott Street. They had plumbing.

She dashed down Orchard Street, past the crowded tenements where the poorest souls lived. She had to end the dreaming and get back to the heat, the stench, the real world out there. Hunger for food replaced her hunger for reform.

She pushed Officer McGlory out of her thoughts. The face-off with the cop was over. But his presence still sent tingles down her spine.

****

Tom watched her walk away. Her proud bearing was not that of the usual immigrant pieceworker. A tough exterior fronted the delicate beauty. Wisps of her auburn hair escaped from her bun, framing her polished features. He could tell, despite her toil in the factory, she took time to care for her hair and her skin. "I believe in you, Vita," he said and didn't care who heard.

Those poor Italians, how they suffered. It broke his heart. This lovely woman now on the streets without a job was one of them, yet she seemed to have risen above that. She carried herself with dignity. Oh, she'd make it out of here someday, all right.

Now she was out on the street because of him. He needed to find her another job. A decent one.

Just as she turned the corner and vanished, his heart leapt. An invisible force pushed him: *No, don't let her go!* He ran after her. "Miss Caputo, wait!"

She turned, eyes wide with surprise.

"Miss Caputo, to make amends, may I please do just one little thing for you?" He straightened his collar.

"No, you done enough for me. Now just—"

"Please." He leaned forward.

She looked him up and down, and her eyes clouded in distress.

"I just thought of something. I know a bank that's hiring clerks. They have immediate openings. Please go there. They'll hire you. I'll make sure of it." The words rushed out in one breath.

She shook her head, strands of hair following the delicate curve of her cheekbones. "Oh, no, forget it. I'll get my own job. I know nothin' about banks, I can only sew and do piecework. For now, anyways."

"They're not looking for someone highly skilled. They want young energetic people they can train their way. It's the New York Bank and Trust on the northwest corner of 20th Street and Fifth Avenue. You'd be perfect for the job."

"No, I don't want nothin' from—"

"Vita! Hey!" Her brother Butchie stalked toward them, his hulking chest straining under a cotton skivvy shirt. "What the hell you doin'?" He shot Tom a dirty look. "Leave her alone, you!"

Butchie shoved her behind him, spitting out accusations in Italian. "What ya doin' wit' my sister, ya dirty cop?" he growled.

"It's all right, Butchie. He's a clean cop." Vita stepped forward. Butchie's eyes looked like bullets waiting to pierce Tom's heart.

"He knows I'm a clean cop, I've seen him get booked enough times," Tom shot back. A few months ago, Butchie'd gotten into a brawl with Tom's cousin Mike in Mulberry Bend. Butchie did time. He'd loathed Mike ever since. Tom knew Butchie didn't give a fig about his sister—he was just being his obnoxious self.

"I'm telling your sister about a job," Tom explained.

Butchie turned to Vita and jerked his thumb in Tom's direction. "Don't trust this crum bum."

"I don't!" She brushed her hair off her face.

How badly Tom wanted to touch that hair, just to see how soft it really was.

"I was telling him to leave me alone." She shot Tom a pleading look as if to say, *Just go away. My brother is embarrassing me.*

Butchie stepped up to Tom, reeking of stale cigarette smoke and garlic. "Stay away from my sista." He poked Tom in the chest for emphasis.

Tom could've run the ruffian in for assault, but he didn't bother. Italians touched everybody when they talked. He longed to make eye contact with Vita as she gave her brother a deadly glare. His last sight of her was Butchie tugging her away as she swatted him with her bag. Tom had to laugh through his sadness. He hoped she'd turn around and look at him, but she didn't. Oh, he had to get her that bank job.

****

Butchie dragged Vita home, his hand clamped around her wrist like a handcuff, jawin' about what a disgrace she was. "You cavortin' on the street with that crum bum cop…" She didn't bother arguing back. Most things weren't worth arguing about with her family.

They trudged up the dark stairwell, past the festering garbage piled in the corners. She almost stumbled into the toilet on the landing between the flats as he shoved their door open. It banged against the wall and wobbled. She tripped on the warped floorboards. Gathering her skirt, she sat at the scarred table. As usual, her stepmother had removed Vita's prized possession—her tablecloth.

Papa shambled in, buckling his belt. She took a good look at him. Daylight slanted through the dirty window, lighting the streaks of his thinning hair, the same gray as the ship railing she could never forget. He coughed and wheezed, blowing his nose into a hankie.

"You know where she was?" Butchie started in. "She was on the street with McGlory, that cruddy cop."

"Why?" Papa's fist pounded the battered kitchen table. "Why you do this to us? He hates us, they all hate us."

"It was nothin', Papa," she answered. "He was tellin' me about some job. I wasn't interes—"

"Don' you talk to no Irish cop." Papa's voice rasped, thick with catarrh. "They think they better than us, make us sit in back-a the church, and you talk to one of 'em? You lucky he don' run you in for a streetwalker, just cause he feel like." He grabbed his wine jug off the windowsill and took a swig.

She couldn't tell them what had happened that morning. He hated her being with this cop for one reason, his name. McGlory.

She thought of Tom, hiding a secret smile. Maybe he did want to help her. He thought enough of her to send her uptown for a job. What a noble gesture! But if she didn't get another job, would he really care? Of course not. His job was on the streets; he dealt with tramps and vagrants and street arabs. "Nobody but family cares," Papa had taught her. The Italians who set their fellow immigrants up with jobs were as brutal as bums slitting throats for pennies.

No, the cop didn't care. *Ptui* on him. Her smile vanished into a snarl.

The door swung open and in flounced her stepmother, Rosalia, sporting ankle-high button-up shoes. She'd either bought them with grocery money or swapped with one of the neighbors. She dutifully kissed Papa on the cheek. But there was nothing dutiful about Rosalia's role as Papa's wife. They all knew she slipped in and out of rum-holes on his card-playing nights and stayed out till minutes before he got home. Vita couldn't blame her; Rosalia was only ten years older than she was, sent here to marry Papa after Vita's mother died.

Rosalia had worked in a feather factory when she first got here, but the swirling fluff gave her asthma. She'd never worked a day since.

"Whatcha screamin' about?" Rosalia pulled off her shoes and tossed them under the table.

"None of your business what we're screamin' about." Butchie got up and leaned out the window, his muscles tense underneath the thin shirt.

"I'll see ya's later." Vita headed for the door. She had to get a job—fast. She pinned her hair back up into its tight bun.

"Where you go, back with that cop?" Butchie cracked his knuckles.

"What cop?" Rosalia turned from the sink, tipping a pan over, droplets of grease splattering on the floor.

"Hey, I scrubbed that yesterday." Vita sopped it up with a towel.

"That crum McGlory. Butchie caught him talkin' to her in the street," Papa said.

"Mike McGlory?" Rosalia's amused smirk brought out the wrinkles around her eyes. Her face soured again when Papa glared at her.

"Not Mike. His cousin or somethin'," Vita interjected.

"Why ain't you at work anyway?" Papa turned to Vita, as if he'd just realized she wasn't supposed to be there.

"I got fired."

"Ah, *madonna mia*," Butchie spat.

Vita ground her teeth and headed for the door, calling over her shoulder, "I'll have another job by tonight, and it'll be better than anything you can get!"

"Yeah, you go, you get anudder job." Papa's last words died inside his wine jug as he swigged some more. "Butchie, walk 'er down."

"Don't bother, Butchie." She turned her back on him and strode out.

"No. I walk you." His voice tight with apology, he

followed her.

She went down the stairs, holding the wobbly banister. The place was a nightmare—the arguing, the heat, the bugs. It made them all say cruel things they didn't mean, and they had short tempers to begin with. It all came out of the endless struggle to survive.

Vita and Butchie headed east on Bayard and made a left onto Bowery. Neighborhood Italians owned all the shops here. Factories would be her last resort.

They stopped in front of Gallucci's Millinery Shop. "I'll be fine, Butchie. You ain't gotta follow me around."

"I wanna make sure you won't get cornered by that leatherhead again."

"Butchie, there's a lot worse that can happen to me than a cop cornering me, believe it or not. He was—" She knew he would never believe this. "He was tryin' to be nice to me, me gettin' fired and all. Forget about him."

"Then I see you tonight." He turned and loped away.

But she wasn't going home until she had a job.

Gallucci's had nothing. She hadn't thought they would; she'd just wanted Butchie out of her way. Wanting to do this right, she went to her friend Angie Paluzzi's on Elizabeth Street to map out a job-seeking route. Their front tenement faced the street. Mrs. Paluzzi took in boarders, but during the day she worked at home alone. On the way over, Vita gave half her change to a bum, wishing she could buy him a decent meal.

"Vita! *Avanti!* Come in!" Mrs. Paluzzi called from two floors up. Vita climbed the stairs and held her breath to block out the stench of garbage. But here she'd have a view of the street instead of dead chickens falling down an air shaft.

Vita's stomach growled, but she didn't want to ask Mrs. Paluzzi to feed her. Mercifully, her friend's mother fixed sausage and peppers without asking. Vita devoured it in three bites.

"Why ain't you at work?" Mrs. Paluzzi asked as Vita wiped her hands on a towel.

"I got fired. I'm gonna look for another job when I leave here. I just wanted to come here and think for a while. You know how hard that is to do over our place."

"Wha' happen?" Mrs. Paluzzi cleared the table. "My Angie, she get fire too?"

"No, it was a…just a misunderstanding, but I'll find somethin' better, I know it."

"I know you will too." Mrs. Paluzzi went back to her work, putting yellow centers into forget-me-nots. Her nimble fingers made more than the standard three cents a gross. "Where you gonna look?"

"I'll start with the shops. Martinelli's, Ugo's, the others. Then, next year, I'll try something on Wall Street—maybe one of those places where they sell stocks."

Mrs. Paluzzi beamed at her. "Ah, I can say I knew little Vita. Now she deals in big money!"

"Oh, I don't know if I'd be dealing with any big money. All I could get to start is a clerk's job. But I'm gonna dress nice, hold my head up, show them what a hard worker I am, let them know I graduated grade school…and use a different name."

"What kind of different name?" Mrs. Paluzzi's

fingers didn't stop.

"An American name." She went over to the sink and got a glass of water. "So I'll take no chances. I'll still be Vita Caputo around here, but I gotta be a real American to get a good job."

"You *are* a real American." Her voice rose.

"Yeah, but in places like Wall Street they don't think so." Vita went back to the table and sat.

"What you call yourself, then?" Mrs. Paluzzi broke the thread with her teeth and expertly threaded another needle.

"How does Violet Greene sound? With an extra 'e' at the end?"

Mrs. Paluzzi smiled. "Like-a something you plant in your garden."

"I think it sounds cultured." Vita waved a pretend fan through the air.

"Why Greene?" She kept on stitching.

"It's a solid American-sounding name, and those money people love anything green."

Mrs. Paluzzi laughed. "You lucky you don't look Napolitan. But you also smart girl. You go uptown, you use American name, you won' get kicked around."

Now Vita needed to tell her about the decision to stay away from home till she got a job. "Signora P., can I come back here for supper? I'm ashamed to go home."

"Why you ashame?"

"I told them I won' be back till I got a job. I don' wanna go back on my word. So—just in case I don' find nothin', can I come back here?" Her throat still dry, she gulped more water.

Mrs. Paluzzi nodded. Thank God she understood.

"You come back here for supper, but I want you right back with your family where you belong."

There it was again. Family. Oh, how she wished she'd been born into a different one.

****

She tried the paper-box plants, the artificial flower shops, even the candy factories. "I'll carry trays and shell nuts," she promised. But they all turned her away. That didn't discourage her, though—she marched on, the fire of determination in her belly. She still had the streets east of Bowery to cover. But she didn't go past Fourteenth Street. She didn't belong there. Yet. She'd get there someday, but in small steps, not leaps. Wall Street and uptown seemed like a million miles away in both directions.

****

"You comin' up for supper?" Angie Paluzzi asked Vita as they went up Angie's stairway at six o'clock. Vita leaned on Angie's arm for support. Her parched throat hurt as she swallowed. Sweat drenched her blouse. "When Mama tol' me you got fired, I acted surprised, but they was buzzin' about it all day. The gossip buzzed louder than the machines! What the hell happen?" Angie lowered her voice to a whisper as they approached her apartment door.

"I stopped a street arab from pickpocketing a cop," Vita said. "The cop came to the factory to thank me, but old Wrench Neck threw me out. I ruined some of his blouses, and he thought I stole 'em."

Angie's gasp echoed through the hallway and died in the depths of the plaster peelings all around them. "Oh, *Madonne!*" She blessed herself.

"Of course it couldn't be any cop. It hadda be the

one who Vinny had that fight with's cousin." She let out a heavy sigh, going over those events in her mind, stopping at the same place—when her eyes first met Tom McGlory's. "Don't tell your mother any of this."

"No, I won't tell her nothin'." Angie walked ahead of her and pushed the door open. "But she knows you got fired."

"Yeah, I told her." Vita followed her friend inside.

"Okay then. Let's forget it and eat."

****

Mrs. Paluzzi let Vita stay the night there. "But only one night. Then you go back home. Butchie come down here lookin' for you about an hour ago. He's gonna come back again after, I know it." She shook her finger, but Vita was too tuckered out to argue—she closed her eyes and stretched her weary muscles.

"Just tell him you don't know where I am. I don't wanna go back till I get a job. Like I said." Vita rubbed her eyes and helped herself to a glass of water.

Mrs. Paluzzi clasped her hands and raised them to heaven. "I say a novena for you. But don't you be ashame. They your family, Vita."

"I know that. But I'll go back tomorrow. After I get a job. A good one. I'm no use to them right now." She gulped down her water.

After supper, she took a pillow, loosened her clothes, and slept out on the fire escape across from Mrs. Paluzzi's eight-year-old son Nicholas. At least the air out there circulated a little.

By noon the next day, not having found a job, Vita offered to watch Mr. Mongibelli's cart for a few hours, while he went to tend his sick wife, in exchange for three oranges and a bunch of grapes. The cart stood kitty-corner to Joey Cap's Saloon, where the cops always went for a beer after their beat. *Is Tom in there?* she wondered. Her heart danced. She stared at the saloon's frosted glass doors, hoping to see him, praying he wouldn't see her. An image of him flashed in her mind. She counted so many emotions in those eyes: compassion, interest, and...pity. She realized she hadn't thought of him all morning. Then a flash of light hit her from across the street. A dressed-up Rosalia slipped into the saloon's ladies' entrance, the sun glinting off the frosted glass as she threw the door open. Her open blouse buttons exposed her neck. *So she's on the prowl again.* Vita sighed, shaking her head.

****

Tom, hot and sticky in his uniform, longed for another horn but had to be content with the two beers he'd just had; he was going on duty. He ran a finger under his collar. He sat in Joey Cap's with Mike, his fellow police officer and cousin.

"Hey, what's bothering you, Tom?" Mike slurped his beer. He'd just gotten off duty and tucked into his corned beef sandwich. After two nickel beers, "Moose" Murphy, the owner, gave cops a free lunch.

Tom slapped together some cheese and cold ham between two slices of rye. "Just tired, I guess." He took a bite. Tom didn't want to repeat yesterday's events. Then they'd get talking about Lorenzo Caputo and his sons, and he knew Mike didn't want to hear that name again. But ever since Vita's brother dragged her away, Tom couldn't stop thinking about her. How had she made out? Had the father beat her? He wished he could've escorted her home to make sure they wouldn't lay a hand on her.

Mike nodded, taking a long draw of his beer. He knew when to leave Tom alone.

When Tom stepped outside, back on duty, dazzling sunshine startled him. Then he saw her—Vita—tending Mr. Mongibelli's pushcart. His heart skipped a beat.

Tom watched her talking to Mongibelli, her hands waving in lively gestures. Her hair's luster winked back at the sun. Her eyes accented her fair skin, flushed with a pink tinge, the color of blossoms. She held her head high with a proud composure. Her presence graced the ugliness around her. He wanted so badly to part those lips in a kiss…

Mongibelli gave her a few coins. She thanked him, slid them into her pocket, looked up, and saw Tom. Her face turned ashen. Tom walked toward her with a big grin. *Oh, thank God she's all right.*

"Hello, Vi—Miss Caputo." He plucked his hat off, grabbed an apple off the cart, and overpaid Mongibelli. "It's nice to see you again. You're looking well."

The color came back into her cheeks. Her posture eased. Guilt stabbed at him—how could he be so selfish? He shouldn't want to talk to her so soon after yesterday. She must still be shaken up over that. "Have you found another job?"

"No, no, I haven't. Not yet." She turned to the peddler. "*A presto.*"

"May I walk a ways with you?" Tom asked as they headed down Canal Street, sidestepping heaps of trash.

"No, you better not. I mean, I better not." Her eyes darted around, no doubt on the lookout for her brother.

"Don't worry about him seeing us together. I'll protect you now, and I'll protect you later," he promised.

21

She raised a brow and took another glance around. A corner of her mouth lifted. She looked at him and nodded. "Okay. Well...at least I won't get robbed now. But you might." She gave him a sideways once-over before turning back to watch where she was going. He hoped she'd stumble like she did yesterday, so he could catch her in his arms again.

"Hey, some of these street arabs are good at their trade. Even a cop can be blindsided." He didn't want to let her go. He needed to know if she was okay, if she had enough money, enough to eat. Although these things were none of his business, he wanted *her* to be his business.

He wanted her.

"Did everything go well for you yesterday, with your family, I mean?"

"It's really none of your concern, Officer." She kept her voice steady.

He'd expected that reply, so he didn't even wince. "I was just hoping you'd be all right."

"Well, you can save your time. You caused me enough trouble already." She quickened her pace, her shoes clumping on the pavement.

Why should she confide in a nosy cop? he asked himself. Italians didn't trust anyone, especially cops. He wouldn't dare offer her charity in the form of money, food or shelter, so he repeated the bank job offer. "Go see Mr. Liam Johnson," he urged. "I wish you'd do yourself a favor and go up there."

"I wouldn't be able to work in a bank. I've never even been inside a bank."

He tried to hide his surprise, but while his family certainly wasn't well off, he had to remind himself that they were a long way from the bottom. "There's places I've never been to, either. But that doesn't mean you shouldn't try." They reached the corner of Mulberry and Broome, surrounded by shabby wooden houses, storefronts, and the jostling crowd. "This is where my beat starts. I want it to work out for you, Vita. I mean that."

She nodded and went on her way. He watched the curve of her hips, trying to keep his eyes averted from her derriere but unable to resist. *Oh, to have that body pressed against mine*—his imagination took over as he lost sight of her. He fought back even more forbidden thoughts as she disappeared into the crowd.

How he hoped she'd take that bank job! He clenched his fists and pounded the air. In a way, he could almost guarantee it. The bankers owed him a favor. If she got a job there, they'd be connected, however remotely. At that moment he decided Vita Caputo would be a major part of his life, even though it would be ages before she even knew it.

Chapter Two

The Church of the Transfiguration's bells chimed four times. Vita's empty stomach growled again. Shriveled oranges hardly made a meal. Not as poor as most Mott Street immigrants, they'd always had enough to eat, even before they had a table to put it on. She remembered the day Papa brought up that scarred old table, dripping in frozen rain, last Christmas Eve. The Dragonetti brothers managed to hoist it up the stairs sideways and shoved it against the kitchen wall. After she dried it off, it looked forlorn. She took pity on it, like an abandoned animal. Her heart lifted; now she had something to care for and pretty up. She bought red-and-white-checkered fabric and made a tablecloth. It was like dressing a doll. Since she never had any dolls, she took pride in caring for that old table. Rosalia hated the cloth and kept yanking it off. But, cloth or not, that table became part of the family—the catch-all for butt-filled ashtrays, pastry-piled plates...and a centerpiece of paper violets stuck in an empty wine bottle.

She spent her last penny on an apple and sat on a nearby stoop to savor every bite. It took the edge off her hunger for now but didn't ease her fatigue and the crushing humiliation she'd suffered all day. Every respectable establishment shooed her away. Now she went to the less respectable ones.

At the last place she wanted to work, the Bowery

Shirtwaist Factory, she approached the ruddy-faced boss and held her hand out. "I'm Vita Caputo, sir. Do you have any job openings?" She'd barely finished her introduction when he stood and shoved her toward the door. "I heard you been fired for gettin' in trouble wit' coppers and stealing blouses."

"*Madonne*, how stories get twisted around here! I didn't get in no trouble or steal a thing!" She threw her hands in the air. "And I saved the cop from getting robbed!"

"Aah, get outta here," he spat. "Scram."

She dragged herself to Mulberry Bend and leaned against a rubbish can, her spirit crushed. Now she'd hit rock bottom—no hope of a job and one meal from starvation.

She gave herself a shove and left Vita Caputo leaning against the rubbish can. A shop window caught her reflection and she stopped to look. "Hey you don't even look like a Vita Caputo." Moving closer, she stared into her eyes. She studied her face, free of stray hairs. She could've come from anywhere but Southern Italy.

That thought gave her the push she needed—uptown.

Heading north, away from the tenements, she gawked at stately mansions and shiny carriages. The New York Bank and Trust Company stood on the corner of Fifth Avenue and 20th Street, palatial, imposing. She climbed the marble steps, her heart pounding so hard she couldn't catch her breath.

She pushed on the polished brass bar across the glass door and stepped inside. A rush of cool air refreshed her. She wrinkled her nose at the strange aroma, a musty old-book smell—it must be all that cash seeping through the vault walls. *Does gold have an aroma?* she wondered. Her heels clicked on the floor and echoed through the high-ceilinged lobby. Bejeweled women in plumed hats and men in tailored suits dipped fountain pens in inkwells and filled out slips of paper at the marble counters. Nobody talked. Italian funerals were livelier than this.

Her world knew no such reserve. Poverty went hand in hand with noise—singing, shouting, the El's grinding wheels, carts clattering over the cobbles. *So this is the world of business?* she marveled. *How do they stay awake with all this quiet?*

Now in the role of Violet Greene, she squared her shoulders and lifted her chin. Though she'd never owned a bankbook, she knew how to match these uptown dandies with her wits.

Glancing around the cavernous lobby, she spotted a Fifth Avenue-style lamppost of a woman tapping at one of those typewriter machines.

Vita approached the woman and cleared her throat.

She looked up, fingers poised over the keys. "May I help you?"

"I'm here to see Mr. Johnson about a job."

"Name, please?" She swiveled her chair to face her appointment book.

"Violet Greene. With an 'e' at the end," she added.

"Do you have an appointment, Miss Greene?"

An appointment! *Mama mia*, who made appointments? "Why—no. I didn't think I needed one."

The woman's lips compressed into a pencil-thin line. Vita realized she'd acted very brazenly in this world of protocol. "Mr. Johnson never sees applicants without an appointment. He doesn't even see *customers* without an appointment." From where she sat, she managed to look down her nose at Vita.

Someday I'll be a customer and he'll see me without an appointment, she wanted to retort in her wine-bottle-shattering shriek.

"Who do—with whom should I make this appointment?" Vita asked.

"Unfortunately, he's booked solid until Tuesday of next week—" She slid her manicured pinkie nail down the page of the appointment book.

A surge of panic ripped through her. "I don't have that long to wait. I have to see him today," she insisted.

The woman glared at her. "We cannot let anyone who wanders in here—"

The paneled door opened and a mustachioed man lumbered out, working a gold pick between his front teeth. He looked at Vita, smiled, and held out his meaty hand.

"Hello, I'm Mr. Johnson. You must be next. Step into my office, and we'll start the interview."

A surge of energy shot through her as she crossed the threshold. *Violet Greene won't walk out of here without a job*, she vowed.

****

Mr. Johnson stood aside to let Vita enter his office. Shaded lamps cast a soft glow on a marble fireplace. Charts, fountain pens, and inkwells covered his desk. Heavy red velvet drapes shut out the slanting sunlight. Only the bars across the window reminded her that she was in a bank. They got to chatting about New York's spread uptown, the vast development, and the growing bank industry that clearly made him filthy rich.

He leaned back in his leather chair, lit a cigar, and blew out of a stream of smoke. The pungent haze threatened to choke her. "Ah, the good old days when the land we're now sitting on was an open field where I brought my father's horse to graze." He gestured out the window at Fifth Avenue. "The place was piled with horse dung, and now it's piled with money. Ah, America!" he chortled, waving his cigar through the air, adjusting his dollar-sign-shaped tie clip.

Ah, America. She'd never seen a pile of money, but she knew horse dung.

"I'm from humble beginnings, Miss Greene," he went on.

This is a job interview? She hoped he didn't expect to hear about *her* humble beginnings.

"I was brought up in the shantytown north of here." He leaned forward and tapped his cigar on a crystal ashtray. "My father was a blacksmith, and I lived by my wits. Worked as his apprentice until I'd saved enough money. Then got in with the right people."

She didn't ask who these "right people" were.

She wanted to discuss the future, but he seemed intent on digging up the past.

"I can see Manhattan spreading the entire length of the island, Mr. Johnson." She straightened her back and sat tall, tugging on her skirt. "When I'm older, I plan to purchase some property north of here while it's still affordable. And I don't mean Forty-Fifth Street. I mean way north. The other tip of the island. That is, if I can find a good solid bank that'll do business with me," she added with a smile, knowing she'd flattered him. It didn't take much.

"My word, a lady with vision beyond her lace

curtains!" He gave her an admiring once-over, but his eyes didn't linger anywhere. "Ah, yes, that wilderness up north very well may be built up someday. I'll keep that in mind. Yes, I'll keep it in mind." He sucked on his cigar.

Oh, if only she *had* lace curtains! "Well, I can't start saving for property unless I have a good job, which I'm hoping you'll offer me."

"Why isn't a nice girl like you married and raising a family?" he asked.

"I haven't met any nice men yet, Mr. Johnson."

"I'm sure that will change in no time, working here at my institution. You'll have many suitors. But I don't want you running off to get married and quitting your job here after we take the trouble to train you." He sniffed at the money-scented air.

"That won't happen, sir," she assured him. "Even if I did marry, I'd keep on working."

He gave her a quizzical eye. "You're not one of those suffragettes, are you?"

"No, sir." She shook her head. "I'm a reformer."

His eyes popped. The cigar fell from his mouth onto the desk. "Will that take time away from your job here?"

"Absolutely not. It never has before. And I've worked much longer days and nights than banker's hours." In the same breath, she asked, "Does that mean I get the job?"

He retrieved his cigar and slid it between the grooves in his ashtray. "I know a worthwhile investment when I see one. You start tomorrow. The pay is fifteen dollars a week. We even have a pension if you stay long enough. Which I hope you can."

"Sixteen dollars a week is fair, sir." *Mama mia,* fifteen was a fortune, but why not push for sixteen?

He stood and walked around his desk. "After you're trained." He held the door open for her.

"Fair enough."

New York Bank and Trust's newest employee skipped down the bank's steps, gazing out over the splendor of Fifth Avenue. She almost felt like a Violet Greene. She'd left Vita Caputo leaning against the rubbish barrel on Lower Broadway.

A tinge of disappointment niggled at her elation because he'd hired Violet Greene. Vita Caputo wouldn't have gotten past those spit-shined brass-and-glass doors—no matter if Tom recommended her. But she planned to tell them her real name after a few weeks. Then she'd know if Mr. Bank and Trust valued his word as much as his money.

****

As she strolled down Broadway, she glanced into the fashionable shops of the Ladies' Mile. Now she would earn more in one week than her father and brothers could scrape together in a month at the railroad yards. But something weighed her down like a hunk of bread sopping up olive oil. She now owed Tom McGlory a favor…even though the prospect of seeing him again lit a fire deep inside her.

She glanced down at her high-buttoned white blouse and trim skirt—her Sunday best. She couldn't have interviewed at a bank in her everyday sweat-stained blouse, frayed skirt, and scuffed shoes. Since all her money went on food and rent, she never owned any new clothes. She bought them second or third hand. She didn't even own a corset. Thank the Blessed Mother she didn't need one.

She always averted her eyes passing the shops that displayed lavish millinery, ribbons, and silks. The new high-button shoes, all the rage, cost far too much, even at her new salary. One day she'd have a wardrobe of fashions to go with her uptown brownstone.

In the midst of all this dreaming about fashions—and Tom—she hadn't figured out where to sleep tonight. Mrs. Paluzzi had told her, in her motherly way, that she wanted Vita back home. This would be her third night with them. She knew of some clean boardinghouses with good plumbing, fewer roaches than people, and windows that let light in. She couldn't bear to go back to Mott Street. It just wasn't home anymore.

****

Later that evening, after finishing their beat, Mike and Tom spotted Liam Johnson sitting on a bench facing the river, leaning on his walking stick. They approached him and said hello.

Oh, I hope he hired Vita, Tom silently pleaded.

"I won't be doing the beat tomorrow, Tom. I'm on another detail. G'night." Mike turned and went on his way.

Tom sat on the bench beside Liam and gave his legs a good, long stretch.

"So, did you hire her?" Tom asked the overfed banker patting his bulging belly as he sat back.

"Hire who?" Liam asked.

"Vita Caputo. The young lady I told you might come around for a job. Remember, I asked you to hire her to repay me those wee favors my Da did you fellows."

He shook his head. "No, she never did come by. I had a feeling she wouldn't. Probably got a job at another factory."

Tom's shoulders slumped, his spirits dashed. He gazed out over the river and the Brooklyn Bridge. So the little fox got a job somewhere else after all. But he doubted it was in another factory.

Chapter Three

For the first time since Vita could remember, she wasn't in a hurry, clutching her skirts to run somewhere, her ankles exposed. Nope, she basked in her first real luxury—watching kids play stickball and toss bottle caps, hearing the tempo of accents come and go as she strolled past. The setting sun painted the tenement windows a warm orange. The aromas of garlic, sweet basil, olive oil, and gravy wafting from open windows made her mouth water. She smiled at folks sitting on their stoops whether she knew them or not.

It wasn't the new job that made her smile. It wasn't even the refreshing breeze tickling her face. A handsome policeman brought that smile and stirred up a fantasy—gliding over the Waldorf ballroom's polished floor in his arms, his eyes sparkling under the chandeliers. Oh, for that to come true someday!

With an urge to hobnob around Greenwich Village, she turned onto Bleecker Street. She peeked into café windows and gazed at the brownstones with swept porches and scrubbed steps. Maybe she couldn't afford a room here, but its offbeat stylishness and genteel shabbiness enchanted her.

On Bleecker Street, she noticed a flight of stairs leading down to a door painted violet, the color of the paper flowers she'd strung together for three cents a bunch. A sign shouted "Madame Callisto—Fortunes Told" in swirling pink letters. She didn't know what drew her down those stairs to knock at that door. It must've been that pink and violet, so festive, so feminine. She'd never been to a fortuneteller before; the gypsies on Hester and Broome Streets all hawked their talents the way Italians peddled *baccala*. Papa had called an exorcist into the house when he thought his "evil" uncle had cursed him by bilking him out of five dollars. Italians feared and revered the supernatural, but Vita never believed the clues to her destiny waited inside a crystal ball. Praying to saints was one thing, but how could a crystal ball or a stack of cards tell the future?

But tonight, more than a soft bed to rest her aching body, more than a hot meal, she hungered to explore her future. So much had happened since yesterday. It all came out of nowhere and hit her in the face. She needed to know if her hunches would prove right—if she would fulfill her mission in coming to America.

She rapped on the door. "Come in," sang a melodious voice.

She walked in and sang back a hello. Swirls of smoke surrounded her. She inhaled a sweet scent similar to the frankincense they waved around at mass. Directly before her, green beads dripped in strands from a doorway. The beads parted as wild black hair and a white smile burst through.

"Hello, I'm Madame Callisto." She flitted in like a butterfly and greeted Vita with a thicker New York accent than her own. She clasped Vita's hands, and her chunky rings dug into Vita's palms. Her hair seemed to float to her slim waist, cinched with a gold chain belt.

Colored stones hung from her neck. Bare feet peeked out from under her ruffled skirt. Vita knew she looked downright drab next to her and wished she had some jewelry. Maybe with her first paycheck…

"Here, siddown, cookie. You look beat. Lemme getcha a Chianti."

"You read my mind. Well, I guess you're supposed to." She sank into a cushioned chair. Madame brought in a glass of red wine and plunked it down on the table. "Oh, yeah, this is what I've been dying for." She sipped at it, rolled it around her tongue, savored it, inhaled it, and let it trickle down her throat. Not as robust as the wine in her neighborhood, it offered a sweet smoothness.

"Thanks, I needed that." She rolled the glass over her forehead. "But I guess you already knew that."

"Now—I ain't what they call clairvoyant. You do have to tell me a few things about yourself. Start with your name." She buffed a silver ring on her frilly blouse.

"My name is Vita Caputo, and I'd like a reading, but I don't have that much money. Maybe you can tell me a few things instead of the whole shebang. I mean—just give me fifteen or twenty cents' worth."

The woman laughed, showing a gold tooth that gleamed in the fading sunlight. "Oh, it's different with everybody. Some people don't give me good readings at all. We just ain't in tune with each other. You, though, I can tell, have a busy history, and I think what may be in store for you could be even more busy than that."

"You mean my future looks as bad as my past?" Vita chased away a chill of foreboding.

Diana Rubino

"Your past hasn't been that bad, Vita, now, has it? I'm sure it ain't been nowhere near as bad as mine." Madame raised a dark brow.

"Well, how 'bout this? I've never walked this far unescorted." She lowered her voice as if Butchie could hear.

"So what made you?" Madame asked.

"Raw grit," she answered.

"You never had grit before?"

"Oh, sure, I was born with grit. I think my mama gave it to me. It's been bottled up. I been saving it— like in a bank." Vita giggled, thinking of the coincidence. She'd be saving money like that, too, very soon.

"You like money, don'tcha, Vita?" Madame gave her a friendly grin.

"I'm striving for success. The money will come along with it. I'm starting a new job tomorrow, at a bank." Her voice lilted with pride.

Madame Callisto pointed a long-nailed finger at Vita. "I knew it, I knew it! Good for you, kiddo. Good for you."

"In the last few days, life tossed me some very strange lines, and now I wanna try and toss a few back." Vita smoothed her skirt down.

"Oh, you and life'll get along just fine, kid, I can feel it." She nodded at Vita, her gaze penetrating.

"Is that my reading?" Vita's shoulders drooped with disappointment. "Ain't you even gonna get your crystal ball out?"

"I'd rather do the Tarot with you." She stood. "That okay?"

"What's the difference?" Vita asked.

"About fifty cents." She whipped a cloth bundle from a heavy chesterfield and unwrapped it to reveal a stack of colorful cards. "But I think I can get a better reading on you this way." She shuffled and spread them out on the table, arranging them this way and that, turning some over as she spoke.

The cards looked hand drawn and painted. They displayed fancy-costumed mythical figures, swords, chalices, and wands in bright colors. Vita laughed. "And the world thinks Italians are superstitious pagans!"

"There's somebody new in your life, and you're afraid to admit how you feel about him. And it is a him." She looked up at Vita with a raised brow.

"It certainly is. Those cards told you that?" Vita stared at the mélange of colors, meaning nothing to her.

"No, you're telling me that. The cards are just helping me connect to you. Kinda like a wireless."

Vita sat in wide-eyed fascination. "I want to hear more, especially about him." Her heart tripped as that tingling returned.

Madame turned over another card. Vita saw crossed swords—or were they shovels? "He's become a big influence in your life. I take it you care a heap about this person?"

"I—don't really know him yet. Well—when I say 'yet' I mean—" she stammered. "I'd like to get to know him, but—"

"Is he somebody who can wield power?" Madame asked.

"You mean like a policeman?" Vita ventured.

"Oh, he's a leatherhead?" Her tone turned flat and sour.

"Yes, but he's one of the good ones." Vita closed her eyes and conjured up Tom's image.

"Yeah, well, I'll find that out soon enough." Madame turned over another card. "For your sake and the sake of this wretched city, I hope he is," she muttered as her expression turned icy. She pressed her lips into a tight line and shook her head.

Vita peered over at the card, a bent-over skeleton.

"Oh, no." Madame's face paled, and she whistled low and long. "But you did want the bad with the good, didn't you?" she asked, her tone foreboding.

"Of course. What? He doesn't care about me? He's corrupt? What is it?" She pressed her hands against the tabletop to keep them from shaking. If it had anything to do with Tom, she wanted to hear it.

"No, it's nothing to do with him. This is the Death card."

Vita swallowed. The lingering taste of wine soured in her mouth. "What's that mean? Somebody's going to die?"

Madame Callisto opened her mouth to speak.

"No, no." Vita cut her off. "I don't want to know. Not yet. Tell me another time. Next week. But not now. I've got enough on my mind. Let me handle one thing at a time."

Madame turned over the other cards in the spread, plucked a pen and paper from the chesterfield, and scribbled down a few words Vita couldn't see. She didn't want to. "Well, but compared to that one, the rest of it ain't so bad."

"Tell me the good. Then I'll come back for the bad."

"Tell ya what, I won't charge you for this." She

folded the paper. "Come back when you want, and I'll tell you the rest of it. I'll keep the reading in the chest here. It doesn't mean someone's gonna die. It means transition, finishing up, conclusion." She opened a bottom drawer and shoved the folded paper inside. "Want more Chianti?"

"Sure." Vita sat back and rolled her head around, massaging her neck. "I never believed much in that stuff anyway. I keep an open mind about it, but I wouldn't lead my life by a skeleton on a card."

"And you shouldn't. They're only for guidance. I can see changes in your life just from what you told me. A new job at a bank. A fella." She filled their wine glasses. "Believe you me, Vita, if my life don't make yours look like a fairy tale, nothin' will. Ever meet a Catholic Polish Jew with three names, one of each? Well, here I am. Jadwiga Ann Wisen, at your service." She raised her glass. "The Wisen was Americanized from Wisniewski. The moniker at the front is spelled with a J and a W, but we say 'Yad-*VEE*-ga.' Now ya know why I call myself Madame Callisto." She grinned her gold-toothed grin.

"Callisto's a beautiful name. I'm sure the bank would give you a job in a minute! They were quick enough to hire Violet Greene," Vita said.

"Who's she?"

"Me." She pointed her thumb at her chest.

"Oh!" Madame Callisto snickered. "Let 'em think you're a lily-white Anglo. Just be good at it, and it don't matter whatcha call yourself."

"That's why I'm gonna get real good at it—great, in fact—and then tell them they hired a peasant's daughter." Vita spilled her plans.

Jadwiga wheezed a laugh. "Let me be there, hah? I wanna see the looks on the faces a those big bugs when ya tell 'em you're Signorina Capuuuto!"

Vita gestured at the crystal ball. "Can't you just watch from there?"

"No, it don't work that way. But I do see stuff I don't wanna see in there. I've scared the gazonkas off some 'peter players' who look like gone suckers already. They could lose an arm, a leg, that don't scare 'em. It's the loss of self-respect—bein' thrown outta work, a lot of 'em go from guttersnipes to street arabs—they'd rather die another death than live like that again."

Vita nodded. "I can understand that. Work equals self-respect in my family. I was out of work for twenty-four hours and it was the worst day of my life. That's the way I was brought up. Nothin's worse than being reduced to begging, or even asking. It's really all we got, our pride." Her voice faltered.

"Ah, you got more than that, kiddo." She gave Vita's shoulder a squeeze. "You got brass. I heard it clanging when you opened the door."

"Thank you. And after Violet Greene has settled into her job, I'll send Vita back here to hear all about the death card." Somehow it didn't scare her like real death. It was only a card.

"Tell ya the truth, I get that card a lot, and hey, I'm still here." She gestured up and down. "It don't mean physical death. Not by a jugful. Truth be told, it was a combination of cards that predicted my husbands' deaths, both of 'em, who I was married to at the same time, and none was the death card. Pretty bang-on, since they died one after the other."

"What happened?" Vita forgot about looming death in the family, the new job, and her family combing Mulberry Bend for her. Even the image of Tom blurred as her life shrank in comparison to Jadwiga's.

"One was a sailor. The other was better known. His name was One-Armed Charley Monell. He ran the Hole-in-the-Wall, a brawlin' den on Dover Street." She sat and propped her elbows on the table. "One night they found out about each other. Jerry, my sailor husband, was in the Hole-in-the-Wall, so Charley went over to Cherry Street, rounded up a few crimps, and they clobbered Jerry with knockout drops, ya know, chloral hydrate, after he got stinkin' drunk. Charley had an arrangement thing with the cops, always dumped the bodies where the cops could find 'em, so they could round 'em up later. But Jerry never woke up. Charley was killed in a brawl the next day. Didn't die right away. Staggered out into the outhouse and died sittin' there. What a way to go, hah?" She poured herself another glass, licking the rim. "But each one gave me a beautiful kid. Born Danuta and Zygmunt. Fourteen and sixteen. Great kids. Musicians."

She stopped to light a small pipe and offered Vita some. She politely refused, not so sure it was tobacco. It smelled normal enough, but she wasn't that ahead of her time—yet.

Jadwiga lit a few candles as the room grew dark. "Gotta economize." She peeked through the drapes. "Slow night. They come like a herd a elephants right before the new year. Always wanna know what the new year brings. Imagine the line I'll have waitin' here if I last till nineteen hundred."

41

"Maybe we'll both start the new century as big successes," Vita encouraged.

"Oh, not me, cookie, just you. And tomorrow's when it's all gonna begin."

"That reminds me, I'd better get going." But to where? Vita asked herself. To the Paluzzi house one more time? Risking Butchie's and Papa's fits?

"You can stay here if you wanna," Jadwiga offered, as if she'd read Vita's mind—well, maybe she had.

"How did you know?" Vita asked.

"Cuz if you had such cozy happy diggin's and a warm family bosom, you wouldn't be hangin' around here this late."

"You're right." Vita let out a relieved breath, knowing she wouldn't have to sleep on a bench. "I left them when I lost my job, not wanting to be a burden. I just can't bring myself to go back."

"I hear it at almost every session, toots. It don't bother me no more." She turned her pipe upside down and banged it against an ashtray. "They all get to sound the same after fifteen years."

"I'm sorry, but—I don't have any advance money to give you." Vita cringed.

"You're workin' in a bank, dearie." She gave Vita a narrow-eyed stare. "Somehow I don't think you're gonna honey-fuggle me."

She led Vita through a doorway to the back room, past a woodstove and a cupboard stuffed with mismatched dishes and cups. She showed Vita to a long rack hung with dozens of skirts, frilly blouses, and shawls, each more loud and garish than the next.

"Borrow anything you want." Jadwiga brushed her

hand along the variety of fabrics.

Her own brother wouldn't recognize her dressed like this. But to work in a bank? "Oh, Jadwiga, I don't think I can wear any of th—"

"Here." She swept a black skirt off the rack and held it up to Vita. "This is the plainest thing I got. You could be buried in it."

Vita decided she could get by with it after tearing off three layers of ruffles. Jadwiga gave her a white blouse and a pair of black stockings. "You can keep those." She then perched a hat on Vita's head. "That I want back. It's my newest."

It was one of those green wide-brimmed numbers with a saucy ostrich feather, so uptown, so classy. "Oh, it's the end!" Vita shivered with delight.

Jadwiga was still asleep when Vita left the next morning. She left a note thanking her and promising she'd be back with payment for a night's stay. She didn't search the bottom drawer for her Tarot reading. *I'll come back and face Death later*, she promised herself. *Much later. Now I got some living to do.*

Chapter Four

Vita Caputo never got the respect Violet Greene commanded as she reported for work that first morning. Customers greeted her with smiles, guards tipped their hats, a gent held the door for her!

The name change, the fancy new clothes, and the hat made her stand a head taller.

She finally had her own window, even if it was behind a counter. She learned how to cash bank drafts, handle deposits and withdrawals. When her first depositor handed her his passbook, she skimmed the columns to the ending balance. Then came the awkwardness of peeking into someone's private life. But handling this new and powerful set of duties was a huge responsibility. That, she realized as she handed the customer back his passbook, was where this city's leaders had gone wrong. Their cheating of the helpless masses drained every drop of dignity from the offices they held, reducing them to common thieves. That was the true test of integrity and honor—give someone power and see how they use it.

As Vita learned the intimate details of these strangers' lives, she learned an important fact: no area of a person's life was as private as his finances. Marriage secrets and wild fantasies paled in comparison. No matter how much they flaunted their wealth on Fifth Avenue, they guarded their passbook balances with fierce jealousy.

As she practiced with the adding machine on her lunch break, footsteps approached her window. She looked up to see the shiny black hair and green eyes. Her jaw dropped.

And so did his. "Vita!"

"Shhh!" She held a finger to her lips and glanced around. Good. No heads turned.

"You did it!" he went on, his smile lighting up the entire lobby. "You got the job! I'm so proud of you. When did you start?"

"Today." She kept her voice down. "I was going to send you a thank-you note."

He waved her mannerly intention away. "You don't have to do that."

Mama mia, he's a depositor here! As it hit her that she might be seeing a lot more of him, he gazed at her like some long-lost treasure. His eyes mirrored all her delight in this new world.

The picture of authority in his uniform, brandishing gleaming buttons and a badge, he made her proud to be a citizen.

"Officer McGlory..." she whispered, her eyes darting this way and that. "I'm Miss Violet Greene here. So please address me that way."

"Now why did you do a thing like that?" He tilted his head, his eyes puzzled with bemusement.

"Banks don't hire Southern Italians." She stated the obvious. "No place like this hires us."

"Don't you think that's a bit extreme?"

"Not at all." She kept her voice down. "I plan to tell them who I am. Then I'll see how much they really want to keep me. When I'm secure here. But, please, don't say anything."

"They would have hired you anyway." He gave her a knowing nod. Too knowing.

"How are you so sure?" She suspected something now. Was there some kickback involved here? In this city, anything was possible. Her palms sweated and her chest tightened with unease.

"You're bright and ambitious and have enormous potential. I knew they'd like you." His eyes so steady upon her, he didn't even blink.

"Well, your respectable Mr. Johnson just figured I was one of his flock and made a few not-so-respectable remarks about mine."

"Well, I'll keep your secret. If you keep mine." He winked as he slid his passbook under the row of bars separating them. "And after you make this deposit for me, may I have the pleasure of escorting you to the ice cream parlor?"

How forward, how brazen, how presumptuous! But then, so was she. "You certainly may."

She flipped the passbook open and placed the crisp ten-dollar bill in her drawer. She tried, oh, how she tried to keep her eyes away from that balance, but his, above all, she wanted to know—more than J.P. Morgan's if he'd come in here. She already knew Morgan was worth millions, but Tom McGlory was still a mystery to her. So she peeked. She wrote the deposit amount in and added it to his balance—the not unhealthy sum of $300. How did he save all that money? Was he enterprising or just plain stingy? Did he do work on the side? For all she knew, he could've been hoarding all his life, starting with pennies. As she slid his book back and he brushed her fingers retrieving it, she realized all these questions about him only frustrated her.

****

She tried to stop wondering about Tom's background as they sat at a marble-topped table for two. She savored her vanilla eggcream, a wild extravagance.

"You got that job on your own, Vita. I recommended you for the job but told Johnson your real name." He twirled his straw. "He didn't know who you were. So you're not obligated to me at all. I know that was bothering you."

"Good. That makes us even, then. But I want to thank you for suggesting it and believing in me." It still hadn't sunk in that she was working on Fifth Avenue and sitting across from the cop who'd accosted her only a few days ago. "But it all happened so fast. It's not just the job. I left the tenement behind."

His eyes widened. "What happened?"

"It was completely my decision. Something pushed me out of there, but it wasn't them."

"Where are you staying?" he pressed on.

"With a friend." She didn't elaborate. She wasn't sure if she'd spend another night at Jadwiga's. But she didn't want him knowing where she lived—yet.

"How about this?" He leaned forward and folded his hands. "We take boarders in my house. We live on Pearl Street. My father and I own the house. I live on the top floor with three boarders. We have two female boarders in the attic. My father lives with my sister and her kids on the lower floors. It's a comfortable enough house—nothing fancy, but there's always room there." His eyes didn't leave hers. "How about it?"

She broke his gaze. This offer took her off guard.

"I appreciate it, but—let's face it, Tom, what would my family say?"

"Do you still care?" he probed.

"No, not any more," she admitted.

She settled her gaze on the depths of her glass as she imagined living in his household, under the same roof with him.

Her senses returned, and she shook her head. "No, that's just—so out of the question, I can't even consider it. That would be way too bold. Moving out of the tenement is one thing, but—"

"We take in female boarders all the time." His tone lilted with encouragement. "It's not so unusual, not in our house. The females have one floor, the males another. My father wants a houseful of people. He can't stand to be alone, ever since my mother died back in Ireland. He wants to be surrounded by people, like a big family."

She looked into his eyes. "Oh, I'm sorry. I didn't know you lost your mother too."

"My mother and baby brother died during the last potato blight. My father couldn't afford their passage when he came over, so he promised to send for them, but they died before he had a chance to. He's also on the New York City police force. Lieutenant. I guess you can say I'm the glue that holds them together. They all depend on me, but I'd be extremely lonely if I didn't have them. I'll be the first to admit I need them as much as they need me." He took a sip of his malted.

"I couldn't board at your house, Officer McGlory." She shook her head. "It just wouldn't be right."

"I'll tell you what's not right." He smiled. "You not calling me Tom."

She forced a smile, wishing he'd take his eyes off her. What did he find so fascinating anyway?

"And what's not right about your boarding at my house, Vita?"

"We're natural enemies. My family—they'd never respect me if I had anything to do with you. I can't lose their respect. I don't live there anymore, but they're still my family. There are rules. Italian rules." She didn't dare touch on the reason she held even more deeply inside—she was falling hard for him.

"Do you respect them?" he asked.

"Of course." That question was so simple it didn't bear thinking about. "A huge part of our culture is the importance of respect, especially for my elders and the sanctity of the family. No outsider could ever overstep family rule. And we do have our rules. Old world rules, but they crossed the ocean with us."

"I know that's what you've been taught, but those aren't good reasons to respect someone. Respect has to be earned. And if they respected you, they'd treat you better. They'd trust you. Your brother wouldn't go dragging you down the street like a caveman." As his voice gained volume, she glanced around. No one had abandoned their treats to listen.

But what he said got her thinking. "To me, respect is instinctive, like hunger pangs. It never occurred to me that it had to be earned." She bent her straw. He waited. "You just don't understand Italian culture, Offic—Tom. I've moved out, which is very untraditional, but they're still my family." She shrugged. "No, it's not perfect, and we're not always smiling. But it works—something holds it up and keeps it going. It's the honor, the strength of the family unit,

49

how we feel the family is more important than any one of us. Sometimes I wish this city was run that way."

"For the good of the city instead of the citizens? That doesn't sound very democratic, Vita." His tone took on a patronizing hint.

She argued back, "The city has to thrive before its citizens can thrive. It's not every man for himself. Look at this place—" She gestured around. "Nobody cares. Nobody. In our family, we don't steal from each other. We're there for each other. We put the family's needs before our own. We look out for each other instead of ourselves. Can you say that about this city?"

"No, but it could change." He folded his arms on the table. "But probably not, the way things are going."

"Oh, yes, it will change. It can't go on like this. It'll collapse on itself. Read about the Roman Empire."

He gave her an approving nod. "Sounds like you've thought this out quite a bit."

"I read the papers," she informed him. "I have a daily habit. I open the *New York Times* and go straight for the editorials attacking Tammany Hall, the corrupt ward heelers, the assorted crooks, graft, and other payoffs. They're day-old papers people threw out, but one day never seems to make a difference. The corruption's still as evil, the living conditions still as brutal. The criminals who run the city make life miserable for honest workers."

"I know." He nodded. "Don't I know it. It's a hard world out there. Nobody knows that better than a cop. Sometimes it's tempting to take a payoff or do a favor—just once. But it's not worth it. I still have to live with myself."

Respect for him filled her heart. "It's good to know

an honest cop." She gave him a genuine smile.

"There are a few of us around," he assured her.

After another round of eggcreams, he walked her to the corner, where she hopped aboard the Fifth Avenue bus. She released a long breath. "Whew. Now we're even. I owe him nothing." *And he's coming back anyway!* Her heart leapt as the bus lurched.

****

She entered LaFamina's Tailor Shop. "Hey, Vita!" She spun around to face her brother striding toward her on the verge of a jaw-jutting fit.

"Papa's gonna kill you when I get you home," he warned.

"Papa don't have the strength or the will to kill anyone, least of all me. You're not taking me no place, Butchie. It's not my home anymore."

"Where you living?" he demanded. "The streets, Bandits' Roost, or Bone Alley?"

"Do I look like I've been living in Bandits' Roost?" She gestured at her skirt and blouse. "I got a job, a respectable one, and I'm doing just fine. I'll go back and see Papa when I feel it's right, not when you feel like dragging me back there."

"What kinda job?" His sneer didn't intimidate her one bit.

"You don't need to know, Butchie. Now I gotta get some clothes made." As she reached for the shop door, his hand gently touched her shoulder.

"Vita. Wait."

She turned to see the pained look in Butchie's eyes, his mouth curved downwards. A rush of love for her brother made her give him a hug. "No, Butchie, I'm not going back. I've had enough of it. Just tell Papa I'm okay."

"Where are you living?" he repeated.

"With a friend."

His eyes darkened. "You're making our family look real bad, Vita."

"I'm the one making us look bad?" She jabbed a thumb at her chest. "Has Rose entered a convent?"

"I don't want you turnin' out like that one." He never called Rose by name.

"I couldn't be like her if I took acting lessons. I left because I didn't have a job. Now I've decided to stay away because I have to make it on my own. I'll send you plenty of money. Don't worry about that." She waved her hand for emphasis.

"Come on, what's this job?" he goaded, giving her a brotherly cuff on the chin.

"In a bank. And that's all I want to tell you. I was saving it for a surprise. I get paid on Friday, and I'll be back on Saturday for the block party."

"You workin' in a bank?" His eyes bugged out. "How you get a job there?"

"I went for an interview and got hired," she told him the truth.

"Just like that?" He snapped his fingers.

"Yes." She didn't tell him it was Violet Greene who got the job "just like that."

"You still see me as a six-year-old folding paper forget-me-nots." Well, why shouldn't he be surprised? She'd never shared her dreams with him. All he gave a damn about was the family image. That's why they'd dragged Rosalia home a few times.

"You wanna know where I'm staying, Butchie? I'm at Madame Callisto's on Bleecker Street," she told him.

He screwed up his face. "Who the hell's that?"

"A fortuneteller lady who I'm boarding with. She's got great diggings, with a bright purple door. You can't miss it. That's where I am if you need me in an emergency."

"You staying wit' a damn gypsy?" He let out a low whistle. "Papa ain't gonna like that."

"She's not a gypsy. And he's gonna like the money I bring him on Saturday. You'll see." She gave Butchie a peck on the cheek and entered the tailor shop.

Sure enough, he still stood there when she came out with Mr. LaFamina after closing the shop. "I walk you down there, to this Madame Calypso," Butchie said as Mr. LaFamina turned the key in his lock.

"No worry, Butchie. Vita, I walk you," the tailor said, and even Butchie couldn't argue with that.

"See you Saturday," Vita told her brother as she and Mr. LaFamina headed west on Spring Street.

"Where you go now?" Mr. LaFamina asked.

"Madame Callisto, on Bleecker."

"Ah, *si!* I know her." He nodded with a smile. "She tell my *fortuna*, long time ago."

"Oh? What did she say?" Vita asked, curious.

"I do big business!" He held out his hands and shrugged.

"Well, I think she just may be right." Vita nodded.

When they got to Jadwiga's, Vita asked Mr. LaFamina if he was coming in, but he shook his head, waving his hands. "I gotta nice lady I'm courting tonight," he said.

"Well, good for you! I'm happy for you." Since his wife died, those lights in his shop burned at all hours.

"Hey, before you go, let me ask you—did Madame Callisto say anything about love when she did your reading?" Vita asked as she knocked on the door.

"Ah, *meraviglioso*!" He kissed his fingertips. "She say some-ting about me takin' a wife. Sure enough, one week later, I take Mario Scrudato's wife!"

He tipped his hat and scooted off down Bleecker Street.

She knocked again, but Jadwiga didn't answer. It was open, so she slowly nudged it till she could see in. Jadwiga sat giving a card reading to a man. He fidgeted, wringing his hands. Vita backed out, closed the door, and walked around the block. A shroud of impending doom made her shiver. She slowed her pace as she remembered her own reading, the final fate waiting for her in the bottom of the chest. Maybe he'd gotten the death card, too.

Chapter Five

Tom muddled through the next few days. They couldn't have been duller or more routine. Pound the beat in the sweltering heat, duck into the saloon for lunch, pound the beat till supper, go home. In summer the crime rate always shot up, but the last few days proved too hot for the crooks. The city lay quiet. He itched to do something, even nab a pickpocket, but there wasn't so much as a cat stuck up a tree. Fruits and vegetables withered in their carts. Vendors waited for customers to come to them instead of grabbing passersby and shoving *baccala* in their faces. Not a breeze stirred. Nobody sang or shouted out windows. It was just too damned hot.

He longed to see Vita but couldn't go back to the bank so soon. Instead he had a single rose delivered from Murphy's Florist every noontime for the next week. His reveries didn't do much to cool him down in all this heat, either. He always spent moonlit summer nights on his roof. He did his best writing there, but he never showed a word of it to anyone. Aside from his daily journals, he wrote the occasional story based on his life on the force, like the ones he read in the *Police Gazette*. Getting it down on paper served as an emotional outlet, after seeing so much crime and death. But the words didn't flow like liquid gold. He reread them every year to measure his emotional growth and reset his priorities.

One night he sat at the writing desk in the parlor, adjusted the lamp, and started a journal entry. As his pen scratched over the paper, the words took a shape of their own, the form of a letter. Before long, he realized he was writing to Vita.

To keep himself from indulging in forbidden fantasies on those sweltering nights, he read Dickens till he fell asleep. *Hard Times* was his favorite. It made him appreciate what he had.

Now, his feelings for Vita spilled onto the page so fast it came out as a scribble. He needed to get his growing fondness, caring, and affection out of his mind and into words. But he couldn't send her this. Not yet. He'd never written a love letter in his life, and he wanted to get it right.

"Tommy, please come fix the basin again—an egg fell down the plug hole!" His sister Bridget's voice funneled down the hall. He went upstairs to lock the page in the trunk. The plug hole had to wait.

****

Vita climbed her tenement's stairs and entered the kitchen. It seemed like she'd lived a lifetime since she walked out. Had it only been five days? A pall of hostility hung in the stale air. The railroad flat dared her to leave again and find something better. And she was going to spend an entire eighty cents for a curtain? What could she have been thinking, to even consider decorating this dump?

She'd spent the last three nights at Jadwiga's and had to find a room somewhere. Why not the Village? She liked its eccentricity, its carefree vagabond flair. She wanted to be a part of that exotic, bohemian scene.

But 124 Mott Street pulled her backwards. If only she could take Papa with her and share her new world with him. No, they'd never escape Mott Street. An overwhelming heaviness came over her as she gathered her few belongings and dropped them into a potato sack —her Bible, a battered copy of *Billy the Kid*, an Italian cookbook, and *Bloomingdale's Illustrated Catalog*, filled with beautiful clothes, accessories, and housewares she planned to own someday.

She didn't take a wistful look around, didn't stand at the threshold reliving memories. She walked out of the darkness and into the light. The Village beckoned her. She tripped over her feet to get there.

When she turned the corner and saw Tom McGlory, she ran smack into a moving cart. She dropped her bag, but her stuff didn't scatter all over the street this time. Her heart took a sudden leap even before her mind registered the excitement of seeing him. She pulled down the brim of Jadwiga's hat to hide her face as she observed him. Dressed in well-fitting black trousers and a clean white shirt, he stood talking to two men in suits. One of them slipped Tom a large envelope and he stuffed it into his pocket. They shook hands. She ducked into a store as he headed in her direction, but he didn't see her. No one from around here dressed like those fops. They had to be politicians, or worse…

What was in that envelope? Her mind rattled with questions. He couldn't be taking bribes. Not after what he'd told her over eggcreams. Gripping her bag's straw handles, she forced herself to trust him.

But the most baffling question of all: why did she care?

****

She got off the streetcar Saturday morning and followed the noise—accordion music, singing, laughing. The block party must've started at the crack of dawn. As she turned onto Mott, the mingling aromas of garlic, sausage, peppers, and onions made her mouth water. Her box of pastries didn't smell half as sweet. As she headed closer, the lively strains of "Danza Danza Fancuilla Gentile" grew louder. Revelers danced in a circle, jumping and kicking. A wave of nostalgia brought tears to her eyes—these were her people. But she remembered why she'd left.

She got a sausage sandwich from Cappuchine, giving them away from his cart. She sat on her old stoop and savored each juicy bite, wiping her hands with her hankie. Now it was grease-stained for good. Then it dawned on her: she could afford a new one!

After indulging in that temptation, she went upstairs.

She greeted her brothers Butchie and Vincente, sitting at the kitchen table reading the papers. Now that she no longer lived there, they talked to her with a kind of awe, like she was a superior instead of their kid sister. "How pretty you look," came from Vinny, and Butchie managed to admit, "It's been quiet without you around."

Vinny had never been much of a fixture in Vita's life. They were so far apart in age, he was like an uncle rather than a brother. But as Papa's firstborn son and therefore his favorite, Vinny went by whatever Papa thought or said.

"So where's this bank?" Vinny poured her a glass of wine.

"Fifth Avenue." She took a sip. "You going down later?" She changed the subject to the block party.

"Just got back up. They been at it since the sun come up." Butchie yawned and grabbed a cruller from the open box on the table.

"Hey, last night I seen that leatherhead McGlory talkin' with John McGurk. Short-Change Charley and Eat-'Em-Up Jack McManus was with 'im. They was all talkin' and shakin' hands like they was real pals," Butchie announced as he dove into his cruller.

"When was this?" She tried to sound casual but feared she spoke too quickly. They all knew John McGurk. He owned the Mug, the worst dive on the Bowery. He armed his waiters with knockout drops. Charley was his head waiter and McManus was his bouncer. He'd gotten shut down a few times, along with the other suicide halls where addicts and the otherwise doomed went for liquor laced with camphor or benzene. They had names like the Hell Hole, the Dump, and the Cripples' Home. And they were all in her neighborhood.

"McGlory seen me." Butchie talked as he chewed. "Then he grabbed McGurk by the arm and went around the back of the Mug. I wanted to get him back for what he done to us, so I went on the roof and peeked down. McGurk handed McGlory a wad of cash. He stuffed it in his shoes." He took another bite. "I couldn't hear what they was sayin', but I caught 'em. I went straight to the station and told the sergeant there. The sergeant's a decent guy, Frank Munn. He's one of the straight ones. He took down a few notes and thanked me. If they nail him, maybe I'll get a reward. That's what McGlory gets for dealin' with them guys and their bahbah."

Disappointment rattled her. So Tom McGlory was as corrupt as he was two-faced, running her in for such a minor offense as disobeying orders, then turning around and taking bahbah—graft.

She didn't want to tell her brothers that she'd also seen Tom taking what was probably a comfortable payoff from two crooks. So he *was* on the take. A thief, just like the rest of them. After he'd told her how honest he was. She tried to tally up his undesirable characteristics—and damned if she could come up with one. But wasn't this enough? *He's a thief, a liar, a crook...* she repeated in her mind.

Papa came in and sat at the table. "Is it safe where you staying, Vita?"

"Very safe, Papa." But she didn't tell him where.

He poured himself a glass of wine from his jug, and she bent over to kiss him. Knowing she'd leave him again tore her heart in half, but she didn't belong here anymore. No one on Mott Street had goals or ambitions—their lives revolved around survival.

He left the kitchen, and she figured he was going for a nap, but he came back out with a tiny box. He placed it on the table in front of her.

"This belonged to your mother. I try to give it to her when I try to court her. She no like me and give it back, but took it when I ask her to marry me—five time." He held up five fingers. "Took me five year to get her to marry me. She took it and wore it over her heart. So you take it now."

Vita opened the box. Nestled into tissue paper sat a cameo brooch no bigger than her thumbnail. She marveled at its simple ivory on black, a delicate oval rimmed in filigree lace. She misted over and stood to give him a hug. He hugged her back with his free arm; his other hand clutched his wine jug.

"Thank you, Papa." She said a silent prayer of thanks that Rosalia had never found it, or it would have been sitting in Schiavone's Pawn Shop right now, its heartwarming history locked inside it forever.

Before they all went down to revel in the festivities, she went back to her old dresser and grabbed her prayer beads, her St. Anthony statue, and a few dollars she'd stashed under the floorboard. She gave the money to Papa. While learning the adding machine, she'd figured how much she'd need for night school and living expenses. She hadn't included this stash. Before now, she couldn't afford night school. Papa wouldn't have let her go anyway; it was something she would've had to do on the sly. But not anymore.

The party didn't break up till way past midnight, everyone toting greasy sacks of leftovers. Empty wine jugs clinked as the revelers stumbled home. She stayed at the house that night. Papa and Butchie went to bed early out of habit, even though Sunday was a day off. Rosalia stayed on the roof yapping with neighbors. Their voices tumbled down the air shaft like the garbage they threw down there. Vita took one more bite of a cannoli and savored the creamy taste all the way to bed, where she fell onto the lumpy mattress, exhausted. In that ethereal edge-of-dreaming stage, Tom McGlory's face came into clear focus. He spoke to her in a dreamlike babble. She yelled back at him, turned, and walked away, ignoring his calls, finally falling asleep with a calm satisfaction. In her dream she no longer cared.

Chapter Six

The next morning, Vita splurged on eggs and bacon from the grocer, a fresh loaf of bread from the baker, and made breakfast for everybody. Still hung over from the party, they all ate in the silence of the ravenous. After grabbing the last slice of bread, Rosalia pushed away from the table, announced, "I'm goin' to mass," and left Vita with the dirty dishes. Men didn't go to church. Worship was a woman's job. Papa stopped making Vita go after she made Confirmation. She went because she wanted to.

This morning she'd gone to mass before breakfast. She sat way in back and didn't pay much mind to the priest chanting away in Latin. This was her private time for praying and remembering her mama. She looked up in the familiar far corner. The image of an angel with dreamy blue eyes looked down at her. As she pretended that angel was Mama, a protecting comfort always warmed her. She wanted to be married in this church, her mother-angel watching over her with those heavenly blue eyes. Even if it meant coming back to the old neighborhood.

That's why she went alone. To be with her angel.

****

After she washed the dishes and scrubbed the kitchen floor, she told her family *ciao*.

"Where you goin' now?" Papa asked.

"To look for a nice boardinghouse." She wet her comb and smoothed her hair back. "Butchie, you can come help me look," she added, knowing this was the last thing he wanted to do, but it reassured Papa she wouldn't land in some bawdyhouse.

She kissed Papa behind his newspaper and followed Butchie down the stairs.

Her gaze darted around for Tom walking his beat, but she didn't see any police at all. The streets rested in silence as they headed for Jadwiga's.

"You wanna see where I've been staying?" she offered, wondering what Butchie would make of her bohemian friend. He'd probably drag her home after seeing Jadwiga in her ruffles and skinny pipe—oh, she hoped the fortuneteller wasn't wearing lipstick!

"Yeah, I never been to Bleecker Street. It's full of *strambi*, ain't it?"

She laughed at the word she hadn't heard in ages. "Some of them are weirdies, but that's what gives it character."

They went down the steps. As she knocked on the purple door, Jadwiga's singing floated out from inside.

Butchie looked around with a crinkled brow, puffing on his cigarette. "How'd you find this joint?" He backed up and looked at the door, like he couldn't figure out what kind of place this could possibly be.

"I just was passing by and it caught my eye. Jadwiga's a fun gal." She knocked again, and the high-pitched caterwauling stopped.

"She ain't one a them gypsies, is she?" He scowled.

"No, Polish. Smart. Great sense of humor." She hastened to add, "Just like us."

Jadwiga opened the door. "Well, if it ain't bub and sis!" she greeted them, her yellow ruffled blouse louder than her voice. Out billowed some of the sweet smoky stuff. Vita inhaled its essence. Ah, that exotic scent, so in tune with the freewheeling Bohemian lifestyle she admired.

"Jadwiga, this is my brother Bruno. Call him Butchie. Butch, this is my friend Jadwiga."

Jadwiga held out a ringed hand and squeezed his. "Hiya." He peered over her shoulder into her flat, looking like he didn't know how he got here.

"Hey, Butchie, you should come down here." Vita gave him a little shove. "You'd enjoy it, all the different nationalities and non-Catholics and free expression…so unrestrained."

"Who says I'm restrained?"

She laughed, but she could see him fitting in, even if it was just sideways. "Well, you're not, but you're a great accordionist and have a great singing voice, and that makes you an artist, don't it?"

Jadwiga hustled them in. "What can I offer you, Butchie? Some wine?"

He nodded, taking in her diggings. "Yeah, nice place. You make wine down here?"

"Nah. Just vodka. Want a horn of that instead?"

"No, thanks. Vodka's too rich for me." Butchie patted his stomach. His eyes flitted around, trying to avoid Jadwiga, but after all, she was the focal point.

"Jadwiga, I'm going to be getting out of your way and finding a place." Vita pulled up a chair. "You know of any nice boardinghouses around here? I want to stay in the Village."

"Yeah, matter of fact I do. Just the perfect place for

a gal like you." She sat across from Vita. "A friend of mine, calls herself Madame Branchard, she has a three-story rooming house. You'd love 'er. Her boarders are all writers, poets, reformers—"

"Hey, uh—what kinda madam is this madam, anyway?" Butchie wedged his way into the spirited exchange. "I don't want my sister stayin' with no—ya know—" He gestured with his hands, and Jadwiga nodded him on.

"Yeah? Ya know what? Can't say it, can ya? Well, nothin' like that goes on there. I'm there a few nights a week. So are a lot of my friends, all writers, social reformers—thinkers. Vita likes to use her brain, and I'd like her to meet some of these people anyway."

"Well, I'm goin' over with her," Butchie declared. "If I like the looks of it, she can stay, but—"

Vita jabbed at her brother's arm. "Hey, excuse me for butting in, Butchie, but I feel like a pound of sausage the two of you's are haggling over. You can walk me over there, but I'll stay if *I* like it, not if *you* like it." She turned back to Jadwiga. "Now—what's the address? I'd like to call there now, if you think she's in."

"Oh, she's always in. She has her salons three nights a week and spends the rest of the week getting ready for the next one. Ya know, putting out tea and biscuits and cups and saucers. She's at Sixty-One Washington Square South. Just the other side of Third Street. Make a left on Broadway."

"Great, Jadwiga, thanks! Let's go, Butchie. I can't wait to meet her." She stood, rubbed her hands together, and headed for the door.

"If you don't see it right away, it's the one with the

big knockers—door knockers—in the shape of lions,"
Jadwiga said. "Charges real cheap rent."

Vita took Butchie's arm and skipped up Broadway.

"She's too old for you, Butchie," she kidded him,
knowing he'd never woo someone like Jadwiga.
Butchie was in the market for a bride and courted only
young neighborhood girls to Papa's liking.

The first thing Vita saw when Madame Branchard
opened her door was her short shock of bright red hair.
Round wire glasses rested on the bridge of her nose. A
black cat curled around her shoulders. She held a book
in her free hand. Her bare legs showed under a sacklike
dress, her feet shod with the kind of sandals Jesus wore
in pictures.

"Hello, I'm Vita Caputo. My friend Jadwiga Wisen
told me you might have a room? Oh—and this is my
brother Butchie, but he's not looking."

The woman let her glasses slide a bit farther and
looked at Vita over the rims. An eyebrow shot up, along
with the corresponding corner of her mouth. "Yes, I do.
Jadwiga! She's sent me more boarders—well, it's way
up on the third story, and it's small, under the eaves.
Nobody here sleeps at night. That's when they come
out. Like vampires." She smiled.

"Oh, that's fine with me." Vita glanced inside.
"She told me about some of your boarders, and they
sound fascinating. You see, I'm a reformer myself. I'm
not an artist or anything, but I'm active in tenement
reform and—well, I work in a bank, so you won't have
to worry about me skipping rent or anything."

Madame Branchard laughed. "Yes, do come in.
You, too, honey." She nodded at Butchie, hanging
back, staring at two men walking down the street side

by side, their arms wound round each other.

She hadn't been joshing when she said her attic room was small. Vita mopped her forehead with her hand and pulled her blouse away as it stuck to her body. The room was hot as holy hell, the bed nestled in the alcove under the dormer window. "This is just what I want! My very own garret room!" She twirled around and flopped on the bed. Butchie checked the lock on the door. "Yeah, clean as you always kept our house," he admitted. "Not a speck of dirt or a bug in sight."

"I'll take it!" She gazed around her new room, leaning out the window that fronted the street. "My very own window! Now that's worth the rent!"

****

Vita spent the next few nights sitting in on Madame's salons with the other boarders and assorted drop-ins. She didn't dare open her mouth and join the conversations about subjects and people foreign to her—existentialism, Nietzsche, Dostoyevsky—and sexual freedom. Needing a break from all the philosophizing and titillation, she went to Jadwiga's for a reading on Tom.

Jadwiga offered Vita something clear that she drank from a long fluted glass. It was probably the vodka she'd offered Butchie.

"I don't think so, Jadwiga." She scrunched her nose. "I can smell it from here."

"Nah, that's the *golombki*." Jadwiga put down the glass and dished out a meaty concoction, fragrant with herbs. "*Golombki* means pigeon, but it ain't the kind that flies. Though we eat that too. It's a stuffed cabbage with pork." She smacked her lips.

Vita took a bite and savored the rich taste. "My

first taste of Polish cooking, and it's every bit as good as my own meatballs. *Delizioso!*" As they ate, Vita got around to asking her to do another reading.

"On your beau?" Jadwiga asked.

A dash of hope shot through Vita. "He's not my beau," she had to admit. "But maybe someday."

As Jadwiga laid the cards out, Vita waited for some kind of contradiction, a hint that she knew something Vita didn't.

But the cards told of deceit, treachery, and dishonesty. When Jadwiga asked the question, "How do other people see Vita?" she turned over The Fool. "Naivety. Innocence. Ignorance. It don't mean *you're* a fool. People see you as not as smart as you really are. So not a bad card to get."

But she still came away with an empty, unfulfilled void in her heart. Nothing good came out of this reading.

"Have you seen your man since our last reading?" Jadwiga lit her pipe.

"Yeah, then I saw him the other day, but he didn't see me," Vita replied in a low tone. "I didn't want to believe what I was seeing, but Butchie confirmed it, and these cards just took away the benefit of any doubt I can give him now."

"What did you see?" Jadwiga puffed on her pipe, her eyes fixed on Vita. A pungent gray smoke rose from the barrel.

"He was taking a huge envelope from two well-dressed big bugs. Then Butchie said he saw him taking money from John McGurk, who owns a suicide dive on the Bowery. And anybody who didn't fall off the boat yesterday knows they weren't swapping colcannon recipes."

"Man alive." Jadwiga shook her head, blowing out a thin stream of smoke. "Well," she said after taking a thoughtful sip of her homemade potable, "he is a cop. Tryin' to find an honest one of them's like tryin to find an Italian who don't swim in garlic."

"Much as I love garlic, I try to stay away from it," Vita confessed. "It makes you reek when you eat it."

"Well, maybe he ain't a lot dishonest." Jadwiga winked. "Look, honeybun, just 'cause he's a crook don't mean he can never love ya. All crooks got families, and they take care of them. Just take a stroll down Fifth Avenue. They take care of their ladies, all right."

"Fifth Avenue mansions and fancy carriages aren't expressions of love. That's not what I want." She shook her head. "No, it could never work with someone like him. I told you my ambitions. To make things better for my people, and for all poor immigrants. He stands for everything that keeps us down."

Jadwiga turned her pipe upside down and tapped it into the ashtray. "I want to meet this Tom of yours. I want to search his aura. I need to shake hands with him, look into his eyes, hear his voice. Then I can get a much better idea of what he's about. Not all crooks are crooks for life. They're not cops for life, either. They gotta retire sometime."

"I'm more mad at myself than anything." Vita sighed. "I can tell if someone's on the up-and-up or not. If you live on Mott Street, you get to be real good at it."

"You been taught not to trust anybody outside your family so you won't get flim-flammed." Jadwiga got up and emptied the ashtray. "You'll also never really love anybody if you're on your guard all the time, thinkin' everybody's out to honey-fuggle ya."

"I want to be able to trust Tom McGlory. In a way, I want to—to bring out the good in him." But she wondered if that would be harder than reforming the entire city.

"If he's got any good in him at all, believe me, he'll show it." Jadwiga went over to the stove and dished herself up another helping of *golombki.*

"It's a war that neither of us can ever win, Jadwiga. I've got my own agenda. He's got his." She couldn't help arguing—she needed convincing.

"Yeah, and it looks like he's on yours. It sounds like you want this fella, change or no change, crook or no crook." Jadwiga sat down with her heaped-up plate.

"No!" Vita slapped her palm on the table. "I can't pine away for a corrupt member of the Metropolitan Police Force. I'll honor my family's wishes and marry a nice Italian boy."

"Come on, Vita." She took a few bites and wiped her mouth with a hankie. "A nice Italian boy would bore you to bitter tears. You're hoping Tom's got some savage in him, so you can tame him. What fun would he be otherwise? Where's the challenge? That's like bein' a politician in a clean city."

"You think I enjoyed seeing him taking graft from those thugs?" She shifted her weight on the creaky chair. "All my faith in him went plunging like a sinking ship."

"You don't want to lose all your faith in him," Jadwiga insisted. "If you'd given up on him already, we wouldn't be sitting here with a deck of Tarot cards spread out between us and our *golombki,* now, would we?"

Vita sighed, reaching that point of surrender every time a wise soul hit her with a truth she couldn't deny. "No, I'm too practical for that. Too practical for my own good, maybe."

"Sure, you're upset you saw him taking what could be graft." Jadwiga put her fork down. "You can easily bring him down a peg, say he's not good enough for you, 'cause he's an outlaw. It'd be real easy to get hitched to a nice Italian boy who'll work on the docks all day and eat your homecooked pasta every night, while you do your reformin' and politickin'. But if Tom McGlory's a crook, you'll be fighting him all the way. And I have a feeling I know who's gonna win." Pushing her plate aside, she gathered her cards and wrapped the cloth around them with a motherly gentleness. "And ain't success sweet?"

"I don't know yet, but I'm gonna find out. It sure looks sweeter than failure." Vita let a slow smile spread her lips as a streak of energy shot through her, like a steam train revving its engine.

"Here." Jadwiga offered her a pipe, and this time she took it.

"Try it on. If you're gonna live at Branchard's, you may as well learn to smoke, 'cause they all do over there."

She captured it between her teeth and liked the sensual feel of her lips wrapped around it. After a few sputters that turned into coughs, Jadwiga came over and slapped her lightly on the back. "Smooth, take air in with it, don't breathe in a lot of smoke."

Vita took another drag without choking it down. She glanced at herself in the mirror across the room.

She looked so chic holding the stem between her thumb and forefinger, mimicking Jadwiga's relaxed posture. She delighted in this activity of smoking. "This feels so glamorous, and it's so taboo! Maybe someday I'll make it acceptable."

"Hey, there ya go. You got the hang of it," Jadwiga congratulated her as she crossed her legs, hiked her skirt up past her knee and swung her leg, puffing on her pipe. "Looks like you're enjoying it as much as I enjoy the company of Phoenix here." She tapped her pipe.

"You named your pipe?"

"I name everything I own. Even body parts, like some fellas give pet names to their little friends." She settled into her chair.

Vita wasn't aware that men named body parts. "What little friends?"

Jadwiga stared into Vita's blank expression and burst into laughter. "You really crack me up, you sweet little thing. You're like a rum cake with none of the rum."

"Well, I just wasn't sure what you were talking about." Her head felt fuzzy and light. Just the sound of Jadwiga's lilting voice made her want to giggle. "Hey, what were we talking about?"

"They name the part of their body that gives them the most pleasure. And it ain't their stomachs." She gave Vita a nudge. "Get it now?"

Vita gave her friend another blank look, then something in her brain started figuring, the same way she arrived at a sum when adding numbers. She gasped in surprise, and this triggered a new spurt of coughing.

Jadwiga filled a glass with water and held it up to her.

"No. Not their—" Vita pointed downwards.

"I've heard fellas name that body part just about everything: Junior, Johnson, Percy, and of course there's the old standby for those who don't have any imagination, Dick," Jadwiga said. "Now Polacks, I've heard them name 'em Stosh. Greeks, always Jimmy. And Irish—ah, I don't even think Irish know they have 'em."

Although Vita reveled in this titillating subject, she couldn't believe this conversation. If anyone else had even touched on this forbidden topic, she'd have cringed with embarrassment. But it seemed so natural to be talking about this with Jadwiga. Her body glowed with a strange excitement. Her senses of smell and taste seemed heightened.

"So how about Italians?" Vita asked. "Do they name their—parts?"

"I've never known any Italians." Jadwiga tapped her teeth with the stem of her pipe. "Now Germans, they're a different breed altogether. They give theirs numbers."

"This is all so new to me, Jadwiga. I know how the woman's cycle functions, and how a man's seed can beget a child, but beyond that, I know nothing." She shook her head, imagining this conversation at her dinner table. "No one ever broached the subject, and I'd never dare ask. But I've always been curious, I mean, about the way men's bodies look. I've never seen one." Heat crept into her cheeks.

"All those brothers in such close confinement?" Jadwiga's eyes widened. "Don't they ever take their clothes off?"

"Of course, but nowhere near me. I'm their sister!"

"Well, depending on the fella, it can be the most beautiful sight you'll ever see." Jadwiga closed her eyes and smiled dreamily as if savoring a work of art. "But they're not all Michelangelo's *David*. Some are big, some are small." She showed Vita with a spread of her thumb and forefinger, just how big and small.

"And—what do you do?" Vita's curiosity burned like hunger. "Once he puts it in you?"

"I'll tell you what not to do." She leaned forward. "What you must never, never do."

"What's that?"

"We live in very prudish times, Vita. Mothers teach their daughters not to enjoy the sex act. It's just for having babies, it's your wifely duty, it's your job to give your man pleasure. It's all hooey, you hear me? All a lotta hooey!" She stabbed a forefinger at Vita. "Don't ever think you have to settle for that. You have every right to enjoy it. God gave us parts of our bodies that we're entitled to enjoy as much as men are. So don't you ever just lie there with gritted teeth, watching that mantel clock and waiting for him to finish his business. You move with him."

"Move?" She blinked, completely stumped.

"It's all right to writhe and squirm and moan as loud as you want. It's your right, too!" Jadwiga delivered her words like a reformer, as if to a theater full of rapt listeners.

Vita gasped. "Really?" The smoke's fuzzying effects turned to plain shock. "What's all this moving and squirming you're talking about? I thought it was just a joining of two bodies and a rapid buttoning-up afterwards." She gestured at her buttons. "Do all women do it this way?" She imagined Mrs. Paluzzi for a fleeting second. The thought turned her stomach inside out. Never!

"They ought to. I don't see any point otherwise." Jadwiga smiled and patted Vita's hand in a motherly gesture. "I don't wanna scare you. Come back next time and I'll tell you more, but I don't want to spill it all at once. That would be like knowing everything about Tom McGlory. It'd be no fun after that, would it? He'd be like broken-in shoes. Learn a little at a time. Lots more fun." She gave a sharp laugh.

Vita drained her water glass. As she sat and let her mind wander around those forbidden pleasures, she wiggled her toes in her comfortable worn-out shoes.

"I've been hearing about it—well, not 'doing it' like you just told me, but the last few nights I sat in on Madame's salons in the parlor with all the existentialists, reformers, and poets. Inez usually shows up to talk about sexual freedom. And not just between men and women. They get into deep discussions about homosexuality." Her cheeks grew hot. "It embarrasses me, and of course I don't say a word, but I just sit there, fascinated. Then I'm ashamed of myself."

Jadwiga gave her a dramatic eye-roll. "Oh, come on, Vita. We're at the brink of a new century here. You, so ahead of your times already, ashamed for listening to talk about sexual freedom? You gotta change with the times, young lady."

That odd tingling stayed with her as she walked back up to her attic room and unpacked her few precious belongings. She would let her imagination loose tonight, in bed.

Now she considered something much closer to reality. She wanted nothing to do with corrupt policemen. She set a patched skirt inside the wooden chest at the foot of the bed. Pulling a loose thread, she thought of Tom and that first meeting. Although now, the more he repelled her, the more he piqued her interest. How perverse. But then, fate brought her to this city for a reason. And it wasn't to live and die on Mott Street. Her destiny lay in New York City—and on some level, her future involved Tom McGlory. Either as friend or foe, she knew they were fated to meet again—and again.

Chapter Seven

Vita tallied up the day's receipts as a customer approached her teller's window. She looked up to see Tom standing before her. He gave her a heart-melting wink, said, "Hello, Miss Greene," then turned and headed for Mr. Johnson's office.

Her crush of disappointment—*Why didn't he stop to chat?*—battled with her curiosity. *What kind of business could he have with Johnson?* She sneaked a look in at his account in the file drawer. Nope, no more deposits. If he was taking graft, he hid it, just like the rest of them.

She forced herself back to her job and started adding again, her fingers now adept at punching those numbered buttons.

He came out of Mr. Johnson's office and strode over to her window. Her entire body tingled.

"So, Miss Greene, it looks like you're really enjoying your job here."

She drowned in those eyes of his. "I'm blessed. And I have several people to be thankful for, one of whom is standing in front of me."

"Hmm, fancy English." He smiled. She tore her gaze away, remembering how she'd vowed to keep her distance. But those dreamy eyes, the lines etched around his mouth, the black shadow shading his chin— all her vows crumbled to pieces at the sight of him.

"It's good to see you happy, Vita." His kept his voice low so only she could hear. "Your eyes are bright, your hair is shiny—you never looked better. Not that you weren't gorgeous before."

Their gazes held.

"Sorry." He glanced away. "I overstepped my bounds."

"You did? When?" Italian men didn't compliment their women like this. Not because it was improper. They just didn't bother.

After the disastrous Tarot reading and her catching him taking money, she wanted to hear something good from him—to assure herself that he wasn't all evil and corrupt.

"I'll finish it for you. I'm wearing a new blouse, a new skirt, and new shoes." The clock struck five and the vault slammed, the official closing of the bank.

"Vita, will you have dinner with me this evening?" His voice floated to her ears as smooth as the bank's marble columns, his demeanor as polished as the brass and glass all around them. No hesitation fell from his kissable lips. No awkward bumbling tainted his hopeful words. It made her wonder how long he'd practiced.

"I'm afraid that's impossible, Tom." She lowered her eyes. Her face fell in disappointment. Escorting her to the corner was risky enough, but…dinner?

"It's your family you're worried about?"

"No." She made a cutting gesture. "Not anymore." *It's you*, she wanted to say. She wanted to confront him, to condemn him, to tell him what she'd seen him do, but she certainly couldn't let him court her. "I can't make it tonight, Tom, but I would like to talk."

"How about a short soda, then?"

Her mouth puckered at the thought of sipping a luscious eggcream from a candy-striped straw. That would certainly sweeten what she had to say.

"That sounds dandy." She took her purse from under the counter and said goodnight to her co-workers. They didn't notice the fellow she was leaving with. No one seemed to mind anyone's business around here. Uptown certainly was a different world—even the ice cream parlor he brought her to, with heart-shaped chair backs and frilly tablecloths.

"Tom, I'm not going to hold this back, and I hope you'll be honest with me," she said after some small talk. Her heart finally slowed to a mere tap. She imagined herself as a city councilwoman talking to one of her constituents, and she pictured him as someone else—an underling, a crooked cop, anything but this exciting man who stirred up a mixture of fear and longing, pulling her in, yet driving her away.

He nodded. "I could tell something was bothering you the minute I walked in. What is it?"

She twirled the striped straw and ran her fingers over it. "I saw you with two politicians, slipping an envelope into your pocket. I don't think I have to say any more." She didn't mention who Butchie said he saw Tom with. After all, her brother could have been mistaken. Lots of guys had broken noses, missing teeth, and walked with a limp like McGurk.

Tom didn't blink, blanch, or blush. He didn't squirm. He didn't move a muscle. He only sipped at his soda. "So you saw me with two politicians. And you jumped to all kinds of conclusions."

"Somehow I didn't think they were handing you a church donation."

"I was conducting business I can't discuss. And that's all I can say about it." His abrupt tone told her the conversation was over.

"You're not going to defend yourself?" She pushed on. She cared too much to let this drop without hearing more.

"There's nothing to defend because I wasn't doing anything wrong. Now, I suggest you stay out of my business and just take care of your own." He broke eye contact.

Wasn't doing anything wrong. That could mean he was crooked but didn't think he was doing anything wrong. Oh, if only Jadwiga were here! What Vita wouldn't give to have her talents.

"Vita…" He clasped her hand. She curled her fingers around it, savoring his touch. The tension between them made her jump as if hit by lightning. This was their first physical contact aside from the morning he was ready to run her in, and there'd been nothing affectionate about that. If her brothers saw her handholding in public, they'd lock her away in a convent. Against the morals of a good Italian girl, she tightened her grip on his hand. She shouldn't have, but a deep longing screamed for his touch. What would it be like to hold him, to kiss him? She forced her fantasies to a halt.

"There are so many more things we can talk about. Why does it have to be this? When I'm off duty, I don't want to think about the job. Especially when I'm with you. So let's enjoy what little time we have together." He caught her gaze and held it.

Oh, he was almost as persuasive as she was! Her heart lightened as she took another sip at the straw. Just for this small slip of time, she chose to believe him—he'd done nothing dishonest. She welcomed all these scary new emotions that confused and excited her. She'd have to sort through them later—when he wasn't around.

"I've got no dinner plans tomorrow evening." The words fell out of her mouth. But just one dinner…

"Tomorrow I'm on duty. Would you care to have dinner on Friday evening at Astor House, then a carriage ride uptown?" he asked.

Dinner at Astor House! It wasn't for the filthy rich, but she'd never been anywhere as nice. The big word "obligation" flashed in her mind like a warning signal, but a fast "Yes!" escaped her lips as heat flooded her cheeks.

****

That night she went to a reformist meeting at Cooper Union with her cousin Baldo, the "mayor" of Mott Street. They joined the group of disgusted citizens who wanted the city cleaned up. Plain sense told her she was fighting against everything city cops stood for—*Oh, don't let Tom be one of them*, she silently begged.

Butchie blocked the side aisle with a bunch of Italian *paesani*. Surprised, she made her way through the sweaty bodies and approached him. "What are you doing here, Butch? I didn't know you were mad enough to actually come to a meeting." She spoke over the agitated voices.

He gave her a quick shrug. "I just wanna see what's goin' on."

Vita looked around the room at their neighbors. Most were poorer than her family, but no one took these meetings more seriously than she did.

"Hey, uh…" Butchie's eyes softened with concern. "Sis, some of these guys can get ugly. The new ward heeler's here, and he's supposed to be a jackass. Maybe you better go home. Somebody might start fights." He jerked his thumb in the direction of a few nearby ruffians.

"Ha!" she scoffed. "Don't worry about me, Butchie. I've been coming to these meetings a long time, and fights never break out. I don't expect one will tonight, either. So you better tell your *goombahs* there"—she gestured at the slick-haired fellows, their faces shadowed in a few days' growth, yabbering away in Italian—"like I'm telling you now, there better not be any trouble. I think you're the ones who oughta leave."

"Hey, I don't want no trouble." He looked away, his eyes following a group of some uniformed cops walking past. "What you doin' here, McGlory?" he called out.

Vita's gaze flew to the leather hat. Her heart leapt. He turned halfway around, but it wasn't Tom.

"Just keepin' the peace." It had to be his cousin Mike. He was a younger version of Tom, shorter and not so broad-chested.

Although she usually sat in the first row, she brought Butchie to the back, squeezing through aisles of wooden folding chairs. Just in case the meeting got his temper up.

****

She went to see Jadwiga on Saturday. "Hey, want to go to dinner at the Waldorf?"

"You mean the hotel? Nah, that's a bit out of my price range. Maybe someday." She poured Vita a glass of wine.

"No, not the hotel. Madame Branchard told me about this place. It's one of the hottest Village spots. It's a small café on Sixth Avenue, always packed with writers, artists, and—the people I want to meet—reformers."

"I ain't much on cafés, the poseurs all flicking their scarves, sipping coffee with their pinkies extended..." Jadwiga mimicked the typical café dweller.

"C'mon, Jadwiga, I passed by there, and it's hopping! My first week's pay is burning in my pocket, and I feel like celebrating. Tomorrow I'm going by the house to see Papa and give him a contribution, but before handing it over, I want to enjoy some of it."

"All right, I'll put on something presentable." Jadwiga stood, hands on hips, facing five or six skirts hanging on her wall. A spiky tree branch in the corner dripped with silver necklaces, colorful beads, and other dangly baubles. One glance into the mirror showed Vita looking like a refugee in her plain shirtwaist and skirt, Mama's cameo pinned to her high-buttoned collar. How would she look draped in gold and beaded jewelry?

As if reading Vita's mind—and she probably did—Jadwiga swept one of the skirts off the wall and held it up to her. "Perfect! That is you, Vita. Well, it's a more colorful you, but it's you—you with a capital Y-O-U. You gotta wear this tonight."

She walked over to the tree branch. "Can I wear some of these?"

"Of course! You wouldn't be dressed without 'em."

Jadwiga heated a pair of tongs over the fire, curled Vita's hair, and pinned it up—not in her tight little bun, but with a cascade of curls falling around her face. She squirted some musky perfume on Vita's neck and wrists from a fancy bottle with a black bulb. "I've never worn perfume before. I hope I don't attract bees—or something worse."

When Jadwiga finished with her, she looked every bit the Greenwich Village bohemian. She dragged her finger over the row of red buttons up her skirt front and twirled in front of the mirror, her blouse red, her black hat brandishing a scarlet feather. Gold filigree bracelets flowed from her wrists. Square ruby rings dazzled at her fingers. The little pouch that Jadwiga gave her created a brilliant finishing touch. She opened it. Inside rested a clay pipe, exactly like hers, but in white.

"Oh, God, Jadwiga! I can't smoke in public!"

"And why not? You look through any café window, you see gals smokin'. Gals always smoke in places like that. They also smoke where we're going afterwards."

"Where did you have in mind?" She hadn't even thought about afterwards. That was bedtime to her.

"I thought we'd go to Tony Pastor's Music Hall. A loud fun place. Nobody cares whether you're escorted, if you smoke, who you are." She held out her hand as if to introduce her. "You'll meet some interesting people there. They get all kinds. From top to bottom—the usual variety of writers and artists, the political hopefuls, business moguls out with their mistresses, working class slobs like me—but I manage to fit in." She smiled, fussed with Vita's hair one more time, and they headed out.

After dinner they walked through the Village to what looked like a real dive from the outside—

whitewashed cinderblocks, worn steps leading to the door—but inside, smoke rose to the whirring fans on the ceiling. Pots of wispy ferns hung from above. The polished dance floor gleamed. Tables and chairs lined the perimeter of the room. Laughing, drinking men and women sat at every one of them. Up front, a combo consisting of a piano, a bass fiddle, and a horn played lively music.

Jadwiga led Vita to a table near the stage, where three people sat in animated discussion, trying to shout over one another. At closer view, Vita saw a girl about her age, smoking a pipe. One of the men wore a jacket and tie, while a striped scarf hung around the other man's neck. Both men's unruly hair touched their shoulders. They gestured as they spoke, pinkie rings flashing glints of light in the electric lamps surrounding them. When Vita and Jadwiga approached, the scarfed man dragged a pair of wooden chairs from the shadows.

"This is Billy Strong." Jadwiga introduced Vita. "He's in politics. And this is William Sidney Porter, a writer."

"But I like to say I'm an author." Smiling, he corrected her and motioned Vita to sit.

The pipe-smoking girl held her hand out to Vita and introduced herself as Inez Mulholland. Her firm grip nearly crushed Vita's hand. She wore her blonde hair short. A waitress came by and they ordered cocktails, but Vita asked for seltzer.

"They're unsurpassed at the art of mixology here," Inez encouraged Vita, but she wanted to break herself in slowly.

The music was so loud her throat went raw from shouting over the blaring horn and the piano, but she pulled her chair up next to Strong and they got talking about their mutual interests. She looked into droopy blue eyes. The name didn't suit his physique. Still, she'd remember that name and what he told her: "I plan to be mayor of New York someday." She looked around with a satisfied smile, smug in her independence. These free spirits celebrated free expression—and now she was one of them! She relished this first step on her way to achieving her goals. In her borrowed clothes and jewelry, she raised her head high. Nobody knew who she was, and that was just fine with her. As she sipped her seltzer, watching Jadwiga put away a gin-and-something, she glanced at the dance floor. Couples swayed to the music, women twirling, their skirts flying around them. She turned back to the men at her table, hoping for an invitation to dance. But these fellows didn't look like dancers. She added that to her agenda—dance lessons—after night school, of course.

Jadwiga took out her pipe, and Porter lit it for her. She gestured to Vita, pointing at her satin bag. Vita loosened the drawstring and pulled the pipe out. She didn't relish this bold and brazen act, but women smoked those thin cigars everyplace. She tapped some tobacco into the bowl, and Strong lit it for her. As she took that first fashionable drag, she made sure to take in enough air so she wouldn't choke.

She crossed her legs and dragged on her pipe. Ah, so New York.

When the band took a break, Jadwiga started chatting about books. Vita learned she and Porter enjoyed western novels. He mentioned a few authors she didn't know, and she added a trip to the library to her list of must-do's. Oh, she'd missed so much. Twenty years old, and she'd never set foot in a dance hall.

She rested her cheek in her propped-up hand, hanging on Porter's words about his struggle to get his short stories published and his decision to use the pen name of O. Henry. Her gaze roamed the room, fueled by her curiosity to see what the other women wore. Her glass slipped from her fingers and she spilled seltzer down her front when she saw him. Tom and Sergeant Munn nudged through the crowd in plainclothes, looking very dapper—starched shirts, neatly pressed trousers, shiny shoes. Tom's hair glistened with sapphire highlights in the blue light fixtures on the walls.

"Look—" She shook Jadwiga's shoulder. "It's him—" Jadwiga read her lips, stood, and craned her neck. Vita pulled Jadwiga back down and rasped into her ear, "Don't face that way…don't…don't let him see me. He's heading for that table. The tall one with the balding guy."

Jadwiga's gaze fell upon him. She squinted and nodded. "Oh, yeah. That's him, all right. I'd know him anywhere. Exactly as I pictured."

Even the two Williams leaned over their drinks to see who'd caused her to spill seltzer down her front.

Tom walked toward a table across the room and waved Munn over. She lost interest in everything about this place—he outshone it all. He stood the tallest, his eyes shone the sharpest, his mustache the trimmest. Women turned to stare at him before dragging their gazes back to their own escorts.

Jadwiga gave Vita a wink, stood, and left her with

the three bohemians. She cut across the dance floor and headed toward Tom. The crowd blocked Vita's view until she saw Jadwiga brush against Tom's shoulder and drop her handkerchief. He bent to pick it up, handed it to her, and gave her a polite smile. Jadwiga walked on toward the lavatory, and in a few minutes she rejoined Vita and their group.

"You didn't talk to him, did you?" Breathless, Vita dunked a napkin into her seltzer and mopped her face.

"Didn't have to." Jadwiga leaned over to say goodnight to Inez and the two Williams.

"Nice meeting you," Vita mouthed, for they wouldn't have been able to hear her, and skirted the dance floor as she and Jadwiga made their exit. She didn't feel Tom's eyes on her this time. As a doorman hailed a taxi, Vita asked Jadwiga, "So did you read him?" A taxi pulled up.

Jadwiga chuckled. "Oh, yeah, I read him, all right. He's a quiet one, that's for sure. Keeps it all inside. He's proud, very proud." She gave Vita a wide grin as the taxi jounced down the street. "What I'm getting is that he's dedicated to his work and could not be compromised. But I can get a lot more from him with this." She held up a brown leather billfold and opened it. It contained an identification card and several bills. She fanned them out like her Tarot cards.

"Where have I seen that billfold before?" Her jaw dropped. "That's his!" She gasped, not believing, not wanting to believe that Jadwiga had taken it right out of his pocket.

"He'll get it back," Jadwiga assured her, counted the money and stuffed it back into the billfold.

"You picked it right out of his pocket? My God,

that's what he thought I was trying to do to him!"

"Don't have much luck with his billfold, does he?" Jadwiga laughed, leaning forward to signal the driver to drop them off.

They entered Jadwiga's flat, and she poured herself another horn. "Nightcap?"

"Nooo, thanks." Vita wagged her hand.

Jadwiga took a mouthful, put the glass down, and held the billfold between her palms.

"He's ardent, impetuous, feckless, and loves to drink, dance, and fight, although he'll never admit to the last one. He's egalitarian, democratic, tough, generous, friendly, witty, physically courageous, proud, and opinionated."

"That's a real mix." Vita sat and pulled her shoes off. "Why didn't you find 'corrupt' in there?"

"I don't feel it."

"Maybe that's because he doesn't think he is. A lot of them don't." She rubbed her aching feet. Too bad the fashionable shoes pinched.

"That's what I'm getting on him, Vita. It's up to you if you think he's worth sticking around to let him prove it."

"I need to be able to trust him." Her doubts screamed at her as she tried to fight them back.

"Would this help?" Jadwiga took out a creased piece of paper from the billfold. She unfolded it and dangled it in front of Vita's face.

Vita's eyes grew wider with each line. "My whole life changed the day I met you," she read out loud. "You are so brave and determined, not like any woman I've ever met. I dreamed of having a lady like you all my life; I thank God our destinies have crossed. I'm not one to voice my feelings, nor am I one to have much control over my emotions. Whatever our differences, I know we can work them out. Do not turn me away. Now I know why God spared me from starvation and brought me here. You are the flower that dares to bloom in my garden when blight threatens. You are the sun that peeks through the clouds on a day that wants to remain night. You are the fire that warms me on a cold night. You are what I've been missing. I was always there for you; you just never saw me. Together we can conquer these demons that are threatening to keep us apart. Just give me a chance to show you how I feel."

"Jadwiga, this is so beautiful." She pressed the note over her heart. "Did you read it?"

"I read it, all right. In the ladies' lavatory."

"I wonder who it was meant for," she mused as tentacles of jealousy niggled at her.

"Well, it don't look too old, so unless he's got another fire goin' to warm him on a cold night, I'd guess it was you."

"Oh, if that was only true," she said over a sigh. But what right did she have to expect this outpouring of emotion from him? A realization hit her: although she could never put them into such beautiful prose, her feelings for him had become just as intense. She held the letter close and inhaled the billfold's leather scent—his scent.

She folded it back up. "I can't jump to any conclusions, Jadwiga. This may not be for me."

"Don't sell yourself short. It's for you, all right. I know it. Looks like you got yourself a suitor, dear heart."

Vita's body warmed at that. "I've only had one

suitor in my entire life. Marco Manziano."

"Yeah? What happened? You give him the mitten?" She took a pull of her drink.

"No." Vita rubbed her feet some more. "He died of a bad heart, only twenty-one."

"Ah, what a shame."

Focused on the memory, she went on, "I didn't like him that much, but Papa did. His and Papa's great-grandfathers had been brothers. But he never uttered a word that'd come close to the outpouring of this letter. I wonder if or when he was planning to send it to me, then."

"When the timing is right." Jadwiga slid it back out of the billfold and skimmed it again. "When he's sure of your feelings for him. Like I said, he's proud. He can't make a fool outta himself. Maybe he got hurt before and wants to be sure this time. He's a good writer, though, I gotta say. Ought to do it for a living, instead of pounding a beat."

"I've got to get this back to him somehow. He'd be mortified if he found it missing." She took it from Jadwiga and clutched it, not wanting to let it go.

"Yeah, he should get the billfold back," Jadwiga agreed, tapping brown powder into her pipe bowl. "But you oughta keep the letter."

"I can't keep this! We've got to get this back to him just the way you found it. He's probably frantic looking for it—all of it."

"Frantic?" Jadwiga waved a be-ringed hand. "Nah, not him. Nothing makes him frantic. If he's as crooked as you think he is, he ain't gonna miss the dough much." She snickered, blowing out a stream of smoke. "I'll bring it back to the dance hall tomorrow. I'll tell them I found it on the floor. Or you can take it. Whatever."

"I'll take it. I should take it." Vita's voice trembled. "If I personally bring it back, I won't feel so guilty about snooping."

She took the letter from Jadwiga and slid it back into the billfold. "Just out of curiosity, how much money did Tom carry?" she asked.

"Hundred, hundred ten, something like that," she replied.

Graft? Vita wondered. "Whew, that's some pocket fulla rocks." Either way, it wasn't hers.

"When he does give you that letter," Jadwiga warned with a wink, "don't forget to act like you never seen it before."

****

Sunlight dazzled in a clear sky as Vita stepped into the cool darkness of Tony Pastor's Music Hall. Dust mites floated on a slant of sunlight streaming in from the window above the bandstand. The wooden round-seated chairs rested upside down on the tables.

Vita's heels clicked on the floor as she walked back to the far corner. A gas lamp cast a yellow glow onto the closed door. She knocked.

"Yeah? C'min."

"I found this on the floor last night," she explained to the well-fed manager sitting at his desk poring over papers. She placed the billfold at the edge of the desk.

"Yeah, a leatherhea—a policeman was lookin' for a billfold." He grabbed it with pudgy fingers, flipped it open and rooted through it. "McGlory, he's the one." He looked up at her and gave her an approving once-over. "Thanks for your honesty, miss."

"It's nothing." She turned to leave. She bowed her head, ashamed of Jadwiga for having done such a thing.

"Uh, miss…"

She stopped. "What?"

"There's a reward." He held some folded bills between his fingers. "Twenty-five clams. He said somethin' real valuable was in that billfold."

The letter? Or his money? she wondered. "I don't want any reward. Just return it to him. You can give him back his money."

His eyes brightened and he smiled, as if he'd never met anyone who refused free money. She wished she hadn't read that letter, only because he might have written it to someone else.

****

After she stopped at Mr. LaFamina's to pick up her new apparel, she browsed in a used bookstore, walking out with two bags of books. She'd found an author William Sidney Porter had raved about, and the others were about New York history.

When she got back to the boardinghouse, Madame Branchard rose from her seat in the parlor. She went up to Vita and handed her an envelope. "A very handsome young man just brought this over 'for Miss Caputo,' he said. I couldn't convince him to stay and wait for you. He said he had to get to work. If he's courtin' you, Vita, don't let him get away!"

"No, he's not courting me," she mumbled as she took the envelope. Madame Branchard stood and waited. Did she expect Vita to open it right then and there? She said, "Thank you," in a polite tone. But Madame ignored that, nodding expectantly, her eyes roving from Vita to the envelope and back again. Vita slipped the envelope into one of her book bags and hustled up the staircase, her hand sliding up the banister. As much as she loved her new home, thoughts of Tom tightened her stomach with longing.

She didn't rip the letter open till she closed her room door. Twenty-five dollars fell into her lap. She recognized the upright penmanship, but she studied the bold lettering written with a flourish. It almost spoke to her.

"Dear Vita, thank you for your honesty. Johnny the owner described you; the red hair, the cameo brooch…"

If he knew she'd found his wallet, he must know she'd probably peeked at the letter. But she couldn't keep his money. She thought of bringing it to the station, but handing it back in person would be a more genuine gesture.

Chapter Eight

When Vita reported to work dressed in her new green blouse and skirt from the Ladies' Mile, co-workers and customers commented on how lovely she looked. That apparel was her first extravagance, a dream come true.

She kept it to herself that Tom McGlory was escorting her to dinner that evening. They weren't courting, and she didn't want word to get around that they were. A few female heads turned when he strode through the doors. He carried himself with such poise. Her heart lunged, her eyes riveted to his graceful bearing. He looked resplendent in a dark jacket, crisp white shirt, and perfectly knotted tie, graced with a gold tie clip. He waved hello and went to Mr. Johnson's office.

That gave her a chance to catch her breath and get back to her job.

She counted the minutes till he approached her window. "Good afternoon, and you do look lovely today, Miss Greene."

She caught the faint trace of a spicy shaving lotion that she could actually taste. Her mouth watered. He slid a passbook and some bills under the bars, and she brushed his fingers with hers. "Just so it won't look like I'm simply chatting here, you can post this to the account I opened the other day."

It was twenty-five dollars, almost her entire savings. If he'd been taking graft on a regular basis, he'd be depositing a lot more, but of course he wouldn't be banking it. So she assumed this was honest money. But why had he opened a new account?

It was not her business why customers did what they did, and she certainly couldn't ask him why he'd opened another account. Twenty-five had been the amount of the reward he'd offered for his billfold. Maybe he was setting up an emergency fund. But why would he need this if he was raking in a fortune in graft? Her curiosity made her dizzier than the sight of him.

She asked no questions, simply handed him back his passbook and took her purse from under the counter.

If only she could have freshened up before he arrived, but she'd been too busy. So she excused herself to the ladies' lavatory, stood at the mirror, and let her bun down. She hadn't cut her hair since she left Italy. She barely recognized herself. The woman looking back at her brandished a spark in her eye she'd never seen before, a confident glimmer behind a hint of wisdom. Ladies never went out in public with loose hair, so she pulled it back and twisted it into her familiar knot. She dug in her purse for the vial of Madame Branchard's toilet water. She splashed some on her pulse points as she'd shown her. "I didn't even know I had pulse points." Vita smiled at herself in the mirror. She wondered if men did the pulse point ritual or if they just slapped it all over their faces. She couldn't picture Tom dabbing cologne on his wrists, but she couldn't imagine him taking graft, either. Just for tonight, she'd promised herself, she was going to believe him and trust him and enjoy his company. Because after tonight, what?

Either the carriage was hired or it belonged to someone reasonably wealthy—black and polished to a sheen, it displayed a shiny gold eagle on the door and lamps next to the windows. He helped her inside, and she sank into the cushioned velvet seat. As he sat next to her, his thigh brushed up against hers, sending a forbidden thrill through her. She should've moved aside. *I'll go to confession Sunday*, she silently promised.

They clip-clopped up Fifth Avenue past the fancy mansions with floor-to-ceiling windows, ladies strolling with lacy parasols, and gents in silk top hats. Tom pointed out the Vanderbilt, Carnegie, and Astor palaces. "And there's Madame Restell's house." He showed her the brownstone on 52nd Street. Vita remembered reading about the famous abortionist who slit her throat in her bathtub. *All those poor souls*, she thought. Not a pushcart or squawking chicken in sight—only refinement and elegance. Tom gazed out of the carriage, a wistful expression saddening his eyes.

"Is this what you want?" She gestured at the palaces. "Tell me your hopes for the future, Tom. I know you have them."

"Oh, yes, I want it so bad I can taste it." He clenched his fists, staring at the carriage floor, his gaze fixed on an innermost thought. "The mansions, the carriages, the servants, the membership in the Century Club. If they can have it, why can't I?" From his hesitant tone, she could tell he didn't share his dreams with just anyone. "I want it all. I want to go as far as a man can go in this world."

She didn't want to ask him how far he'd already come. She was treading too close to her suspicions. What she really wanted to know was why he wanted to be one of the nabobs, not so much how he planned to get there. But there had to be more to it than wanting a mansion and custom-made coaches. She distrusted people who craved immense riches. Comfort was one thing, but to want more than enough to spend in a lifetime fell into the clutches of greed. But could Tom be this way? She hoped not—it would shatter her image of him—the image she'd begun to adore.

There was no reason for this vulgar display of wealth, not to this extreme—each mansion and carriage more outlandish than the next. And hearing Tom say he wanted it all made it hard to separate him from all these nabobs.

He must have sensed that from the way she suddenly went quiet. "How about you, Vita? You want the finer things in life, the comfort, the style. I know you do. If you didn't, you wouldn't be going to reform meetings, trying to improve your quality of life." He took her hand. She tried not to clutch his too eagerly. "You deserve it all. You're special. Very special." His tone expressed true devotion.

She wasn't used to flattery. After a simple "Thank you," she went on, "All this"—she waved her hand at the displays of ostentatious wealth—"is each one trying to one-up the other. I don't care if my next door neighbor has more than I do. I'm going to be a success, Tom. I'm not going to spend my life on Mott Street and exist on slave wages. But I don't want to be obscenely wealthy, either. I want just enough. No more, no less. Just enough."

"That's very noble of you. You're stronger-willed than I am," he admitted. They passed a magnificent coach drawn by six matched grays parked at the curb. A splendidly dressed couple alighted and glided through iron gates to their elegant townhouse. "Now that's living."

But she wished they were in the Village among the artists, poets, and men strolling arm in arm. Her lips craved the feel of her new pipe. Here she sat straight and stiff, like a player on a stage, leading a cast of props. A woman in voluminous skirts swished past them in a rustle of silks and crinolines. *Could she actually be comfortable in all that?* Vita wondered. "*Mama mia*, look at her, she looks a walking window dressing!"

As the carriage turned down 42nd Street and headed back downtown, he said, "I know you want to be successful, and I admire you for it. But the more you get, the more you'll want. It's human nature. We'll start right here. Tell me you'll be satisfied eating eggplant from a pushcart after one meal in this place." His tone challenged her as the carriage pulled up at the entrance to Astor House. He helped her down, and she linked her arm in his as he escorted her in.

"But Tom—" His nearness created a deliciously scary feeling, like the first time she'd taken a whiff of Jadwiga's smoke. "If you did this all the time, you'd tire of it."

He looked down at her and smiled, but his eyes still held a vague sorrow. "There's always something new. This is New York. This country is in the stages of late infancy—how can there not be anything new to find in every single day here? We're young. We have to grow with America. It would be a sin to just stand back and watch." He squeezed her arm as the maitre d' showed them to a table overlooking Broadway. Tom nudged the maitre d' aside and held her chair out himself.

"I have to admit, I might get sick of this if I did it every day, but it would take a lot of days," Tom said as a waiter filled their water glasses.

"So how often do you go to Tony Pastor's Music Hall?" He scanned the menu. "Do you like music?"

"I love music, but I never went to Pastor's before. How about you?" As she studied her menu, she noticed it didn't list any prices.

"It's a popular place for cops. Makes a nice change from the taverns and the oyster houses, but I don't do either very often. I spend a lot of time at home with the family. There's always something that needs to be done in the house, somebody who needs a hand with studies, or a personal problem to be worked out—always a tiff I'm expected to referee. I'm the family peacemaker." He chuckled, his laugh lines etching a genuine quality into his smile.

"Our family could sure use a few of those. One for each of us."

"But you all love each other." He closed the menu. "All families squabble."

She didn't want to discuss her family. "Leaving was the best thing I ever did," was all she'd say. Then on second thought, she decided to share more. "I don't even know if Papa loves me. He's never shown affection to any of us. I have a dark cloud hanging over my head, Tom. My mother died after having me. They all blamed me for that, especially Rosalia. She was happy in Italy, and they dragged her here to marry

Papa."

"Look, Vita, none of this is your fault." He reached for her hand. She grasped it back, public place or not.

"All right, now that I'm out of the house, I want to look to the future and enjoy the present while I'm living it. I wanted to tell you about Mama dying and all that, but with a present and a future like mine, who needs to think of the past?"

He nodded his agreement.

"Let's change the subject, Tom. Let's talk about you."

"Sorry." He gave her a shaky grin. "I thought maybe getting you to talk about them would help a little."

"I'd rather talk about you." She feigned interest in the menu, more eager to talk about him. "I already know my family."

"There's not much to tell." He sipped his water. "We came here to avoid starving to death, and I'm determined to make the most of being here."

He didn't elaborate, and she sensed a double meaning behind his words.

He ordered for both of them, and the prime rib with buttery mashed potatoes and mushroom gravy melted in her mouth.

"You amaze me, Vita. It would be so easy for you to just climb those tenement stairs every night after a day's work at a factory and start all over again the next day."

"Easy? There's nothing easy about that life. It's a brutal life, and I know I can make it better someday. And not just for me. It takes a lot of reasoning, some cajoling, even some whining." She dabbed at her lips

101

with her napkin. "The main thing is we're nice to the people we have to be nice to. So we have a good chance the ward heeler or the district boss will come to our reform meetings at Cooper Union. There's always a reporter there taking notes, and an article about the meeting always gets into the press. During the cholera outbreak last year, we pushed the Health Department to get the Disinfecting Corps to bring disinfectant to the Lower East Side."

"I heard about that." He nodded, his eyes brightening.

"They started to come around about every ten days after that. We're pushing for indoor plumbing in all the tenements by the turn of the century. The immigrants who work so hard should have a reason for immigrating, instead of leaving a starving village to come starve here."

"I'm proud of you, Vita. You don't know how proud I am." He smiled, rapt, with an interest she could never command.

Just like Mrs. Paluzzi, who listened with an open mind between cooking and cleaning and piecework, Tom was nearly demanding in his encouragement. "Do it," he urged, "follow your dreams, don't let anyone stop you. This city needs someone like you."

"The bank's the best thing that ever happened to me, and I thought you and I were even before, but it looks like I owe you a lot more," she confessed. Now she didn't mind being indebted to him. Just as long as something remained unsaid between them, she'd have a reason to see him again.

"You don't owe me a thing." He waved away any chance of a returned favor, but her senses alerted her:

He knows I still suspect him.

After ice cream with raspberry sauce, they left the carriage parked and strolled up Broadway. She linked her arm through his and held her head high. No one halted to sneer at her. No one knew who she was. She basked in this obscurity, another luxury she'd never had before. In the old country and on the East Side, privacy didn't exist.

He strutted like a proud peacock. She sensed that he pretended to be one of these nobs. But Fifth Avenue wasn't her style. The obscene display of wealth made off the backs of the poor sickened her. *Tom wants a piece of this?* She itched to talk him out of it.

They turned and headed back for the carriage parked at the curb, behind an even shinier one with bigger wheels. "The strive for success should be the best part, not getting there, Tom. And don't be miserable along the way because you're not there yet."

"I'm not miserable. This is the best evening I've spent in months." He gazed down at her, his eyes twinkling.

She told him with all sincerity, "Me too, except it's been much longer than that."

He helped her into the carriage, and she turned to him. Their gazes held as she moved closer, their lips within kissing distance. He lowered his head, caressed her cheek with his fingertip and met her lips in a teasing kiss, leaving her hungry for more. She locked her arms around his neck and pressed her lips to his. A flutter in her lower region captured her unawares. *Dear God, what's coming over me?* She suppressed a shudder. Hot with shame, she pulled back and slapped herself across the cheek.

"What's wrong?" he breathed, pulling away.

"This isn't right, Tom. I'm supposed to be a good girl." All the Catholic rules invaded her conscience as her body betrayed her, yearning for more kisses, more touching, more of this closeness so new and scary, yet so exciting.

"You are a good girl, Vita. But we want each other. What can be wrong with that?" He claimed her lips before she could argue about the church, her honor, or original sin.

She fought this wild desire, but this was the moment of a lifetime. Her arms wound around him. His tongue pressed forward and mingled with hers in an exquisite rhythm. This new thrilling sensation took her breath away. She needed to gulp for air, but her lips hungered for his once more. She pulled him into another kiss, savoring his warm embrace as a symphony of sensations washed over her—delightful tingling, the clean scent of soap on his neck, his hard body against hers…

When he kissed her goodnight at her door, she fought with all her strength not to prolong the sweet moment. "I'll see you again soon, right?" She knew that bold question defied the courting ritual. But her desire to be with him made a mockery of the courting game.

He looked at her as if she'd just given him a precious gift. Warmth infused his eyes and touched his lips with a grateful smile. "Of course. Tomorrow. And I'll count the minutes," he whispered it as if in prayer.

Chapter Nine

When Tom reported for duty, his uniform didn't stick to his body. He breathed without choking on foul odors. A cool breeze ruffled his hair. Anybody curious about hell should visit New York City during a heat wave.

Lamplighters lit the gas streetlamps with their long sticks. The peddlers shouted their final wares of the day on every bustling corner, and the harried customers shouted back. The sun sank behind the precinct station. The shade cooled him as he climbed the steps.

As he walked through the precinct door, a pall of tragedy hung in the air. Nobody one looked up, greeted him, or joked around. He didn't smell the usual aroma of coffee. This could only mean one thing. Sergeant Munn confirmed his suspicions when he approached Tom, his face ashen.

"Who died, Sarge?"

"Tom, God almighty, I don't know how to tell you this." His voice broke. "Mike was shot while on duty last night, Tom. We lost him." He wiped his eyes with a handkerchief. "Jesus, I'm sorry."

An invisible blow struck his chest and knocked the wind out of him. "Mike? My Mike?"

He nodded and wrapped his arm around Tom's shoulders in a fatherly hug. Shock gripped him and numbed him. He didn't fight it, but he built a barrier against the grief that would flood him later.

Mike at every age flashed through his mind: playing stickball in the street...

Leaping out of the path of a wagon clattering toward them...

Helping Tom climb the tree in their yard...

Swinging from the rope...

Wrapping his coat around Tom as they walked home New Year's morning...

...all these memories, all their lives, Tom and Mike, Tom and Mike...

"Who did it?" He slammed his fist on the desk. He fleetingly suspected the Italians, but stopped himself. *No, they can't always be guilty.*

Still too numb for grief, he savored that numbness. But he knew it would abandon him and leave a raw gaping wound. "When did it happen?"

"Last night. They found him just before daylight."

A few rookies started to put up black bunting. Seeing the flag lowered to half mast would be the worst part. He could never bear to see that flag sliding down the pole and stopping halfway.

"Where?" It didn't seem real. They couldn't be talking about Mike.

"A fruit vendor found his body at 124 Mott Street, in front of the alley between two tenements."

"That's the Italian section." Still numb and not thinking straight, he looked up the Caputos' last arrest report.

There it was. 124 Mott Street. The Caputos' building.

He didn't say anything else to his sergeant. He just wanted to be alone. He walked over to St. Andrew's

Church, took off his hat, and went in.

The door groaned shut as he walked up the aisle. One woman knelt in a back pew. He dropped some coins into the poor box and lit a candle. Then he headed for his usual family pew. Pausing to genuflect, he entered the third row and dropped to his knees on the cushioned kneeler. The scent of candle wax enveloped him. He fixed his gaze on the lifeless face of Christ, immortalized in sculpture on the massive crucifix towering over him.

"Oh, Mike…"

Mike's spirit filled the hallowed space, from where he sat to the high arches reaching toward heaven. In life, Mike was the most curious fellow Tom knew. Always wanted to know how things worked, why things were the way they were. Their lives just didn't allow for the asking of such questions. Who had time to sit and speculate about how humans fit into the universe? Tom would sit with Mike for hours, debating, guessing. Mike would've made a brilliant detective, with his sense of curiosity and thirst for truth. Now he'd passed that quest on to Tom. And his first duty was to find out who'd cut his life short. He didn't even want to know why. He just wanted to know who. *Why* was a moot point. Why? Because they were murdering bastards. Rotten New York bastards.

He laid his head on his arms as Mike's presence surrounded him, more strongly than yesterday when they'd walked side by side.

"Oh, I'll find the bastards who killed you," he answered Mike's silent question. "I'll get them, buddy, if I have to die trying. Dammit, Mike, I'll get them…"

Then Mike's presence vanished. "Yeah, yeah, I'm

going." He pulled the heavy wooden door open and exited God's house.

****

He sat alone in Joe's, trying to dull his pain with yet another beer. Just as he expected, the numbness gave way to the grief that crushed his spirit. The fact that Mike had been found outside Vita's building ate away at his gut. Had she heard about this? If so, what was she going through? If only they'd met years ago, she'd be sitting here next to him. He'd be sharing this with her instead of suffering through it alone.

Then something hit him like a physical blow to his gut. *What am I thinking here? Not wanting to suffer alone?* He'd done his best thinking, his best planning, grieving, and praying, while in silent solitude. Why this sudden longing to share this with someone—namely her? Was he weakening? Did he need her? *No, stupid idea—you're half crazed with grief, McGlory. You're in shock.* He was physically attracted to her and longed to know her intimately—he could even say he was falling in love with her. But need her? He'd have to think long and hard about that.

****

Tom and his fellow cops draped his house in black bunting. The entire Metropolitan Police Force streamed in, offering condolences. The parlor was so jammed with cops, friends, and priests bringing food and whiskey, Tom slipped out and went to a quiet tavern down the street. He sat in the back, nursed a beer, and prepared for a world without Mike.

Two of the meanest cops this side of the Weehawken swamps swaggered toward him. He didn't see their faces, but he knew them by their bulky outlines. Their daysticks obeyed their arrogant gait. And they weren't here to offer condolences, although he expected their sanctimonious attempt.

Jimmy Mulligan and Eamon Murphy looked like brothers, with the same black hair and deep-set eyes. They'd been cops since he was a rookie kid.

"Tom—sorry to hear about Mike." Jim spoke while Eamon nodded, his eyes shifting downwards.

What a load of bunkum. He scowled. "I appreciate your sympathy." *Now scram,* Tom wanted to add. But did they have something to say worth hearing?

"Do you two know something?" Tom knew they'd spill at least half of what they knew, if anything.

"Mike was taken out because he wasn't smart like you, and he didn't mind his own business," Mulligan mumbled, his tone menacing.

Tom didn't need to hear any more from these two bad eggs. "Yeah." He waved them away. They returned identical nods, made an about-face, and ambled off. Even the smoke seemed to get out of their way.

"Oh, Mike, what did you get yourself into?" he moaned. "You were straight, too, and look where it got you, cousin." But it had to be more than that. He must've known too much. Tom shook his head in helpless bewilderment. *Oh, Mike!* He'd been too trusting, and it backfired on him. Tom rested his head in his hands, fogged by grief, reaching no conclusion. He drained his beer and got out of there. A whiskey-soaked father and a houseful of mourners waited at home.

****

The next day Vita went to the tenement straight from work to pick up a few things she knew Rosalia never used: a bedsheet jammed in the dresser drawer, a pillowcase, a pair of nylons. In no mood to argue about how the men suffered without Vita there to cook and clean, she didn't want to bump into Rosalia. Still floating on clouds from her date with Tom, she knew last night had been a brief escape from reality. The way her body had responded to that kiss made her cringe in shame. Here she was, moved out of her father's house, a woman on her own, letting a man kiss her like that— surely he questioned her virtue now. But she pushed that old-world guilt behind her new mask of independence. She let a man kiss her. So what? That wasn't so taboo in the world she now lived in. Jadwiga and Madame Branchard would knock back an extra shot of gin if she told them.

As she climbed the stairs, the putrid odors strangled her. The toilet on the landing looked more spattered and stained than usual. God, how did she ever live here?

She opened the door and stepped into the kitchen. "Anybody home?" No. Good. She went to the back room and set her potato sack down.

****

"You better sit down for this one, Tom." Sergeant Munn took him by the arm and sat him in a stiff-backed chair.

"Oh, no," he groaned. "What now?"

"The Caputos were arrested for Mike's murder. The old man and the son—Lorenzo and Bruno."

"God, no. Not those two." His vision blurred. A sickening wave choked him. He swallowed.

"Eamon himself just made the arrest," Munn went on. "He found the same kind of gun that killed Mike in the Caputo apartment, found some things belonging to

Mike up there. Eamon figured it was them 'cause Mike had arrested them before and was comin' down on them for gambling shenanigans."

Tom nodded, facing the ugly truth. Eamon had hauled them in a few times. The Caputo father and son beat Mike up—twice—when Mike booked them for thievery. The last brawl happened two months ago. He'd booked Bruno himself once, but witnesses vouched for him, and nobody knew who started it, so he got off.

"You know they had it in for Mike," Munn affirmed. "Him and Bruno were the prime suspects. The evidence was all over the place. Pointin' right at 'em."

A new wave of shock stunned him. He thrust his hands in his pockets, jingled his coins. He paced in circles, head bowed, staring at the scuffs on the floor. He shut his eyes and envisioned his Vita—how beautiful she looked last night, how her eyes sparkled. He'd longed to kiss her all evening, burning with desire. He'd taken terrible advantage of her in the carriage, but she'd responded with a fervor that matched his. Now she had to suffer this.

"You okay, Tom?" Munn placed a hand on Tom's shoulder. "Wanna go for a beer or somethin'?"

"No." He rubbed his eyes. "Poor Vita must be in such shock right now."

Munn leaned over him. "What's that?"

He shook his head. "The Caputos—Vita. She's— never mind." He couldn't share this with the sergeant right now. He stood and faced Munn. "I'm going back on the beat. I need to get back to work." He left the precinct and headed for his beat.

His eyes burned, his throat ached. But he had a job

to do. As he patrolled the crowded streets, he made a vow: "I'll find the bastards who killed you, Mike, but for the love of God, don't let it be the Caputos."

****

At seven sharp the next morning, Tom walked up to Sergeant Munn scribbling out a report at his desk. "I need to go undercover, Sarge. I need to find out who killed Mike."

Munn put his pen down and flexed his fingers. "You're being too noble for your own good, Tom. Leave it to the rest of 'em. We don't need another fly cop."

"No, I don't trust the rest of 'em. They'll come up with some cock-and-bull report and bury it in the dust along with my cousin's memory. He deserves more than that, and you know it." Tom stared the sergeant down.

Munn opened his mouth to speak, but Tom cut him off. "Either I'm a fly cop, or I'm quitting the force and doing it on my own." He paced back and forth. "I mean that. I can live on the few bucks I have. I'm up for a promotion."

Munn sat in silence and nodded his approval.

Tom went to Mike's wake in plain clothes, on duty but undercover. He got his way.

Chapter Ten

Vita worked late and strode up the quiet street, everybody at their kitchen tables eating supper. With a spring in her step, swinging her pastry boxes by their strings, she turned the corner of Mott. She'd promised to come back and cook tonight.

Mouth-watering aromas of garlic and sausage floated through windows as she passed the endless rows of tenements. Her stomach rumbled. She reached 124, leapt up their stoop steps, and pushed the door open.

Vita climbed the narrow stairs and halted. Mrs. Rizzoli stood at the landing, her girth blocking Vita's way. *"Buona sera, Senora Rizzoli! Come va?"* She gave the rotund *nonna* a smile.

But she didn't smile back or pinch Vita's cheek.

Vita peered at Mrs. Rizzoli clutching a wadded-up hankie, her eyes red and swollen. "What's wrong?" Vita reached out to her.

"Go into my apartment." Mrs. Rizzoli gestured to her door.

"Why your apartment?"

As Mrs. Rizzoli nudged her along, Vita walked in on what looked like a wake. Almost the entire building milled around in there, along with some neighbors. The crowd hushed as she entered. *Papa? No, don't let it be!*

She clutched Mrs. Rizzoli's arm and dropped the pastries. "What happened?"

"They took them away, Vita, your papa and Butchie." Mrs. Rizzoli gave her the staggering news. "The cops come and take them in a black Maria."

"Cops? Why?" she shrieked.

A neighbor hugged her, and she stumbled back. Someone shoved a wine glass into her hand. Her fear of Papa's death vanished, but she shook with worry.

"The cops took your father and Butchie to the police station." Mrs. Rizzoli draped her arm around Vita. The woman reeked of garlic and body odor, but Vita needed the comfort of a mother, even if it was someone else's.

"What'd they—what'd they do?"

"I don' know, I don' know. Sal, take Vita to the police station. Maybe they can tell her what happen," she addressed her son. He lumbered up to her, a replica of his mother but a foot taller. Her breaths came in gasps. The wine glass vanished, but someone pressed a glass of water into her trembling hand. She sipped just enough to wet her mouth.

Pop Bullets, one of the local bookies, stood behind Mrs. Rizzoli. He took Vita's hand and clasped it between his two sweaty paws. "A coupla cops take 'em in a black Maria. I says, 'Hey, where you takin' 'em?' but they don't answer me. They no talk to us."

"Take her to the police, Sal." Mrs. Rizzoli's voice pierced the air, conditioned from years of giving orders.

"First let me go upstairs." Vita elbowed her way out. "I want to bring them some things."

"I go with you." Mrs. Rizzoli nudged Pop Bullets aside and grabbed Vita's arm.

"No!" she insisted. "Let me go alone."

Vita climbed the stairs and entered her own empty

rooms.

Oh, God, what could Papa and Butchie have done now? Both of them this time! Not another brawl with a policeman. She had to get some bail money! She mentally calculated how much she had. No, that wouldn't be enough.

She saw Papa's crucifix under the kitchen table. She picked it up and noticed a gash in the bottom, as if someone had flung it. *He'll want this*. She placed it on the table, turned, and headed for the back rooms.

Chapter Eleven

"Tom, I know you want to work this case, so go to the Caputo joint and give it an overhaul for further evidence," Sergeant Munn ordered as he laid a hand on Tom's shoulder, his tone gentle. "Since you and Mike were so close, you'll be able to tell if anything there belonged to him."

"Yeah, I'll have to—I'll go." But his feet wouldn't move, as if nailed to the floor. Questions hammered at him, but he had no answers. "The Caputos have been arrested?"

"Yeah. They're bringin' 'em to the Tombs tomorrow."

The Tombs was aptly named. The city's main prison, it covered an entire block. Urchins caught for stealing bread rotted in there with murderers. As a rookie, he used to shudder every time he passed that dungeon.

Another pain for Vita stabbed his heart. Seeing her father and brother in that hellhole was more than any woman should have to bear. Even a woman as strong as Vita. He dredged up a torturous memory: his own destitute father, jobless and stripped of his pride and dignity. He forced that long-ago nightmare from his mind once more. He couldn't even bury it by spilling it into his journal. It still crept up and haunted him.

"How about the other family members?" Tom

asked. He didn't want to mention her name.

"The wife was brought in for questioning," Munn said. "The daughter might be brung in later."

He knew she'd be called as a witness at the trial. A flood of pity washed over him. *Lord, don't make her testify at her own father's murder trial,* he begged.

Sergeant Munn sent Petey Murphy, a second-year rookie, along with Tom to the Caputos' tenement. Oh, how he didn't want to overhaul that place. All he wanted to do was find her, hold her close, and feel their hearts beating as one. If her father and brother had killed Mike, of course he'd want them behind bars. Until now, he'd prayed for a future with her, against the odds. But this would tear them apart, their precious courtship doomed to shatter in the horror of this ordeal.

He wanted to ram his fist through the wall and feel the agonizing pain of his bones crunching, just to prove he was still alive.

But he forced himself back to his job and the emotional detachment he'd been trained for. He had to be a cop—now—but, by God, a cop was the last thing he wanted to be.

He led the way up the stairs to the Caputos' rear tenement. Petey knocked on the door. "Open up, police!"

No answer. They waited. Tom kicked the door in and it wobbled open. "Police!" They stepped in, fingers wrapped around their gun handles.

A scream shattered the silence.

Tom pushed Petey aside and ran to the back bedroom. Vita huddled in the corner.

She clutched a book to her chest, like it was all she had left. The fear in her eyes tore him apart. But he

117

wasn't here to comfort her. He had this detested job to do.

"What are you doing here?" She heaved a deep breath and flung the book onto the bed. Her eyes narrowed with that mistrust he'd seen the first day they met.

"Looking for further evidence," he replied, his tone flat.

As her eyes widened in horror, a bare fact seared through him like he'd been shot: *She doesn't know yet.*

"Evidence for what? What's going on here?" she demanded.

"Your father and brother are in jail, Vita." He didn't want to delay it, to approach it cautiously, or sit her down and break it to her. He had to tell her the only way he knew how.

"I know, but—" She took a step forward and held out her hand.

He thought she wanted him to take it, so he willingly reached out, but she only steadied herself against the open dresser drawer. "What'd they do? Nobody could tell me."

"My cousin Mike was found shot to death next to this building. Your father and brother were arrested for his murder. I'm sorry, Vita. I'm so sorry." He approached her with caution, longing to hold her, to cradle her in his arms.

She backed away. "No. Oh, dear God."

As a cop, he'd learned about denial, that most basic human reaction. If people didn't have denial to ward off the initial shock, they'd all be running around insane. He waited for her shock to set in. He didn't move any closer or offer comforting murmurs. As much as he ached to hold her, he kept his distance.

He turned to Petey. "Wait in the hall and don't touch anything."

"Tom…" Her voice reached him, strong and even.

She stood upright, brows furrowed, eyes hardened and dark. "It's not true. They didn't do it. It's a frame-up. My father and brother are not murderers. You don't believe this, do you?" Her eyes pleaded with him.

Of course I don't believe it, he wanted to assure her. *Of course it's a frame-up. Your father and brother are innocent.* Oh, how easy it would be to shower her with hope and tell her what she wanted to hear. But he didn't dare. He stood before her, torn between his job and his love for this woman. Cops looked at homicides with a detached eye and stayed out of domestic squabbles, but nobody trained him for anything like this.

"I don't believe anything yet, Vita. It only just happened. Now please let me get you through this." His barriers shattered, he gathered her into his arms.

She stiffened, unresponsive as a statue. She trembled under her starchy blouse; her brooch scratched his neck. But he held her tight. "I won't let go until you calm down," he whispered.

She softened and clung to him. How he wished he had someone to comfort him in his grief. He thanked God he'd been the one to tell her this horrible news. He couldn't stand her hearing it from some stranger. He didn't give a damn about the job right now. All that mattered was seeing her through this.

She broke away from him and sat on the bed. She picked up a plain gold ring from the nightstand and slipped it onto her thumb. Her father's? "Where are they now?" she asked in a small, yet brave voice.

"At headquarters on Mulberry Street."

"I'm going there." She stood and headed for the doorway.

"Vita, I need to toss—search the place first." He didn't need to force the apology into his voice. It was just too damn hard to be a cop right now.

"Search it for what, what for?"

"Further evidence." He was sure she hadn't heard him the first time, and he didn't blame her.

"Further? What evidence do they have? What kind of stuff was planted in here?"

"A gun," he said.

She nodded in resignation, as if she knew they stashed a piece in here someplace. "Yeah, then. Go ahead. Look. Don't let me stop you. It's your job. Do it." With an expectant nod, she folded her arms and stood in the doorway, waiting.

The first place he looked was in that open drawer. He turned it over and emptied it onto the bed, sifting through gray underwear and sheets. Then he came upon a money clip and watch fob. His heart fell and crashed into pieces.

"These are Mike's." Oh, how he didn't want to find anything of Mike's in here.

He turned to her, holding the items out in his palm.

She rushed up to him and swept them out of his hand onto the floor. "No, Tom! No, this can't be! They didn't kill anyone, don't you understand?"

"Vita, I'm not the judge. I don't know who killed my cousin. But there's evidence here. That's all I have any power to do right now, is bring that evidence in."

"No, Tom!" She clutched his sleeves with

trembling hands. She leaned into him, standing on her toes, their lips inches apart. "Tom, just forget—please forget you ever found anything here. Just like it never happened. They'll find the killer. Tom, don't do this to us."

"I can't forget it. Withholding evidence is against the law. Vita, we've got to get to the bottom of this. My cousin is in a cold grave. Somebody murdered him, and I need to know who, damn it!"

A horrible thought broke through his reasoning. Did she believe they were guilty? How could she let them walk free after snatching away his cousin's life?

"But it wasn't them, Tom. I know it in my heart and my soul. I know my father and brother. They're a lot of things, but they're not killers. Don't let them hang for something they didn't do."

"I can't *let* anything happen. I'm a cop, Vita. I'm not a judge. We'll go to the station, and you can explain everything to Sarge. We'll go through the chain of events. Throwing away evidence is not the right thing to do. How do you think I feel?"

She lowered her fists, and they fell to her sides. "All right. I'll go. I'll answer questions. But I want to see my father and brother. So let's go." She stopped trembling and held her head high. "But I'll tell you one thing, Officer McGlory." She stared him down. "There's no justice for people like us. None!" She turned on her heel and strode out the door.

He and Petey escorted her to headquarters. She ignored the hostile stares and murmurs. Despite the torment her family was about to suffer, she knew they couldn't hurt her with dirty looks and snickers behind her back. Not anymore.

No one spoke on the walk to the station. Tom's hand cupped her elbow with no affection, just a rigid grip. The physical contact sent shudders of revulsion through her. And only twenty-four hours ago she'd cozied up to him, kissing him, adoring him. Now he believed Papa was a murderer.

As they walked, she sensed his disdain. She even tried to forget herself for a moment and understand how he felt. But she couldn't. Her own emotions clogged her heart, leaving no strength left over for empathy.

When they got there, Tom asked the sergeant, "Where are Mr. Caputo and his son?"

"Down the hall." He jerked his thumb at the holding cells. "Smokin' some guinea stinkers."

Tom brought her to a holding cell. Papa and Butchie sat on beds suspended from the wall with chains, talking. Papa's hands punctuated his muted tones as he spoke. Butchie puffed on a cigar, a cloud of smoke hovering above their heads.

When he saw her, Butchie laid the cigar on the wooden floor and came to the bars that separated them. She clasped his hand and blinked against stinging tears, but when Papa came over and took her hand, she broke down.

"What happened, what happened?" Vita squeezed his hand. "Dear God, somebody tell me what happened!"

Approaching heels clicked on the concrete floor. She turned to see Rosalia reach through the bars, cupping Papa's face, playing the dutiful wife. Was she behind this? Vita should have hated herself for thinking this, but her judgment had vanished. She hated the faceless, heartless excuses for human beings who did this to her family.

"Tell me the truth, Butchie." Vita looked into her brother's eyes. "Did you kill that man?"

"No," he answered emphatically. "I didn't, and no, Papa didn't either. We was all sleepin' then—they can't even tell us when the cop dropped dead. He could'a been brung there and left there."

"I swear on your mother's grave, Vita. We're innocent." Papa's words echoed and died.

She longed to trade places with him just to get him out of there. This was just as much punishment for her.

"The entire building's doing novenas," Rosalia offered, as if that would change things.

Vita gripped the bars, itching to smack her. Papa turned away and went back to sit on the bed.

Needing to cancel out Rosalia's inane remark with something practical, Vita said, "I'm going to get you out of here. If I do it with my dying breath, I'm going to get you out!"

"The only way that's gonna happen is if they find who really killed the guy." Butchie's reply carried a defeatist tone. *No, that's not Butchie*, she thought, all his belligerence, his rambunctious spirit, gone. Well, she had plenty to spare.

"They'll find them, I know it. They have to!" Why she believed this, she didn't know. "Someone in this city must be decent enough to help us."

A thought of Tom swept through her mind. When he'd burst in to do his search, he hadn't looked at her with the loathing of an Irish cop. He'd looked bewildered, but as determined to find his cousin's killer as she was to clear Papa and Butchie. "Don't trust nobody outside the family," Papa had warned her over and over. Now she knew what he meant.

****

Sergeant Munn escorted her into a stuffy windowless room with wooden chairs and a beat-up table. She sat in a hard chair and stared straight at him.

"My father's been ill," she said. "He shouldn't be in a place like that."

The sergeant scraped his chair forward and propped his elbows on the table. "That's not for you to decide, miss." He didn't make eye contact.

The door opened. Tom walked in, holding a yellow pad and a pen. He took the chair next to the sergeant. As she fixed her eyes on an obscene word carved into the wood, she felt his eyes on her. She longed to meet his gaze. But she didn't.

"I'm going to ask you a few questions. You're not under suspicion of any kind. We just need to know a few things to help us with our investigation," he explained, his voice gentle and calm. Against her will, it soothed her. She didn't want that—she wanted to scream out at the injustice they'd been forced to suffer. She knew she'd fall apart if she looked into his eyes. Having Tom McGlory question her like a common criminal degraded her. So she willed herself to stay calm—she had to, for Papa and Butchie.

"Then ask me what you want to ask me." She forced evenness into her tone and clasped her shaking hands. She wouldn't expose the terror that engulfed her.

"Where were you on the night of August fourth?" Tom's voice remained steady.

"I was staying at Jadwiga Wisen's. On Bleecker Street."

"When did you see your father or brother after

124

that?" he asked.

"Not until the next Saturday, when I went to a block party," she answered.

"Had you ever seen weapons in their possession before?"

"Never!" She gripped the table's edge. "I mean— they never let me see them. I know they have a gun, but I don't know where it is. They hide it and never let me or Rose see where. They never used it. I know it!" She stared him down. "It's just for protecting us, they'd never dream of killing anybody just—to murder them!" Pleading crept into her voice.

"Come on, now," Sergeant Munn spoke up, his voice harsh and abrasive. His stale-cigar breath blasted at her. "They've been arrested enough times, and at least once on a weapons charge. We found a gun on your brother. Has he ever waved it in your face or your stepmother's face in a fit of anger? Don't lie to us, Miss Caputo. Unless you want to join them in there." He jerked his thumb and his head toward the door.

"My brother or father would never pull a gun on me, no matter how mad they were." She stabbed him with her furious eyes.

"Your father has hit you more than once, hasn't he? He's taken a strap to you?" Munn badgered her. "That's a weapon. He's used physical force on you more than once. Don't deny that. These are two violent and dangerous men we're talking about here. Don't try to cover for them."

Munn was playing "bad cop." She knew that routine. But she lifted her head high and stared him down. "It's none of your business whether he's laid a hand or a strap on me, and it has nothing to do with any of this." She sat rigid, too stunned to let him rile her. She knew he was hammering her so she'd break down and make some sort of false confession. Well, she'd sit here for days without a morsel of food or a wink of sleep before she'd let him force her into saying anything but the truth, and that only as it related to the current situation.

"Sarge, be easy on her." Tom's voice feathered over her ears, just as his lips had. "She's under enough pressure. I'm not ashamed to admit I sympathize with her."

"Sympathize on your own time." Munn's snarl turned his tumescent face into a parody of a rotten tomato. "Look, girl. Look at me when I talk to you!" He pointed at her in a weak attempt to degrade her.

She wouldn't let this creep humiliate her. He deserved no more respect than the dung on her shoes. "You know about their other arrests, don't you? Your brother had a brawl with Mike McGlory and did time for assaulting a policeman. Well, answer me." His spittle sprayed on the table as he talked. "Answer me!" he demanded.

"Yes." Her shoulders drooped. "I know about the other arrests."

"Did either of them threaten to kill Mike McGlory after those incidents, mention that they wanted to kill him?"

She stiffened. "Of course not."

"They ever threaten to murder anybody?" His cold gray eyes narrowed with malice.

"Never."

He sneered. "No, they just go out and do it, right?"

"Now, Sarge—" Tom interjected, throwing down

his pen and scraping his chair back.

She glanced up but didn't make eye contact.

"Let her alone. We have all we can get from her." He turned to Vita. "We'll call on you later if we need any more information. Thank you for coming in."

They stood, and she pressed her palms on the table, needing to push herself into a standing position. Munn stalked out and left Tom standing across the table from her.

"Vita…"

She welcomed his calming voice, but needed air. She thrust a hand out and grabbed the table edge. Her knees gave out. She collapsed. As her head hit the floor, she smelled dirt. That, too, faded as darkness closed in around her.

"Vita!" He sprawled out over the table in an attempt to catch her, then dashed around it and knelt beside her. He pressed his fingers to her wrist. The pulse beat rapid and steady. Cradling her head in his lap, he brushed wisps of hair from her forehead. "Hey! Somebody get me some water in here! She fainted!"

One of the rookies came in with a glass of water. Tom dipped his hankie in it and pressed it to her forehead as he stroked her face. He'd wanted to touch her like this for so long, to run his finger over the curve of her cheek and along her slender neck. "You'll be fine, baby, I'll take care of you…" He murmured the soothing words. As her hair tickled his cheek, an unwelcome surge of desire tore through him. How beautiful, so soft and feminine, yet so willful and determined to make a difference in this world. His heart swelled with pride and respect for her. If he could ever make his dream woman appear before his eyes, here she was, her head in his lap, their hearts beating together. Oh, how he wanted her to share his joys and sorrows, to watch her fulfill her destiny.

"Oh, dear Vita…" he whispered, inhaling her sweet fragrance as her hair caressed his cheek.

Her lids fluttered open. She looked up at him, her eyes unfocused.

"Here, take some water," he offered as he lifted her head.

"What happened?" She rose to her elbows, bewilderment darkening her eyes as he placed the glass to her lips.

"You fainted. Nothing serious. I just think this whole ordeal did you in."

"I never faint. It must've been—oh, of course. Your sergeant. Trying to make me admit Papa is a murderer." She took a gulp of water and struggled to free herself from his hold on her.

"It's all right, Vita, I'm not going to hurt you."

She clung to him, then gave herself a shove and knelt, clutching the table's edge. He stood and helped her into the chair, handing her his dampened hankie.

As she wiped it over her face, he handed her the glass of water and she drained it.

"You need to eat something," he said. "You also need to get some rest. I'll take you back to your boardinghouse."

"No!" Her protest wasn't that of a woman who'd just fainted. "Forget it, Officer McGlory. I'll take care of myself. I've got a father and brother in there about to hang for something they didn't do, and you're not going to help me ever again. Let's just forget we ever met. This can't go on. No more dinners, no more promenades, no more carriage rides. It's over. I need to think of my family now. You obviously have your own agenda, finding out who killed your cousin and nailing my family for doing it. So just go and leave me alone."

"Vita, I'm not letting you go. You're not walking off into the night alone." But his heart verified its double meaning; he didn't want to let her go. At all.

"I'm going to see my family one more time, and then I'm getting out of here." She tried to stand but dropped back into the chair.

"You're not going anywhere by yourself for a while." He stood behind her and placed his hands on her shoulders.

She teetered, so fragile under his touch, a delicate shell protecting such inner strength. He should have called a cab right then, but some primitive male instinct wanted to breathe his strength into her. She sank back in the chair. He knew she didn't want him to leave. He knew they stood on opposing sides, yet they needed each other.

****

He waited while she spoke with her family one more time; then he walked her out to the street. "You're taking a cab, and I'm going with you. I don't want you in a streetcar."

"I can go myself. I don't want you following me there," she pleaded rather than demanded. She looked everywhere but at him and fidgeted with her sleeves as she leaned against a lamppost.

He wanted to stand behind her and be her support. The sight of her face, so pale in the growing darkness, tugged at his heart. With her world crashing in around her, she looked so tiny. He wished he'd had the power to make this nightmare disappear. *How will we ever work through this?* he pleaded. *How can I make it all as it was only twenty-four hours ago?* Something from his Catholic upbringing told him this was a test of their souls' endurance—and that God would give them the strength to see this through. He began praying for her family's innocence. He didn't believe in the brutality the police inflicted on the city's helpless—under the system, their chances were slim to none. That was one thing he wanted to change. The gross injustice.

When the cab arrived, she hurled herself off the lamppost and hopped up onto the seat, ignoring him. She was either deep in prayer or planning how to get a decent meal to her family. He followed her, his mouth shut.

They sat in silence. She leaned away from him as the cab jounced down the street. They stopped in front of her boardinghouse, and he helped her down.

"I want you to eat," he urged. "I'm going to tell your landlady to feed you something nourishing."

"Stop fussing over me." She shooed him away. "I've got two other lives to worry about now."

At her door, he wanted to prolong their parting as long as possible, but she slid the key into the lock and stepped in. She was just about to close the door when he leaned on it, causing her to stumble backwards.

He caught her by the waist, and she clasped his hands. There they stood, making no move to break away. Footsteps whisked down the steps, and a frizzy-haired woman came to the door, wire specs perched on her nose. "Good afternoon, Officer. What's wrong? Is Vita all right? What happened?" She clutched her shawl around her thin shoulders.

"I'm fine, Madame Branchard, I just need to lie down." She waved her hands and turned away from Tom.

"Please make sure she eats. Something good like chicken soup. She's had a very difficult time," Tom told the woman. He'd expected Vita to live with an offbeat type like this and admired her for it.

"Do you want to come in for a whiskey or a smoke or something?" Madame Branchard asked.

Vita shot her a warning look. "No, he's got to go. Goodbye, Officer."

He feared this was the last goodbye he'd ever hear from her.

He turned and wandered off, not knowing where to go, not caring. He strode down the street, obsessed with finding Mike's killer and bringing the bastard to justice, whoever it was. He feared he'd lost Vita forever. But he'd nearly starved to death once and survived. He could certainly find a way to get his life back now.

Chapter Twelve

The horror didn't hit Vita until Angie came over. "Everybody was in church all day. Father Genzale held a mass for your father and Butchie—like they'd already died." Angie approached Vita with outstretched arms, but she backed away and sat at the table.

"So it's real, it really happened." Vita propped her elbows on the table, her head in her hands.

Angie dragged a chair next to her and sat. "Yeah, Vita. It happened. You know that. What can I do? Just tell me, and I'll do it for you."

"No, it's just—" She raised her head and stared at Papa's crucifix on the table. "Look at this. This gash in its side. It takes away its purity." She slid it closer. "Before you told me about the mass and all, I guess I still hoped this was a nightmare and it didn't really happen. But now I know it's real. And that's why I feel like I just got run over in the street." She rubbed her stiff neck muscles.

Angie leaned over and placed her hands on Vita's shoulders. "Oh, no, Vita. It's my fault. I'm sorry, I'm sorry!" Her voice cracked with sobs.

"No, it's not your fault, I didn't mean that, Ange. You had to tell me. Now I know. It's true, so I gotta find out how to help them. I'm glad you come over here and told me that. I'd been hoping I still dreamed it all this while. Now I need to do more than say novenas."

Before now, if the entire neighborhood marched on that police station to vouch for Papa and Butchie, it would've amounted to nothing. They said novenas because no mortal could make this right. But now she knew differently. She had to be their salvation—here on earth.

"Mama says you should stay with us a while. You can't be alone." Angie waved around the empty room.

"I'm not alone. I have Madame Branchard and the other boarders." In a way she couldn't explain, the last thing she needed was to go back to the smells, the crowded rooms, the wailings to Saint Jude.

"You should be in your own neighborhood, with us," Angie demanded, her pitch charged with surprise, as if no other solution existed than to let the Paluzzi family carry her.

"I'm sorry, Ange, but I've come this far. Stepping back into anybody's sagging bosom would only weaken me." She took a deep breath and thrust out her chest. "I'm going to stay right here and see what I can do about finding the real killers." She traced the figure of Jesus on the cross with her finger. "How I'll do this, I don't know yet. But it's so obviously a setup, the fools must have left something behind. When Tom tossed the place, he only found what he wanted to find—the stuff he said was his cousin's. If they really were his cousin's. I have my doubts. I don't trust nobody now."

"But are you all right in this place with a bunch of poets? They don't look like they eat much." Angie squeezed Vita's hand on the crucifix.

"Yes, I love it here. I'll be fine, Ange. Tell your mama thank you. I'll come by if I have to."

Angie watched Vita with vacant eyes, and Vita

133

didn't blame her. Solving a murder was way beyond Angie's scope. She knew who *could* help her—and it was nobody from Mott Street.

After Angie left, Vita washed her face, loosened her bun, and went to Jadwiga's.

****

Her friend stood there, eyes and mouth wide open, as Vita explained what had happened.

"You want a reading?" She placed a glass of Chianti in front of her.

"No, not this time." Vita pushed the glass away. "For once, I don't want to be told what to do. I'll do this myself, surprise the saints and those cards that think they know so much. I'm beyond trusting everything now—all I have is my own self, my wits, and my strength."

"Well, with all that, who needs saints and cards?" Jadwiga's words rode out of her mouth on a stream of tobacco smoke.

"But it exasperates me that Tom thinks my father and brother killed his cousin. I begged him to throw that stuff out, and he wouldn't!" She pounded a fist on the table.

"He came out and said he thinks they did it?" Jadwiga pulled out a chair and sat across from her.

"No—he didn't say—he doesn't know what to believe. But I do. I know my family is innocent."

"Look. He didn't accuse them, did he?" She leaned forward and smoothed stray strands off Vita's face. "In light of what happened, I really can't blame him, honey. His cousin's dead. His agenda is to find the killer and bring 'im to justice. He didn't betray you as much as protect his cousin."

"Well, of course." She spread her fingers, palms up. "How can I expect him to care for me more than his cousin?"

"It's not a matter of who he cares for more. He's just being a cop. And if he's a decent one, he's the only decent one in New York, and you got 'im. A decent cop wouldn't throw out evidence to protect anyone. If he's as rotten as you seem to think, he woulda threw out all that stuff of Mike's he found. But—on the other hand, if it really is all part of a frame-up, that was part of the act," Jadwiga said. "But I just don't get the feeling that he'd do something that rotten. Even if he is a crook, to do something like that is just—plain heartless."

"That's what I've been torturing myself wondering." She let out a ragged sigh. "If he's in on it."

"You really think he'd do something like this?" Doubt crept into Jadwiga's tone. "I don't think he would, and I hardly know him."

"It really don't matter no more if he is or not. He's nothing to me now. I have to shove my feelings for him out the door—my father's and brother's lives are at stake here. I can't let my silly romantic feelings for a cop stand in the way of that." Vita studied her friend. "You don't believe what I just said, do you?"

"Why wouldn't I believe it? You're no liar. Of course I believe you about that. But I'm not so sure I believe you about throwing your feelings out over him." Jadwiga widened her eyes on the *him*. "He's still out there."

"I know." She took a swig of that wine after all. "He's so entrenched in my soul, I wouldn't do myself any good denying it."

Jadwiga relit her pipe. "Look at it this way, Vita.

Nobody in this world is in a position to help you—except Tom McGlory. He wants to find his cousin's killers and so do you." She sat back and crossed her arms over her bosom. "For God's sakes, don't treat him like the enemy. Get with him and get on his team, find the killers. And when you do—well, then come back for a reading if you want one. But if all this turns out to be a trap, Tom'll be the one to find it."

"And if he's in on it?" Vita cocked her head.

She rolled her eyes. "Glory be, Vita, you gotta trust somebody sometime. If you can't trust Tom, trust the man upstairs"—she pointed upward—"to lead him in the right direction. Sometimes you just gotta jump in with both eyes shut. It's all about faith."

She shook her head. "But that's almost impossible for me. I've never done anything—not even buy a pair of shoes—without weighing the decision, going over the pros and cons. Can I trust this man I've fallen in love with?"

"That'll be the test, honey bunch." Jadwiga puffed on her pipe.

So she forgot logic and planning and even faith, and trusted nobody and nothing—only her instincts.

Chapter Thirteen

She needed to tell her employers the truth. She was not Violet Greene. With Papa and Butchie now accused murderers, she couldn't hide it any longer. They'd find out once the press started blabbing about it. Now she cringed every time Mr. Johnson or one of her co-workers called her Miss Greene. She just didn't want to keep deceiving these nice people.

She went straight in to her boss, past the secretary's squawking beak, through the door, over the thick rug.

"Good day, young lady. Sit, do sit!" His smile outshone his diamond tie pin.

Guilt crushed her even further. She settled into the same chair he'd interviewed her in.

"So, to what do I owe this pleasant surprise visit, Miss Greene?" He tossed his pen aside and sat back, crossing his hands over his middle.

Shame flushed her cheeks at the sound of that name. What a pity this unfair world forced her to lie.

"Mr. Johnson," she began, "I need to tell you something about myself…"

She gripped the chair arms, looked him straight in the eye, and told him. "My name isn't Violet Greene. It's Vita Caputo. I'm an Italian immigrant. And my father and brother are in jail for a murder they didn't commit." She held her breath and waited for the axe to fall. She awaited dismissal like the final sentencing of death.

But he did nothing of the sort. He lowered his eyes and gave her a more valuable gift than anything inside the bank's vault—sympathy.

"Miss Caputo—Vita—" Her name on his lips sounded foreign. "I realize what your people have to go through. I can't fault you for using an American name. I'm sorry for what's happened to your family. I hope justice is served. If you need time off to go visit them, you can have it. I hope it all works out for you. If there's anything I can do to help—" He finished off with a splaying of his hands that completed the offer. She sensed his discomfort saying that. It just wasn't his nature, but she knew he didn't get to be a big-time banker by being nasty all the time.

So he kept her on. The kindhearted banker continued to employ the daughter of an immigrant accused of murder. She didn't wonder why. She just spent an extra few moments in prayers of thanks every day.

****

Tom stopped at Liam Johnson's brownstone after his beat. He needed to tell him to postpone the McGlorys' home remodeling loan. He couldn't possibly think of fixing up a kitchen amidst all this tragedy.

The butler let him in. Standing in Johnson's entry hall, decorated with elaborate crystal gewgaws on shelves and gold-framed photos of well-heeled ladies and gents in front of sprawling summer homes, Tom fought pangs of envy. Johnson had made it, but not by hard labor or going around being nice to everybody. Tom didn't envy the way he'd gotten there. He'd achieved his success at the expense of others—people more trusting than him. Not every road to success was littered with the dumped bodies of the bilked. Someday he'd be out of Pearl Street and in a home to be proud of. It just wouldn't be so soon. As his thoughts turned to Vita, Johnson entered. His satin smoking jacket's velvet lapels matched the wallpaper.

"Tom! What brings you here? Care for a brandy?" He showed Tom into the drawing room and sat him down at the window facing Fifth Avenue. Tom imagined this was his own drawing room, with the initials engraved into the brandy snifter reading 'T.McG.'

"I found something out about one of my prized employees today." Johnson filled his snifter.

"I know about her." Tom nodded with his ready explanation.

"The former Miss Greene? Yes, she—"

Tom cut in, "I'd pledged my loyalty to her, Liam, and I really didn't see any harm in not mentioning her name and nationality. Did it matter in the end? She's a great worker, isn't she?"

"One of the best I've ever had, Tom. She did what she had to do, changing her name. Maybe if the rest of 'em had the brains to do that, they'd get somewhere." He chuckled into his brandy.

Tom fidgeted with his cuffs, more than ready to change the subject. "Just be easy on her," he suggested. "She's going through hell."

"I hope they bring Mike's killers to justice, Tom, whoever they are." He held up his glass in a toasting gesture and took a sip.

Tom found it hard to read the banker at the

moment. Did he think the Caputos killed Mike?

"I admire all Miss Caputo's qualities, Tom. She's intelligent, well-spoken, witty, a damn hard worker, and…" He stopped.

And what? But Tom knew what was coming.

"Yes, she's beautiful. With some lipstick and powder and without that Italian bun, she'd be stunning. And—without that hardness in her eyes," he added.

Tom knew what Johnson meant. Her lot in life gave her that sharp cynical look, turning her eyes from the softness of a spring day to the grayness of a storm.

"You're her employer," he said. "Keep it that way."

"Aha." He raised his glass to Tom once again. "So you are sweet on her."

Tom said nothing, but the look he gave Johnson told him he'd better get back to his wife and five kids. "I'm proud she got the job on her own. I guess you owe me two favors now, pal," he said.

****

"Come on in here, Tom, and close the door." Sergeant Munn led Tom into that stinking interrogation room and sat in the only chair with arms. The war room, as they called it, where they brought accused criminals and witnesses for questioning, looked more like a prison pen without bars.

"What is it?" It had to do with either Mike or the Caputos. Whatever it was, he wasn't expecting it to be good.

"Tom, your going undercover was a good idea after all. We want you to get more involved in it. A lot of cops are sick of having to buy their jobs. It cost me a grand to make sergeant. I know you want to make captain someday, and you know it'll cost you at least twelve grand. Cops are quitting the force left and right 'cause they're so disgusted with the promotion-fee system. We want to see what we can do to pull the tiger's teeth out, if you know what I mean." He scratched his earlobe.

Tom blew out a relieved breath. "Whew, it's not about the Caputos. Oh, yeah, I do want to make captain someday, but I sure don't want to have to pay twelve grand to get there. I'd love to see Tammany shrivel away, or at least tame it."

"Well, the new commish, Ted Roosevelt, just appointed a special detail to do just that. He wants to clean the force up," Munn said. "Wants a detail of honest, aboveboard fly cops. The ones who're stayin'."

"Must be a small detail." Tom let out a cynical laugh. "I have no optimism lately. I haven't felt alive since Mike died."

"I know, son." Frank nodded. "I understand."

"Yeah, for me, this is the ever-risky job of a Metropolitan policeman going one step further, turning against my own in a quest to clean the whole thing up." Tom shuffled his feet.

"It ain't really like that, Tom. We need a few brave cops willing to risk more than the rest of 'em. The clean ones. And we all know the clean ones are the ones with the balls to take the risks."

"We need the young ones," Tom corrected him. "Meaning the ones who don't have families. No wife and kids to leave behind." Tom figured Munn wouldn't hide that reason.

"So we understand each other," Munn said.

"Sure, I got nothing to lose. I won't be foolish, but

I do want to make captain some day. I know the risks."
He thought of Da, and a wave of affection warmed him.
"I also owe it to my father, who took every risk to get
me here, to make this city a safe place for us."

"We need ya to go to Tammany as a decoy," Munn
instructed. "Get into the inner workings of their plots.
Find out what Mayor Grant's up to. You'll be armed at
all times. You just won't be doin' the beat anymore. Or
uniformed. But it's strictly top secret." His voice
lowered. "You can't discuss it with nobody. Not even
your family."

"Well, if this means the beginning of the end of
corruption in this city, I want to be a part of it, Sarge.
So if I die doing it…" His voice trailed off. He finished
the thought in private. It was better than the way his
mother died. "But what about finding Mike's killer?"
Tom reminded Munn. He knew the sergeant hadn't
been too crazy about his sleuthing. Now this coinciding
with the force's new cleanup agenda provided the
perfect opportunity to divert him from it.

"We have detectives, Tom." Munn told him what
he already knew. "There's nothing you can do that they
can't."

"But just imagine if this had been someone in your
family. Wouldn't you want their killers brought to
justice?" He turned the tables. "And, Sarge," Tom
plowed on, "your problem, like the root of this whole
tragedy, is you believe you caught the killers. Best of
all, they're Italian immigrants. But that's what tears at
my gut." His voice rose. "They didn't feel they needed
to prove it. So even if the Caputos killed Mike—" He
didn't mention his loyalty to Vita. "—they deserve a
fair trial."

"They'll get it." Munn's assurance sounded halfhearted.

"Like hell they will." It rendered him helpless, this mishmash of corruption and prejudice, the heart-wrenching agony Vita suffered as a victim of this twisted system.

Now a glimmer of hope gave him a dash of energy. "But this new assignment'll remind me I'm alive."

Munn gave him an encouraging nod. "Look, Tom, there's a possibility your undercover work could help the Caputos. I know you're sweet on the girl. You could help her—"

"Get her family a trial, a chance to defend themselves." Tom finished his sergeant's sentence, as he frequently did. And for the first time since shock had numbed and stunned him, he hoped.

****

Vita sensed Tom's presence in the bank before she even saw him. When she looked up, his gaze sent shivers though her. His eyes weren't lifeless anymore. They sparkled. Something had changed; she knew it. If he'd walked past her in the street, she'd have told him about the prayers she'd been saying for both of them and their families. But now, she could only force herself back to work, hard as it was with him barely a lobby away. She focused on the next customer's deposit slip and the pile of bank notes sliding under the bars. No way was she going to let Tom McGlory interfere with her work. After she helped the customer, she saw Tom entering Mr. Johnson's office. What did he talk to Johnson about all the time? Were he and the banker Johnson planning a big development with graft money? Once again, her suspicions went wild and stabbed her with fear.

She glanced at the clock. Where had Tom gone? Shortly past noon, Mr. Johnson asked her to work late. Fourteen-hour days were nothing to her; a ten-hour shift was a walk in the park.

"I'll make sure you get escorted home," he assured her.

At nine on the button, who showed up but Tom McGlory. She longed to rush into his arms but held back.

Besides the two of them, only the guards stood posted at the door. They intruded, they invaded her privacy, and they could hear every word echoing through the lobby. Tom, on the pretense of carrying out Johnson's orders, obviously had his own agenda. She was so curious as to what he was going to say, it gnawed at her like hunger. She didn't get her hopes up, but she knew his eyes had brightened for a reason. Tom McGlory didn't playact.

"Did something happen?" were her first words. Would she have to pull the answer out of him like tugging on a clothesline?

"I'm here to escort you home. Mr. Johnson said—"

"But did anything happen?" She tried to keep her tone below a shriek and realized how she hungered for a morsel of news—anything.

"The force is letting me devote some time to finding Mike's killers." He took a step closer. "Why don't we work together instead of being on opposite sides of this case? We both want to find out who killed Mike. I don't want to see your family in prison if they're innocent, no matter what our differences are."

Just as Jadwiga had predicted. So that's what had

put that glimmer in his eye. She wanted to burst out of her skin and let her spirit frolic in a frenzy of thanks.

"You—believe they're innocent?" Her voice croaked a hoarse whisper. She wanted to clutch his arm but grabbed the counter for support.

"I believe your family is innocent until proven guilty. A very un-New York thing to say, I know, but it's all circumstantial. I don't want to see you suffer like this, and I know Mike's soul won't rest until we find out the truth. Or at least try."

"But, Tom…" She looked into his eyes, into his soul. "Do you *know* they're innocent *in your heart*?" She pushed him to the limit here, but she had to know.

"Well, they have been arrested before…" He paused. "But not for murder." He added that qualifier. "I'm hoping as much as you that they're innocent."

"Hoping? I'm not hoping. I know they're innocent! There's no doubt in my mind, like there still is in yours!" She curled her fingers into a fist and pounded it on the countertop. It barely made a tap. She wanted to pound the reasoning into him with that fist. At the same time, she burned to defy her culture and trust him. Her moving out to start a new life had worked. Why not trust this one man?

"Vita, arguing will not change anything. We've got to work together."

"All right," she agreed, returning his serious stare. "This isn't about me, it's about Papa and Butchie." Regardless of what Tom McGlory believed or didn't believe, he was willing to bring these faceless bastards to justice. For this, her heart burst with respect for him. She offered him her hand, and he enclosed it in his warm fingers. "Tom, you're my only ally in the world."

She couldn't let any feelings for him get in the way—those silly, fanciful delusions.

They took the Fifth Avenue bus and walked to her boardinghouse. They didn't discuss the murder. He started talking about the stars—how they changed with the seasons, how far away they were, and what it would be like to travel to one of them. He attempted to make her forget her problems for a while, and she clasped her hands in a prayer of thanks.

They got to Madame Branchard's too soon. Where had the time gone? Why couldn't they walk to the end of Manhattan Island and take a ferry ride, gaze at the stars, stroll, sit on a bench, and talk some more?

Just as he said goodnight, Vita saw Rosalia walking toward them. Her red-rimmed eyes told Vita she'd been crying—or drinking—or both. *Oh no, that's all I need*, she thought. Rosalia ignored Tom's greeting and started blubbering. "They gonna evict me, throw me out onna street—" She wiped her nose on her handkerchief and rubbed her eyes with her fist. She wasn't wearing her wedding band.

"Maybe you can get a job, Rose." She didn't hide the irritation in her voice. She couldn't sympathize with this woman. Her inner voice giggled with glee, way back in her throat. Up till now Rosalia had only worked when she felt like it. The rest of them had to pull their weight—and hers.

"You can get public assistance," Tom offered.

"Never! We're too proud for that!" she screamed in his face. "Whatcha doin' with him anyway?" She jerked her thumb at his chest.

"I had to work late and my boss asked Tom to escort me home."

"All right, she's home. Now you can scram," Rosalia dismissed him, walking into the hallway of Madame Branchard's rooming house. She turned and waited for Vita to enter and close the door.

Tom turned to leave. "I'll be in touch, Vita," he called over his shoulder.

She wanted to shake Rosalia...shake those phony tears out of her...shake her until she busted out of her corset. Tom's abrupt exit had left her empty and longing. She whirled around and shut the door.

Rosalia elbowed her way past Vita and into the kitchen, where Madame stood at the sink washing teacups. "You the landlady, eh? I need a place to stay—I'm all alone, my husband's in jail, and I see ghosts all night—"

Vita wanted to shrink into the woodwork. She heard Madame Branchard say something like "Vita's room."

She stalked into the kitchen. "No, Rose. You're not staying in my room no how!" She turned to Madame Branchard. "She can sleep on the floor in the parlor if she wants to get out of her house that bad—but not in the room that I'm paying for."

She turned on her stepmother. "You should've stayed home and kept running the household, at least keeping it clean, but no, you had to follow me here, to scout the area and horn in on my life. Well, I don't want you barging in on it. You're no substitute mother."

"Vita—" Rosalia pleaded, hands clasped, tears in her eyes. But were they real? "Lemme stay with you, just for a couple nights. You don't know what it's like over there all alone. You just don't know what it's like." She stamped her foot. "I see ghosts..."

147

Vita threw her hands in the air. "Ghosts. Oh, *Madonna mia.*"

Madame Branchard adjusted her glasses and slid out from between them. "Vita, having her hang here would be fine, but not on the parlor floor—you know how we stay up half the night gabbing."

She rolled her eyes heavenward. "Oh, all right, stay in my room. But only for a few nights." She remembered Mrs. Paluzzi giving her the same warning. But she let Rosalia stay with her out of pity. Rosalia had never been at the receiving end of any kindness, and now was the time.

"Look, Vita, I ask you 'cause if it wasn't for your father, I wouldn't even be in this country. Now I'm alone 'cause your father's accused of a murder. So just let me stay."

"I said all right." She turned and walked out of the room, and her stepmother followed, each at odds—and alone.

****

That night, lying in the dark on a bundled-up pile of curtains and clothes, Rosalia droned on and on…her arranged marriage to Papa, the suitor she had to leave behind in Italy, how she'd dreaded coming to a strange country to sleep with a man she'd never met.

But something in her diatribe compelled Vita to listen. Rosalia didn't complain this time; her voice didn't clatter with that tinny whine. This genuine outpouring of emotion begged, not just for an audience, but for reassurance that her life hadn't been wasted. "Rose, you can salvage the rest, whether Papa gets through this or not," she assured her.

Rosalia kept talking, now in an advising tone rather

than a victimized plea. What she left out conveyed more than what she did say. That warned Vita to take charge of her life.

"Don't ever let him force you into marriage, Vita. He's your father, and I know you love him and all." Rosalia turned her head away. "But how could he know what's best for you? Does he have to sleep with the *asino* he forces you to marry? No, he marries you off, and his job's done. He thinks he's done best by you. But who has to suffer if it don't work out? Not him. You. You stuck wit' a guy you don't love."

"Rose, your thirty years weren't entirely wasted," Vita reminded her. "You could do a lot more with the life you got ahead of you."

"Nah, I'm not smart and ambitious like you. I can be a wife, but nothing else. When your father asked for my hand, they turned me over like he was the only husband they could unload me on. Not that I was old. They just didn't want me marryin' the boy who was courtin' me. I was in love with him, and him with me. But he wasn't good enough for them."

"Why not?" She couldn't wait for the answer.

"He was a heretic. A religious fanatic. Protestant. They thought he was some kinda—like a incubus, the way they talked about him. How could I ever marry a non-Catholic? He had his little band of followers, and they never hurt nobody, they just didn't wanna be Catholic. But he was a *ladro* to the family. The lowest kind of criminal. It was my bad luck that I fell in love with the wrong person. It woulda been just as easy to love a Catholic, but I just didn't."

Vita nodded. "I understand. I'm really sorry, Rose. A lot of things woulda been different if they'd let you marry who you wanted. I always knew that."

"Yeah, and sometimes I take it out on you's—but it's not you's problem, it's mine."

"Did you ever hear anything about him?" Vita asked.

"My sister Jeannette, she wrote to me once and told me they exiled him to somewhere, I don't know, Sweden or Switzerland, someplace like that. I guess he found what he was looking for there."

"I'm sorry." Vita offered her sympathy. "I know how hard that must have been, giving up the man you loved to come here." Being torn away from Tom to marry someone she didn't love would shatter her. "I don't like to think about this, but Papa won't live forever. You can still find love. And you can find a good job like I did and get out of the East Side."

"Ha!" Rosalia's jagged laugh scraped at the walls. "No, I'd be a-scared to do what you did—go out and march into some fancy uptown bank and get hired, and go lookin' for a room. I don't wanna fancy job, or clothes, or goin' out to dance, all them things you can do. I wanted babies, but I can't have 'em. I'm alive. All I need is a husband to take care of me. If I fall in love with him, it's even better."

"I know you'll do just fine, Rose. You're still young, you're pretty, and you'll find a man to love before you're too old."

Rosalia finally calmed down, and Vita insisted she take the mattress. Vita slept on the bunched-up curtains, thinking far into the future with Tom.

Chapter Fourteen

Another bouquet of fragrant white roses arrived at the bank, the second this week. Vita put it in a crystal vase, on the counter where customers filled out their slips. Everyone, especially Mr. Johnson, stopped by to enjoy their sweet fragrance.

Now they all called her Miss Caputo. Every knowing look and smile made her stand taller and prouder. If anyone heard about Papa and Butchie being in jail, no one breathed a word of it to her. What they twaddled about behind her back was something else altogether. Uptown gossip made Lower East Side prattle look as stale as yesterday's bread. Real scandals festered here on the numbered streets. Infidelity was their parlor game. They swapped spouses the way Italians swapped rum cake recipes. Mr. Johnson never got anywhere near the fray, and if he did indulge in extramarital dalliances, none of the underlings ever heard about it. To her, he was as gracious as ever, letting her have extra time off and not docking her pay.

****

On the third day of Papa and Butchie's jail time, Vita walked through the Tombs' metal door. It clanged shut behind her. She waited in the stone-cold room for an escort to the cell blocks, cringing at the filth—the rodent droppings, the puddle of urine in the corner. It was worse than the tenements. The warden came in and eyed her up and down, making her feel as dirty as the crud on the walls. "Your father's sick," he said without preamble.

"Sick—how? What's wrong?" Her grip weakened. Her bag slid to the floor.

"He's in the infirmary," was his answer, and although she wanted to shake him, she needed to be with Butchie—they shared Papa equally.

She grabbed her bag off the floor and ran down the dank corridor, ignoring the smells. A trickle of relief played over her, battling her dread of Papa's illness. At least he was out of this trap and getting decent medical help. She finally reached Butchie. He grasped her hands through the bars.

"Are you sick too?"

"Nah, I'm okay." His stubble had sprouted into a full beard.

"What happened to Papa?" she asked.

"Nothin', just nerves. He ain't really sick. I mean sick-sick. He ain't gonna die or nothin'. Don' worry about him." His tone, only a little beat around the edges, calmed her.

"Will they let me see him?"

"Prob'ly not." He shook his head. "They wouldn't let Rose in to see him. I'll tell him you was here. They doin' anything on the outside?"

"Yeah, Tom McGlory is trying to find the killer." She waited for his reaction.

His brows drew together and he rubbed his whiskery chin. "He don't believe we're tellin' the truth."

"I think in his heart he believes that you're innocent. But he's just not jumping to any conclusions.

He's not your everyday cop, Butchie. He's different."

"Don' believe it." He scowled. "Don' trust any of 'em, Vita. Most of all him."

"Butchie, please." She let out an impatient huff. "Don't start this again. Just spend your time praying. If you don't trust them, trust me."

He squeezed her hands through the bars, and she tiptoed out because every step of her heels sounded like cannon shots. She didn't want to attract any attention around here.

She stepped outside into the sunlight. Only then did she realize what "liberty" really meant. A heavy sadness weighed her down. Papa and Butchie were no longer free and might never be again. Maybe the courts would show mercy and deport them. Papa never liked America anyway.

The next morning when she got to her teller's window, she found a small envelope with her name on it. She recognized the penmanship from that love letter she shouldn't have read. Her heart leapt.

With trembling fingers, she sliced an opener through it. She really wanted to tear into it like the wrapping on those Christmas gifts nabobs gave each other.

She stared at the short note.

I need you to help me do some detective work. I'll come to the bank at five o'clock.

The hours dragged—she glanced at the clock every few minutes and daydreamed about him between tasks—the way he brushed his hair off his forehead, the tapping of his foot when they waited for a streetcar. Then she chided herself for even thinking his nearness would divert her attention from Papa and Butchie.

When he met her at the glass doors at 5:00, he held out his hand. She clasped it, careful not to let her fingers linger in his. He hadn't tried to kiss her again since that night in the carriage. Maybe he hadn't liked the way she kissed. Oh, these lewd thoughts! His kiss had been an expression of affection—nothing more. But she wondered when he'd kiss her again.

"Care for some dinner?" he asked, and they strolled, in typical uptown fashion, into a bistro on 22nd Street.

Her dress and hat were as fashionable as anyone else's; Tom was by far the handsomest man in the place.

She had onion soup and a bowl of greens while he had a rare steak. Now was a good time to tell him about Jadwiga.

"...so maybe she can help us," she suggested, sitting almost sideways so they wouldn't bump legs under the table. "She does readings—she's very accurate. She's been a good friend to me."

He stopped eating and looked at her. "I'm not so sure, Vita. I never believed in any of that supernatural mumbo-jumbo. Not the way—" He stopped himself just in time and plunged a forkful of steak into his mouth.

"Say it. Not the way Italians do. Well, we're not exactly pagans, like the Romans. We do believe in God, you know. He's even the same God you believe in. He just drinks wine instead of whiskey. I never thought of Jadwiga in religious terms. I believe in her, and I think she might be able to help us." She sipped her mint tea.

"I was hoping we could spend some time questioning your neighbors," he said. "I managed to talk to some of them, but most of those people won't give me the time of day. I need to get some witnesses. Reliable ones. I've already talked to everyone Mike knew, or knew where he could have been coming from, who he could have been with that night, or who had a vendetta against him. Now I'm relying on your territory. They'd be a lot more inclined to cooperate with you. And you want to go crystal-ball gazing?"

"We can do both," she insisted. "But I really want you to talk to her first. Just hear what she has to say."

They clinked water glasses—she'd turned down the offer of wine. "For you—I'd talk to Saint Anthony if he was here," he said.

"You pray to him when you've lost something."

"Can I pray to him so I *won't* lose something?" His tone reverent, his eyes swept over her face. She should have looked away. But she couldn't.

"Only if you're afraid of losing it." She picked up on his meaning, hoping they were on the same track.

He smiled that mystifying half-smile and finished polishing off his steak.

****

Jadwiga opened the door—and in typical Jadwiga fashion she acted like she'd waited a lifetime to meet Tom.

"This must be Tom! Come in, come in!" She gestured with both hands. "I was just brewing a pot of strong Russian tea. Unless you'd like something stronger. But—maybe not. I didn't assume just because you were a policeman off-duty—"

"It's all right, Jadwiga, tea sounds dandy." Vita filled a few empty pauses by admiring the new hooked rug, checking on the plants, and telling Tom about Jadwiga's children and their musical abilities. She

155

would have mentioned that Butchie was an accordionist, but she didn't want to be too wistful about him. She couldn't get too misty over the family or bask in her new-found sophistication until this was solved. Then she'd have plenty of time to entertain all these strange new sensations awakening her body.

"I've seen her before," Tom commented as Jadwiga swished away in a cloud of perfume and white muslin skirts.

"Oh, you couldn't have," Vita countered too quickly. "She—hasn't been around here long."

"Well, maybe not, then," he replied to her relief. "When I meet somebody like her, I usually write it down, along with the date. I would have remembered reading what I wrote about her."

"Did you write it down when you met me?" She slathered her voice in sweetness.

Without answering, he looked straight at her and raised a brow. Jadwiga returned with a tray piled with teacups and a pot.

"Would you do a reading for us tonight?" Vita asked, only to reinforce Jadwiga's validity to Tom.

"Don't see why not. Let's have our tea first."

"I need to see if you can pick anything up about the murder." Vita sipped her tea. She knew her heart wouldn't stop pounding until she heard the answer.

Jadwiga nodded, gazing into her teacup as if contacting an oracle within its depths, her eyes crossed with concentration.

Tom's expression held its mild indifference. "How much do I pay you for this?" he asked.

"Tom, she's contemplating," Vita scolded him.

"Nothing at all," Jadwiga insisted, her eyes

sweeping over him as she stood and brought her velvet-covered crystal ball to the table.

Vita watched Jadwiga's eyes penetrate the ball's depths. Her gaze relaxed, as if admiring a beautiful piece of art. Vita's eyes followed hers down to the ball. Oh, to have the ability to see the visions her friend perceived in there. Vita shifted her gaze over to Tom and resisted the urge to lay her hand over his.

Jadwiga opened her mouth to speak, looking like she'd just come to a painful decision. "There was a strong attachment, a trust, two people sharing a special bond, loving each other very much." Her eyes swept back and forth between Vita and Tom.

Every vein in Vita's body throbbed.

"Do you get anything on the killer? Was there more than one?" Tom leaned forward, his tone impatient, rushed.

Vita cringed at his abrupt grilling. She hoped to hear more about this special love. Was it Tom and his cousin? Tom and her? She'd find out soon enough, so she kept quiet.

"I just began seeing policemen—uniforms—yelling at each other—a brawl." Jadwiga's eyelids fluttered. A crown of sweat beads popped out along her hairline. She focused on deep inner thoughts. Tom bowed his head and clasped his hands as if in prayer.

"They're fighting, kicking—there seems to be a stalemate. They're of equal strength. They're both armed. Reaching for their guns. Two shots. They're both shot, but one is dead."

Tom pushed his chair back and stood. "I've seen enough. I mean I've heard enough. Can you stop now, please?"

"Tom—" Vita clutched at his sleeve, but he strode from the table and stood at the window, his back to them.

Jadwiga, still in her trancelike state, went on: "I'm trying to see his face, but they both look the same."

Vita stood and went over to him. "Are you all right?"

He looked at her with a desperate plea in his eyes. "A cop killed him, another cop. Is that what she's saying?"

"I'm not sure—she says these things are symbols sometimes."

"Hey, you want me to start again? Why'd you get up?" Jadwiga's voice sounded far away, or maybe it was just weak from fatigue.

"No, but thank you, I've heard enough of this. I don't want to undermine your talents, but—" He walked back over to the table and studied the ball as if he saw a vision in there. Vita sensed his desperation to believe what he'd heard, but she knew how he felt about this "supernatural mumbo-jumbo."

"Does that literally mean another cop killed him?" he asked her. "Do you see these things at random? Do you interpret them another way? Or what?" He punctuated his inquisition with gestures at the ball. It was the ball he wanted the answers from.

"Sometimes what I see are symbols," she explained. "I've read a lot about dreams, and it seems the symbols are universal—like emotions that we all share, no matter where we come from or what language we speak. Sometimes I see things that are going to happen, and sometimes I dream these things, and then they happen." She polished the ball with the velvet cloth. "What I just saw could be symbolic—the good cop killing the bad cop, or vice versa. Good overpowering evil, like that. That's why I wanted to see their faces. But it was like in a dream. Sometimes you can see every detail of a face."

"So another cop killed him." Tom leveled his gaze at her.

Jadwiga stood and swept at her forehead with a hankie. "That's what it feels like to me. If not another cop, an equal. Someone just like him."

"Anything else you saw in there?" he prodded.

For someone who didn't want to hear mumbo-jumbo a minute ago, he had sure become a believer fast. His change of heart encouraged Vita. Her spirits soared.

"I got feelings that this had been going on a long time, this antagonism. It wasn't a spur-of-the-moment murder; it was planned, or at least wished, for a long time." Jadwiga circled her fingers around the ball but gazed across the room.

"A conspiracy?" he asked.

"That I didn't get. But long-time enemies. Not two guys passing in the night and one sticking a gun in the other's gut."

"But you didn't see anything at all to do with my father or brother," Vita stated rather than phrasing it as a question.

"No, they never entered it. Didn't feel them at all."

"Oh, dear God." Vita whispered the entreaty over a sigh and sank back down into the chair.

Tom went to her, gently touching his palm to the top of her head. She reached up and clasped his hand, drawing him nearer, and stood on shaky legs.

"It's okay. I'm not gonna faint again," she assured

him with a weak laugh. "I'm just drowning in relief."

"You want a drink, hon?" Jadwiga draped the cover over her ball and circled around the table, heading for her vodka supply.

"No, nothing." Vita shook her head. "I don't know how long I'll feel this relief, so I'm going to enjoy it."

"Until they find the killers, of course," Jadwiga asserted.

"Until *we* find the killers," Tom corrected her, "because I'm not putting my faith in the police force for this. To them, he's just another statistic. But he wasn't just another cop to me; he was my cousin and didn't deserve this."

"Well, you have my blessing, both of ya's. I'm here if you need me. This'll work out, I know it." Jadwiga belted back a shot.

Vita couldn't blame her. She craved a drag on her pipe, but not in front of Tom.

"You two can do it together, I know it," Jadwiga assured them as they left.

Vita's muscles ached and her head spun in every direction like she'd been dumped in the ocean not knowing which way was up. "I believe Jadwiga, yet I can't let go of some doubt," she admitted to him.

Tom kept shaking his head and frowning. "Let's just walk," he said. "I don't want the evening to end." They headed toward the Battery in a silence that comforted her more than words.

At the foot of New York Harbor, he stopped her and drew her close. "Oh, Vita." He spoke her name like a prayer, with the need to bind her to him, to make her his.

In her answer, "I'm here for you," she assured him

she'd always stay by his side. "If we can get through this together, the rest of our lives will be a precious gift."

"It already is," he promised her.

As they stood gazing at Lady Liberty, the breeze picked up. She wrapped her shawl tighter around her.

"We should get back and start questioning your neighbors." He took her hand and guided her away from the waterfront. He flagged down a passing streetcar and they boarded. Streetlamps glowed in the dusk. Sheets billowed from the fire escapes.

As they reached her Mott Street tenement, he asked, "We'll do the questioning tomorrow, but right now I want to look around your rooms again. Is your stepmother around?"

"No, she stayed with me last night. I have a feeling she's gone back there. She didn't want to be alone anymore."

She unlocked the door and pushed it open. While Tom looked around, she lit the lone lamp in the kitchen. It spilled a soft circle of light on the table. She shivered in the eerie absence of her family. Their presence lingered; she smelled their sweat and heard their shouting voices. Papa's wine jug and a crumpled pack of Butchie's cigarettes stood side by side on the table. Rosalia's olive green tablecloth darkened the kitchen even more. She hugged her arms to her sides. It was as if they'd gone to the corner store and would walk through the door any minute.

Vita walked through to the bedrooms. The darkness intensified the smells. But she didn't cringe with shame. Instead, she almost basked in a malicious smugness. Now Tom could see how they were forced to live. She wanted him to be ashamed of his own people for holding her people back.

When he'd burst in here in broad daylight, it hadn't mattered. But now, enshrouded in darkness, the place looked as eerie and miserable as the Tombs. Shadows crept up the peeling walls. A flushing toilet on the landing broke the silence.

They didn't speak as he went on his search under the beds and bureaus. Brushing off his hands, he asked, "Are there any loose floorboards or a corner of the cellar where they keep junk and things?"

"Hardly," she answered. "We barely have enough junk to fill this place."

He then shuffled through Rosalia's clothes, shoes, and unmentionables. She had more stuff than any of them. As he shook out Rosalia's bloomers, nylons and corsets, a question hit Vita: Does he suspect Rosalia? But he shook his head and tossed her things back into the bureau drawer.

"Do you think I should bring Jadwiga here? Maybe she could give us a hint as to who's been here," she suggested.

"You can do anything you want with Jadwiga, but I don't think she'll help us."

She turned to face him. Shadows deepened the lines around his tired eyes and emphasized the stubble on his chin. Aware that they were all alone, she battled her fierce attraction to him. Those wicked urges tempted her once more. She pushed them away like the good girl she was.

"But you listened to her," she argued. "You seemed to have believed what she told you from the reading."

"Even if the ball speaks gospel, we can't use it for evidence. I'm a cop doing my job. If they ever found out I'd even gone there, I'd be laughed off the force."

"So you only went to humor me." She glared.

"Not to humor you, no." He shook his head. "I don't humor people. I was—what you said—trying to be open-minded."

"And now it's clammed up again."

"I don't believe her. I don't disbelieve her." He raised his arms and dropped them to his sides. "I trust your judgment. You wouldn't have taken me to some charlatan. If she was a charlatan, I know you wouldn't be bothering with her at all."

"So your idea of open-minded is not to form any opinion at all," she challenged.

"I'd rather try the conventional methods first. Talking to possible witnesses, trying to collect evidence. I'll follow her leads if they make sense, but I can't come to any conclusions by what somebody sees in a crystal ball. No competent member of the force can."

"Then you still think Papa and Butchie might have done this?" She dwelled on this, unable to stop herself.

"No, I don't think—I don't know, Vita. I'm so tired, I can barely think straight." He rubbed his temples like he had a bad headache.

She dragged her feet, too. She didn't think she'd make it to Washington Square tonight; she would probably sleep here and leave in the morning.

"Then go home, Tom. I'll stay here." She gave him a dismissive wave.

"By yourself?" He stopped rubbing and looked at her.

"There must be at least a hundred bodies crammed into this building. This isn't exactly the Sahara Desert. I'll be fine."

He stood in near-darkness now; she could barely make out his body's outline against the window facing the air shaft. They had no pretty hanging light fixtures.

"I'll see you tomorrow, then," he said. "We'll question your neighbors."

"All right."

But neither of them made a move. She didn't want him to leave, and she knew he couldn't tear himself away. She thought of offering him some coffee, but her better judgment told her not to. Having a man alone in her father's home would mark her as the blackest *putana* this neighborhood had ever seen. Even if not an eye peeped at her, she would have to live with it herself.

So she made the first move of dismissal. "Maybe you'd better go, Tom." She knew that didn't sound as dismissive as it should have. But, gentleman that he was, he picked up on it.

"Good night, Vita." He made a move to turn and leave, but desire pushed her forward, and she opened her arms.

He turned to her, and they fell into an embrace. His hands traced the curve of her back, stopping at the swell of her buttocks. Her arms wound around his neck. She brought her lips to his, and they explored with a sweet mutual need. Their tongues mingled and tasted of each other's surrender. A quiver raked through her, filling her with a tormenting thrill. She brushed off her immediate response—shame and disgust with her body for betraying her like this. She fell deeper into a dizzying loss of control as his hand caressed her cheek and he traced a finger over her ear. She never knew a touch could make torrents of voracious longing ripple through her.

"Tom," she whispered, and with the rapidness of her breaths, her whimperings became moans as his tongue teased her sensitive earlobe. What was this raw thrill raking through her? He pressed the length of his body up against her. An exquisite and delightful sensation swirled through her lower region, her heart thumping with a mounting beat. She felt him harden between her legs and her thighs parted, to savor this delicious new sensation. The world faded away—all except their desperate need for each other. Sensing his desire heightened her thrill. Her need jolted into an ache, but she didn't know how to ease this delicious but painful yearning.

He pulled away, tugged at his clothes, raked his fingers through his hair. "I'm sorry, Vita, I'm sorry…"

Her scruples came rushing back, leaving her cold and ashamed. She'd betrayed God and her family. But she could only blame her body. It had openly deceived her. It wasn't his fault, it was hers—this physical need nestled in her heart for the first time tonight. How they blended, playing upon her heart and her most sensitive parts, like a swirling melody.

"No, Tom, it was me—I don't know how that happened, what made me do that. My body just—" She caught her breath.

"So did mine," he interrupted. He backed away in tentative steps, his arm reaching behind him, his hand groping for the doorknob. "But I couldn't help it. You're just so beautiful—I didn't mean to take advantage of you like that. I'm sorry."

That was taking advantage? That's what women guarded their virtue against? That's what tarnished reputations and labeled women such ugly words? These delightful sensations shared with a special someone in a moment of intense emotion? She couldn't, in all her logic and reason, reconcile the two, any more than she could reconcile two unequal columns of numbers.

Or maybe this was something that no other woman had ever felt, the reason women shunned it and the church condemned it—it wasn't supposed to feel good. She'd shared something with Tom that she never had with another human being, never in her dreams or in her prayers, in religious ecstasy or in the joy of holy celebrations. She longed to share it with him again and again.

But it couldn't be tonight, or any time soon. She'd committed a sin, letting this happen while her loved ones languished in prison, his cousin in a cold grave. She needed to get to the confessional—before she suffered God's wrath.

So he turned and left her alone. She shivered in forbidden delight, still feeling the waves of pleasure from their bodies meeting and pressing, their lips searching, their souls mingling. It left her emotionally and physically drained. She dragged herself to the bed and fell into a deep sleep.

Bright sunlight woke her up. A picture of Tom entered her mind and delicious longing bounced on every tingling nerve. Then thoughts of Papa and Butchie took over and stayed with her as she began her daily ritual.

Before she left, she took a few more keepsakes and

stuffed them into a pillowcase, along with a shirt of Papa's and Butchie's comb. She'd brought them some clothes yesterday, and Butchie had wanted his Mary medal. Rosalia brought them whatever the neighbors cooked.

She hesitated at the door and reflected on these short-tempered, proud, but humble folk she called family. Papa favored the boys, but Vita realized he felt more comfortable with them. He showed protection toward her rather than affection. Rosalia, the odd piece of the puzzle, the necessary wife, refused to fulfill most of her wifely roles, and Papa didn't care. Vita wished she'd known Mama. Papa had said she was a lot like her mama; headstrong and wise beyond her years. Who was this woman who'd carried her? Only when he blew his top in fury did he blame Vita for her mother's death.

But love them she did, and no matter where she wound up, she'd always be Vita Caputo from Mott Street.

Closing the door, watching the shabby kitchen shrink to a thin slice of mottled sunlight, she took a deep breath. Pride swelled her heart—of her heritage, of her wine-swilling, festive culture, of her deeply ingrained work ethic.

New York and Vita Caputo stood at a juncture, destined to meld, to fuse, and to become greater than they could ever be singly. She needed to tame this demon. It was time for reform.

She walked out, not looking back. With nothing weighing down her heart, she left the building and embraced the city now giving her the opportunity to redeem it.

She left some money with Mrs. Del Monte upstairs

for when the landlord collected on rent day. She didn't want Papa and Butchie to be homeless when they got out.

Then she headed to her uptown world. Yes, her uptown world was far more different from the Lower East Side than Napoli was.

Chapter Fifteen

"Let's start with the basement tenants and work our way up," Tom suggested. So she led him into her building and down the stairs. Doors opened wide at the familiar sight of her face, but Tom's rigid line of questioning did nothing to make her neighbors cooperate. Some of them didn't speak English, and Vita had to translate. As they babbled in Italian, she repeated their words so Tom could understand, but the general consensus was, "We don't know nothin'."

Pent-up frustration coiled her muscles like a tight spring. "Look, Tom, they're not opening up to you. They don't trust cops. They're afraid of getting set up or wrongly accused. Their fears are rational, you gotta admit."

"All right, you do the asking. But do you know what to ask? What did they hear? What did they see? Can they give descriptions?" He slid Mike's photo out of his pocket and handed it to her, turning away, as if he couldn't bear to look at it. Crinkled around the edges, a crease ran down the center, cutting through his features. He looked even younger than she remembered him at the Cooper Union meeting. Neither tragedy nor wisdom had etched any lines around his eyes or pleats in his brow. Now they never would.

"I'll do my best. If anybody can get these people yakking away like *chiaccharione*, I can." She gave him back the photo.

"Yakking away like what?" he asked.

She tapped her thumb and fingers together like flapping lips. "People who gab a lot." She allowed herself a smile and headed back inside. "Go to Joe's. I'll meet you there."

As darkness fell, she asked…and asked. They told her again and again, some with pity, some with a slam of the door in her face, "We don't know nothin'."

****

She went in through the Ladies' Entrance of Joey Cap's Saloon and found Tom hunched over a stein of beer. As she rushed up to him, all the emotions they'd shared in the last few days burst out of them in a rib-crushing hug.

"Oh, Tom…" She slid into the chair across from him. How she wished they were alone so she could stay wrapped in his arms. "Nothin'. I got nothin'."

He extended his hand and she clasped it. "Nobody saw Mike before the murder, nobody heard gunshots that night or early that morning. I wish somebody saw something or even recognized Mike from the picture…" She released a long sigh. "We're at a dead end. I know there's still the rest of the block. But…" Defeat dragged her voice down.

"Don't even think of giving up. I know that empty feeling inside. We'll find them, though." But his voice sounded even more defeated. He drained the stein and stood, motioning her out.

"I want to walk past your building one more time." They stepped back into the night and headed that way.

She didn't ask him why. Maybe his returning to the crime scene helped him face it. She heard her angel's voice: "They'll see the truth and you'll all return here as a family." Her eyes filled with tears. "I believe you, Mama," she whispered. As she stepped back with her thoughts, she left Tom alone with his.

When they reached her building, he pointed to a dark, irregular-shaped stain a few feet from the stoop. "This is where he was found. Lying here." He knelt, ran his hand over the stain, gathered a clump of dirt, and let it sift through his fingers, Mike's blood mingled with the earth and refuse of Mott Street. She took a step back, not wanting to intrude.

"Nobody heard a gunshot." He spoke so softly she had to step closer.

She knelt beside him. "Somebody would've heard it, even if it was in the middle of the night."

He shook his head, lines creasing his forehead. He also had stab wounds," he went on. "Here and here." He pointed to his chest, just below his heart.

"No one in my family is capable of stabbing anyone." She jumped to their defense. "We have one small knife, the size of a pen. We use it to slice bread and chop up meat, when we have meat. The knife has its place, above the sink."

"It wasn't that kind of knife." He stood, brushed the dirt from his fingers, and helped her up. She clasped his hand, feeling the grit stuck to it.

"There's really nothing else we can do tonight, Tom, except think some more." She hoped he would suggest a long walk, a ride on the Staten Island ferry— another few hours of closeness, of mutual comforting, so she could relive some of last night's magic. Most of all she needed to understand those confounding emotions. They'd haunted her like phantoms in the night and vanished. She needed to master them, or else.

"Would you like to go for a walk, back down to the Battery, or go across on the ferry, and talk, or just—just think it out some more?" She extended the bold invitation. "Or do you want to be alone?" She asked that to be polite but hoped he wouldn't even consider that.

"How 'bout you coming back to my house? Meet my houseful?" She knew this was a big step for him, an impossible premise for her. She wanted him alone, without the distraction of watching him stand on his family stage and perform.

She pulled her shawl around her shoulders. The breeze from the river carried a chill. "I'm not ready for that yet, Tom. I don't think you are either."

They walked down to Battery Park and sat on a bench, not another soul around. He gathered her to him. She molded herself to his side and leaned back against the crook of his elbow. Her free hand grasped his. This fulfilled her more than those searching kisses. "I'll ask for forgiveness and do my penance when tonight is over, God," she whispered. He would forgive her these few brief moments of self-indulgence.

"I want to bring you home, Vita." Now the suggestion became a demand. "I want them to meet you."

"Not while this is going on. Do they know who I am?"

"If Liam Johnson didn't hold it against you, my family certainly won't. They're not like that." His encouraging tone didn't convince her.

She shook her head. "Let's just leave the families out of this for now. I mean—in the way that we can."

"They don't think they're better than anybody. You know what kind of mix of boarders we've had over the years? Slavs, Germans, an American Indian—we've accepted them all."

"I don't even have to call myself Violet Greene?" She searched his eyes.

As he stroked her cheek, she tingled. "Never. I know how hard it was for you to shun your heritage and change your name for that job. But I'm just as proud to take you home as you are to be who you are."

"You might think they're open-minded and accept all kinds. But you're talking about boarders here. Bringing me home isn't quite the same. They might think you're serious about me." She snuggled even closer.

He lifted her chin with his finger and brought her lips to meet his, but he didn't kiss her. Their lips almost touching, he said, "I *am* serious about you, Vita. Very serious." He caressed her with his words, taking a breath as if to say more but didn't. He didn't kiss her and she didn't raise her lips in expectation. Their gazes locked. Neither of them blinked. "I only hope I'm worthy of you. And I'm hoping that my feelings will be returned someday."

How could she share her feelings now? She didn't have the words, in English, or even in the more expressive Italian, to describe the responses he evoked in her. "There just aren't any words, Tom," she answered truthfully. "Why are words even necessary?"

"You don't have to say anything." He touched his fingertip to her lips. "I'd rather show you than tell you anyway. And we'll get through this. Much better than if we were alone."

"We still can't bring Mike back." She broke her gaze and took a much-needed gulp of air. "It won't ever be all right."

"To us his death is senseless, a tragic waste of a life. A good, honest, clean man robbed of everything the world could give him. But it's only senseless to us. God wanted him and called him. And he went. And here we are." His hold on her relaxed, and they sat in silence as the plaintive wail of a boat's horn echoed through New York Harbor.

He made it sound so logical. The closer she got to his soul, the more she understood the workings of his church and how the Irish Catholics related to God. How their common sense extended through every aspect of their lives, including how they viewed their own fates. After a lifetime of kissing statues and fearing the Evil Eye, this was so refreshing.

"I know we're here now," she said. "But as we sit here, now is over. There's tomorrow. And next week, and next year." She looked out into the blackness.

"God, Vita, I can't possibly think that far ahead. Take one step at a time. It's a straight line. We go through time like we get on the ferry and glide through the water. But we can't rush it, and can't slow it down. So take it as it comes."

She returned her gaze to him. "But you've got to do some planning. I'd rather die than live my life on Mott Street. I wasn't anywhere ready to take those steps when you told me about the bank. I'd planned on another year of saving, then night school, then two years in a clerical position while going to my reform meetings, then working my way into local politics—I had it all planned out. It just happened faster than I planned it. Now I have to plan faster to catch up."

"But you also have to take daily life with the long-range plans. Look at what happened—who could ever plan on something like this? While you're making your great plans, the unexpected hits you in the face. Horrible things like tragedy, and magical things like" —he took in a deep breath—"love."

Her eyes questioned him, but he still gazed out over the harbor. "You mean—" Oh, how she longed to hear him say those words!

But he only smiled, lightening the intensity of the moment. "It comes unexpectedly. But that's the beauty of it when it does come. Don't you agree?"

She nodded, knowing she couldn't be the first to say "I love you." He might be the picture of danger and mystery, with his dirty political dealings, but her growing trust for him chased away the fear. She feared herself now—feared she'd fallen deeply in love with him.

She was the one who suggested they should be calling it a night. And despite this perfect moment, with twinkling boat lights spanning the harbor, a caressing breeze playing through her hair, and not a soul in sight, she fathomed who they really were: the daughter of an accused murderer kissing a crooked cop. She was so glad it went deeper than that.

****

The following evening, she knocked on more doors and showed Mike's picture to everyone she passed on the street—even the streetcar drivers and coachmen.

Mrs. Rizzoli thought she recognized him. But Vita knew it was a dead end when the nonna said, "*Si, si*, my son, he bring the young man home with a few other fellows from the docks last Christmastime. But all these *bambini,* they all look alike to me." Mrs. Rizzoli sent Vita back where she started.

If anyone in the Italian section ever had anything to do with an Irish cop, they wouldn't dare admit it. They brandished outright smugness when they said, "We never seen this cop."

Yawning with exhaustion, she dragged herself to Jadwiga's. Over vodkas on the rocks, Vita said, "Come on over to the Mott Street flat. I don't want the ball or the cards, I just want to see if you can get a feel for anything. Somebody went into the rooms and planted this evidence. If you can feel their presence almost as strongly as Papa's, imagine what you can come up with!"

"I'll give it a whirl," came her answer, and Vita's tiredness vanished.

They headed for Mott Street. Jadwiga brought her vodka bottle and homemade *placki ziemniaczane,* potato pancakes. Vita put them in the oven to heat up as Jadwiga ambled around the kitchen. "Watch that floor, it buckles," Vita warned as Jadwiga stumbled and grabbed the wall for support.

"Thanks." She kicked off her shoes and padded around barefoot. Vita had always scrubbed the floor when she lived here, but it didn't look all too clean now. Grime just seemed to come up through the floorboards.

As Jadwiga wandered through the back rooms, Vita took her checkered tablecloth from the cupboard, pulled off Rosalia's ugly green one, and spread hers over the table. When Jadwiga came back, Vita told her about the bloodstain outside the building.

"Show me," she demanded.

Vita checked the *placki ziemniaczane,* and they went down to the narrow alley next to the stoop. Most vendors had left for the day, and only a few still remained, packing up their wares. The usual piles of horse dung, discarded fruit rinds, and rotten vegetables lined the streets. Nobody sat out on the stoops at this sacred dinner hour. Aside from whoever was peeking through their shabby curtains, Vita and Jadwiga had the street to themselves. Three street arabs squatted in the dirt across the street playing jacks. The blood had completely seeped into the alley's dirt, but studying it, Vita saw the faint outline of the stain Tom had shown her. The urchins swept up their jacks and scampered away.

Vita traced it with her finger. Jadwiga blotted the stain with her handkerchief, and they went back upstairs. Sitting at the table, she held the handkerchief close, squeezed her eyes shut, and pressed it to her cheek.

"Oh, yes, I sense an intruder," she said.

Vita's eyes shot over to the door. The faint banging of cookware came through the thin wall. "Now?"

"No. But—but there was someone in here besides your family," Jadwiga stated, as surely as if she'd been there.

"People came and went all the time. We always had company."

"No. This wasn't company." Jadwiga shivered.

Vita touched Jadwiga's ice-cold hand and shivered herself. "Why are you so cold all of a sudden?" The kitchen was warm; if the window hadn't been open, she'd have suffocated.

Jadwiga opened her eyes, shook her head, and lunged for her vodka bottle. Vita offered her a glass, but she refused, folded her hankie, and pushed it down the front of her blouse. "The *plackis* will warm me up. Let's chow now, and I'll see if I feel anything later. I'm not so sensitive on an empty stomach."

Vita placed three potato pancakes on each plate, but they only nibbled. She grasped her friend's hand. "Are you all right?"

"Yeah," she answered with a shaky smile and took another vodka shot.

"You wanna go?" Vita hoped they could stay longer and Jadwiga could pick something up. "You know I'm desperate. But I don't want to make you sick."

"No, I'm okay now. I just had a real intense feeling. It went right through me." She didn't shiver anymore. But she did knock back yet another shot of vodka.

"From the hankie? From the stain? Or in here?"

"All of it," she said. "I felt a connection. Whoever left Mike's body in the alley was in this room, and this same person was tryin' to shut me up, not wanting it to come through."

"Oh, dear God." Vita clasped her hands. "Maybe they're psychic, too."

That made Jadwiga laugh. Vita laughed along with her, grateful for the release. "Yeah, it's crazy, thinking that, I know. But you know where I come from. I've been brought up to believe that there's a lot around us that we can't see with our eyes or feel with our hands or hear with our ears."

"Well, Polish folks ain't far off it." Jadwiga

grinned. "Heaven's overflowing with saints and angels, and that hot place down below is pretty crowded, too, gettin' more packed every day. Anything's possible as long as you believe."

"Well," she replied, "Italians scoff at earthly things, while the rest of the world scoffs at Italians."

Jadwiga looked at her nearly empty bottle as if contemplating one last shot. "Another psychic would have gotten in touch with me by now, if it was." She slid the bottle around in circles on the table. "They'd know what I was trying to do here. But psychics don't make good killers. We're not violent by nature. We're a big band of cowards, really." Jadwiga began playing with her necklace, Vita's favorite: a gold-and-jade-beaded double strand she loved borrowing.

"I'm glad you were able to feel something here. I did, too, the other night. I felt Papa's presence really strongly, then another one, an evil one. It didn't scare me, though. I'm not a-scared of nothin' these days." Vita allowed herself the indulgence of a smile. She couldn't smile between the bars of Papa and Butchie's cell; she couldn't smile at angry reformers or her Mott Street neighbors. She saved her smiles for those special moments with Tom. But with Jadwiga, she could sneak in a joke or just sit and smoke their forbidden pipes.

"You got nothin' to be afraid of." Jadwiga gave her arm a reassuring squeeze. "Nobody's gonna hurt you. Your pop and brother'll be just fine."

"You really know that? I mean *know* it, instead of just having like—your strange feelings?" Vita wiggled her fingers.

"If they're innocent, they'll get out," Jadwiga declared.

179

"They are! You should know that, everybody knows that, and nobody around here is anywhere near psychic."

"Yeah, that's why I'm here, ain't I? Lookin' for this killer of yours, hopin' he stumbles into my vision?" She drummed her fingernails on the table, staring. "In time, I wanna be able to tell you something you can sink your teeth into, bite off and chew."

Vita perked up. "I have another idea that might throw some more light on it."

"What?"

"What about a séance to contact Mike's spirit?" Little shivers went down Vita's spine at the thought. It spooked her, but she'd try anything.

Jadwiga cocked her head, flinging a lock of hair behind her shoulder. "I ain't done those much."

"Why not?"

"People don't want 'em. They were real vogue about twenty years ago. Every parlor in New York would be blazing in candlelight at night, people sitting in circles at the table, holdin' hands, callin' up spirits. I did a few, but nothing ever happened. They just seemed to go out of style. It was all the rage, though, with Mary Lincoln trying to bring her son back. Madame Lavatsky and all these so-called spiritualists pocketed a wad of dough, feeding off desperate soul-searchers."

"I don't care what's in vogue," Vita countered. "We're trying to find the killer. We've asked everyone under the sun except the man who got gunned down. Mike's got a spirit—we all do. Maybe his will talk. Especially if it's restless. He was so young; you saw the picture. No older than me. Isn't it worth a try?"

"Hey, anything's worth a try." She held her palms

up. "But Tom should sit in on it. He's the one who was closest to him. It'd help a lot if he was here—or wherever we're gonna have it." She looked around and bobbed her head, frowning. "I dunno if a spirit would want to come here."

"Too much garlic?" They giggled, and Vita savored another bite of *placki ziemniaczane.*

Chapter Sixteen

"A séance? Come on, Vita—" Tom looked away. As the bus rattled down Fifth Avenue, raindrops blew in through the window and slapped her cheek as if to chide her.

"Jadwiga wants you there, to add your energy." She clutched his sleeve, urging, "The more energy she can channel, the better. I want to find this killer as bad as you do, and my father's and brother's lives are at stake. How much time do you think we have left?"

He looked at her, apology shining in his eyes. "I didn't mean to—I just never thought of doing any of these hocus-pocus things."

"A lot of strange things happen to people, Tom."

"Yeah, but not to plainclothes New York cops. I've heard all the folk tales and the fairy tales—Ireland's steeped in folklore, but who knows where it came from. It could've come out of the mist. But when you have to risk your life every day, you step out into the street, see the stark ugliness of crime and death, and use these new questionable methods of forensics and criminal science, you get grounded. It's a real earthly existence, being a cop." A frown deepened the lines around his mouth.

"You're a lot more spiritual than you admit," she informed him.

"But I've never had the compulsion to bend down and kiss a saint's feet—or pin money on one. I place it straight into live people's hands reaching out for it."

"You don't have to kiss a saint's feet," she assured him. "I'll tell you something. A lot of Italians just go through the motions because they were brought up that way. Or they're afraid not to. But I can tell you're—" She gestured up and down. "You're spiritual."

"You can see my spirit?" A smile played on his lips, but the question carried a flicker of doubt.

"It's not something you see. It's something you—know." She hesitated at the end, treading on uncharted territory.

"I see what you're saying. I mean—I know what you're saying," he explained, and she understood every word.

"Then you'll sit in on a séance?" She bounced in the seat. "For us? For Mike?"

He pursed his lips. "Well, for a shred of evidence, I guess it's probably worth a few minutes in the dark."

"We are in the dark, Tom. The Tombs is light compared to this."

His gaze caught hers. "Hey, take that pleading look out of your eyes and come here." He opened his arms. She leaned forward, letting the raindrops mist her face. She inhaled the earthy scent of his coat. Yes, everything about him was earthy, here on the surface. Deeper down, his hidden depths lay unexplored.

****

Rosalia overstayed her three-night invitation. Each time Vita entered her room to see her stepmother lounging on her bed smoking or peeling off her nylons and tossing them on the floor, pity softened her heart and she bit her tongue.

Rosalia befriended Madame Branchard, who urged

her to sit in on the parlor discussions with the free thinkers, to speak her mind and leave those old-world restraints behind. When reformers and writers gathered over cocktails, she sat rapt with attention and absorbed it all, wide-eyed. Like a flower in bloom, Vita saw a forward-thinking woman emerge from the old-world Italian bride.

"Hey, I'm happy for you, Rose." Vita took her aside one late night as the party broke up after a heated discussion about women getting the vote. "You may have found your niche here."

"Does that mean I can stay?" Her eyes sparkled like Vita had never seen before. One of her rare smiles lit up the dark staircase.

"Talk to Madame. She might ask you to kick in some rent."

With a delighted squeal, she dashed back down the stairs. Vita hoped Madame would prorate the rent, another useful banking term she'd learned at her job. She had a hunch she'd use it someday.

****

She and Jadwiga decided to hold the séance at the alleged crime scene—the Mott Street apartment.

As dusk gave way to darkness the following night, Jadwiga arrived at the tenement with something wrapped in a bolt of black satin that must've cost a fortune. She placed her bundle on the table and unwrapped it. "A spirit board."

Vita dragged her fingertips over the well-worn surface. "I've seen these in Italy. Gypsies use them." Red block letters faded into the shiny well-worn wood. It displayed the alphabet, the numbers 1 to 9, and the words "Yes" and "No" in the bottom corners. Jadwiga unwrapped a saucer-sized glass oval. "This is called the planchette." She polished it with a white cloth and set it in the center of the board.

Tom arrived, glanced at the board, and hovered around the table, declining her offer to sit. He paced the kitchen, a real noodge, looking antsy to get this over with. As they stood around it silently, Vita sensed the tension between the three of them heightening. "I'm as desperate for the truth as you are." She took his arm and led him to the table.

"We'll get the truth." A calm and whispery Jadwiga broke the silence as she stepped forward and took both their hands. They stood like that, connected, as Jadwiga said a prayer to Saint Michael. She asked Vita, "You got a candle, honey?"

Vita found a white candle in the bedroom where Rosalia kept her Blessed Mother statue. She lit it, and they sat around the table. "Put a pinkie finger on the planchette," Jadwiga instructed.

Nothing happened—yet.

Vita looked at Jadwiga. "Do I have to close my eyes?"

"Of course," she whispered, and once again all fell silent.

Finally Jadwiga spoke, in a low drone that helped calm Vita.

"Mike, are you here? Tell us if you're with us, dear," Jadwiga summoned him gently, like encouraging a frightened child.

"Mike? Hey," Jadwiga said in greeting, as if he'd just walked through the door. The planchette moved toward Vita. She recoiled at the sound of the scraping on wood but didn't dare open an eye.

"Jadwiga…" Vita whispered as she slid her foot over to meet Tom's, but the little glass oval continued sliding.

"It's spelling the word 'frame.' " Jadwiga drew the word out slowly as Vita's pinkie moved around, barely touching the planchette. It seemed to be guided from one side to the other and back again.

Vita pulled her hand away as if she'd touched a red-hot coal. "Ow!" She blew on her burning pinkie finger to cool it and stared at the board. The planchette flipped over, struck the table, and teetered on the edge.

Jadwiga plucked the planchette up and dropped it again. "Hey, this thing's hot as a poker."

Vita held up her hand. "Yeah, it burned my finger."

Jadwiga peered into it, her hair falling over the board like a gleaming curtain. "Look." She took the candle and held it level with the table's surface. Vita inched closer, her nails digging into Tom's sleeve. The inside of the planchette was charred black, as if flames had blazed under it.

"Did this ever happen before?" Vita whispered, not daring to speak out loud. She didn't detect any spirits, but the air grew colder. She ran her hands up and down her arms to warm them.

"Only once, at a séance I went to in London." Jadwiga touched it again and pulled away. "It's still warm."

"What did you say it just spelled out?" Vita felt Tom's body tense, his thigh pressed to hers.

" 'Frame.' A few times. Just 'frame.' " Jadwiga sat there staring at it.

"Like we've been framed?" Vita turned to face Tom. His eyes shut, he muttered something she couldn't hear.

"I'm sorry." Jadwiga looked at him, her eyes glowing like coals in the candlelight. "I didn't bring back Mike."

"You sure?" Tom met her apologetic gaze and let out an uncomfortable chuckle.

"It's encouraging." Jadwiga flounced across the kitchen and lit the lamp. "Anybody for a drink?" She swung her empty glass between her thumb and forefinger like a pendulum.

Neither of them responded. Tom sat buried in his thoughts. Vita studied the table's scars. Then she focused on the spot where the planchette had overturned and cut a nick in the surface. It resembled the gash in Papa's crucifix. Rosalia told her he'd flung it to the table when he was accused of the murder. The table now had a big gash on the other side where the crucifix had struck it.

Leaning over, she ran her finger over it as she had on the crucifix mark—the result of Papa's rage. She sensed hatred and violence flowing from that gash, as she'd sensed in the crucifix. This table had once been new and shiny. It bore scars of age along with scratches, dents, and stains. Some family had taken pride in it, long ago. Now, dark emotions marred it forever.

Vita spread her cloth over it and fussed with the edging.

"Look, I need to step back, to look at this from a distance." Jadwiga wrapped up her board and planchette, corked her bottle, and gathered the bundle in her arms. "I can't think right now. I need to get out of here."

Tom sat, hands folded between his knees, staring at the floor. Neither answered. Vita walked over to Tom and placed her hand on his shoulder. As he reached up and clasped it, his touch warmed her.

"I don't want to hang around here either." He slid the chair back, reached forward, and fingered the tablecloth. "This is the one you were telling me about?"

"Yes, the table's frilly dress, I call it," she declared with a hint of pride.

"I knew it was yours the minute I saw it. Nobody but you would have picked this out." He ran his finger over the lace edging the same way he'd caressed her cheek. "It's so soft and pleasing to look at."

He turned to her. The lamp's glow shone into his eyes. She saw his struggle to hold back tears. She wanted to press his head to her breast and assure him that it was healthy to cry, to grieve; Mike's death was her tragedy too. If Jadwiga hadn't been there, she would have taken that one step closer to let their tears flow and mingle.

Jadwiga must have sensed their need to be alone. "If you two wouldn't mind seein' me home"—she inched toward the door sideways—"I'll call it a night. You'll want to talk it out, you know."

"Thanks, Jadwiga." Vita gave her friend a wink.

They walked to Jadwiga's place, Jadwiga leading the way, letting Tom and Vita walk together. She picked up her pace like she couldn't wait to get out of their way. No one talked. Tom's arm wound around Vita's waist. She leaned into him as they headed to Bleecker Street.

"There's no hurry, Jadwiga. Don't rush on account of us," Vita called out. Her spirit had certainly linked with Jadwiga's, too. She finally had her first true girlfriend. She'd realized that the moment Jadwiga offered Vita her new hat. She cherished that gesture of intimacy, the sharing of a personal item. Now, as Jadwiga rushed home to let them be alone, Vita knew she had a true ally.

"Oh, you know me, always in a hurry," Jadwiga rattled off in short spurts as their steps echoed on the sidewalk.

Yes, of course Vita wanted to be alone with Tom, to talk about what they'd felt during the séance. Had they been so desperate for an answer they'd pushed that planchette by force of will?

They bade Jadwiga goodnight at her door and saw her safely inside. She and Tom faced each other, nearly touching. She caught her breath just in time to stifle a sigh, her body betraying her again.

Their attraction wasn't just physical—it was mental, compassionate, and most of all, spiritual.

"I know I shouldn't be saying this, but I don't feel like going back to my room yet, Tom." She added, "I don't want to be all alone. I need to talk some more."

He glanced at his watch and snapped it shut. "It's half past eleven. I'm not all that familiar with this territory, but if we walk around a bit, I'm sure we can find some little café or something open. It is the Village, after all."

"Why not Madame Branchard's parlor? She doesn't have any salons on Monday nights. It's quiet there, and no one will bother us. We can talk, if we keep our voices down." They headed up the empty street.

"She wouldn't object?"

"Never. As long as we're at opposite ends of the couch." She hoped he'd caught the levity there. A young woman inviting a suitor into her home was a brazen move, but that parlor entertained the most mixed company. "Tom, I'll be honest—and a bit forward here, but I just want to be alone with you."

He grasped her hand and squeezed it. "I like it when you're forward."

A thrill of anticipation shot through her. *Am I falling in love?* she asked herself again.

She slid her key into the lock, and they entered the house, their steps light. She glanced around the dark hallway, listening for voices, shivering with delight. The empty parlor was theirs alone. She turned up a gas lamp on a side table and offered him something from the kitchen.

"I don't need anything from the kitchen. I like what I see right here." His eyes locked with hers, and he guided her to the sofa. She sat much closer than a respectable girl should, but she wanted to be bold, wanton—to take advantage of these rare private moments.

"Did you feel Mike's presence at all during the séance?" she asked, desperate for some understanding from that extraordinary event.

He gave an emphatic nod. "I always feel his presence. He's here with us right now." He gestured around. "He's not in a cemetery. I refuse to believe that."

"But when that glass was moving around the board, did you feel him there, guiding it? Was it him spelling out 'frame'? It wasn't either of us, I know it. Something was guiding it. Some kind of force." Recalling the scene sent shivers through her.

"You're asking the wrong person if you're looking to validate the results of a séance." He shook his head. "You should be asking your friend. I've never done anything like that. I never would have thought to."

"We don't know. I'm sure Jadwiga doesn't even know for sure. But I want to know what you believe," she urged.

He crossed one leg over the other and rested his head against the sofa back. "I haven't radically altered my beliefs after tonight." He spoke with his eyes closed. "I don't know what it would take to convince me that the dead can talk to us through spirit boards, or telegraph wires, or any other medium. Even when they come to us in dreams we don't know if it's really them or our imaginations or whatever makes us dream. I have faith his spirit is always around me, but I haven't heard his voice or seen his image. He hasn't whispered the name of his assailant into my ear or sent any pots and pans flying around our kitchen. But that doesn't mean he's not here."

She shifted, moving even closer. "So you're saying we're no closer to finding any clues than we were three hours ago." If he wasn't a skeptic, he sounded like one. But that was because of her own background—a Roman Catholic who believed her mother could see her through the eyes of an angel on a church wall.

"Clues?" He opened his eyes and looked her way without turning his head. His lashes feathered over his eyes, casting them in shadow. "Cops don't use spirit boards for clues. If any of the fellows I work with knew what I did tonight, I wouldn't just get laughed off the force, I'd get *kicked* off."

"Well, you obviously don't think it's so farfetched, or you wouldn't have agreed to go," she argued, wondering how he'd answer that.

"I agreed to go because I'm open-minded. I don't disbelieve anything. I didn't go expecting Mike to come out of Jadwiga's vodka bottle in a vapor and start rattling off details about what color boots his murderer wore. No, no one convinced me that was him who spelled out 'frame' tonight, but who am I to say it wasn't him?" He gave a one-shoulder shrug. "No one I've ever known has seen a ghost, and I certainly have never seen one trying to spook Five Points, but that doesn't mean they don't exist. That's one thing you learn in criminal science, Vita. The more we learn, the more we realize we need to learn. But clairvoyants have never been any use to the police department."

"Well, what if one did help?" She pressed on. "What if this one tiny word, 'frame'—out of the dozens of letters of gibberish the board might have spelled out—meant something, or if Jadwiga had a vision, or a feeling, and we acted on it, and it led to Mike's killer? Would the police employ them?"

"I doubt it. Maybe some of those small towns would, out there on the prairie. But the Metropolitan Police prides itself on its forensic abilities. This is New York. It's not Naples or a cluster of mud huts in County Limerick. New York professes to be the cultural center of the New World, and it wants to lead the world into the new century. I don't think its citizens would take to the Metropolitan Police engaging in séances and contacting spirit guides in the advancement of their scientific methods. It would be a contradiction. They deal with what's in this world and maybe what's below it. But nothing above."

"Well, I want to believe someone was speaking to us there, Tom. I think the word 'frame' being the only readable word it spelled out is more than a coincidence." She wanted to convince him.

"You sure it didn't spell any Italian words?" He turned his head her way, still resting against the sofa back.

She tucked her feet under her. "No. Jadwiga wrote them all down. There was hardly a vowel in the whole string."

"Maybe it was in her language, whatever it is."

"Her language is English," Vita replied. "She doesn't have any native language. She was orphaned. I don't think she's bilingual at all."

"Ask her. Maybe she chants." Laugh lines creased the sides of his mouth in the lamp's soft glow.

"I hope not, if it's anything like she sings." Vita let out a low whistle. "*Madonna mia*, it's like a werewolf with laryngitis."

"The word 'frame' hasn't told us anything we haven't surmised already." His smile vanished. "I already know it's possible that your father and brother had nothing to do with this."

"Well, I know it's impossible they had anything to do with it." She tried to keep her voice down, but her excitement made her jumpy. "They're innocent, and this reinforces it."

"I know it's hard to accept, Vita, but I'm looking at this like a cop. And if I wasn't, we'd never be able to figure out what happened."

"Do you ever worry about your own life?" she asked, wondering what he really feared.

"Worry? No." He shook his head. "I don't worry about anything. Every day I go out there I'm fully aware I might be brought back home in a box. But at least I'll have died a noble death. Doing my job. Not wasting away to a skeleton by starvation." His eyes slid shut again, and his chest rose and fell in a deep breath.

"I worry."

He tilted his head. "About what?"

"You getting killed."

He rested his arm along the sofa back. His fingertips reached her hair. "You don't have the time to waste worrying about me. It's enough to look after yourself. You're a very brave woman, leaving home, moving in here. I don't want you worrying about something you can't control."

A pang of disappointment pinched her heart. Was it because she wanted some control over him? "Have you ever thought of quitting the force?"

His brows drew together, as if she'd asked him to ponder the impossible—which she was beginning to think he never did.

"Quitting? Of course not! That would be like asking me to quit being a man."

So maybe he did ponder the impossible.

"A cop isn't just my job. It's what I am. It's who I am." He looked at her. "Try to imagine not being Italian."

She smiled as an image of Butchie playing his accordion flashed before her eyes. He'd said he wanted to be buried with it, back in Italy. What would she want to be buried with? She didn't know. But she did know that she wanted to be buried in American soil. "I already have tried not to be Italian, Tom. To get my job.

And I'm sure it'll happen again. Not on purpose. But this is America, after all. We can be one thing deep down in our hearts, but to thrive here, we have to adapt to what's around us, on the surface. There might come a day when you won't want to be a cop anymore. It's who you are now, but you aren't going to be the same person twenty years from now."

He rubbed his temples. "Now where did—what made you come up with all that? Twenty years? Holy Christmas, I don't even know where I'll be in twenty minutes! I mean—at any given time, of course. Tomorrow at four o'clock, I won't wonder where I'll be at four-twenty. But twenty years!" He let out a low whistle, still shaking his head. "We're talking about the twentieth century now!"

"I know." She gave him an eager nod. "Isn't it marvelous? I'll have accomplished so much by then. And Papa and Butchie—they'll be all right, too."

He leaned forward and stroked her cheek. "I hope to God you're right. If I didn't know any better, I'd think you were hanging around with that Jadwiga too much, all this talk about the future and the next century and what you'll be doing."

She moved closer, grasping his hand, knowing how naughty she was. This was beyond forward. "No, it has nothing whatsoever to do with her. It's all me—so far, she's only told me stuff I don't want to hear."

"I know it has nothing to do with her—I knew it was all you." He looked into her eyes.

"And how well do you think you know me, Tom McGlory?" She kept her tone light and inquisitive, although inside she'd begun to boil.

He lifted a few of the wispy strands that had

escaped her bun and let them slide through his fingers.

"I know you're strong and determined and beautiful. I know if I ever touched liquid gold, this is what I imagine it would be like. I wondered what it would be like to touch your hair like this."

His fingertips played through her hair. Her lips met his fingers and planted nibble-like kisses on them. "I've always wanted to touch your hair, too."

"My darling, you can touch me anywhere you want," he whispered, leaning closer.

Heat infused her cheeks. *I invited this. There's no backing out, no refusing, no asking him to leave.* From this moment they could only move ahead.

She smiled playfully, reached over, and touched the soft waves ending just below his ear. Her fingers didn't stop there; they ran down his neck as her thumb toyed with his earlobe. In one concerted move, they embraced. Their lips played upon each other. He teased her with his tongue. As her mouth yielded to his, he led her into a kiss. Their tongues mingled and found an easy but swelling rhythm. Again those riotous pangs gnawed at her—had she invited them, just by suggesting this closeness?

She agonized over whether to nudge him away or let him continue to bedevil her with these intoxicating emotions. His hand played through her bun, working it free. A pin fell down the back of her neck. Pins all over the couch in the morning! But morning didn't exist, only now, her hair free and loose around her shoulders. He brushed it back as only he could, enfolding her long locks and clasping them between his fingers, as if he'd wanted to do this for a long, long time. Their kiss ended, but they played upon each other's lips in affectionate pecks. His breathing in her ear sent searing heat through her. She shivered when he flicked his tongue over her earlobe. "Tom—" she breathed. "We'd better stop."

He eased away and clasped her hand, kissing each of her knuckles. "You should have stopped me a lot sooner." His breath raked over her cheek.

"I just didn't want you to," she confessed.

"You want me to stop now?"

"We're on the couch here, in my boardinghouse. Anybody can come down. I wanted you to kiss me, but—"

"But just once." He gazed at her dreamily, eyes half closed. His breathing quickened. Her heart hadn't hammered this hard since that first day, when he grabbed her on the street.

"Well, yeah. One kiss and—then I wanted you to keep kissing me. But it started getting—" She halted, at a loss for the right word.

"Too hot?"

She blushed, looked away, and concentrated on the portrait of Madame's Uncle Iggy on the table. Anything to cool off.

When she said nothing, he continued, "Vita, I'm a healthy man, and I'm with a beautiful woman I care about very much. Sometimes it's not easy to simply sit on the couch and kiss. Sometimes you might have to slap me—or something."

"Oh, don't be silly. I'd never slap you." She let out a girly giggle that she hadn't planned on. She covered it up with a cough.

"You might have to." His voice became husky. "Because every time I'm anywhere near you like this, I

197

have a voracious longing to make love to you."

She held back a gasp. She'd fantasized about this so many times, but now that it was happening, it petrified her. Her muscles tensed. "Tom, you really shouldn't be talking like this."

"Does it make you uncomfortable when I tell you how I feel about you?"

"No—but about—" She stammered. "Well, what you said about making love, I—think you could have kept that to yourself."

"Vita, I'm not one to share much with anyone. Even with my father, who's the closest person to me in my life, I don't share all that much. I've never spilled my feelings to another human being. I've only spilled ink on sheets of paper. That's how I get it all out. And even that's not easy. I really have to struggle to get it out even then. But getting it out—that's the hard part."

"And right now you don't happen to have any ink and paper." She lowered her head and raised her eyes.

"I don't think I'll ever need it again, as long as you're with me."

No longer touching, they sat inches apart. He didn't move closer. She read the sincerity in his eyes but couldn't think too clearly herself.

"Would you care to tell me how you feel?" he asked.

Oh, she wouldn't dare! So she said, "I feel fine."

He laughed softly. "I'll bet."

She needed to cover that up with something fairly intelligent, so she blurted, "There's just so much going on that it's hard to figure out how I feel about anything. Right now my main concern is for my family." She hadn't meant that to sound as a reprimand.

"I know." He nodded his understanding. "In light of all that's happened—what I'm trying to say is that you're what keeps me going through all this. Having you to think about and to be with, it's saving my sanity. I don't stop thinking about Mike—he's on my mind constantly—he's here with me every second. But you—you keep me going."

"I understand exactly." Through all this, and even after this, she'd be miserable without him. "Through all our differences, all our doubts, I want us to stay together." She stopped and took a breath. "Is this weakness?"

"Absolutely not," he assured her. "It's strength."

Her heart tripped at those words. "Oh, Tom, that means everything to me."

The mantel clock rang out softly, only once.

"My God, it's one o'clock." She straightened her sleeves and blouse, although they weren't disheveled. Her hair fanned around her shoulders and tumbled down her back. How could she explain that to anyone who walked in? She felt around the cushions for pins.

"I wish you'd wear your hair down all the time." He adored her with his gaze. "It's so beautiful, framing your face like that."

"Like Jadwiga does?" She tried to imagine her friend wearing a bun. "She looks so offbeat with her hair all wild and swinging like that."

"Her hair is coarse, like the tail of a horse. Yours falls in silky waves." He wound some strands around his fingers again. "It's like a waterfall. How did it get to be so long?"

"I just never cut it." She smoothed it back with her palms. "I guess I should."

His eyes widened. "No, don't. It's beautiful the way it is." He stroked it one more time, his fingertips lingering on her cheek.

"But I could never wear it down like this."

"Yes, you can." His thumb brushed across her lips. "When you're with me."

"But what will everybody else say?" She wound her hair into a bun and stuck a pin through the knot.

"Nothing. There won't be anybody. I'm talking about when we're alone like this."

She sprang to her feet, smoothed her skirt and glanced into the hallway, hearing footsteps. "Alone? You know as well as I do we shouldn't be alone. This was unusual. I just needed to talk more. I shouldn't be with you unescorted this late at night—early in the morning."

He stood. She faced him, at eye level with the knot in his tie. She didn't look up for fear he'd kiss her, and as much as she wanted him to, she scolded herself. She wasn't supposed to *want* physical pleasure!

"I'll get out of here, then." He turned toward the doorway. "The last thing I want to do is harm you in any way."

"I know, and I trust you. You're a true gentleman."

He gave her a tight smile. "Thank you for inviting me in."

She walked past him, and he followed her to the front door. Her breath stopped as she awaited his kiss. But he only said good night, turned, and left her.

She tiptoed up the stairs, hanging on to the banister in the dark, alone with her wanton thoughts.

****

The next day, Sergeant Munn sent Tom to the

Hotel Brevoort's café to investigate a money laundering scheme. On his way out, he noticed a familiar figure heading down the street on the other side. He recognized Vita's psychic friend, walking with a limp.

He crossed and walked up to her. "Hello. Are you hurt?" He looked down at her feet. Neither looked swollen or injured.

"Nah, just broke my shoe." She held up a black stump. "I was goin' to the cobbler, but he's closed. And I'm starved. You have lunch yet?"

He shrugged. "I could go for something."

So they walked down 8th Street and ducked into Three Steps Down, crowded with lean bearded patrons, scarves wound around their necks, berets perched at artsy angles on their heads. She claimed a table in the center of everything, and they ordered drinks.

"I want to talk about the séance," she said.

"Yeah? I'm trying to forget it." He gave her a half-grin.

"That was the first séance I did since my salad days." Their drinks came, and her gold bracelets tinkled as she lifted her glass to him in a toast. *"Na zdrowie."*

"Even if 'frame' meant Vita's family was framed, it doesn't tell us who framed them." He tried not to sound skeptical. "That's what I need to find out here. I know how important this is to Vita and don't want to make light of it in any way."

"I was desperate to get more out of that session." She frowned and rhythmically kicked the table leg. "I hate to say it, but I didn't feel much of anything coming through me."

As he sat with this oddball woman, curiosity poked at him. "I know I came across as a skeptic last night, but I try to keep an open mind. Not understanding any of this makes me want to learn more," he admitted. "And it's what Vita believes. In order to understand her, I need to understand her beliefs. Have you ever had any visions that led to killers or helped solve any crimes? Or have you ever prevented a tragedy with a premonition or vision—or whatever you call them?"

She tugged at one dangling earring. "Never predicted a disaster or prevented one, but I've stopped people from doing stupid things. For instance, a fella kept coming to me, wanting to leave his wife for a mistress. I told him the mistress was no good for him. The mistress was—" She took a sip of her wine. "I just knew I had to keep this man away from this gal and in his own wife's bed where he belonged. Sure enough, the day he decided not to see the mistress, they were supposed to take a train to Long Branch. He stood her up. Had a pang of guilt, or maybe he just listened to me, but the train derailed and every single passenger was killed. Now, I didn't predict the train accident and say to him, 'Stay off that five-fifteen to Long Branch!' but I just knew—and told him, almost yelled at him—he had to forsake that mistress, and that was the night before."

Tom shook his head in wonder. "Amazing. I wonder if you really would be able to help the police."

She drained her wine, and they ordered ham sandwiches. They chatted a bit about how she discovered she had this strange gift. Then they started talking about Vita.

"She's really gone on you, my good man." She twirled her empty glass.

A rush of affection jarred him and tightened his muscles. "Do I have to tell you anything, or can you just read my thoughts?"

"Well, it doesn't take a psychic to figure out you're in love with her."

He gulped enough beer for three swallows. "You mean it's that obvious?"

She tilted her head and smiled. "Well, if you're not, you oughta be out there on the stage with the Booths. 'Cause you're a better actor than them."

"I haven't been acting." He fiddled with the fork in his place setting. "I've told her I care about her, but I haven't yet told her I'm in love with her. I didn't want to scare her away. At this point we have a few things standing in our way—in the form of a tragedy. It's hard for the both of us—no relationship could withstand all this unless it's strong as nails to begin with. Sometimes I feel like I'm trying to push a locomotive backwards, and it just keeps coming at me."

She nodded, fingering a charm dangling from her bracelet. The waitress brought their sandwiches, and Jadwiga dug in. "Take it slow and don't rush anything. Wait till this all works out before you ask her to marry you," she advised as she chewed.

"Marry me?" He nearly fell backwards. "She'll never marry me."

"Why not? You don't think Saint Bridget and Saint Anthony could get along together?" She signaled for another drink.

It pained him to hear it, although Vita was always warning him about their cultural differences, what her father would say if he knew they were courting. But to marry! "She would turn and run the other way if I dared to mention it—even if I asked her to marry me in twenty years. She has her life planned clear through to the next century, and I don't think a wedding day is anywhere on that calendar."

"Oh, don't be so sure." She spooned mustard between her slices of ham. "She wants a family, kids, all that. I know Vita pretty well now. I'm tellin' ya this without a deck of cards or a ball in front of me. Don't give up on her. Once Vita puts her mind to somethin', she don't give up. Make sure you're one of the things she puts her mind on. Then you'll be ringing in the next century together."

"I could never hope she'll marry me. But good God, I hope some other fella doesn't sweep her off her feet." He knew he'd just exposed his soul, and not on a sheet of paper. He'd probably divulged too much. And to Vita's closest friend! What had made him open up like this? Had she drawn it out of him with her powers? He was too bashful to ask. So instead he asked, "Do cops ever come to you for readings?"

"Changin' the subject, huh?" She chuckled and took a slow sip of her wine. "Don't ask me for any names, but a few cops visit me."

"I don't want to know who. I was just wondering what makes these cops do what they do."

"There's one who comes a lot—now, I'm not saying if he's from New York or not. He's carrying a lot of guilt on his shoulders, and now all these terrible things are happening to him. He believes he's cursed. He wants to rid himself of these curses. This may sound weird, coming from me—well, everything may sound weird coming from me—I ain't no Ziggy Freud, but I think he's bringing these things on himself. Inwardly he wants to pay for what he did, so he becomes his own worst enemy and becomes negative. His spirit suffers and he falls to illness and ill fortune. I told him to go to confession. But he ain't religious. A lot of people who come to me are like this. They think I'm their redeemer." She rolled her eyes heavenward. "They do all these rotten things, confess to me, and think I'm gonna give 'em extreme unction. They come to me when they're at rock bottom 'cause they think I'm gonna tell 'em they're gonna be saved."

"Do you ever get bad readings?" He took a bite of his sandwich.

"Oh, sure. But when I give customers a bad reading, they never come back. But I tell 'em what I see. The sad part is, these miserable wretches don't realize they can make it good. I can't change these people's lives around. They wanna steal, graft, and whatever, and live in their fancy-shmancy mansions, then come to me—and I'm supposed to tell 'em, 'yeah, your wife loves ya, your kids loves ya, God loves ya, the Pearly Gates are wide open,' with a big smile on my face. But that's only in fairy tales."

"You can only save yourself, in other words," he said.

"Yeah. That's what I'm sayin'." She chewed the last of her sandwich as he wondered how he could ever save the police force. That quest seemed almost as impossible as finding evidence pointing to someone other than Vita's family.

Feeling discouraged, impotent and helplessly small, he paid the bill and bade goodbye to Jadwiga. She headed for the cobbler shop on her broken heel, and he went in the opposite direction, toward the church for a think—and a prayer.

Chapter Seventeen

Jadwiga stood at the stove brewing tea as her son came charging through the curtain.

"Some fella wants a reading, Ma. You wanna do it?" Zygmunt removed his cap and scratched his head.

"Sure, Zyg. Send him in." She poured a cup of tea and brought it into the front room.

She knew the gaunt man standing at her window shuffling his feet. It was the cop she'd been telling Tom about. The tortured soul. Since he hadn't been here for a week, she hoped he'd given up on her readings and found a confession box. But as a steady customer, he kept her in bangles and vodka.

He turned and greeted her. His shoulders drooped; dark circles hung under his eyes. A limp handshake was all he could manage today. "C'mon, sit. Let's get some good news this time." She sat across from him and unwrapped the ball.

For all his misery, he dressed very nattily—tailored suit, crisp collar, shiny shoes. He pulled a handful of coins from his pocket and stacked them on the table in size order. She'd seen this routine before—this was a crook's way of handling money. They never just tossed silver onto the table. They always stacked their change in neat little piles, as if they were staking bets in their card or dice games.

"You look like you've recovered from your food

poisoning." She broke the ice with an encouraging note.

"I'll never eat *calamari* again," he snarled, his voice gravelly from too many cigarettes.

She found that unusual. *Calamari*—squid—was an Italian dish. Non-Italians never ate the stuff. Vita had told her it was her father's favorite dish.

"My wife just left me," he wailed, his hands folded, his head bowed.

She didn't want to be his confessor again. "You want her back, I assume." She warmed the ball under her palms.

"She left me"—his voice cracked, and he wiped at his eyes with a hankie—"at the lowest point in my life."

When could that have been? she wondered. Could he have looked worse than this?

"Look, sir, you should see a priest or a minister. I don't know what more I can do for you. I mean this. All my readings on you have brought forth foreboding." Looking into the ball, she saw complete darkness. To her this always meant impending doom, but she didn't tell him this. He'd probably throw himself off the Brooklyn Bridge. No, she didn't want to be the bearer of this news.

"So what do you see?" He leaned forward, and she slid the ball closer to herself. She swallowed her dread and forced a neutral tone. "I—can't seem to be getting anything here. I—"

Most of the people who came to her shared common woes: grinding poverty, sickness, grief. They clung to her words as their last hope. But this man stood at death's door. Despite his attempt at fashionable dress, he exuded a sick pallor she'd seen on the malnourished who skipped meals for readings. Those she did for free. But she knew he was far from poor. He'd told her he was an officer of the law. "I'd better stop the reading and put the ball away. You should take your money back and go talk to someone of your own faith."

With tight-lipped resignation, he swept his silver off the table and put his hat back on. She knew in her gut she'd never see him again. She longed to help him, but no one could help him: not himself, not a priest, no one. As he dragged himself out the door, she bowed her head and prayed for him.

****

Vita visited Papa and Butchie in jail the next day with a steaming pot of *calamari* and two forks. The guard opened the bars and slid the pot into Butchie's hands. "Can I hug him? Please?" she begged as the man clanged the bars shut.

"No." He spat on the floor and stalked away.

She had to make do with a brief clasp of hands through the bars.

"I'm trying all different ways to find out who framed you," she assured them as they dug into the pot and shoveled the food in.

"Stay out of trouble, you," Papa warned, but his half-hearted attempt at authority weighed on her heart. He seemed to have lost his will, even to bark orders at her. He'd always barked and they'd obeyed, like puppy dogs. But no more.

"I'm not getting into any trouble doing it. I know you're innocent, and they'll get caught and pay for what they did." She grasped the bars, her knuckles white.

The guard swaggered back up to her. "Time's up," he announced and escorted her down the dark hallway.

"Bring some *cannoli!*" Butchie's voice reached her ears as she walked down the long dark hallway. She turned and blew him a kiss.

****

That night as Vita flipped through *Godey's Lady's Book*, Rosalia trudged into the attic room. She plopped down on the bed and heaved a loud sigh to get Vita's attention. "The trial's Friday." Her tone flat, she pulled off her shoes and dropped them to the floor with heavy thumps.

The words in the magazine converged into a blur. Vita looked up. "This Friday?"

Rosalia stared straight ahead. "You have to come to mass tonight."

"I need to do something first." Vita grabbed her shawl and flew down the stairs. She needed to find Tom. They had less than four days.

Her family's lives had less than four days.

****

She didn't find Tom in Joey Cap's or any of the other cop-friendly rum-holes. At headquarters, she rushed up to the desk sergeant. "Is Officer McGlory here?"

"No, his beat ended at three this afternoon." He eyed her up and down, as if he knew her but couldn't remember from where. She didn't offer an introduction, just turned and strode up the street, wondering where to look next. The only other place he could be was home. She looked up at the church tower's clock. Each lost minute made her pulse race even faster.

She knew he lived on Pearl Street, near Five Points, once the worst part of Lower Manhattan but cleaned up now—and solid Irish. She hailed a passing taxi and got out at Pearl across from a row of whitewashed houses. She'd knock on every door until she found him.

She didn't care what these people thought of her looking for Tom McGlory unescorted.

"He lives right over the road," an Irish-brogued yellow-aproned matron informed Vita from her swept porch. "The house with the green shutters."

So he lived in a house with shutters. As she lifted her skirt and crossed the muddy street, she guessed what the inside looked like. Did they have plush furniture? Flowered wallpaper? Lace curtains? She'd soon find out, if they were cordial enough to let her in.

Her throat dry, she swallowed, her heart slamming as she spotted the white clapboard with green shutters adorning the windows. Two dormers sprouted from the slanted roof. It stood out from the other shabby dwellings, in fair repair. Lights shone in almost every window, the golden glow homey and inviting.

She knocked and didn't have to wait long. The door opened, and there stood a bonny lass, as Vita had heard the Irish call a pretty girl. Red curls framed a freckled face. Those green eyes looked very familiar.

Vita cleared her throat. "May I speak to Tom McGlory, please?"

"And you are?" Her voice light and melodic, she was probably a wonderful singer. She looked at Vita with a hint of recognition as if she'd seen her before.

"Miss Vita Caputo."

"But of course. I'm his sister Eileen. Won't you step inside?" The "But of course" sounded more like a reinforcement of her guess as to who Vita was. So maybe Tom had told them about her! Joy sprang up in her heart. But what was there for Vita to say besides "I'm Mike's accused murderers' next of kin"? Yet the sister was oh, so polite. It baffled Vita. For an instant she reversed everything. If Butchie had been murdered and his accused killer's sister came to her door—how would she treat this person? Slam the door in her face? Invite her in for *strega*? These were two extremes; no, she would do just what this girl had done—invite her to pass the threshold, no farther, and summon the person she'd called for. But she was unique—no one else on Mott Street would have been so civil. Including Papa and Butchie. Rosalia—maybe.

After a lengthy wait in the hallway as she peeked into the parlor and ogled that plush furniture she'd wondered about, Tom bounded down the stairs. His jaw dropped when he saw her standing there. He'd just thrown on a shirt, she could tell. It was inside out, the seams bulging.

"Vita!"

"Tom, the trial is Friday," she blurted. Suddenly she lost all her courage and broke down into tears, dreading the tragedy that waited four days away.

"It's all right…" His calm tone soothed her, but not enough.

She wanted his arms around her, but here in his own house, full of his family and boarders, she knew he wouldn't dare show anything resembling affection.

"What are we going to do?" She wiped her eyes with her hankie. "We've got four days. Then they get sentenced." She took short breaths as she forced herself to calm down.

She wanted to go back out into the street, walk somewhere safe, and sit with him in the darkness. But he did the last thing she wanted: he brought her into his parlor. No one was around, thank God. He motioned her to a mahogany-backed sofa, worn at the edges but comfortable as she sat. It matched the wallpaper—all pink flowers and green vines. Newspapers and books crammed a stack of shelves. Lamps with fringed shades cast a warm glow about the room. Porcelain flub-dubs cluttered every table. Lacy white doilies spilled over the table tops, and female voices floated through the doorway from a distance. He closed the parlor door to shut out the noise.

"I still haven't talked to everybody I should have talked to." He sat in the wing chair opposite her, hands clasped between his knees, head down, hair falling over his forehead. Blurred by her tears, the lamps glistened like a million stars.

"Oh, how we need hope, Tom. What can we do now?"

"There's nothing you can do now," he said in that calm, reassuring tone. "Just leave it up to me."

"And all you're going to do is ask more questions? You're expecting people to tell you the truth? If people told the truth, my family wouldn't be within four days of their lives." A buildup of anger seemed to twist her heart. She wanted answers, not a dangling "Leave it up to me."

"No, I'm not expecting the truth," he said. "Not at first. But I've learned a lot more on the police force than how to twirl a nightstick. And some of them never learn even that."

"I won't argue that. Seeing the condition of the Metropolitan Police Force, I know they are no match for the Harvard Debating Team. I also know you're intelligent enough to be a lawyer someday," she added, straight from her heart.

He fought back a smile at that.

"But this is now," she went on. "And we have four days. They'll fly by like minutes."

"I know all that, Vita." He paused. "Would you like some tea or something? I'm sorry, I should've offered before."

Her heart softened. Through all this, he still managed to treat her like an honored guest.

"No, thanks. But can you talk to any of these people tonight?"

"I can go to the station and see where they are, who's on duty, who's getting themselves into trouble off duty." He stood and reached for her hand. "Now that you're here, I'd like to introduce you to my family."

"No! Tom, really, I'm in no condition to meet anyone, especially your family. I mean, look at me." Glancing down at her mud-splattered skirt, she got to her feet and headed for the door before any other McGlorys saw her. "Any other time but now. I just couldn't. I'm not dressed in my uptown fashions."

"Nobody in my family cares about fashions. But you did meet my sister." He glanced at the parlor door. "Didn't she let you in?"

"Yes. She was very nice to me—as nice as she could be under the circumstances."

"Why wouldn't she be?" He smiled. "I'm sure you would be just as gracious to her if things were the other way around."

Just what she'd been thinking before. Was he beginning to think like her? Oh, she hoped so! Her legs

213

wobbled, and she clutched his arm for support.

"You look like you need some nourishment." He steadied her with a firm grip. "Why don't we head for the kitchen, and—"

"You sound like an Italian grandmother!" She managed a chuckle. "Really, I'll be all right. I couldn't eat a thing."

"I'll get you back home, then."

She heaved a relieved sigh. Whew, that was close. She was in no condition for scrutiny. On the way out, she asked him about his family and what they did with their free time. By the looks of the house, she didn't think they clustered around a gas lamp toiling over piecework day and night. They were well within the lace curtain Irish class.

"The men build furniture, and the girls like to do needlepoint. We've always got aunts and uncles and cousins dropping by, but it's been pretty quiet since Mike died. That put a damper on a lot of the activity here, and probably will for a while. I expect Christmas will be a solemn affair. Then hopefully we can get on with our lives. I know he wouldn't have wanted us sitting around sulking. He never sat and sulked for anybody. Boy, did he love his life." Tom looked up and searched the heavens. "He never complained once."

They linked arms and walked back to her boardinghouse in silence, except for when they passed restaurants and he repeated each time, "Are you sure you don't want to eat?"

"No, I just want you to question whoever you need to question." An idea came to her. "How about if I go with you? Maybe seeing a family member of the accused will give them a pang of conscience."

"Vita, not too many of these guys can boast much of a conscience. I think it's best if you leave it up to me."

They reached her door, and she fished the key out of her drawstring bag. "Will you come by the bank in the morning and let me know what you found out?"

"Of course. Now don't worry."

What an easy thing for him to say.

"I'm going to pray tonight, Tom. And for the next three days and nights."

He gave her a warm embrace but didn't kiss her. She only wished there were two of him—one to go around asking questions and the other to stay here with her. He was the only person in the entire world she wanted to be with at that moment.

"Tom!" she called out to him as he hurried down the dark street.

She rushed toward him, and he turned to face her. There, in the middle of Washington Square South, she threw her arms around his neck, drew his lips to hers, and claimed them.

"It's all going to be all right, Vita," he promised her between kisses. She didn't care that they stood in public on a New York street. "Somehow this is going to work out, and I'm not going to lose you."

They finally broke apart, and she went back to her boardinghouse. Now it was time to get some strength back. So she went upstairs to her little room, clasped Rosalia's hand, and they prayed together.

Chapter Eighteen

Sleepless from wondering if he'd found anything out, Vita had to get to Tom before work. But she'd pushed her luck with Mr. Johnson far enough. Now she needed the trial day off.

As Vita opened her teller's window, a dark-haired, bearded gent in a tailored suit entered and stopped at Mr. Johnson's secretary's desk. A gold pinkie ring flashed as he raised a cigar to his mouth.

"Why, Mr. Mayor!" the secretary greeted him. "It's a pleasure to see you, sir. Mr. Johnson is waiting for you. Let me show you in."

So that's the honorable Hugh J. Grant, mayor of New York City. Vita stared after him. She'd seen him a few times, riding up Fifth Avenue in his carriage. Passersby stopped on the sidewalk to point, wave, and gawk. Some proclaimed "The mayor!" as if a saint had descended upon them.

She'd read a lot about His Dishonor, as they called him, and gossip about him they did—nearly every night at Madame Branchard's. The topics ranged from his gambling habits to the children he'd sired with a mistress in Paris.

Although she didn't respect him one whit, she marveled at the influence he wielded. How cunning and influential he must be to reach the height of power in a city like New York. His life's work centered on sheer manipulation—the inner workings of Tammany Hall, the police force, the city officials—all of them! Even the governor deferred to him. Grant had bullied his way to the top, but citizens only noticed the dazzling smiles from his carriage.

He got to be mayor at the age of thirty-one for all the wrong reasons.

****

Tom planned to question the Metropolitan policemen who'd known Mike best: his champions and closest allies. Then he'd question the ones who weren't his buddies. None of them got along famously all the time. One week they might be shooting billiards at Kilkenny's, and then, with a petty spat or frustration from the job, they'd be hurling everything from sarcasm to insults at each other. Feelings changed from day to day on the force, depending on what the city threw at them.

But first he had to talk to Da. They'd hardly spoken since Mike's death. Tom didn't share his grief, either; he worked through it alone. He urged his father to keep a journal, too, but Da read the newspaper, and that was it.

He approached his father sitting alone at the kitchen table, drinking coffee from one of Eileen's good china cups.

"We need to talk, Da." He slid into the chair across from him. "The Caputo trial is Friday."

Da nodded, ran his hand over his thinning but still bootblack hair, and rubbed his whiskers. He never shaved before his morning coffee ritual. "I know it."

"It's possible they're innocent, you know."

They never minced words, Da and son. They both

knew time was too precious to waste on idle chitchat. That's why they never had any man-to-man or father-to-son talks. They were there for each other. Nothing had to be said.

Da looked over at Tom, cup halfway to his mouth, his hazel eyes like brass ornaments thrown aside to tarnish. "Why? The evidence and motive were there. What else can you go on? You're trying for Detective now?"

"No. I'm trying for Captain. And by then I'm hoping it won't cost me upwards of twelve big ones. But I'm not doing this to try for points. It just doesn't make sense." He splayed his fingers. "What would Mike's stuff be doing in the Caputo apartment? It doesn't look like Mike even died at the scene. He died somewhere else and his body was placed in the alley there. There was only a small bloodstain on the ground in front of their building. It looks like a sloppy frame-up job." He leaned forward. "The cops are sweeping it all under the rug because of who the Caputos are, their skirmishes with Mike, and their political involvements. Da, can you look at it with a detached eye, like you never knew any of them?"

He gave his son a weak grin. "Well, I was wrong, Tommy. Forget Detective. You ought to be a lawyer." He slurped his coffee and put the cup back down with a clink against the fancy gold-trimmed saucer.

"If we're talking strictly motive here, there are other people who've wanted to kill Mike," Tom said. "Other members of the force. An inside job. It's happened before. He's not the first cop to be killed by another cop. They can get pretty damn mean."

"Meaner than those Italianos, those rowdies?" Da

asked. "And we're not talking motive here, no, we're talking evidence." He rose to refill his cup, and Tom followed him into the parlor. Da sat in his cushioned wing chair facing away from the window. Da liked to look at the furniture he'd built and at the pictures of his loved ones instead of out into the street.

Tom knew this was his father's signal to end the conversation. But it wasn't over yet. Tom sat on the sofa.

"They wouldn't have left Mike's stuff in the Caputo apartment." He clasped his hands between his knees. "They would have sold it and unloaded it. They wouldn't shoot him right outside the Caputo building. They're not stupid people, Da."

He shot his son a knowing glance that, if put into words, could have filled a volume of Dickens. That's why they never talked much. They just knew each other's minds so well.

"I know the daughter was here last night. Eileen told me. You fallin' for her? That's why you're doing this? What is this girl doin' to you?" he quizzed, his eyes boring into Tom.

"Why do you assume she's had any influence over me?"

"You're me only son, Tommy. I've been a cop longer than you. I've also been in love, see." He sat back and stretched his legs.

"I'm only trying to be fair to these people." Tom's tone took on a defensive note. "Don't you think I want to know who Mike's killer is?"

"You seem convinced enough who it isn't," Da said. "Would you be thinking this way if you never fell in love with her?"

219

He couldn't argue with his father about being in love. Da knew. But for all his words about Vita in his journal, the words "in love" didn't appear once. Da always managed to do this—tell him things about himself he didn't dare admit.

"No, Da. No, I wouldn't be thinking this way." He kept his voice low because he'd never have admitted this, not to the priest in the confessional, not to himself, not to anyone but his father. "I'd have left it up to the police. I'd have trusted police procedures. I wouldn't have questioned it. I'd have been satisfied—Mike's dead, and someone's in jail for it. But she's changed a lot of things for me. She's made me see a side of New York I knew was there"—he waved out the window—"but now I've got a personal stake in it. These are real people with feelings just like you and I have. They worship the same God you and I do, and they have it hard. Real hard. The justice system doesn't protect them the way it does the rest of us." He stood and circled the room. "And it took her to make me realize that. That's why I went undercover. I would have lived the rest of my life in blissful apathy regarding the other side of Canal Street if she hadn't come into my life. So, yes, I am in love with her." He halted before Da. "And no, I wouldn't have thought in quite the same way. But she's not blinding me. Far from it. There's still a chance that her family is innocent, and if they are, I want to find out who did it. And I don't only owe this to Vita because I may be in love with her. I owe it to Mike, who I loved all my life." He went back to sit down. For the first time in his life, he'd spoken out loud what he'd written in his private journal.

Da stood, walked over, and placed his hand on

Tom's shoulder. "We never have to agree on anything, son. But that doesn't mean I don't think the world of you, and you know it."

Tom stood and gave his father a hug. Da hugged him back. He'd never been an affectionate man, but knowing he loved his son unconditionally was all Tom needed from him.

Da went upstairs to shave, and Tom sat back on the sofa to think some more. The Caputos didn't have as strong a motive as someone at Tammany. Some politicians were a lot more vindictive than street-brawling Italians.

He sat at the window, looking at nothing in particular. Yes, he loved Vita with all his heart. And it would tear them apart if her family was convicted. Nothing in the system protected immigrants, gave them the right to a fair trial or the right to counsel. Now he had only a few days to prove their innocence as detective, defender, and advocate, all in one. They'd probably kick him off the force for taking so much time to do this. But he vowed to save Vita. Or lose everything he had trying.

He noticed flakes of white paint on the window sill, exposing the worn wood underneath. He walked over to pry the curling paint loose. He didn't want any of the kids eating paint peelings. For no particular reason, he tested the window to see if it was secure. Most burglars didn't climb in front windows, but he checked it anyway. He examined the frame to see if any cold drafts would seep in during winter. His room upstairs was as drafty as a boxcar, but he liked it cold. Yes, the frame held, secure and tight. They'd be warm this winter.

Then his mind registered some obscure connection. The séance flashed into his mind. He remembered the spirit board spelling out the word "frame."

It hit him like a bag of feed.

Frame.

They'd all assumed that if this was a message from the great beyond, the message was clear: the Caputos were framed and innocent. But in their excitement and confusion, it never occurred to any of them that some words had more than one meaning. *Frame!* That one haunting word now had a double meaning for him, and here he stood with his palms pressed against it!

Chapter Nineteen

Lunchtime depositors crowded the bank as Tom rushed in. The raw alarm in Vita's eyes mirrored his own anxiety. He called on every ounce of willpower not to sweep her into his arms and twirl her around that spit-shined lobby like it was a grand ballroom.

She left her window and approached him. Her eyes brightened, but her jaw clenched tight.

"Relax, it's all right," he assured her as he led her to a quiet corner.

She fanned a pile of deposit tickets on the ledge. "What happened?"

"I need you to let me back into your father's house. I might have come up with something."

"What? Tell me!" She clutched his arms.

"Someone might have forced their way in there, planted that evidence, and sneaked out. I need to look at that kitchen window."

"They climbed in the kitchen window?" Her voice quivered.

"Well, they wouldn't climb up the front fire escape in full view of Mott Street. There was no sign of a break-in through the door. I never checked the kitchen window when we were there. Aside from that, there aren't any other points of entry, are there?" he asked her.

"No, unless he came up through the drain."

"I'll try that, too," he said. "But first, the kitchen window. If you can take your lunch break now, we'll go."

She held fast to his arm during the entire ride as the taxi lumbered past the factories and stores. He told the driver to hurry, and hurry he did. They swerved past a wagon at Bowery and East Houston, missing it by inches.

"Maybe this is it, Tom. Maybe we can find whoever did this. Dear God, please let this lead to something!" She clasped her hands and prayed to Mama, too.

He hugged her close, inhaling her sweet fragrance. At that moment he knew he was going to spend the rest of his life with her. Even if her family was guilty. But he needed to find evidence. This was the challenge of his career.

As they hurried down Mott Street, she ignored the narrow-eyed glares and mumblings. She led the way up the stairs, tripping in her scramble to the third floor.

"Vita, be careful." His hand shot out and accidentally touched her derriere. He caught his breath and snatched his hand away. The toilet between the two flats flushed as she unlocked her door and shoved it open.

"Isn't your stepmother staying here anymore?" he asked.

"No, she's been staying with me," she said. "She swears she won't ever come back here. But I don't give up that easy—I've been paying rent here to keep the place going for when my father and Butchie come back."

He didn't know she'd been paying rent. Then it

occurred to him he'd never wondered why the place was still vacant. Admiration and respect filled his heart.

She made a dash for the kitchen window, slid the table aside, and wedged herself into the small space. "Well, it's always been pretty beat-up looking." Her words tumbled out.

Tom shoved the table out of their way and opened the window. He ran his hand over the frame, starting at the bottom, where burglars usually jimmied a window to gain entry.

His trained eye saw where a jimmy had been jammed between the frame and the sill. So either this place had very organized termites or someone had forced this window. Jagged slivers of wood lay on the floor under the curling linoleum. He traced his pointer finger along the floor and picked up some of those wood chips. A brown smear ran down the wall to the floor. He swept his finger over the brown stain and held it up to his nose. He knew its distinct odor immediately. In his career, he'd seen clues, and he'd seen bizarre clues…but this?

"Look at this, Vita, but not too close. In fact, let me wash my hands." He stood and walked over to the sink.

She handed him a sliver of soap. "What did you find there that you had to wash off? Blood?"

"No. Excrement." He soaped and scrubbed.

"What? On the wall?" She dashed over there.

"Don't touch anything!" he warned.

"What do you think happened, Tom?" She turned back to face him.

When his hand looked and smelled clean enough to get him through to his next meal, he dried off with a rough towel hanging from a nail.

"He couldn't find the backyard privy?" She threw her hands in the air. "You think he got scared and just—well, let go, here, halfway through the window?" She bent down to look at the brown streak. "I need to clean this up! This is disgusting!"

He lunged forward. "Don't touch a thing. It could lead us to him. Don't ever touch anything at a crime scene."

"What do you plan to do, take it to a lab and look under a microscope?" She placed a fist on her hip.

"No, I'm more interested in the table—I just noticed something else." He scanned the tabletop. "Have you given this table a good looking at?" He removed the dirty plates, yanked the cloth off, and dropped to his knees to inspect it.

"Not really. Just that one gash Rose mentioned, where Papa threw the crucifix. It matched the nick in the cross, and that nick there—" She moved to the opposite side of the table and ran her finger over another mark. "That's where Jadwiga's planchette flipped over when we had the séance. It put this mark in the table. I asked her to show me the planchette the other night. It has a chip in it. I didn't bring it back here to match them, but she said that chip was definitely new."

"Well, look at this." He pointed at a long black streak at the table's edge, on the side that faced the wall. "Have you tried to polish this table black recently?"

"Of course not. I always keep it covered. Rose always took my tablecloth off, but in those last days, she left it alone."

"Then the cloth was probably off when this

window was jimmied." He leaned over and gave it a good look.

"You mean somebody really did climb in here?" She looked at the window. "Who could climb up an air shaft?"

"Someone very nimble. And he's overly concerned about his appearance. Has his shoes shined even before he goes breaking into houses to plant evidence. This black streak on the table is shoeshine polish." He clasped her hand across the table and climbed out onto the fire escape. "I'll check for anything else left behind." The only sunlight came from the small square above him. He faced a narrow air shaft that opened up into an alleyway between this building and the next. Above and below him, sheets and long johns hung from lines strung between windows.

She held a hand out to him as he climbed back in. He needed no assistance, but he let her help anyway—he needed her touch.

"So you've been asking the wrong people the wrong questions." Her hands rested on his chest. "You should've been grilling shoeshine boys."

"And maybe barbers. If he took the time to get his shoes shined, he may have got a shave and a haircut, too," he deduced.

"But we don't know who he is."

"Not yet." He snapped his fingers. "But I can narrow it down. I'll start with my prime suspects. If reliable witnesses recognize one of those faces, we're in luck." He took a few rapid breaths. "And I hate to say this, but these aren't the brightest people in the world, either. They're sloppy. They've been known to leave evidence lying all over the place. But I just need something to lead me to that evidence." He tapped his fingers on his chin, thinking.

"All right, let's find the shoeshine boys." She made a dash for the door.

"You can go back to the bank, Vita. I can handle this." He followed her.

"Not a chance, Tom." She shook her head. "We're too close to finding—no. I don't want to leave your side for a minute."

They stood in the doorway. "Vita, if I get closer, and I'm hoping I do, it's going to get a lot more dangerous. I don't want you anywhere near any of this. You can't be with me during this chase. Go back to the bank where you're safe."

"But I'll be fine. Please—" she pleaded.

"No! I don't want anything to happen to you, Vita. I love you too much." The words fell out of his mouth before he even realized it.

She stared at him, her eyes round with hope. A flush spread over her cheeks, and her lips twitched. "Oh, God, Tom…" She rested her head on his chest. He held her tighter than he'd ever held another human being. He kissed her hair, taking in her fragrance, wanting to imprint it on his memory forever. They stood like this, swaying together, for a long time. She finally pulled away. "Please let me know what happens."

"Of course I will." He walked her down to the street.

They stood at the corner, and he flagged down a taxi. She climbed in and pulled her skirts in after her. He blew her a kiss as the vehicle lumbered away.

Hot blood rushed through every vein in his body.

His heart raced like a stopwatch from anxiety, the rush to beat the trial, and the most overpowering of all—love. Love moved him to do this; love breathed the life into him.

He went to the precinct to collect some photos before he headed up Mulberry Street, on the lookout for shoeshine boys.

The first boy, perched at the corner of Mott, saw Tom walking toward him and hurried to open his box.

"I just need to ask you a question, son." Tom bent down to eye level with the boy. "Then you can shine my shoes. I need to identify someone. A man whose shoes you might have shined very recently, early in the morning. If I show you some pictures and you recognize him, could you tell me who he is? There's a reward in it for you either way."

"Ukay." He nodded, his eyes bright. Then Tom asked him the easy part. "I need all the shoeshine boys in the neighborhood to look at these pictures. Can we go find them?"

"Some are in school."

He didn't want to pull kids out of school. Not yet. So he asked the lad to lead him to the others who weren't in school. And with the prospect of a few more coins in his pocket to jingle, the boy led Tom down the block, fast.

****

Five eager shoeshine boys of varying ages stood around Tom's kitchen table as he laid out six photographs. To keep it honest, he threw Sergeant Munn's in there. Then he thought again: if one of those boys picked the sergeant out of a lineup of thugs' photographs, things could get real interesting.

They all studied the photos, their young eyes squinting as their brains worked.

Finally, the next-to-tallest pointed to the second photo. "I shined his shoes real early in the mornin'," he informed Tom with a slight Irish brogue.

Tom picked the photo up. It was Owen Rooney, on the force longer than Tom. And he'd only talked to him two days ago. He'd looked innocent as a puppy with his cherub cheeks. He had suspect number one.

"Are you sure it's him, son?"

"He was my first shoeshine of the day," the boy affirmed.

That made sense, if he was going to break into the tenement early in the morning after they found Mike's body.

"Did he tell you his name at any time?"

"No, sir." He shook his head.

"Did he say where he was going after you shined his shoes?"

Negative again.

"Was he wearing a uniform of any kind?" Tom asked.

"No, sir, just trousers and shirt."

"Do you remember the details of the shoes?" Tom pressed on.

"They was real muddy. The mud was dried. Then on the bottom of one shoe there was some kinda shite. It stunk like he just stepped in it. He told me to clean the shite offa his shoe for a extra dime. I cleaned it offa the sides but not offa the bottom. I don't never shine shoe bottums. Folk just scrape 'em themselves."

Tom stayed calm. "What color was his hair?"

"A kinda dark orangey. Like a rotten carrot."

Tom reached into his pocket and began distributing coins. He had his man. No one had hair like Owen Rooney. And only a klutz like him would step in horse dung and leave a trail of it while trying to plant evidence.

Tom slipped an extra dollar to this informer. The lad didn't show joy in any way. Tom knew he'd do that when he got to the candy store. Then Tom kept his other promise—every pair of shoes in the house gleamed, newly shined, when they all left.

Owen Rooney. The cop who'd arrested the Caputos. After planting evidence and stepping in horse dung with his shined shoes. Tom wanted to find that horse and reward him with the world's biggest bag of apples.

"Thanks, boys. You have no idea how much you all helped me today." The boys went scampering in all directions as Tom skipped down his front steps. With a spring in his step, he headed for the precinct. Now to find out the location of Owen Rooney's diggings.

Chapter Twenty

Vita returned to the bank, but her mind just wasn't on her work. She gave one customer ten dollars too much, and he was honest enough to point it out. Before she started giving away all the bank's assets, she feigned illness and went home. She saw her co-workers exchange knowing glances. It was no secret what she was going through. They all knew about the murder and the accused; it was in all the papers. She needed to be at Tom's side every minute of this ordeal, especially now they had a lead.

As she sat on the Fifth Avenue bus heading south, passing the gated mansions and shiny carriages, she realized how much she loved him. But she couldn't sit in Madame's parlor squawking about reforms while he risked his life. This tragedy afflicted both of them. So would the triumph.

She got off the bus at Mulberry Street and headed for the police station.

She saw Tom appear at the doors. But instead of racing up to him, she hung back. She watched him lumber down the steps. He turned left, and she wedged her way through the crowded street to catch up with him. As he walked toward the Bend, she followed half a block behind.

His rapid pace increased with every step as he turned onto Baxter Street. He strode with purpose, as if the initial glee of finding evidence had given way to the rage of injustice. He turned in at a shabby clapboard house, kicked the outer door open, and vanished inside.

****

Owen Rooney lived on the top floor of a dilapidated three-story clapboard. Like every house on Baxter Street, grime streaked its windows and piles of stinking garbage rotted on the porch. Tom clutched his pistol, kicked the front door open, and took the stairs two at a time.

Teeth clenched, his chest about to explode in rage, he banged on Rooney's door, ready to kill the bastard with his bare hands. "Rooney! Open up!" Nothing. The faint thumping of hoofbeats and rumbling of carts drifted up from below. His blood surged.

His pistol at the ready, he kicked at the door. It swung open.

Crumpled, sweat-stained shirts, filthy socks, empty bottles, and half-eaten sandwiches lay scattered on the floor. The tattered curtains billowed in the breeze. Tom shoved them aside to let some light in. The stained mattress smelled of stale urine. When Tom tossed it, cockroaches scampered in all directions. He emptied a beat-up dresser one drawer at a time. Three wads of cash tumbled out with the ragged socks and underwear. He flipped through old newspapers piled on the floor and found more cash under a moth-eaten rug. A Bible lay on a crate next to the mattress, along with a dirty glass half-filled with whiskey, a dead fly floating in it. He thumbed through the Bible. A scribbled piece of paper slid out and fell to the floor.

He unfolded the paper and read the short message: "Do the hit—Mike McG." with Mike's badge number.

"Plant Mike's goods in 124 Mott St. rear tenement, 3rd floor. Will pay a thou on acceptance & another thou after it's carried out." It wasn't signed, but the handwriting looked familiar. His stomach turned.

Loud footsteps pounded into the room behind him. He spun around and cocked the pistol. Rooney stood in the doorway, shaking like the coward he was. That blaze of hair assaulted Tom's eyes like the flames of hell. He leveled a gun at Tom's heart.

"You son of a bitch," Tom heard himself say.

"Mike got what he deserved, just like those guinea bastards who double-crossed me. What I do for Dick Croker is between me and him." His high-pitched caterwaul screeched like nails scratching on a chalkboard.

Tom fired first, but not to kill. Yet. The shot hit Rooney in the shoulder. It knocked him off balance. He fired back, but his shot went off above Tom's head. Plaster rained down all over him.

Rooney howled in agony and doubled over. A figure hovered in the shadows behind him. He turned and stumbled, clutching the door frame. "You bitch!" Then he pitched forward, flat on his face. A knife was buried in his back, up to the handle.

Tom now saw who'd stabbed Rooney. "Vita! Christ Almighty, what are you doing here?"

Her eyes wild and glazed over, she heaved a deep breath.

Tom sidestepped around Rooney's body and clutched her shoulders. "You could've got killed. What are you doing here?"

But she didn't answer, and he didn't ask her again. He knew why she was here—she had to be.

They clung to each other, catching their breath. She went limp in his arms, yet her strength seeped into him. He wanted to scream, *Why did you put yourself in that kind of danger?* But he kept quiet.

He stepped over Rooney's corpse to get the handwritten note. "Vita, just stay calm. Walk over to the precinct. Get them to send a patrolman and a detective here." He knelt and prayed. How happy he and Vita would be now. He kept thinking these calming, encouraging thoughts, thanking God. Owen Rooney's death marked the beginning of their own lives.

****

Two detectives compared the handwriting with Tammany boss Richard Croker's. They turned to Tom, nodding in unison. "It's a match."

Vita leaned against Tom. He raised his head to heaven and thanked the Lord once more.

"Please, let's get my father and Butchie out of there," she begged, clutching his arms.

He wanted to marry her even before they left the police station. He didn't want to waste another minute—more crazy thoughts of a man in love.

"Release her family," Tom told them.

Vita and another patrolman went to the Tombs in a black Maria. Tom almost told her to give her family his regards, but he kept his mouth shut. He'd get his thanks later.

Chapter Twenty-One

Her fantasies about Tom couldn't match the joy flowing through her at this moment. "God, thank you so much for giving Papa and Butchie back to me, thank you, thank you," she repeated, hands clasped, on the taxi ride to the Tombs. She didn't care if her police escort heard her.

Before the taxi halted, she jumped out, ran up to the prison, burst through the door, and rushed to the startled guards. "I want to see my father and brother! They've been released! Oh, please let me see them!" She wanted to spring the lock herself and pull them into a three-way hug.

"Do they know they've been cleared?" her police escort asked one of the guards.

"Not unless some angel flew in here and told them," he replied kindly enough, but with a touch of irritation. Vita tore down the hall to their cell. The guard caught her and pulled her back. "Hey, this ain't an Italian festival." He clamped his hand around her arm and walked her to their cell.

She stopped at the bars and peered in. "It's empty!" A terrifying flood of panic tore through her. "Where are they?" she shrieked.

"Their trial was scheduled for today?"

"Yes!" She gripped his arm. "Where did they take my father and brother?"

"They must be at the courthouse."

"Oh, dear God." She leaned against the stone wall. The bone-chilling horror of the dungeon seeped through to her skin.

****

Vita and her police escort climbed back into the wagon and headed up Centre Street. In the Criminal Courts Building, he led her through a maze of musty hallways, one wooden door after another with brass knobs and high transoms. She dodged clerks and almost collided with a judge draped in black robes. The place reminded her of the factories she'd worked in, only this place was ventilated.

Vita's weakened legs couldn't carry her another step. Sweat soaked her back. She mopped her brow with her sleeve.

He opened the door to a courtroom and motioned for her to stand at the back. Her neighbors, all dressed in funeral attire, packed the benches. They expected Papa and Butchie to get the death penalty. Vita craned her neck to see the front row over their heads. What must Butchie and Papa think of her not being there? But it didn't matter; in a few seconds, they would be free.

The judge began speaking, but she couldn't hear his garbled words. The excited clamor drowned them out. He struck the desk with his gavel. A collective gasp rushed through the courtroom like a gust of wind. Wailing sobs filled the air. Hankies fluttered. She stood on her toes to see a guard pull Butchie to his feet.

She tore up the center aisle, straight to the stunned judge. He shouted and banged his gavel, but she shrieked above the noise: "They're innocent! We got the real killer!"

On tiptoe, she reached up and clutched the edge of the judge's bench as if hanging from a cliff. "We found him—Owen Rooney!"

The judge stood, a big black cloud looming above her, sleeves billowing. "Young lady, you are out of order!" The sounds faded. Her eyes closed. Someone caught her before her legs gave out. She fell onto someone and spun into darkness like water swirling down a drain.

She woke up lying on a couch in what looked like a library. Then it all came rushing back. A woman sat at her side, wringing out a cloth over a bowl.

"Where am I?" her voice croaked.

"The judge's chambers." The woman pressed the cool cloth to Vita's forehead.

"Who are you?"

"A court clerk." She dabbed the cloth over Vita's cheeks.

"What happened?"

"After you fainted, so I heard, someone brought you in here. The judge asked me to give you some water and sit with you until you came to. Have you eaten today?"

"No. Where are my father and brother?"

"The officer and detective are following them, trying to catch up with them. They were to be taken back to the Tombs after sentencing. But when they catch up with your father and brother, they'll tell them they've been released and let them go. Your sister was with them."

"Sister?" *Rosalia!* "She's not my—" Ah, why bother? "Does my family know we found the killer, Owen Rooney?" She struggled to sit up, but a wave of dizziness slapped her down again.

"Lie back," the clerk ordered. "A police officer came in with a detective and spoke to the judge. Yes, they all know the killer's been identified."

"He's dead," Vita stated.

"Who is?"

"The killer. Owen Rooney." As an image of Tom flashed through her mind, an overwhelming need for him came over her. "Was it a tall well-built black-haired cop with a mustache who came into the courtroom?"

The woman nodded with a dreamy smile. "Yes, I don't know his name, but he really was very handsome."

"That's him." Vita knew. The "very handsome" was all the confirmation she needed.

"Who?"

"The man I'm going to marry." She turned her head away to smile in private.

****

A black Maria brought Vita to Mott Street, and she jumped out. Neighbors gathered around her, wringing hands and thanking saints. They grabbed her arm and pinched her cheek. Old nonnas jawed in Italian about God's mercy and how He'd saved their souls.

Up the stairs she went, as fast as she could. The darkness didn't bother her. The smells didn't register. She burst through the door and rushed to Papa and Butchie at the kitchen table.

They kissed, they hugged, she sobbed. Butchie's eyes shone under the light of a lamp. They mumbled Italian prayers, bits of endearments, lines of prayers, and the names of every saint they'd ever known.

Neighbors brought wine, sausage, and pasta with garlic gravy. They stood around drinking, eating, and talking with their mouths full, as always.

"Mangia, mangia!" Papa ordered as Mrs. Paluzzi thrust a sausage sandwich into Vita's hand. Still too jumpy to eat, she started to give it back. But it smelled so good she shoved it in her mouth and clamped her teeth down.

"Rooney's dead, you know," she informed them between bites. She didn't tell them she'd stabbed him. They'd find out soon enough.

"We know." Butchie raised a wine glass to his smirking lips.

"Why'd Rooney do it, Butchie? Why'd he set you and Papa up?"

"I double-crossed him once, on a bet," he said. "I don't wanna go through all the messy details. He wanted to get back at me, show me a lesson in honor. I hope it's nice and honorable down there where he is. And I don't mean in the ground six foot under. I mean down below even there."

She didn't want to talk anymore; just being with them, seeing them free, was enough. "C'mon, let's take this party into the street." She led them downstairs, and before long it looked like a saint's feast day—eating, drinking, dancing, singing…and somebody even brought a Saint Anthony statue. They just couldn't celebrate anything without inviting an Italian saint.

She kept an eye out for Tom, but he never showed. This was his victory, too, and she wanted him here with her. Her mind rambled on: How long would it take for her family to accept him, if at all? But she tried to think like him—take one step at a time. *Mama mia*, she was starting to think like him!

As the celebration went on, she put all those worries out of her mind.

Butchie got corned. He slapped his *paesani* on the back. He danced with every girl who caught his eye, and plenty did. He lumbered over to Vita and gave her the tightest hug ever. He lifted her and twirled her around until they fell over each other on the stoop.

"You okay, you okay?" he panted, hugged her again, and pinched her cheek till it stung.

"Yes, Butchie, I'm fine! Oh, Butchie—you're free, you and Papa. Thank God you've been given back to me."

He released a deep sigh and flopped on the stoop steps, rubbing his hands over his eyes. "Am I exhausted. I never been so tired in my life. You sure I ain't dead?"

She smiled and sat next to him. "You're breathing, aren't you?"

"Well, I'm drinkin' and pissin.' That should tell me I'm alive enough. I'll let you know tomorrow."

She knew he was corned, but sometimes he made more sense with a few belts in him. "Butchie—you know who's really responsible for getting you out of there, don't you?"

"Oh, yeah, your leatherhead?" He managed a smile and propped himself up on his elbows. "Yeah. I know it was him." He rested his head on the step and gazed up into their very own little patch of sky.

"Do you still hate him?"

"I never hated him." He flipped his hand. "Cops and us are natural enemies, but I don't—can't hate nobody."

"Hate is so horrible." She shuddered. "It's so ugly. I wish Papa wasn't like that."

"He don't hate either. He wants you to think he does, but—you didn't see him there in that cell, waitin' to die. You forget who you're mad at, you forget revenge, you just do a lot of heavy talkin' to God, thinkin' over your life and convincin' God that you ain't so bad after all, so you can get to heaven. I wasn't gonna spend my last days hatin' nobody."

"And now that you're free—can you thank Tom for saving your life?" she dared to ask him.

"He did it for himself, too, Vita." He yawned. "Didn't he wanna know who killed his cousin?"

"Yes, but it wasn't entirely self-serving. He did it for me, too. He loves me, Butchie. And I love him," she admitted to her brother. "So I wish you would try to get along."

"Haay, I get along with everybody!" He stood and did a jig. Then he staggered back to the stoop and collapsed on the steps in loud rhythmic snores, his head lolled over to one side.

She cradled her brother's head in her lap. "Hey, Cappuchine, come help me get Butchie in, willya?" she called to her neighbor.

He loped over to them, the last bite of a sausage sandwich in his hand. "Come on, *paesan'*, up ya go." He draped Butchie over his shoulder and helped him up the steps while she followed. Then, with her brother poured into bed, she had a party to get back to.

****

When she reported to work the next day, they greeted her with flowers, cakes, hugs, and good wishes. Mr. Johnson handed her a vase of fragrant red roses.

242

She hadn't expected so much as a reaction from him. "How did you find out so fast?" she asked between thank-yous.

"Officer McGlory told me last night. They had a celebration of their own over there. That's the one I went to," Mr. Johnson added with a smug curl to his lips. "They were hoping you'd turn up." He managed to add a dash of sincerity to that afterthought.

"I only wish it could have been one big party," she lamented, still missing Tom.

All day she worked with one eye on the door, hoping Tom would come in. When five o'clock came and he still hadn't turned up, she debated going to his house but didn't want to impose so soon after all this.

Instead she went to Jadwiga's. "Let's have a celebration dinner at the Mad Hatter." She entered the front room and sat at the table. The *New York World* lay spread open like a tablecloth.

"Looky here." Jadwiga slid the newspaper over to her with one hand while splashing vodka into a horn with the other.

KILLER OF POLICEMAN FOUND AND EXECUTED, the headline screamed. She skimmed the article, and her eyes halted at the sight of Tom's name. Thankfully, her name hadn't made print. She closed the paper and folded it with a contented sigh.

"Go into my closet and take anything you want," Jadwiga offered. "Then go into my jewelry case, wear whatever you want tonight, and keep it."

Jadwiga knew Vita loved her clothes and jewelry. She'd begged a few garments right off her friend's back: the cherry red jacket with the white trim she couldn't live without, the ruffled blouse with the

243

ribbons that matched her blue shoes. And her jewelry was just divine. Of course Vita couldn't dress like this at the bank, so she'd started building a wardrobe for Greenwich Village and no farther uptown.

She had a ball rummaging through Jadwiga's ruffles, lace, and bangles. She sauntered out modeling a bottle green blouse with billowing sleeves and satin ribbons down the front, a spring green skirt, and three dangling mother-of-pearl bracelets that reflected the blouse's emerald hue. They reminded her of Tom's eyes. Green was now her favorite color, ever since she'd first looked into his eyes

"So where is your fiancé?" Jadwiga came over and smoothed the ribbons down Vita's blouse.

"*Mama mia*, Jadwiga." She gave her friend a dramatic eye roll. "He's not my fiancé. Let's not rush things."

"Well, if he ain't yet, he will be. He won't waste any time in popping the question. No ring yet?" She lifted Vita's left hand and dropped it when she saw it was ringless.

"Of course not. I haven't even seen him since yesterday." She paused. "Jeez, was it only yesterday? It seems like ages. So much has happened." She took a deep breath. "He didn't come by the bank or the block party last night. I think he's just letting me have time with my family."

"Could be." Jadwiga gazed into the glass like it was her crystal ball.

"What do you mean? Do you see something in there?" Vita peered over into her glass.

Jadwiga laughed. "No, but you seem to forget, in the wake of all that's happened, and it's perfectly understandable, that he might've been involved in some shenanigans he didn't have time for when he was sleuthing. Now, with Rooney pushin' up daisies and Tom's cousin's death avenged, he has to get back to the business at hand."

"No. I don't want to think about that. You already convinced me that, besides being model suitors and husbands, men still do dishonest deeds for a living." She sipped the wine Jadwiga plunked in front of her. "It's something we'll have to work out."

"Well, if you're wondering where he is, that's probably where," Jadwiga said.

"Where's where?"

"Wherever he goes. Clip joints, pool halls, I don't know. They go everyplace. Just watch him. But he might be ring shopping, too." She gave Vita a wink.

"I don't want to think about engagements or killings or men anymore tonight. Tonight is girls' night." But it nagged at her like a bad headache for the rest of the evening. Where could he be?

They headed for the Mad Hatter dressed like Village bohemians in their feather hats and tall heels and colorful blouses. In a bold move, Vita took out her pipe, lit it and puffed, not waiting for a gent to light it for her.

"Atta girl," Jadwiga encouraged, puffing away at Phoenix as Vita tried to stifle a cough. She pushed her water glass over to Vita. "If you become mayor, every dame in New York'll be puffin' on white pipes. They'll be a fashion accessory!"

Vita marveled at that—women imitating her, her style of dress, her bold behavior. She wondered how strong a leader she really could be. The idea got her pulse racing. "But before women imitate my dress and pipe, I want them to adopt my ideals—that it's okay for a woman to use her brain, to have a decent job for decent pay, to marry who she wants and have him treat her right."

"Just make sure yours treats you right," her friend warned.

"I haven't got one yet," Vita shot back.

"Oh, you will, you will. Sooner than you think." Jadwiga nodded. All thoughts of cleaning up New York vanished as Vita admired her new bracelets. They winked up at her as if they dripped with emeralds. Tom's eyes.

"We've got a lot to work through, Jadwiga."

"What? Your families?" She flicked her wrist. "They now know who did the killing. So it was a setup and a very tragic event. But Tom wasn't in on it."

"Try telling that to an Italian who has to sit at the back of the church," Vita countered.

"Then elope."

"Huh?" Vita looked up in surprise.

"You heard me."

Oh, yes, with Jadwiga there was no mistaking it.

"And come back and get into politics and face the world, expecting women to model themselves after me? I'd gain a lot of credibility that way. Honest Vita Caputo runs away to get married. No, I couldn't hurt my family that way," she stated with conviction.

"And they're not hurting you? Forbidding you to see him?"

"They never hurt on purpose," she explained. "It's all for the good of the family. Good Italian girls just don't elope."

"How 'bout bad Italian girls?"

Vita didn't answer that because she didn't know any.

"You think your voters'll give a hoot how you got hitched, once you're sweeping grime from Tammany? You'll be a breath of fresh air, somethin' we never had. They'll respect you for it. You love your man, your family looked down on your marrying him, you said screw them and married him anyway—you ain't less of a daughter because of it."

"Oh, you don't understand the way we do things, Jadwiga. I'm lucky I wasn't married off already. Papa never tried again after Marco Manziano died. Maybe he thought it was a bad sign, the evil eye sneering at him. I could never hurt him like that."

"Think about yourself, honey, for once." Jadwiga's tone scolded. "For once, put the family second."

"They'd never forgive me." Vita shook her head.

"Then that's their problem, ain't it?"

"It's my problem, too," she informed her friend. "I'd have to live with it."

"They'll get over it. Believe me. You're gonna be so rich and make them so proud, they'd even forgive you if you birthed a child out of wedlock."

She choked on her wine. "Please! Watch what you say around here." Sometimes Jadwiga really did like to play for shock. But this time she sounded dead serious.

Jadwiga laughed and whistled the waiter over to order Vita another Chianti.

And after another downed drink, Vita put the elopement idea out of her mind. It would never happen. She'd find a way to make everyone happy. Even if she had to wait to marry Tom. But she'd find a way.

Jadwiga, on her third vodka, got awfully quiet.

"What's bothering you?" Vita badgered her. "We're supposed to be celebrating, and you look like your best friend leapt off the Brooklyn Bridge."

"I just wish I could have pinned the killer down for you. Your family might be more understanding about you and Tommy if they hadn't had to go through all that. They were bitter enough about cops to begin with."

"For God's sake, Jadwiga! None of that's your fault," Vita assured her.

"Yeah, but I'm—I feel like I failed you." She studied her pipe barrel as if it told fortunes.

"Failed me? The word 'frame' led to everything. Tom kept it in his mind. That wouldn't have happened without the séance."

"Vita." Jadwiga inhaled deeply and took Vita's hand. "Rooney used to come to me for readings. I recognized his picture in the paper. I had horrible thoughts about him. His last visit to me, I knew that was going to be his last but didn't know exactly how. He looked downright peaked. I knew he got in with the wrong people and was involved in crime. His aura was black, like the inside of that planchette at our séance. He had a cloud hanging over him. If only I could've done something before…" Her voice faltered.

"You couldn't have stopped him from killing Mike. It's over—Just forget it." And she really did want to forget it.

"Maybe I should stop doin' readings."

"Why?" Vita prodded. "You can't save the world, Jadwiga."

"You're gonna try, ain't ya?"

"No, I'm going to enter politics to do what I can," she answered. "But I don't expect to change the entire city. It's been here longer than I've been here and will be here a lot longer."

"Then let me help ya. I'd love to help ya campaign, or—whatever you do."

Vita smiled. Her dear friend had a gift, and Vita didn't want to see her give up on it.

"An Italian and a Polack—broads, yet!" Jadwiga held her glass up in a toast. "What a city it could be!" They clinked glasses. *"Na zdrowie!"*

****

As the taxi clattered down the street to her boardinghouse that night, Vita's thoughts returned to the tragedy of Mike's murder and her family's ordeal. Resting her head against the back of the seat, she forced those thoughts away and gave her imagination free rein. *Whatever you want to think about, this time is yours and yours alone!* she told herself. This rare and decadent luxury didn't cost a dime but was truly indulgent because time was precious, too. She wanted to accomplish so much, and she wouldn't let one chance slip away.

She handed the taxi driver his fare and glanced into Madame Branchard's front window. The pink-shaded lamp glowed in the darkness. They'd either had an early night or couldn't find anything worth arguing about. She planned on taking the longest bath ever, in the little room off the kitchen—maybe even bring a glass of wine in there and luxuriate like the ancient Romans.

On her way up the stairs, she glanced down the hall and noticed the closed parlor door. Maybe one of the other boarders was in there with a beau. She smiled in the dark. Let them enjoy themselves. All the girls here had beaux, and they needed privacy without chaperones breathing down their necks during every stage of courting.

As she gathered her soap and towel, Madame Branchard tapped on her door. "You have a gentleman caller, Vita. A policeman."

"Tom?" His name lingered on her lips as she repeated it. She dropped her things and crossed the room.

"No, hon, not him. Another policeman. Theodore something, I think he said."

No. There can't be anything wrong. "Thanks," she whispered, gently nudging Madame Branchard aside. She descended the steps, gripping the banister to support her wobbly legs. *Stay calm!* she warned herself. But of course it was no use; staying calm just wasn't her nature.

"Theodore something" stood before the closed parlor door. *He's a policeman?* Curious, she looked him up and down. Tall and hefty, a bold pink shirt peeking out of a buttoned waistcoat and fitted jacket, he looked way out of place against the dainty patterned wallpaper.

He removed his hat. "Miss Caputo." He strained to keep his voice soft as he held out a piece of paper.

"Yes?" Her voice shook.

"I'm Theodore Roosevelt. I have a summons for you, Miss Caputo." He held it out to her. But she stood rooted to that spot.

He stepped closer, and she took it from him, unfolding it with icy fingers. Why would she be served with a summons? Was someone arresting her now for something she didn't do?

A shot of anger tore through her at this system, at everything she wanted to change. It eclipsed her fear, made her blood boil. She flipped it open and saw the word "Summons" in fancy script at the top. Her eyes widened with each sentence as she read. "I can't believe what I'm seeing."

I hereby order Miss Vita Caputo to enter into holy matrimony with Mr. Thomas McGlory immediately following service of this summons.

Signed and witnessed, it looked very official. She looked up at Theodore Roosevelt. He flashed her a toothy smile.

"He's *pazzo*, he's just nuts!" She read it again and again, laughing, her eyes filled with tears of relief and happiness.

"Deeee-lightful, isn't it, Miss Caputo?" The door to the parlor behind him opened and he stepped aside. There stood Tom in the doorway. Roosevelt cuffed him on the chin and vanished.

"I would have arrested you, but I was afraid you'd resist." He gave her a playful grin.

She leapt forward and embraced him with every bit of strength she had left, crushing the paper between them.

"You are just crazy!" was all she could think to say. Still dizzy from the shock, the fright, and the anger that blanketed it all, she juggled a new jumble of titillating emotions.

"You're the one who should be crazy, crazy enough to marry me, that is."

All her doubts vanished at that instant. "Oh, yes, together we are stronger than any force that would dare keep us apart." Then, in a guarded tone, she asked, "You don't mean tonight, do you?" Jadwiga's one-word suggestion flashed through her mind: *elope*. She wondered if the two of them had planned a slick coup. Was a priest in the parlor waiting to officiate?

He laughed, a halo around his head from the lamp's glow. "Any night you want. Tonight, tomorrow, next week—just don't make me wait too long."

"How long were you sitting in there?"

"A few hours. I figured you were with your family. Your landlady was nice enough to let me wait. I told her I wanted to surprise you, and I think she figured out what it was. So she didn't interfere. Teddy there, who considerately left us alone, is our commish, and the jokester on the force. He'd have to be, to have gone along with this!"

They went into the parlor. Quivering in naughty delight, she shut the door. As she sat on the sofa, he dropped to one knee. He slid his hand into his pocket and brought out a sparkling ring, took her hand, and slipped it onto the third finger of her left hand. "Vita, will you marry me?"

"Oh, Tom…" She held it at arm's length, turning her hand this way and that. It glittered in the lamp's glow.

She would have eloped with him if he'd asked. If a priest had stood in the room, they would have been married by now. She threw her arms around his neck, dizzy with happiness, dizzily in love. "Of course I'll marry you! Tonight, tomorrow, whenever you want! Oh, how I love you!"

He sat beside her, and she pulled the pins from her bun. Her hair tumbled to her waist, and he stroked it lovingly as she nestled against his chest. Their lips met and parted. Her mind raced...*We need to set a date!*

Chapter Twenty-Two

Vita sat at the kitchen table Monday morning, dressed for work, her diamond solitaire sparkling in the autumn sunlight streaming through the window. She sipped her coffee and opened the morning edition of the *Times*. No more day-old papers for her.

She read the first article about the upcoming mayoral campaigns. Hugh J. Grant was running for reelection. But she had to read the next paragraph twice before his opponent's name sank in, a Republican banker. A conservative reformer, his platform centered on taming the Tammany tiger. She knew that name from somewhere. Of course! She'd met him in Tony Pastor's Music Hall. He attended Madame Branchard's salons, always discussing the reforms he intended to make. His name was William Lafayette Strong.

She ignored the smug editorial. Obviously no one in the Tammany machine wanted this man to win. In fact, they would do everything in their power to make sure he lost. But if he was going to lose, he'd lose with dignity. At that moment she decided to help him win.

She planned a busy day: after work, she'd find campaign headquarters and offer her help to elect Strong, and then she'd tell her family she was engaged. Telling them who she was engaged to would be the hard part. She planned to soften the blow with a Strong campaign placard and tin buttons from headquarters.

That and five pounds of fresh tomatoes from Mr. Stromboli's cart.

****

"Hey. You like?" Butchie sat and stuck his legs straight out for her to admire the new shoes she'd bought him.

"They fit?" she asked as Papa came into the kitchen grumbling about his dyspepsia and the overflowing commode in the hall.

"Then go in the back-a-house! Or off the roof!" Rosalia waved her arm, the flab swinging like a saddle bag. Yes, things were back to normal.

They talked about what a great mayor William Strong would be as Vita handed them each a campaign pin. Butchie helped her nail one of the placards onto their door for everyone to see the honest weatherbeaten face on their way up and down the stairs.

Thankfully no one noticed the ring. Not even Rosalia.

She decided to tell them over the exotic Chase & Sanborn coffee she'd brought. "I'm glad you're all sitting here, because I have something to tell you."

For once, they sat silent. She had their attention, something she was never able to get.

She took a deep breath and licked her lips. "I'm engaged." She waited.

"Engaged? To do what?" Papa spoke first, clanking his spoon against his coffee cup, tossing the dripping spoon onto her tablecloth.

"To be married."

"You—gettin' married?" Butchie stuffed a hunk of pastry into his mouth. No surprise there. But he hadn't heard it all.

Then the inevitable came. "To who?"

"Tom McGlory."

Butchie's jaw stopped in mid-chomp. "Nah, him?"

Papa didn't look like he'd heard anything. Rosalia waited, as if expecting Vita to say, "Ha ha, gotcha! It's all a joke!"

"Yes, it's him, and we're getting married." She didn't wave the ring in their faces. She didn't have to. Rosalia grabbed Vita's hand and shook it at them.

"Looky, he gave her a ring. Made of tin, just like the Billy Strong buttons." Rosalia snickered and dug another pastry from the bakery box. Vita bristled at how amusing her stepmother found this whole thing.

"You ain't serious, are you?" Papa ran his tongue over his bottom teeth.

Vita threw her hands in the air, palms up. "You'd think I just told you I'm goin' out to Tombstone to join a band of outlaws!"

Papa mumbled in Italian. Butchie stared down at his new shoes. Rosalia stuffed her face with a cruller.

She went on, still on the defensive, "We're going to be married because we're in love." Her voice remained steady. She tried to think like Tom now.

"But he's Irish," Papa stated, as if to inform her of one crucial fact she'd overlooked. But if being Irish was the only thing Papa had against Tom now, that encouraged her.

"I know he's Irish," she verified. "So what?"

"So what?" Papa pointed at her, condemning her to the gates of hell. "You can't marry into the Irish. They hate us."

"Oh, come on, the whole world doesn't hate us!"

"He might'a told you he loves you, but his family

won't take it," Butchie warned.

"I appreciate your concern, unfounded as it is. Tom has never said anything bad about you, Butchie. He's the one who found the man who framed you for murder, remember? He could never hate you. And you said you couldn't ever hate him, remember?"

"Yeah, so he ain't so rotten, and I don't hate him, but I don't gotta let him marry my sister." He struck a match on the sole of his shoe and lit a cigarette.

"You don't gotta let me do anything. I'm twenty-one years old. I don't need your permission or Papa's." She stood and turned to leave. "That's the way it is. See you's on Saturday."

She knew Butchie would pop up and insist on taking her home. He did, and she let him. A crisp breeze kept the stenches at bay. As they walked, she assured her brother her future was now secure. "I know you don't hate Tom, but expecting you to accept an outsider into the family is expecting a lot. But I still do expect it from you."

Butchie gave her an affectionate cuff on the jaw. "Hey, the guy saved our lives. What can I say? If he's gonna be my brother-in-law, I'll learn to love the paddy."

Chapter Twenty-Three

"I told them." Vita and Tom sat on a blanket in Central Park, a picnic basket between them. On this glorious Saturday, not a cloud dotted the sky. The sun bathed them in warmth. A calm breeze played through the orange, gold, and red leaves. Couples just like them, young and old, strolled hand in hand. Scampering children kicked a ball. She relished this day to be free, to enjoy life.

He dropped the basket lid and looked over at her, the plates and cups a respectable barrier between them. "What'd they say?"

"I've already sold Butchie on it, but Papa's still in denial."

"I told you I should have gone to your father first and asked for your hand in marriage." He drummed his fingers on the basket's lid.

"He only would've said the same thing to you, Tom. He wouldn't have let you in the door. It would've made it worse."

"Yeah, you're right—all I did was find the real killer and save his and his son's lives and prove their innocence. Maybe I should do something really noble, like open a gambling casino on Mott and Canal." His voice dripped with sarcasm.

"He's stubborn, Tom. You have to understand him. He thinks someone up there saved his life." She pointed to the sky as a leaf fluttered down and landed on her shoulder.

"Well, maybe someone up there did. But they usually need an earthly conductor for help. Doesn't he think I had anything at all to do with it?"

"Of course he does." she said. "He's just too proud to admit it."

"Well, someone down here wants to marry his daughter." He clasped her hand. "And never having wanted to marry anyone before, I'm at a loss for what to do now."

Jadwiga's suggestion loitered in the back of her mind—that one simple word that would hurt a lot of people, including herself, but she had a decision to make: how badly did she want to marry him? Elopement sounded exciting, impulsive, and romantic, but in her family, excitement was limited to wine-soaked block parties. Impulse only applied to bursts of anger. As for romance—that was a luxury only the French seemed to be able to afford.

"I'll keep talking to him." She peeked into the basket.

"I told you I don't want to wait till the next century, Vita."

"I'll get through to him somehow," she promised. "Deep down he's a softie."

He stretched out, his elbow propping up his head. He played with a stalk of clover with his free hand. "You haven't met my father yet."

"And that's the other half of the problem." She took out a drumstick and nibbled on it.

"What, that they won't like you?" He gave her a warm smile. "They know about you."

259

"How much?" She peered down at him. The light gave his hair a sapphire glow. "Besides being part of the family that didn't kill Mike. You didn't tell them we're engaged, did you?"

"Not yet. I wanted to wait until you were with me. I want to tell them together, the whole lot. Just like I wish I could have been with you when you told your family."

She chewed and swallowed. "The thought of in-laws scares the wits out of me. I know they won't approve of anything about me."

He closed his eyes and laid his head down. She knew getting their fathers to approve of their marriage would be harder than getting William Strong elected. But she didn't want to bring that up in the middle of this discussion.

"My family aren't a pack of wolves," he said, eyes still closed. "They won't tear you to shreds. Just come home with me tonight, and I'll make the announcement—we'll make it. Together."

"I can't tonight, Tom. I've got something to do at six and probably won't be finished till late." She nibbled some more.

He opened his eyes and stared at her as if she'd just robbed the Manhattan Bank. "What have you got to do?" he asked as if interrogating a suspect.

"I'm working at campaign headquarters. I've signed up as a volunteer." She finished eating and wiped her hands.

"For who?" he asked.

"William Strong."

"You're campaigning for *him*?" Disbelief rang in his tone.

"Yes. He's going to be the best mayor this city has ever seen. And this is my best chance to get involved in politics."

He laughed, and she found it very condescending. She raised her chin. "And what may I ask is so hilarious about that?"

His eyes glittered. Difficult as it was, she tore her gaze away from them. She couldn't manage to look at him without melting into the ground.

"I'm not laughing at you. It's just the thought of this fella running for mayor. He's wasting his time." He snickered. "And you'd be wasting yours, campaigning for him."

"Why?" she probed. "Because he's honest? Or because he's Republican?"

"Face the facts, Vita. New York might have an honest mayor someday. Someday in the far, far future. But not while there's Tammany Hall. It's a meat grinder. And it's going to tear Billy Strong to pieces. The majority just won't vote for him." His eyes narrowed. "Not only that, you can bet Tammany'll get Grant double and triple votes out of some people—they'll rig it for sure. It happens every time, and it'll happen again this time."

"Well, then maybe some honest citizen can demand a recount."

"Possibly." He gave a one-shoulder shrug. "I don't think it's ever been done. But some reforms are happening around here." He beamed at her. "I'm very proud of what you're doing already, Vita, with the tenement reform, with your cousin there on Mott Street. Don't get mixed up with mayoral elections. They'll chew you up and spit you out."

She rested her elbows on the picnic basket. "Look, Tom, most of the people in this city want decent housing and working conditions and don't even know who William Strong is. I want them to know him. The reforms I've been trying to bring about aren't going to happen anywhere near as fast with a Tammany mayor. So who are you going to support? The man who's part of the machine that had your cousin killed?"

He twirled a blade of grass. "No, of course not. There are other candidates. Grant is a piece of dirt, to be sure. But Billy Strong—he just hasn't got a chance."

"We'll see."

"We're not going to let this come between us, are we?" He sat up, pushing the basket aside.

She turned away. "I'm not going to. But it looks like you are."

"I'm not trying to tell you what to believe in, I'm just telling you you're wasting your time. Help one of the other candidates, if you have to do this."

"I've seen the others and read about them, and they're no better than the rowdies in there a'ready. Strong wants to clean this place up," she rattled off as if she'd started campaigning for him already.

"A Republican trying to clean up Tammany— wanting to clean up the city. I'll see your father give us his blessing first," he said.

"Maybe you will. Maybe you'll see both. Then maybe you'll be big about it. Or am I expecting too much?" She cast a glance at him. He looked hurt, his eyes downcast, his lips tight. But he didn't sound any better than the rest of them.

"After all we've been through, I can't let politics stand in our way. But we need to get a few things straight here. You know I believe in this city. I believe it can be cleaned up, and we have to start somewhere." She gave him a nudge. "Why don't you come with me tonight and meet Billy? I'll bet you've never laid eyes on the man. What do you know about him, besides that he's a reformer?"

He stuck to his guns. "I know he's got a lot of spare time to waste because he's not going to make mayor."

"Just meet the man before you make any more judgments." Annoyance crept into her voice.

She put him on the spot, but he could be as stubborn as Papa. If she was going to spend the rest of her life as Mrs. Thomas McGlory, she needed to learn what really mattered to him.

"Tom, I think you're against Billy Strong not so much because he's an underdog but because he wants to purge the city of Tammany and its corruption— which supports the police force—the political machine. That's it, isn't it?"

"Don't be naïve, Vita." He shook his head. "Everybody helps out their friends. You'll see that if you go into politics. It's about favors. It doesn't matter how much they make on the side, as long as the system keeps running. Strong's not a politician. He makes donuts, for goodness' sake."

She gave him a puzzled look. "Donuts?"

"Yeah, I read in the paper he comes from a family of bakers."

"Bankers, bankers!" She threw her hands up. "You read it wrong. Or it was a drunk typesetter."

He shrugged. "Well, if any Metropolitan cop is seen at the headquarters of a reformist candidate, he'll get kicked off the force. But I'm not that interested in politics."

She knew better. "All cops are involved with politics." But she no longer wanted to argue with him. "Let's get cleaned up here, Tom. I'd like to get back early."

"Vita—" He got to his feet, stretched, and stepped around the blanket to face her. "Just think, if you get involved in this campaign, I'll never see you."

"Join in the campaign and we'll see each other all the time." She picked up the dishes and stacked them in the basket.

"I won't interfere in this. You can campaign for whoever you want. But don't be disappointed on election night when the embarrassing returns come in." His voice sounded smug.

"I only hope you'll come down to headquarters after Grant concedes and have some wine with us," she shot back.

"I hope we'll be married by then." He knelt beside her. "And that's something we can control."

He kissed her there in the middle of Central Park full of people. She was sure no one even glimpsed them, but she didn't care if they gawked. There were too many things she did care about.

****

Too wound up to sleep at bedtime, Vita grabbed her shawl and walked over to Jadwiga's, interrupting her friend's reading of an Ignatius Donnelly book.

"So Billy Strong's running for mayor." Jadwiga puffed on her pipe as they sipped coffee at her table. "I had a feeling he had the guts to do something like that."

"I like him a lot, Jadwiga, and I trust him. So what

if he's surly and serious? He's got a warm streak. He can make people howl with laughter when he wants to."

"Not your professional politician," her friend remarked, thumbing through the pages of her half-read book.

"He worked his way through college and got a degree in economics." Vita began the hard sell. "Billy Strong is book smart the way Grant is street smart. If nothing else, he'll earn votes with his honest, hardworking manner the way Grant buys them with his filthy money. His headquarters looks like a bakery— cakes and pastries all over the place. People come in off the street for the free pastries. Then they pick up the leaflets about him. I have a feeling he'll get a lot of publicity that way."

"Do you really think voters would rather have a banker who gives out pastries than a politician like Grant, who gives out favors and feeds Tammany?" Jadwiga challenged.

"You may not have noticed, but a lot of them have been rounded up and hauled off to prison. The police commissioner, Ted Roosevelt, is doing a lot to end favoritism and corruption. When people realize Billy Strong isn't part of the machine, they'll vote for him."

"He's got an uphill battle," Jadwiga argued.

Vita glanced over at the crystal ball, tucked under its velvet cover as if sound asleep. "Jadwiga, can you tell me who's going to win?" she asked in a conspiratorial tone.

"Of course I can." She dropped a splash of vodka into her coffee and licked the bottle neck. "Grant. By a landslide."

"No, I mean with the ball." She jerked her head in

that direction.

"I don't need the ball, honey bunch."

"Well, I'm not so sure Grant's got it tied up." Vita gave her honest opinion.

"But you wanna know now, so you can defect to the other side in time?" Jadwiga pursed her lips, smearing her lipstick.

"No, I'd never do that." Vita crossed her arms. "But although I hate to admit it, I probably have more in common with Mayor Grant than with Billy Strong. We're both streetwise. We're both cynical. We're both tough. But that's where it ends. The guy is as corrupt as an excommunicated saint."

"Well, why don't you use that to your advantage?" Jadwiga winked.

"How?"

"Next time His Dishonor comes into the bank and gives you the eye, sidle up to him and start a conversation. Don't tell him you're campaigning for Billy, but get to know him—if you know what I mean." She refilled her lipstick-rimmed cup.

"That's crazy." She waved the idea away. "I'd never resort to spying."

"Even if it's to bring a crook down?" Jadwiga probed.

"The mayor is a powerful man. I'm not going to start messing with the machine, Jadwiga."

"You're not going to beat the powerful mayor by giving away pastries and telling voters how honest your guy is. You should get to know the other guy better and find out his weaknesses," she instructed, like a campaign manager.

"Well, I already know he's got a penchant for malt

whiskey and gambling and money. But so does every politician in this city." Vita sipped her coffee.

"Then maybe he likes pastries even more. You know—the sweet Italian ones—like the ones you'll find at Strong headquarters."

Vita knew what her friend was suggesting. But she was only willing to go so far in securing her future in this city. She didn't stop thinking about it, though, as she drew on her pipe.

****

"Vita, you got comp'ny!" Madame shouted up the stairs. Vita, just home from work, was changing into her comfortable flannel shirt and skirt. She descended the stairs, and there stood Tom holding a bouquet of flowers. Her heart wanted to tumble out and embrace him.

"Happy anniversary." He handed her the posies. She inhaled their sweet fragrance as the soft petals tickled her chin.

"They're gorgeous, thank you! But—what anniversary?"

"Ours. Two months. We're going to dinner. Then I'm bringing you home to meet my family. I want to formally present you to them and show them the woman I'm going to marry."

She stiffened. "I think it's too soon to meet your family."

"When do you want to meet them, at the church when you're walking toward the altar?" He pressed on. "Come on, Vita, what are you afraid of?"

"I'm not afraid." She kicked at the woodwork. "I just think it's too soon."

"You wouldn't let me formally ask your father for

your hand, so at least do this for me." His eyes pleaded.

"Don't you think I should wait till I'm invited?"

He hesitated, and she buried her face in the fragrant bouquet, picturing herself in an English garden with fountains.

"You've been invited. They're expecting you."

She should have been annoyed with him for his presumption. But she couldn't put this off—these were her future in-laws, whether they liked it or not. She couldn't be so rude as to avoid them. "All right. Let me put these in water and get dressed."

"You look fine."

She looked down at her blouse and skirt. "These are my hanging-around-the-house clothes. I need to put something decent on."

He grinned as Madame swept the bouquet from her hands. "I'll take care of these. You take care of your future in-laws."

****

When Tom and Vita entered his parlor, the entire family stood there waiting for them. She thought she'd walked in on a wake. The women stood on the left, the men on the right, whiskey tumblers clenched firmly in hand. Four children sat on the floor, surrounded by blocks. The whole family had the same pinkish complexions, freckles, and shiny hair except for one girl with a mass of red curls piled on her head—Eileen, the sister who'd opened the door for Vita that night.

Tom introduced Vita to every one of them. The ladies nodded without a word while the men reached out for tentative handshakes. She'd never remember all their names—Bridget, Eileen, Patrick, Eamon—then the children, Patsy Jr., Colleen, Doreen,

Maureen...whew! And Mr. McGlory, who Tom introduced simply as "my father." He didn't reach out for a handshake, but he said more than the rest of them put together. "Welcome to our home, Miss Caputo." He shortened the "u" and pronounced it as in "put."

Eileen rose to an imposing height and offered her a seat and coffee. Vita declined coffee. The thought of it was enough to pierce holes in her stomach.

"No, thanks so much, but we've just had a huge meal."

Mr. McGlory settled in a wing chair by the window, obviously his chair, just like Papa claimed his at the table. She vowed to buy Papa an even bigger chair than this one. "Have you set a date yet, son?" He addressed Tom, as if the bride had no say in the wedding date.

"Not yet, Da."

"I expect your family is aware of your plans." He turned to Vita. Tom sat at her side, squeezing her hand. She pulled it away.

"Oh, yes, they're aware." She nodded, hoping this was all he'd ask about it. She didn't want to rehash the scene in her kitchen last night.

"How are your father and brother, Vita?" Bridget broke in with her bell-like voice. Vita wanted to kiss her.

"They're fine now, thank you for asking."

"And they survived their ordeal in the Tombs?" Eileen pressed her. "Oh, I've heard about that place. It's like the dungeon in Blarney Castle." Her curls bounced as she gave an exaggerated shiver.

"I hope nothing like that ever happens again," Vita said. "To anyone of any nationality."

269

"As long as they stay honest, nothing will," Mr. McGlory affirmed, sounding much less like a future father-in-law and too much like a Metropolitan policeman.

"Vita, that's a lovely dress. Who made it?" Bridget interjected, and Vita knew then and there Bridget would be her only ally.

"Thank you. My tailor, Mr. LaFamina. He does beautiful work."

"And how long have you been wearing tailor-made clothes?" Eileen's brows jumped.

"Since I started working at the bank. But I only had a few things made there, for work. I usually just go to Bloomingdale's."

"Oh, yes, the job Tom got you. You tell them who you really are yet?" the other sister chimed in, talking over Tom's "Ei-leeen—"

"I told my employers my real name when my father and brother were falsely accused of the murder."

"Imagine—having to lie about who you are just to get a decent job." Eileen shook her head in ill-disguised pity. Bogus or not, pity was one thing Vita didn't need.

"I told Vita she didn't have to do that," Tom said, his tone firm. Vita guessed he used that tone with his sister a lot. "But she knows how prejudiced some people are and didn't want to take any chances. She wasn't trying to deceive anybody, Eileen."

Vita appreciated his defending her, but she could have done better herself. She would have sent Eileen running into her Dada's arms in tears. *I'm off to a great start with this family.*

"I did what I felt I had to do to get the job," she explained, looking into every pair of eyes with all sincerity. "I hope someday we can all understand one another instead of letting our differences get in the way."

Everyone shrugged and *hmmf*'d, as if pondering whether her wish would be worth the effort. Only Bridget nodded.

After another round of whiskey, they seemed more at ease—postures relaxed and they looked her in the eye. But the clock chimed ten, and Tom seemed to have caught Vita's signal when she stifled a yawn. She told them all how nice it was to meet them, and they said their goodbyes. So they didn't welcome her with open arms, but compared to Vita's family, they'd laid out a red carpet strewn with shamrocks.

****

As they walked up Park Street, she commented, "Tom, you're too quiet."

"We're going to your family now, Vita."

She couldn't argue with that. They made a left onto Mott and dodged the street cleaner as it rolled by, followed by two sweepers. "More political favors disguised as jobs," she murmured.

"You carried yourself so well back there with my family. I'm very proud of you. I owe it to you to face your family now," he said as they approached her building.

"Oh, if only we didn't have to do this." She led him up the stairs, past the toilet on the landing, their footsteps echoing.

The door gaped open, and she walked right into the kitchen. Papa and Butchie sat there playing cards. Rosalia leaned out the window gabbing with Mrs. Labrizzi across the air shaft. They glanced at her but didn't register any expression until they saw who stood behind her. Papa strained to focus like he couldn't believe his eyes. He'd looked this way once before—when he caught Rosalia smoking a cigarette at Owney Geoghegan's Hurdy Gurdy.

Butchie tried to hide behind his cards. Rosalia grinned like a delighted kid at a Punch and Judy show—waiting for some first-class entertainment.

Tom strode in and stood before Papa. "Mr. Caputo, I know Vita has told you that we're engaged, but I wanted to formally ask for her hand."

Papa dropped his cards onto the table. The wine jug toppled, and Butchie caught it. He wiped the rim and licked his hand.

"Who this guy think he is, askin' to marry my daughter!" Papa didn't address Tom, but the rest of the family, expecting them to answer him. Why not? To Papa it was a reasonable question.

"Look, McGlory, maybe you better just scram. Make it some other day. With some notice." Butchie's warning was calm as he gestured toward the door.

"Listen, all of you, and listen good." Every head turned as Vita spoke up. "I'm going to marry this man. Papa, Tom doesn't have to ask your permission. He's asking because he's a gentleman. It's not enough he saved your lives. You've still got to treat him worse than I've seen some people treating us. I love all of you and don't want to disappoint anyone, but instead of hating him for no good reason, be glad for my happiness, and that I found someone who loves me very much and wants to take care of me. And—that's all I have to say. Tom, let's go."

They turned and walked out the door. No one came

after her, no one shouted for her to get back up there, and no one threatened. Only one person hadn't spoken the entire time up there. Rosalia.

Rose is on our side, Vita realized, with a silent nod. And she knew why.

Chapter Twenty-Four

Vita never discussed her private life with her superiors at work, but somehow they'd found out Tom had proposed to her. Mr. Johnson called her into his office, closed the door behind Secretary Lamppost, and handed her a stock certificate. "Here's to all the happiness in the world with your marriage."

"Mr. Johnson, I don't know what to say...thank you. This is the most valuable thing I own now." She looked at the face of the parchment—fifty shares of a new company called General Electric. With a fancy blue border and script lettering, it looked like artwork suitable for framing. She knew then and there she wouldn't fritter it away on gewgaws.

"This is the foundation of my future, Mr. Johnson." She looked over at the bank president. "Thank you so much, but I don't feel like I've earned anything. All I did was accept an engagement ring."

He laughed, his fingers stroking his dollar-sign tie clip in a way that embarrassed her. "Marriage is hard work, Vita, you'll see that. And considering whom you're marrying, it'll be even harder work," he added with a note of empathy she'd never heard from him. "It's been hard for you. You came through splendidly, and, I'll be frank, none of those gals out there would have withstood it with half the grace and dignity you did. Sometimes the going will be tough. But you'll get through it, I know you will. So will Tom."

"I'm hoping our different backgrounds will be an asset." Working at the bank, she'd picked up a lot of jargon she applied to regular life. She just loved using all those financial terms. "But you've been just wonderful to both of us, and we appreciate it."

"Don't mention it," he said in a weak attempt at modesty.

The door opened, and the impeccably dressed Mayor Grant stood there. He rapped on the door frame a few times with his walking stick and regarded Vita with his usual pleased eye, a beat longer than usual this time. He strode past her to Mr. Johnson, who extended his arm like a beacon. She turned as they shook hands. Halfway out the door she heard the mayor say, "Miss Caputo, will you stay here a minute? I'd like to talk to you."

She froze for a second, then regained her poise, raised her chin, and turned with a confident smile. "Yes, Mr. Mayor?"

"Please have a seat." He held out his hand as if it were his own office. In a way, it was. "You don't mind, do you, Liam? This'll just take a minute."

She saw the mayor struggling to keep his eyes focused on her face and off the rest of her. His too-even, too-white porcelain teeth made his smile look about as sincere as a wolf baring his fangs. "Will you campaign for me?"

She recoiled, not sure she'd heard right. "Campaign for you?"

"I know you're active in the reformist movements down on the East Side, and I know about your cousin there, the, uh—the mayor of Mott Street. Liam told me you live at Madame Branchard's, where all those progressive-minded types meet."

"Gee, you know a lot about me, don't you, Mayor Grant?" She cast a sideways glance at Mr. Johnson, nodding proudly, as if she were his own daughter. The pride in his eyes softened her anger.

"Yes, I like to learn more about people I find interesting and different," the mayor continued. "A cut above, if you know what I mean. That brings me to William Strong. Now, he's a good man, good man, but not right for the job. Frankly, you're wasting your talents, helping him campaign. Even despite your best efforts, why, we all know he hasn't got a chance. Not a chance." Tom's voice echoed in her ears. *Did the same can oil the entire machine?* "You work for me, and you'll get places." He fixed his eyes on her, as if daring her to refuse.

Yeah, like jail, she wanted to say, *after they're finished wiping the dirt off these streets.* But she didn't refuse him. She had something in mind.

"I'll have to think about this long and hard, Mr. Mayor. I've already begun working for Mr. Strong, and it would disappoint him terribly if I just turned around and deserted."

He gave her a rather patronizing tilt of his head. "That's the world of politics, dear. You live with disappointment every day, every day. That's what democracy is all about. You can't win them all. And you can't let personal, er, loyalty get in the way of what's best for this city."

"I'm working for him because he is going to do what's best for this city," she informed him. "Just like what Commissioner Roosevelt's doing. Cleaning the place up."

"Oh, it's not all corruption, Miss Caputo." He flashed the wolf-smile. "You're a true American. Come over to our side. The winning side. We need good, hard-working campaigners that we'll reward lavishly when we emerge victorious." He turned to Mr. Johnson. "Won't we, Liam?"

Mr. Johnson nodded at the mayor and that confirmed her suspicions about him. *Rewarded how?* she wondered. Would he buy her a bank?

"I'm not working for lavish rewards, Mr. Mayor," she spoke in her most polished tone. "I believe in the city, too, and we'll all be rewarded. Politics shouldn't be self-serving. That's what democracy is all about."

"Then come work for me. Why, we'll have the best campaign team this city has ever seen, only the best." He didn't skip a beat, just thumped his walking stick on the floor for emphasis. She tried not to laugh when he turned it and the brass duck head looked straight at her, its eyes comically crossed.

He skirted her comment well enough. She wanted to snap, "I wouldn't work for you if you made me Treasury Secretary of the United States!" But for what she had in mind, she couldn't commit herself. Now or ever.

"I'll consider it and inform you with my decision, Mr. Mayor. Thank you for the offer."

"I'll be here tomorrow at two for another appointment with Mr. Johnson. Can you tell me by then?" He tried to pin her down.

"I'm not so sure. I like to think things out," she hedged again.

"Very well, then, until tomorrow." He nodded,

bowed, took her hand, did everything but click his heels, the picture of chivalry. He must've practiced for years. She bade them good day and resumed her post.

She knew why he tried to lure her into his camp. He needed the Italian vote. Now it was just a matter of who was more clever.

****

When she returned to her boardinghouse that night, she found a cream-colored envelope with her name written in fancy script propped up on the table. She was in a hurry to get to Strong's headquarters, but couldn't go anywhere without looking at this first.

She tore it open and unfolded an elegant invitation. William Strong certainly wouldn't go around sending these out. It was way too pretentious, too—Mayor Grant.

And sure enough His Dishonorable had personally written and signed this invitation to dinner at the Plaza Hotel tomorrow evening. Dinner at the Plaza! The first of her daydreams as a sophisticated New York woman. But not with the corrupt mayor.

The invitation said a courier would be by to retrieve her RSVP tomorrow morning. She wrote an acceptance. That would be one interesting evening.

****

After work the next day she dashed over to Jadwiga's. "I need to borrow your most uptown-looking hat, and I need jewelry that dazzles."

Naturally Jadwiga had questions. "Where you going all dolled up like that? With who? Do tell!"

"I can't stay. I really gotta go. I'll be back tomorrow and tell you everything," rushed out in one breath as she adjusted the long white ostrich feather and angled the hat just right. She still needed to fix her hair. "Can I borrow some of that lipstick?"

"The red stuff?"

She blanched. "God, no, the pink."

She handed Vita a gold tube, and she dropped it into her purse.

"You want perfume?" Jadwiga asked.

"No!" she blurted. Perfume on a dinner date with the mayor? She wouldn't dare.

"Tell me who, already! Do tell!" Jadwiga demanded as Vita lovingly placed the hat in Jadwiga's biggest hatbox, removing five others to make room.

"It's a long story. But once again, you planted the seeds, and now they're about to bear ripe, bursting fruit."

"Not garlic, I hope." Jadwiga gave her a delicate gold timepiece to wear around her wrist. "Here. So you don't stay out late like a floozy."

Vita laughed, blew her friend a kiss, and ran back to her attic room.

****

Darkness had already fallen when the mayor's carriage rolled up to her door and an elegant footman stepped out. She met him halfway; she didn't want him ringing the bell or attracting any attention. She climbed in and greeted Mayor Grant sitting on the velvet seat. He held out his hand to her and she grasped it. His own grasp lingered a bit longer than protocol demanded. His teeth gleamed in the streetlamps, looking like he'd polished them to match his pearl cufflinks. She nearly caught her hat feather in the door. She had to get used to dressing up and riding in carriages.

"Mayor Grant, I still haven't made up my mind

about campaigning for you, so can I please ask that no one hear about this dinner?"

"First, let's dispense with the formalities and this Mayor Grant claptrap. If you're going to be part of my campaign team, call me what they all do. Call me Huey."

She couldn't, she just couldn't. Much too familiar. Way too uncomfortable. She only called Billy Strong by his first name because they'd already known each other socially. "How about if I call you Mr. Grant?"

"Well, if you insist, Vita, but—oh, do you prefer to be addressed as Miss Caputo?"

"Maybe just for now." Dear God, she didn't want him to think he could take any liberties. Her riding in a strange man's carriage would have melted Papa's crucifix. But in the world of politics, she had to forget everything she'd been taught in order to play along.

He rattled on about his racehorses, his art collection, his new estate up the Hudson. She nodded politely and lined up the questions she'd fire at him later. He seemed impressed with her interest in New York history and her growing library. His eyes glowed with admiration when she shared her knowledge of banking and finance. Men weren't used to hearing women talk about bonds and mortgage rates. They weren't used to hearing women talk at all.

****

The Plaza dazzled, just as she imagined. Crystal chandeliers cast light upon the crisp white tablecloths and shiny silverware. She glided across the gleaming floor like a queen as the maitre d' led them to Grant's favorite table. Coiffed heads turned. Plucked brows cocked. She caught a few hostile glances from the women. But no rude gestures. Well, of course. This was the Plaza. No Mott Street finger-wagging here.

The staff fawned over them as if serving royalty. Over the four-course steak dinner she picked his brains as if she really planned to work for him.

"Miss Caputo, if you come work for me in this campaign, I assure you, when I'm reelected, you'll be a very respected city employee." He held his glass up to her in the gesture of a toast.

"You're offering me a city job?" She sipped her champagne. The bubbles tickled her nose. He seemed unaware nobody drank champagne within fifty trolley stops of Mott Street.

"I'm giving you a job. It's not an offer. It's a gift. Well paid and respected. Just like all my appointments. Even if William Strong did become mayor someday"— he harrumphed into his linen napkin—"I frankly doubt he'd give you or any of his campaigners jobs. He doesn't seem to be a man of his word, from what I've seen of him."

Oh, and Hugh J. Grant was a man of his word, all right. For what his word was worth.

He went on, "Tell me your salary there at the bank. I'll match it and add half."

The offer flattered her. But she still didn't trust him. "What about Mr. Johnson? He's been very good to me."

"Liam will understand. Business is business. How do you think Liam got started? With a city job. He left politics and became a banker. We don't all stay in politics till we die. It just depends if you're a true public servant."

"Isn't it possible to do both?" Why, she wondered,

did he feel there had to be a choice? But she knew what he meant. Politicians made so much money, they didn't need to do anything else. She just wanted to see how he'd worm out of it.

"Why, yes, you can do both. But public service is a noble calling, not just a job. Business is more self-serving." He bobbed his head as if he needed convincing to believe his own hooey.

"Oh, it's a calling, I believe that, Mr. Grant." *And who called these politicians when they died?* she wondered. She didn't think it was anyone up above.

In the carriage on the way back, his leg slid just a bit too close to hers, and she pulled away. She crept closer to the door, almost leaning on it.

The carriage halted outside her boardinghouse. The driver opened the door, and Grant leaned toward her. As she smelled the cigars on his breath, she slid out of the carriage. She wasn't going to give him the opportunity to get anywhere within groping distance.

****

Reading under the dim bedside lamp, sleep nowhere near her, she let her mind wander. She imagined Tom here, as her husband, lying beside her, their differences behind them, secure in a well-paying business that they ran together while they both held important public offices.

It seemed as distant as the next century, even though 1900 was only six years away.

Chapter Twenty-Five

As Tom and Vita sat at the soda fountain sipping their malteds, he hit her with a daring proposition. "Vita, I want you to come to my house for Christmas and spend the holiday with me and my family," he said in one breathless rush, as if he'd rehearsed it.

She sipped from her straw and inhaled the vanilla fragrance, but couldn't enjoy that last mouthful. "That's not a good idea, Tom."

"We're engaged, Vita! They're going to have to accept you." His tone intensified.

"Not if you have to force me down their throats, on Christmas of all days."

"You don't want to spend Christmas with your future husband?" He leaned toward her.

"I haven't even thought of Christmas. The future scares me right now. Even a few months into the future. There's so much going on." She pushed the glass across the counter. Since the first time she'd discovered the sinful delight of them, she'd never failed to suck the last drop out of a vanilla malted.

As his hand covered hers, she wished they were alone, his arms around her. That led to her old factory-worker daydreams: the elegant brownstone with the cozy parlor fireplace—and no worries.

"We're going to be married, Vita. You're going to be part of my family. Christmas without you wouldn't even be like Christmas. The families are just going to have to respect our wishes and live with it."

"My family has never respected much of anything." Her voice dripped with bitterness. "I don't know how to convince my father you're the only man for me."

"I want us to be married by Easter," he insisted, his voice calm and even, but with a quiver of desperation.

"I don't think that'll be possible." She shook her head sadly, wishing she could have married him that night in Madame's parlor. "That's way too soon."

"Are you sure it's just your family? Or are you beginning to have doubts?" His voice turned grave.

"No!" She found his foot with hers under the counter and pressed against it. "I've got the campaign to think about now. And what I'm going to do after election day."

"You'll just go work at the bank as usual."

She held up a hand. "Oh, no. Nothing's going to be as usual. And I don't plan on going back to the bank."

He winced. "Huh? Why not?"

"Because Billy Strong is going to win," she declared in triumph, giving him her sassiest grin.

She ignored his snicker, took her glass, and sucked heartily on the straw. His doubts didn't bother her anymore. Because, in a few weeks' time, she'd be the one laughing.

"I'll tell you what I'd like to do after election day," he said. "If Strong loses, will you marry me the day after election day, no matter what your family says?"

She shook her head. "You know I can't do something like that, Tom. One's got nothing to do with the other."

He went on, "And if he wins, just take as much time as you need."

"I told you—"

He cut her off. "Can I get the marriage license and set it with the justice of the peace?"

"No! I want a church wedding."

He grinned. "Aha. So I'm closer. Now I know where you want to get married, and I think I know why. I just don't know when."

"Two out of three ain't bad." She twirled her straw.

"I just can't wait for you to be my wife, Vita." He grabbed her hand.

"When the time is right, you'll be the first to know."

"You're not giving me the mitten here, are you?" he asked with mock caution.

"Of course not. I accepted your proposal. I will never change my mind." She stared into her empty glass. "I just can't make any promises right now."

"Then I don't think you'll make such a great politician." His cocked brow matched his haughty tone.

"All right!" She released a huff of breath. "I don't want to wait any longer, either. I want it all, I want it now, and what's the sense of having a wonderful job without a new husband to make my life complete? Why wait?" She looked at him and said, "I'll marry you after the election. But I have to choose a wedding dress— bridal things. And I can't do that all by tomorrow. That's as close to eloping as we can get without actually letting you sweep me away."

"Oh, yeah." A smile played on his lips. "Eloping's romantic, all right. But there's no anticipation. And the anticipation of your wedding day is the most exciting part."

"Almost," she teased.

****

The next morning, another invitation arrived from the mayor's office, engraved in the same elegant script. She unfolded the creamy parchment, wondering how she could decline politely this time. But it wasn't for dinner. It was for a gathering at his country estate in Croton-on-Hudson on Saturday.

She'd promised to take Jadwiga out for a birthday dinner, so that night as they preened in front of the full-length mirror, Vita spilled about the invitation.

"You're on dangerous ground, kiddo," Jadwiga warned. It always amazed Vita how Jadwiga could apply lip color and talk at the same time. "Pumping Mayor Grant, having dinner with him, now accepting an invitation at a political—watchamacallit—soirée. When I said spy, I meant do it so he wouldn't know."

"I'm not spying." Vita wound a lock of her hair around the curling tongs. "I'm just trying to see how Grant's mind works, what makes him tick. Find out his good points, and he does have some. Besides liking good Italian wine. He's got an amazing mind. He's smart and shrewd."

"So are you. What can he teach you?" She blotted her lips. "You could prob'ly teach him."

"Yeah, but he's been at it much longer than me. I know he's corrupt and crooked and manipulates people. But he's also a brilliant politician, and I think the best way to learn the ropes is by spending time with the hangmen." Vita set down the curling tongs. "Jadwiga, you know I want to be in his position someday, or close to it. If not New York's first female mayor, then at least councilwoman. What better way to learn than from the master himself?"

"I think you're skatin' on thin ice." She turned Vita to her and swirled peach rouge on her cheeks. "Don't let him charm you too much."

"Charm me! He could never charm me, as much as he's tried. I'm always a step ahead of him." She kept her face as still as possible while Jadwiga rouged her cheeks.

"But it's dangerous," Jadwiga warned as Vita moved her head to sneeze. "Hold still! You'll make me smear it."

"I know politics is dangerous, but it's exciting." She tried to talk without moving her lips as Jadwiga dabbed red lipstick on her. "In that position, I would have the power to do as much good as they've done bad." She blotted her lips with a cloth. "Maybe when Mayor Grant is just a name in the history books I can tell my grandchildren that I knew him and, in a roundabout way, without knowing it, he gave me my start."

"If he don't finish you first." She drew a beauty mark on Vita's cheek with a brown pencil.

"I got men like him figured out. They're not all that hard to figure out. It's simple. They're all variations on my papa." She looked at herself in the mirror and admired her glamorous reflection.

Jadwiga spritzed perfume on Vita's wrists. "You're dealing with the machine here."

"Yes, and it's about to break down." Vita took the bottle and spritzed a bit extra on her neck. Just in case she ran into Tom. He loved kissing her there.

****

Butchie stopped by to see Vita at Billy Strong's headquarters the following evening as she made up placards and flyers. Coffeepots and boxes of pastries sat on tables all over the room. Before coming up to her, he helped himself to a cream horn.

"Hey, Vita, it goin' okay?"

"Swell." She wiped ink from her hands and held up her newest placard that shouted WE NEED A *STRONG* NEW YORK.

"You got some black stuff on your face." He wiped her cheek with a finger.

"Oh, it's more ink. We've been making these placards."

"Gimme some. I'll take them down the club," he offered.

"I thought they had a bunch down there."

"Nah, they all took 'em home and put 'em in windows." He bit into his cream horn.

"They're not supposed to be window coverings, Butchie."

"All right, then when he wins, we'll all be rich and buy curtains." He grinned.

Vita gave her brother a hug. "So what brings you here, Butchie? Want to join the campaign?"

"Nah, Papa wants ya to come home to eat. He wants to see ya."

"Then why did he send you?" She held up another placard.

"You know Papa." He gobbled up the cream horn.

"Is he sorry? For what he said about Tom?" She waved the placard through the air to dry the ink.

"You know Papa," he repeated.

That was her answer. "Butchie—" She hadn't

planned to tell him, but couldn't hold it in any longer. "Tom wants to marry me the day after election day."

"He wants? Can't wait, huh?" He *tsk*'d.

"I told him yes, Butchie. Now if only I could have Papa's blessing, it would make everything perfect."

Butchie's eyes brightened. "Hey, if you love the guy, then—ah, what the hell." He raised his hands and dropped them to his sides. Since the murder ordeal, he'd lost that fighting spirit. But he seemed to savor each day now.

"He really is a good man, Butchie. And don't forget, he saved your life," she reminded him.

"Yeah, you'll never let me forget it."

"You've been acting like you've been given a new life, and that really makes me happy," she told him in all sincerity.

"Yeah, makes me happy, too. That was a close call." He let out a low whistle as his eyes darkened.

"Oh, Butchie, I'm so glad I got you and Papa back." Tears filled her eyes, and she clutched her brother's hand. He pulled away. He wasn't one for public displays of affection either. "So why doesn't Papa realize?"

"He's Papa." Butchie shrugged. "He lived most of his life. He feels he's gonna die anyway. In the cooler, he kept sayin' he wanted to die. Even when we come home, he said the same thing. 'Oh, I wished I could'a died!' He's just pissed off at everything, pissed off at everybody. That's Papa. He's just Papa."

"How about Vinny?" she asked.

"He don't ever think for himself. He always does what Papa does. Papa says 'shit,' Vinny squats. You know that."

"Rose say anything?" she asked.

"Nah. Not in front of Papa. But the jail thing scared her, too. She's been behavin' herself." He patted his pocket for a cigarette pack. "So you comin' or what?"

"I planned on working here tonight. Tell Papa I'll come by tomorrow. I have some money I want to give him anyway."

"See ya." He turned and walked away, grabbing an armful of placards on his way out. She thanked God for Butchie's second chance at life as she got back to writing her placards. NEW YORK IS WEAK WITHOUT STRONG! shouted her next one.

So she wasn't Emily Dickinson. But it got the message across.

****

She walked into her family's kitchen the following night to see a young man sitting at the table drinking wine and playing cards with Papa. He looked up at her, stood, and brushed his trousers down. She saw him struggling to make a forced smile appear sincere. He looked like he'd spent the summer sailing around Sicily. His olive skin glowed. His black hair and eyes shone. He dressed like a dandy, with that Republican look—tailored suit, crisp white shirt, gold cufflinks.

"Vita, this here's Roberto Riccadonna. Roberto, this is my daughter I told you about." Papa jerked his thumb toward the poised gentleman.

Roberto stepped up to Vita, took her hand and kissed it. A politician in the making. If Billy Strong had his looks, he'd be president. She nodded a polite hello and knew right then what Papa was up to. Well, it wouldn't work. Even if she did find the *bellimbusto* attractive, which she didn't. He looked like any of a hundred *paesani* pushing carts, digging ditches, and working the railroads. Besides, she was in love with Tom. But that didn't matter to Papa, and that made her blood boil.

"His father owns Riccadonna Music Company," Papa boasted, as if Riccadonna Music Company were Consolidated Edison. *Now he's trying to stick me with an organ grinder.* She scowled.

"We publish music," Roberto Riccadonna informed her.

She wasn't very musical, so she didn't have much interest in the business.

He named a few songs she'd never heard of. "I'd like to serenade you, Vita." He pointed to his mandolin in the corner.

So Papa had dug up a musical Dickens. She glared at Papa shuffling his cards, brandishing a smug grin.

Rosalia lumbered in, looked at Vita, then at Roberto, and tried to keep a straight face.

Vita ignored her ill-fated suitor and walked over to the stove. "Don't tell me you actually cooked something, Rose." Sauce simmered; meatballs sizzled in a pan, ziti boiled in yet another pot. Rosalia opened the oven and pulled out a loaf of bread. "Who did all this for you?" Vita whispered through the side of her mouth as she took a stack of plates off the shelf.

"Neighbors," she murmured back.

Vita turned to the table with the bread and caught Rosalia wistfully gazing at Roberto, as if she were thinking, *Oh, what I've missed!* Well, she could have him. Vita's appetite vanished. But she didn't want to storm out of there leaving Papa upset and poor Roberto all alone with his mandolin and nobody to serenade.

She couldn't let Papa down. She'd almost lost him, and she had to put up with his pathetic attempt to find her a suitor. She'd explain it all to Roberto later, out of Papa's earshot.

So the four of them sat down and ate supper. Papa and Roberto did all the talking and Rosalia did all the eating.

Vita was too busy missing Tom, wishing that was him sitting there with Papa beaming instead of this poor dupe. She turned and gave Roberto a good hard look as he spoke in perfect English, held his knife and fork just so, posture erect, elbows off the table.

She measured him up to Tom. No, he didn't even rate. He didn't have Tom's street-hardened wisdom in his eyes, the frisky smile that creased his cheeks. Tom's genuine demeanor outshone this man's practiced slickness.

She saw nothing genuine about Roberto Riccadonna. She could tell he'd been through this charade before and struck out every time. She itched to ask Papa, "If he's such a gem, why is he still single?"

He gave freely of his compliments and flattery. Rosalia lapped it up like the frosting on a rum cake.

"An extraordinarily pantagruelian meal," Roberto remarked, patting his mouth with his napkin.

"What's panta—whatever you said?" Rosalia smacked her lips; whether it was over her cannoli or him, Vita couldn't tell.

"It's a gigantic meal. The term derives from the name of a character, Pantagruel, invented by Rabelais in the sixteenth century. I learned that on a tour of the Touraine. That's in France."

Vita figured he enjoyed educating Rosalia with this

historical geography lesson.

"Oh, yeah." Rosalia nodded as if she'd known it all along, rolling her eyes over to Papa, who looked at Roberto like he'd just invented Gaglioppo.

He sang a few songs in Italian and played his mandolin with practiced skill. But although his voice lilted and played over the melodies and his fingers expertly strummed the strings, it just didn't move her. He was a performer at heart, but she didn't warm up to performers. Mayor Grant was a performer, always on stage, hiding behind a mask of style and refinement. Tom's face was his own, and though he didn't wear his heart on his sleeve, his feelings ran deep. It just took a keen sense and a caring heart to bring them out.

After the final strains of the third song faded into the peeling plaster, Vita jumped to her feet. "No time for an encore. I'm beat."

Papa surprised her by asking Roberto to escort her to her boardinghouse. So Papa trusted him that much. Of course Roberto had to act the perfect gentleman. That one kiss on the hand was for Papa's benefit—the only physical contact he'd ever have with her.

As they walked, without any prompting from her, he began telling her all about himself, his autobiography even better rehearsed than his singing.

"I was born on the ship coming over, halfway through the voyage. I was blue and thin. I almost died. I started showing signs of survival, and all the *signore* nursed me to health. Then poor Mama, they wouldn't let her enter Ellis Island because she had trachoma. They sent her back to Calabria. My poor Mama died, and my father married my Zia Anna. He started as a street musician and now the store takes the whole corner of Varick and Broome."

He went on and on, proudly, his speaking voice very much like his singing. She listened politely, nodding and interjecting with an "oh, really?" or a "my word!" here and there. But she looked forward to the excitement of getting home and washing out her stockings.

They reached her door, and now it was her turn to speak.

"Roberto, I don't know what my father told you, but I'm not available."

He tried to pretend he didn't know what she was talking about, but he didn't have his mandolin to hide behind. A pang of pity stabbed at her. Aside from the delicious meal their neighbors had cooked and let Rosalia pass off as hers, he'd wasted his entire evening, letting himself in for a shattering disappointment. "Your father didn't tell me anything, Vita."

She gave him a narrow-eyed stare. "Then how'd you wind up at my father's place? You were taking a stroll down Mott Street with your mandolin and decided to stop in?"

"No, of course not. He invited me ahead of time and told me he'd like for you to meet me—"

"Aha." She raised her chin. "So that's it, then. He did set it up. Well, I'm telling you, Roberto, I'm sorry you came out for nothing, but I'm just not eligible."

"But I thought we got along very well together." His lips spread into that slick smile that didn't reach his eyes. "You like my singing, I'm sure you'd like my family, and they'd love you."

His family! Dear God, he sure planned ahead.

"It's nothing personal, Roberto. Believe me, it's

nothing to do with you." She didn't want to be responsible for him trudging back to his Gramercy Park brownstone and flinging his mandolin off the balcony, never again to woo a prospective bride with song.

"Ah. I know what it really is." He gave her a nod with a cocked brow. "You're smitten with someone else."

"It's much more than smitten." She breathed a longing sigh as Tom entered her thoughts. "I'm very much in love with him."

"Then it wasn't me your eyes were lighting up for when I was singing or flattering you."

She shook her head. "I'm sorry, Roberto. But my father tried to manipulate both of us. I'm sorry it didn't work out."

"If you ever fall out of love, you'll let me know?"

"That won't happen," she confirmed

"I should have known." His gaze raked over her. "That sparkle in your eyes, that smile—it's too real. It's not the starstruck look of love at first sight. I think too highly of myself sometimes." He looked down at his polished shoes.

"Well, too much humility isn't good either," she said.

"I feel very humbled right now," he said as if in confession.

"Somehow I don't think it'll last long."

"Your papa's going to be very disappointed," he said. "I think he saw us being together."

Somehow she didn't think Papa's disappointment dragged the melancholy into his voice. "He's been disappointed before and gotten over it. Don't worry about Papa."

"Well, *buona sera*, then, Vita. I do hope we get to meet again."

"Good night, Roberto." She got her kissing hand busy digging for her key and her other hand occupied holding her bag. His walk, in retreat, was nothing like his cocky strut of the early evening.

She concluded, as she climbed the stairs, they must've struck some deal. She had no dowry. He was from a well-to-do, well-respected family. Well, she wasn't a commodity to be traded on Wall Street. She wouldn't let Papa do to her what he'd done to Rosalia. Oh, how badly she wanted Tom here!

****

She also wanted Tom at Billy Strong's fundraising dinner at Delmonico's. At fifty dollars a plate, she'd been invited to bring a guest of her own. But he had to work. She doubted he would've gone anyway. He wouldn't be seen at a fundraiser for the opposition. Cops were Tammany men, bought by Tammany and just as good as Tammany property. So she brought Butchie instead. He had a ball.

This was how she imagined a high-class wedding would be: a string quartet, gourmet cuisine, gents and ladies in finery they owned, not borrowed or rented.

"Butchie!" She tugged on his sleeve when she saw two familiar figures rising from their table. "Those two guys—I saw those two giving money to Tom once. They're on Grant's payroll. What are they doing here? Spying?"

"Dunno." He shrugged. "Could be. Want me to go talk to 'em?"

"No, of course not. I'll tell the campaign manager."

She informed the campaign manager she'd seen

those two before and thought they were on Grant's payroll, but she didn't elaborate.

Still, she wondered.

Chapter Twenty-Six

The following morning, dressed for Mayor Grant's upriver soirée, Vita sat in Madame's parlor, her shaking hands spilling her tea into the saucer. The collar of her new blouse scratched her neck. But if Jadwiga were here, she'd have told Vita she looked positively "deeeee-vine!"

The polished cream gold-trimmed carriage arrived at nine sharp. The driver escorted her out of the boardinghouse and into the carriage. Nosy neighbors hung out their windows, gawking. *What must they be thinking of me?* Then she shrugged. *Eh, who cares?*

So she sat back and closed her eyes as the carriage glided up the street and out of the city. Now she did the gawking at the rolling countryside. She'd never been north of Central Park. She'd never been to Haarlem, the Bronx, or Brooklyn. She felt like a princess in a fairy tale. She wondered if this was all a dream and she'd wake up slumped over her worktable in a factory with a half-sewn sleeve in her hands. But she knew she'd pay a price for all this.

She breathed in the crisp autumn air. The leaves shimmered in their deep reds and golds, aflutter like confetti. She wanted to reach out, grab a bunch in her hand, and keep them, to freeze this beautiful day in her mind forever.

The carriage turned into a wide gravel drive

between two marble posts. As the ornate gates swung open, she craned her neck to see the graceful white mansion. Even the two-story carriage house was larger than her dream home. The driver helped her down under a portico, and she entered the double doors opening to a marble-floored foyer. A white-jacketed butler greeted her and escorted her to a grand ballroom. A woman played a shiny grand piano as guests milled about, speaking in soft tones. Waiters darted around with sandwiches and drinks on silver trays.

The mayor appeared, casually dressed in brown trousers and a tailored tan jacket. "Miss Caputo! Welcome! So glad you could come!"

"The house is just beautiful," was all she could manage to say as she tried not to gawk. Could those Fifth Avenue mansions be any more opulent inside than this?

She mingled, not saying too much, and when anyone badmouthed Billy Strong, which was about every other sentence, she shut up or excused herself and moved on to the next loose circle. She avoided the tighter circles. The tighter the circle, the more loyal to the machine, so she stuck to safe territory.

She wandered off and found herself on a flagstone terrace overlooking an emerald green lawn that sloped down to the river. She knew Tom wanted to own something like this someday, but a manicured estate with stables, tennis courts, and carriage houses wasn't for her. People bought these things for one reason—to show off.

She strolled back into the house, observed a few paintings on the walls, and peeked into a room displaying marble statues.

What is this, a residence or a museum?

Returning to the ballroom, she heard a familiar voice. Stunned, she turned, and there he was, her fiancé, laughing and dallying with two poised, coiffed, richly dressed ladies. He saw her. With shoulders squared and head high, she walked away. "Vita!" he called after her as she headed down a corridor covered in framed oil paintings.

He followed her out to the terrace. She knew he backed Grant, but she hadn't known he was hearty enough with the mayor for an invite to this shindig.

"What are you doing here, Vita?" he asked as she watched a man rowing a canoe up the river. "Will you mind telling me what you're doing here, and how you got the mayor to give you a personal invitation?" His eyes blazed.

She met them with her own, unblinking. "Mayor Grant comes into the bank a lot. He sent the invitation."

"Just like that?" he inquired with a sharp eye. "How well have you gotten to know him?"

"No better than you, I'm sure," she replied evenly. "We're not on a first name basis, if that's what you're hinting at."

"I'm not hinting." He crossed his arms over his chest.

"I'm just as curious, Tom—what prompted him to extend an invitation to you?" She turned the tables.

"He invited the higher-ranking police officers. I came in Sergeant Munn's stead." He didn't skip a beat, not that she'd expected him to.

"And you hardly know Grant at all?" she quizzed, curious to get it out of him.

"I've met him once or twice." He paused and took

a breath. "We're not personal friends, no. And what is a Strong supporter doing here at Mayor Grant's house?"

"I told you. I met the mayor a few times at the bank, and he invited me."

"Come on, Vita." He smirked and shook his head. "This is the mayor we're talking about. He doesn't go inviting bank tellers to his country estate. What's really going on?"

"That's what I'd like to know about you. What is going on, Tom? With you and these politicians. Exchanging envelopes in alleyways, going off your beat, working all these odd hours. I know I can love you despite all that, but I hoped it would all change. And it scares me. Especially since I want to enter politics as one of the honest ones. It makes me wonder."

He nodded, his eyes sliding shut. He reopened them, focusing directly into hers. "Vita, I don't want anything to come between us, and— Good Lord! Especially politics. So I'll be up front with you if you're up front with me."

"About what you've been doing?" she asked.

"Yes."

Just then the mayor came trundling out onto the terrace, leading a small group, their jeweled fingers clasped around cocktails, ice clinking in their glasses. "Ah, here's one of my trusted colleagues and one of my newest campaigners, I hope," he said with a jovial air.

Tom, one of his trusted colleagues?

"Just going to give these folks the grand tour of the grounds. Then it's time to sit down to our midday meal. Come join us." He clutched Tom's shoulder and whisked him away. His dedicated lackeys followed.

So he did have something to tell her. Her stomach churned, despite the enticing midday meal.

A dinner bell rang, and she joined the crowd in the dining room. Three huge tables stood side by side, covered with pure white linen, delicate china, and glistening crystal. Sunlight streamed through the French doors. It looked like a state dinner at the White House. A waiter seated her in a velvet chair between a ward heeler and the chairman of the election committee. Tom sat at another table, his back to her. It was obvious they couldn't do any more talking alone. After dinner, the groups broke into twos and fours for tennis and croquet. When the mayor corralled Tom into a tennis foursome, she'd had enough. After paying her respects to the host, she called for the carriage. Enough of this high society. She needed to get back to Bohemia.

****

She expected Tom to call on her after she got home, so she stayed put. She sat in the parlor, chatting with Madame Branchard and Stephen Crane, an author who'd just taken a room there. When they asked her to join them at Three Steps Down, she declined. She wanted to wait for Tom. Alone she sat, halfheartedly reading one of Stephen Crane's short stories, glancing out the window every five minutes. When darkness fell, she fetched her pipe and came back down the stairs. One of the boarders answered a knock at the front door. Her heart leapt as she heard Tom's voice. She dashed back upstairs to pull the pins from her bun and shake her hair free.

His eyes followed her all the way down the stairs to the entry hall. Alone, finally!

"Why did you leave Grant's party?" He followed

her into the parlor, taking his usual spot on the sofa.

"I'm no good at tennis or croquet." She sat in a chair opposite him. "And I didn't want to raise any more suspicion. I didn't want you accusing me of being, as you said, 'friendly' with the mayor."

"Vita, seeing you there was the biggest surprise I've had in a long time. I had to look twice to make sure it was you. I never expected you to be there. The last place I could ever imagine running into you was at Mayor Grant's country home."

"All right, so he took a liking to me. He wants me to campaign for him." She brandished a grin which she hoped looked cavalier enough.

"Does he know you're supporting Strong?" he asked.

She nodded. "He sure does. But after what he thinks will be his victory, he promised he'd give me a city job."

"On what basis did he offer you all this?" He cocked his head, sounding skeptical.

"Mr. Johnson must have told him I'm a good worker. But I can see what he wants. He knows I'm active in reform and my cousin's the mayor of Mott Street. He did some digging on me, all right. Luckily, he likes what he sees. But he also needs the Italian vote. Maybe Tammany's starting to realize there's a lot of us out there, and some of us can read and write English well enough to vote." She gave him a repeat of that grin. "He's afraid of Billy Strong and of Ted Roosevelt, no matter what he says from behind his whiskers. Billy's gaining a lot of support, and it's scaring Grant."

"So what are you doing?" he pressed on. "Campaigning for the both of them?"

"No, I'm just getting to know Grant to see what I can learn from him." She got up and sat next to him, but not courting close.

"Listen, Vita." He sat forward. "Either you're with one candidate or the other. Don't play both sides."

"I know what I'm doing," was all she'd say. "So what were you going to tell me, that you should have told me months ago?"

"I never should have told you, and I shouldn't be telling you now. But I need to be honest if we're going to be husband and wife. Nothing like politics is going to stand in our way. I've been working undercover, Vita."

Her heart surged. "How?"

"That's why I've been dealing with those wardmen. We're just beginning to investigate Tammany's ties to all the corruption."

She blinked and inhaled a sharp breath. "You're part of the Lexow Committee? I've been reading articles in the *Times* about them investigating Tammany's dirty work."

"No, I'm not on the committee, but they've been doing a good job. We even have a minister, Charlie Parkhurst, going around in disguise to all the saloons, rum-holes, and clip joints, and reporting back to us what goes on there, how much the wardmen are taking in protection money from the business owners, how much they've been handing over to the police captain"—he counted on his fingers—"and where it all goes, all the way up the line to Tammany. I've been doing things just like that, in disguise, too. But I can't tell another soul about any of it, except my father. I'm telling you because you're going to be my wife, and I'll never keep anything from you."

She craved that surge of relief, but a knot in her gut just wouldn't go away.

"These are dangerous people you're dealing with. Do you really have to do this? Look at what they did to your cousin. I don't want that happening to you!" She inched closer, now within courting distance.

"Mike was in over his head." Now he moved closer. "His problem was that he didn't keep his mouth shut. That's why I had to keep mine shut. If what I just told you never leaves this room, we'll be just fine."

"But why do you have to do this?" she badgered him.

"Because I care about this city as much as you do. I'm one of the few honest cops on the force. Roosevelt and the rest of us are trying to change it. We needed a few brave souls to start, or it never would have happened. So that's where I am."

She leaned forward till their knees touched, but she stopped short of an embrace. Boarders always came into the parlor at this hour. A lamplighter lit the gas lamp outside. A soft glow reached Tom's eyes.

"Tom, I'm worried. I don't want you in any kind of danger. But I'm so relieved you told me. Dear God, I was thinking—never mind what I was thinking." She waved her hands. "I'm relieved that you told me, but I'm still worried something's going to happen to you."

"Nothing'll happen. This won't go on much longer. I'm up for a promotion—one that I won't have to pay for—and I'm doing what I feel is right. I don't want you worrying about me now."

"Doesn't it make you feel better to have shared it with me?" A surge of relief swept over her.

"Now that I have, yes." His shoulders relaxed. "It's

a load off my mind."

As they shared a smile, sweet music started floating in through the open window. She recognized the song. That voice, that melodic strumming…oh, no! Roberto Riccadonna serenading her!

Tom turned toward the window, where a shadowy figure stood in the light of the streetlamp. "That's awful loud. Not only that, it's just plain awful."

"Er—excuse me." She went to the window and leaned out. "Stop it!" she demanded through clenched teeth.

His shoes shone in the streetlamp. He stopped playing and bowed to her.

Two other boarders came in, and Roberto took that opportunity to slither his way into the hall. "Nobody invited you in here, Roberto." She faced him in the parlor doorway.

Tom stood and swaggered over to them. "Do you know this person, Vita?" He stared Roberto down. She saw his attempt to keep that detached cop's eye.

"Allow me to introduce myself. I am Mr. Roberto Riccadonna." He offered Tom his hand.

Tom extended his hand and pumped Roberto's once.

"I've come to serenade the most beautiful lady in New York City." He held out his mandolin like a trophy. Tom puffed his chest out, looking ready to bust that mandolin over Roberto's varnished head.

"He's an Italian singer, Tom," she jumped in, desperate to keep her voice calm, but it wasn't easy. "He serenades women all the time. Then he—leaves." She emphasized that last word, trying to wedge her way past Roberto to the door to usher him out.

But his feet stayed fixed to the floor, his arms spread wide, giving her no room to pass. "I don't leave until I sing you the song I wrote just for you, *cara.* May I accompany you to the parlor?"

"Is this one of Strong's favors to campaign workers, Vita, musical errand boys?" Tom moved closer, forcing her back to the wall. She now stood between the two of them like a slice of bologna.

"I am no errand boy, Mister McRude. My family owns Riccadonna Music Publishing. It's got a saloon on one side and a brothel on the other, so you must have noticed it, stumbling out of one and staggering into the other." Roberto punctuated the end of his statement with a strum of an angry chord on the mandolin.

Tom reached across her and gave Roberto a shove. "Well, she doesn't need any serenading. Now get out of here before I book you for trespassing."

"Trespassing? Just what this city needs. Another leatherhead who makes his own laws." He stepped back and brushed his collar where Tom had touched him. "Well, take another look in your little rule book, because there's no law against courting."

"Courting!" Tom advanced, and she flattened closer against the wall. "Who do you think you're courting?"

She clutched at his arm. "Tom, stop it!"

Roberto retreated another step and swept his mandolin behind his back. "You're not serious about this—this street cop, are you?" He cocked his head and locked quizzical eyes into hers, like she'd just sprouted a third ear.

"I told you the other night, Roberto," she said

through clenched teeth. "I told you you were wasting your time."

"What did you tell him the other night, what other night?" Tom's furious breath blew hot in her ear.

She couldn't turn to face him, wedged between them and the wall. "It was my father!"

"So he's arranging a wedding with his daughter and one of his own countrymen? Then I hope you will be very happy together." Tom strode past her and Roberto, who'd backed up onto the first step, shielding his mandolin behind him. In a calm and dignified manner, head high, Tom walked out.

"Tom!" She dashed after him, but he shut the door in her face.

Roberto grabbed her hand. She pulled away. "Get away from me, you *asino!* Look what you've done!" She flung the door open, ran outside, and peered both ways, but he'd vanished.

Traffic clogged the street, and pedestrians crowded the sidewalks. She'd never find him in this mob. She couldn't go calling after him with so many people around. She didn't even know what direction he'd gone in.

She stomped back into the hallway. Roberto lounged on the steps, his mandolin cradled in his lap.

"Who do you think you are?" She set clenched fists on her hips. "You have a lot of nerve! You are *not* courting me. I told you I wasn't interested!"

"Then are you interested in this, *cara?*" He stood, placed the mandolin on the hall table, and reached into his pocket. He held out a blue velvet box and flipped it open. A diamond bigger than Mrs. Paluzzi's meatballs twinkled up at her. She slapped it out of his hand, and it landed on the rug. He bent over and swept it up.

"Vita, this is an expensive genuine diamond. It cost two hundred dollars. You don't just go tossing it around." He slipped it from the box and held it out to her. She couldn't stand the sight of it, or of him. "I've loved you from the moment I saw you, and I want you to be my wife. I can give you a life of luxury and comfort, a life that street cop could never dream of giving you. Even with all his payoffs. Say you'll marry me, *cara bella*."

She seethed in fury, chest tight, blood hot. "I never want to see you again! Get out of this house and don't come back." She pointed to the door as she backed down the hall toward the kitchen. "If you don't get out, I'll have you thrown out!"

He laughed, a devilish snicker that made her skin crawl. He slipped the ring on his pinkie and buffed it on his jacket.

"You're going against your father's wishes?"

"Damn right I am!" she shot back.

His looked down at her with disdain in his eyes, a sneer on his lips. *Good,* she thought. *Let him think I'm less than a lady.* She could make herself extremely undesirable if she wanted to.

"Vita, don't swear like that. It doesn't become you." He let out another sardonic laugh.

"Get the hell out," she repeated. "And if you come near me again, I'll have you arrested."

"By who? The copper? Somehow I don't think he'll be around here anymore."

"Get out, you smug bastard," she hissed.

He shook his head, *tsk*ing. "Such terrible language. I'll have to do something about that. Wash that little mouth out with soap." He finally turned to leave, and she gulped a tense breath. "*A piu tardi.*" He swept his mandolin off the stairs and vanished.

She ran up the stairs to her room. She found the pretty writing paper she'd bought on impulse, sat, and composed a heartfelt letter to Tom.

This was all my father's doing, she told him. *I only met this man once, and now he won't leave me alone. Please understand.*

She went in circles, explaining over and over.

She left it on the hall table for the postman to pick up first thing in the morning. She never wanted to hear mandolin music again.

Chapter Twenty-Seven

"Vita's got a head like a rock!" Butchie swore under his breath as he walked toward the Village looking for his sister's diggings. He stopped on the corner of West Third and Broadway, scratching his armpit, trying to remember if Vita's joint was on Washington Square North or South. He cut across the park and recognized the queer-looking gal with bright red hair standing in her doorway smoking. Vita's landlady, Madame something.

He walked up to her. "Hiya, remember me? I'm Vita's brother. She around?"

"No, she left early this morning. Said she was stopping by campaign headquarters and she'll be back late tonight." She clamped her lips around her pipe.

Butchie bent down and petted a black-and-white cat. "Okay, I'll see her there." As he turned to leave, he noticed an envelope addressed to Tom McGlory on the hall table. "Oh, I'll take this. I'm passin' right by the police station." He swept it up and stuck it into his kick. "Love letter from my sister to her beau, ya know."

She said goodbye and closed the door. When Butchie turned the corner, he ripped the envelope into pieces and threw it on the nearest rubbish heap.

His sister would be Mrs. Roberto Riccadonna by next Easter, if he had anything to do with it.

****

With election day exactly one week away, the campaigners ran around headquarters making last-minute placards, telling jokes, and trying to ease the tension. Candidate Strong made speeches all over the city. He'd developed a loyal following, and Vita thanked all her Italian neighbors for supporting him.

Tom didn't come by at the bank or at the boardinghouse. He had to have gotten her letter at least two days ago. Three days had passed since the disaster with Roberto. But Vita was so wrapped up in the election and work, her only thoughts of Tom came late at night when she fell into bed. Every night she dreamed they were bride and groom, on a whirlwind tour of Europe, no one and nothing disrupting their happiness.

She pictured him sitting and reading her letter over and over with that special smile of his. But why hadn't he called on her?

****

She got to campaign headquarters at seven that night. The air seemed to vibrate with tension as it got close to the wire. Nervous giggles flitted through the room as everybody scuttled around. Candidate Strong's speechwriter huddled in the corner, chewing on a pen. Vita brought him a cup of coffee. "Oh, no, thanks, Vita, I'm jumpy enough as it is." So she kept it for herself. She held it to her lips, about to take a sip.

"Hello, *cara*." The voice in her right ear startled her.

She turned, faced a beaming Roberto, and accidentally spilled coffee on his jacket. He smiled and brushed it off, flicking drops off his fingers.

"What are you doing here, Roberto?" She couldn't

keep the loathing out of her voice.

"Working. I'm William Strong's newest campaigner." His phony smile turned her stomach. He smelled of tooth powder. Wintergreen. Ptui!

"Why can't you leave me alone?"

"Face it, Vita. Your father wants us married." The phony smile stayed plastered to his lips.

"And why don't you face it. I don't want us married, so we're not getting married. Now get lost." She headed for the door, not looking to see if he followed her.

She jumped onto a streetcar, rode uptown, and walked around until nine o'clock. She passed rows of elegant brownstones with fancy railings. As she peeked into the floor-length windows hung with heavy drapes and lighted from within, she let her mind wander to her future. Here it was—on one of these numbered streets, behind a lacy iron gate, in a cozy living room cuddled up with Tom on a plush velvet couch. *What's going to happen with Tom now?* If only he would just answer her letter! God, he must have been hurt bad. Or maybe he's just too busy with his own work. Or…

She stopped asking questions she couldn't answer and planned to straighten it all out tomorrow—after the election. Billy Strong's election.

****

Tom entered an empty St. Andrew's and walked up the center aisle at two in the afternoon. He entered his favorite pew, genuflected, knelt on the padded kneeler, and clasped his hands. "Hey, Mike, you there, Shorty?" Mike's face came into focus in his mind. Tom smiled. "Hey, buddy." His dear cousin's spirit filled the church, warming the chilly air.

"I don't know if the big date's ever gonna happen now," he whispered, seeking the reassurance only Mike could give him when he was alive, whether it was pulling Tom from an oncoming streetcar or getting him through another night on the beat. "There's this Roberto guy, a suitor her father arranged. He comes up to the window strumming a mandolin, singing '*O Sole Mio.*' Then she insists it's all her father's doing and she's not engaged to him at all. Right out of *Romeo and Juliet*, except I couldn't figure out where I fit in." He shook his head, cradling it in his clasped hands. "I felt like scenery in a really bad play or something. Like it wasn't for real. It would have amazed you, Shorty."

But would it? Mike was in heaven with their crazy Uncle Eddie. What would amaze him?

"Our big day was supposed to be the day after election day and—that's what we'd planned. But of course we want to get married again in church. Right here, with you watching us."

All of a sudden he knew he shouldn't be here any longer. An almost physical push brought him to his feet. "Yeah, I'm going." *Get out of here and win her back!* He heard Mike's voice in his ear, pushing him out of there, back into Vita's heart where he belonged.

And for God's sakes, vote for William Strong.

"Yeah, I was gonna do that anyway." He chuckled as he swung the door open and stepped back into the light and sounds of the real world—here, no spirits dwelled, just mere mortals. He stepped into the busy stream.

He'd already decided to vote for William Strong. Tom's appearance at Grant's country soirée had only been part of his undercover job. He saw what he wanted to see and took an accounting of who showed up. But he'd had too powerful a change of heart to support Mayor Grant any longer. Too much had happened for him to stay in Grant's camp. He'd heard some Tammany scuttlebutt about Grant getting double and triple votes from cohorts and dead people. That was nothing unusual, but it wasn't helping Strong, a good, clean reformist candidate with no Tammany connections. Strong believed in what Tom believed in. But most of all, he was Vita's candidate. Although he didn't think the guy had a chance, especially with Grant's vote-rigging, he really wanted Strong to win the election.

But first he had to win Vita back.

He strode through the bank doors, heels clicking on the polished floor. Three tellers were working. But not Vita.

Oh, God, where is she? "Excuse me, please." He politely jumped the line. Patrons stepped aside for the uniformed cop.

"Excuse me, is Miss Caputo here?" he asked the nearest teller.

"No, she's out, Officer."

"Alone?" He just had to know.

The teller hesitated, then blurted out, "No, sir, with a man. I don't know who he is." She cowered, as if expecting a line of questioning. Tom thanked her and walked away.

So where to go now? He didn't want to lurk around and confront her when she returned with "*O Sole Mio*." But tonight was the election, and she'd be running over to headquarters. She wouldn't want to stop for ice cream or go back to her parlor to meld hearts. There just wasn't time for a romantic encounter in the next twenty-four hours.

So he decided to go to Strong's headquarters and watch the returns come in. She'd be there. He planned it all with the precision of a choreographer: arrive with flowers, meet her on the way out, and have a rented carriage take them to Astor House. They'd sit at a reserved table, hold hands, and make glorious plans for the future.

****

He alighted from the carriage, straightened his necktie, and entered Strong's headquarters. The returns were due any minute now.

The place was jammed, and not just with rich Republican bankers. Strong had amassed quite a following. Tom couldn't help but beam with pride for the guy. He had the guts to do this and get the glory he deserved. But in a few minutes he'd be facing a crushing defeat. His heart swelled with even more pride for Vita. She'd put her soul into this.

Streamers and bunting hung everywhere. It looked like one of those Italian block parties. Pans of sausages and pasta covered every table. Wine glasses clinked. He heard Italian, Yiddish, Greek, and English in a dozen different accents. Nudging his way through the crowd, he made his way up to a five-piece combo playing Italian music. Couples danced to the lively tune. He peered above all the jostling, bobbing heads. Then he saw Vita, dancing, laughing, like she was having the time of her life. His heart sank.

Then the band stopped, and a voice announced, "I'm going to play a song I wrote for Billy's campaign!"

The crowd roared. Tom glanced at the stage, and there stood Vita's Romeo. So he was a composer, too, not just a midnight serenader. He struck the opening chord on an accordion. Everyone stomped their feet and clapped along.

"The returns are in!" someone shouted. The music stopped. The crowd cheered.

Tom stood at the back and waited, tapping his foot, trying to stay calm. But he did have a stake in this. A very important one. This meant a lot to all of them, not just personally but for the future of New York City.

The place hushed, as quiet as a church. The voice echoed through the hall from the stage: "The returns are as follows: 57,492 for William Strong, and 59,337 for Mayor Grant. Mayor Grant is re-elected."

Gasps, groans, curses, sobs filled the room. Strong climbed up on the stage and faced his constituents with his head held high. "Please." He leaned over and wiped a woman's tears away. Standing back up, he swept his own moist eyes over the crowd. "You people have become my family. I can't tell you how much I appreciate all the hard work you've done for this campaign. Some of us might never meet again, but there will always be a bond between us, wherever life takes us, if we choose to stay here in New York or move away to the far reaches of the land. We'll always be part of that brave group whose first sight of America was that beautiful lady standing in New York Harbor with her torch held high." He raised a fist in the air. "Some of us left loved ones behind, never to see their faces or hold them in our arms again—all in the name of a better life for our children, all in the name of a faceless promise in a land where the abolition of slavery is only a few decades in the past, and corruption crawls out of City Hall into the streets. But we did it for a better life." He paused as applause thundered. "Somehow we knew America would give us something our native lands couldn't. And tonight we tried to make it an even better place. They beat us this time. But we can't ever give up. This isn't a defeat—it's merely a setback. We'll be together again someday—and we'll be stronger and wiser than we are tonight. And together we'll win." Applause burst out again. He didn't leave a dry eye in the house.

Tom fought back tears himself. His heart went out to William Strong. He saw Vita across the room weeping, and it destroyed him. He wanted to take her in his arms and hold her. Her sadness reached him like a physical blow to the stomach. He wanted to be up there with her, sharing this with her.

It just wasn't right. They'd buzzed about it at the precinct for weeks, those Tammany cronies of Grant's. The double and triple votes. At their picnic in the park, Vita had suggested the possibility of demanding a recount. "Never been done," had been his blunt answer. Nobody had ever dared. Not till tonight.

William Strong had rallied more support than anyone ever would have expected. The Tammany cohorts grumbled about that, too. So how hard could it be to rally an assembly and demand a recount?

Then he saw Vita and her Romeo embrace. "I gotta get outta here," he muttered. He returned the carriage early and didn't bother to ask for a refund.

****

Vita didn't want to get out of bed the next morning. She forced herself from the warm cocoon. Her feet hit the cold floor. She glanced out the window at a dark cloud enshrouding the city. As for herself, she wanted to burrow under the covers and let sleep reclaim her.

It was over. Her mind kept re-running that moment when they announced the returns. She'd started weeping. Roberto took her into his arms and as much as she detested him, she fell into his welcoming embrace, desperate for the comfort of another human being. It all came out at once. She'd sobbed her heart out, for all the hard work they'd done, all the convincing and hoping—she hurt so badly for Billy Strong up there on that stage, telling them he loved them all like family. Then the shock wore off, and she realized she was in another man's arms. She'd felt a familial bond with him because of the disappointment they'd just shared. But Roberto held her like he'd never let her go. She pulled away when she felt him pressing up against her a bit too suggestively with his male parts.

Whenever Tom held her, their hearts beat as one; their bodies melded; they fit so well together.

Oh, how she missed him!

So now what? Her political career was at a standstill, but she had other things to do.

After work she didn't want to go to her boardinghouse and gab, especially about politics. She'd been so used to running straight to headquarters, she wandered around with no place to go.

Newsboys stood on every corner shoving extra editions of the paper at passersby. People milled about in storefronts, at pushcarts. A buzz filled the air. She bought one of those papers and scanned the front page. Startled, she yelled out loud, "*Mama mia!*"

They'd done a recount. The election had been

fixed. The authorities hauled Grant and his cohorts in for questioning.

William Strong was the true victor.

She read the rest of the column. Her eye caught his name as if it were made of glue—Thomas McGlory. He'd consulted with Strong, and together they'd demanded a recount. It went on to say that Tammany bosses had bribed citizens to vote three and four times for Grant. In a daze, she read as she walked, bumping into people also reading and walking. She stumbled off a curb and fell. She headed to Jadwiga's place. Jadwiga threw the door open and shoved the front page at Vita.

"I got one too!" They tossed their papers in the air and danced around the room.

Jadwiga lit their pipes. As they puffed away, Vita even drank some of Jadwiga's crazy moonshine.

"Your beau's a hero! A recount! Who woulda had the guts to do that?" Jadwiga belted back another glassful.

"Jadwiga—" She took a ragged breath. "I don't think he's my beau anymore."

"What now?" She tossed a lock of hair over her shoulder and banged her pipe on the ashtray, not taking her eyes off Vita.

"Papa arranged for this *bellimbusto* to court me," she explained about Roberto. "He stood under the window, serenading me with his mandolin and his olive-oiled voicebox when Tom was there. Tom gave him a shove and…and that was the last time I saw him." Her voice quivered with a sob.

"He's just stewing in his own *golombki*. That's not all bad." She soothed Vita with a pat on the arm. "He'll be more flavorful the more he stews. But how deliciously romantic! The two of them with you in the middle! You musta felt like a real femme fatale." She smoothed wisps of hair off Vita's face.

"I felt like a slice of bologna between two slices of pastrami."

"Ah, hooey. Two handsome fellas sparring over the beautiful damsel? It's every girl's dream, honey. Tom might even challenge what's-his-name to a duel, you know…choose your weapons at dawn, ten paces, all that. Maybe the same field in Weehawken where Aaron Burr gunned down Al Hamilton."

"Don't even say that! No, nothing like that is going to happen." She cut the air with her hands.

"Then how you gonna stop Romeo from courtin' you?" Jadwiga pressed her.

"Just like I have been," she answered. "Just keep giving him the mitten till he gets the message."

"Ha!" Jadwiga let out a sharp New York laugh. "It'll come down to who's stronger, not how loud you can tell your organ grinder to pizzle off."

"What do you mean who's stronger? I don't want to talk about duels or—"

"I don't mean physical combat." Jadwiga waved her be-ringed fingers. "I mean who's stronger in staying power. Willing to pursue you till he gets you. And how hard has Tom been banging on your door?" She tilted her head with a quizzical eye.

"I told you, I haven't heard from him," she snapped.

"Then it's time for him to hear from you. That's if you still want him."

"Of course I do!" Vita turned away and stared out the window.

"Tell ya what. Let's go celebrate your new mayor's victory. We'll go to Tony Pastor's. Then I'll help ya figure out what to tell Tom when ya go see him tomorrow. If he ain't doing handsprings over you showing up, then maybe they did have a duel, and Roberto stabbed him in the wrong places. But let's go have fun."

Already on a high from Billy Strong's victory, Vita jumped at that suggestion. "Okey dokey, but I don't know what makes you think Tom would be tucked into his beddy-bye this early."

When they entered the jam-packed dance hall, she halted in her tracks, stunned. Showgirls, businessmen, politicians, their wives and mistresses, admiring citizens, the young and the old, crowded around a uniformed Officer Tom McGlory as if he'd been elected mayor. Mayor-elect Strong, who should have been sharing the glory, was nowhere to be seen.

"Let's get out of here." Vita nudged Jadwiga, but she shook her head.

"No! Go up to him. Let him know you're here."

As she turned to leave, Tom pushed through the crowd to get to her. Her heart slammed against her ribs.

"I don't want to interrupt your moment." She tried to keep her voice even as he approached. "Go back to your adoring public."

"Vita, this should be our celebration." He clutched her shoulders. "Your man won! I'm so glad you decided to come here. I wanted you to come here with me. They're throwing a big victory party here. Billy Strong was just here, but he went to his own round of parties. So—" He glanced over her shoulder. "Where's Romeo?"

"He's not my Romeo, Tom. Why can't you understand that?" she shouted above the crowd's cackle. "Didn't you read my letter at all?"

"What letter?" His eyes pinned her.

"The one I wrote you the other night." She leaned forward and stood on her toes as he bent over to hear her. "It got mailed the next day."

"I didn't get any letter." He shook his head.

"Now, how could that've happened?" she said, mostly to herself. "I know the postal service is slow, but—no, it couldn't have got lost."

"Maybe one of your poet friends decided to borrow it for inspiration."

"No, nobody in the house would ever do anything like that." She hoped.

"Well, no matter—what did it say?" he asked.

"I explained that the matchup was all Papa's doing—I'd never set eyes on Roberto Riccadonna in my life. Besides, he's the farthest thing from a suitor I would have chosen for myself anyway." Her words rushed out to convince him.

"Then why were you hugging him on election night?" Curiosity tinged his voice. It was not the tone of a jealous beau.

"I was so shattered, I just fell into the first pair of open arms I saw, and they were his. How do you know?" she asked. "Were you there?"

"Briefly. When I saw that, I turned and left."

She tilted her head in confusion. "But wait—why the sudden defection to Billy Strong's camp?"

He released a long breath. "There was nothing sudden about it. I couldn't vote for Grant. I didn't think Billy had a chance of winning, but I felt it was the right thing to do, to support him. All the cops did, in the end. We all knew he needed the support."

"Thank you," she told him in all sincerity.

They stood quietly, eyes locked, not hearing the voices or the music around them.

He peered at her hand. "Where's your ring?"

"At home." She glanced at her bare ring finger. "I didn't think I should wear it anymore."

"You mind if we go back and I put it back on for you?" He took her hand and held it to his lips.

"And leave your party?" She looked around. A few hangers-on still milled around him.

"It's not my party, Vita. It's the mayor's party." He nodded and smiled at a gent who patted him on the back on his way out.

"You don't care about all the crowds, the adoring and fawning?" She gestured around them.

"Couldn't care less. In fact, I hate it. I'd rather be in a nice quiet parlor alone with you. And I do mean quiet." As he spoke, a platinum blonde admirer circled his arm with her claws and whispered into his ear. Her escort tugged her away.

Vita waved to Jadwiga, deeply engrossed in conversation with her two poet friends. "Sorry to interrupt, but I've got him all to myself, and we're leaving."

"And don't you dare come back!" Jadwiga whispered in Vita's ear, giving her cheek a pinch.

Chapter Twenty-Eight

"I have this till noon tomorrow, so let's enjoy it."
Tom helped her into the two-seater, two bay horses in
the front, an elderly coachman at the helm. "Take us up
Fifth Avenue and around the park, please," Tom
instructed the driver.

He wants to be a nabob tonight, she thought.

She slid inside. The seats were a bit worn, nowhere
as showy as Mayor Grant's barouche, but she preferred
this.

"There'll be a lot more carriages, Vita, and they
won't be rented," he promised her.

"As long as we're together, I'm happy standing on
a streetcar." She settled against him, and he wrapped
his arm around her shoulders. "I don't need a Fifth
Avenue mansion," she told him once again as they clip-
clopped down the street.

"You don't buy a Fifth Avenue mansion because
you need one," he countered.

"No, you buy one to show off to snooty neighbors,
fellow country club members, and anybody else you
might feel you have to impress. That's not for me."

"I'm not trying to impress, either." He glanced past
her out the window. "I've had nothing, and now I want
it all." Burning desire hardened his tone.

"It's bad business to invest too many funds on one
of those anyway," she explained, realizing this was

325

their first serious discussion about their future. "Mansions don't produce income. Sure, they appreciate over time, but collecting rents—that's where the revenue stream comes in. And you also get the capital gain when you sell it. I plan to buy tenements, fix them up, and rent them. With the rental income, we can build nicer apartment buildings, parlay our profits, keep renting, keep parlaying. There's a fortune to be made in real estate."

"And where does the initial down payment come from?" he quizzed.

"From our friend at the bank, Mr. Johnson, of course. You did say he owed you two favors, didn't you?"

He cupped her chin. "Vita, do you realize we're actually talking about our future and for the first time it doesn't sound like some faraway dream?"

"I know!" She squeezed his hand and met his gaze. She saw their future in those eyes; they shone as bright as the future would be. "But there's just one thing."

"Your father," he answered for her.

"And yours," she added.

"He's not as opposed to my marrying as yours is."

"But he's not doing a jig over it." She looked down at the floor, a discarded cigarette butt between her feet.

"My folks appear standoffish when they don't know someone, Vita. They have trouble opening up, that's all. It's not that they don't like you."

"How come we never had that problem, opening up to each other?" She met his gaze and held it.

A streetlamp lit up his eyes as they rode by it. "If I recall correctly, we didn't exactly have a warm beginning. We weren't jumping into each other's arms unable to tear ourselves away, were we?"

"Not at first, but it was always there, wasn't it?" She engaged him in her flirting game.

"For me it was there the second I clamped my hand on your shoulder that morning." He touched it now. "I have to confess something to you, Vita."

She waited for a ton of bricks to drop on her head—he'd been hiding a fiancée, he'd been married and divorced, those adorable children were really his—she knew how seriously the Irish took confession.

"Remember I told you to stay put after that urchin lifted my wallet?" he ventured.

She nodded, expelling a relieved breath. No ex-wife. No children. No shady past.

"When I got back there and you'd gone, I was shattered. I felt like I'd found a pot of gold and lost it. I wouldn't accept the possibility of never seeing you again. I had to get you back. And on the way to Mr. Violino's shooting scene, I stumbled over something on the ground." He grasped her hand. "It was a shirtwaist in the same blue as all that material you'd been holding. I made the connection and swept it up. I planned on going to every shirtwaist factory in New York and asking if they made that particular item, and describing you. Then when I saw it had the factory label on it, I felt like I'd struck gold again. It was so much easier to track you down, then." He sighed and closed his eyes. "I just couldn't wait for you outside the factory and start courting you. I had to go in and ask your boss about you. I didn't realize it would backfire the way it did, you getting fired. It was at that moment I knew I always wanted to take care of you."

"Not 'cause you felt sorry for me, getting me

fired?" Her eyes grew wide.

"No, I didn't feel sorry for you. You're not the type of person to be pitied. But once I'd found you, I vowed I'd never let you go again after that." He spoke as if reciting a vow.

"But what if I wasn't interested in you?" She always enjoyed what-iffing.

"But you were."

Yes, that was the truth.

He went on, "You knew deep inside your heart that we'd wind up together, didn't you?"

"Yes, I did." She nodded. "I didn't know when, though."

"Then there's no 'what if.' I planned to make you my wife someday, and nothing was going to get in my way. Not even you." He kissed her, and she snuggled close to him, wishing this ride could last forever, or at least till their wedding day.

****

With former mayor Grant and half of his cohorts doing prison time, Tammany's power fizzled. As a reward for all her hard work, Mayor Strong gave Vita a job as his assistant bookkeeper. When she gave notice at the bank, she promised Mr. Johnson, "I'll be back—as a customer."

****

Butchie came to get her on Sunday for dinner, and they walked to Mott Street in the cold but invigorating air. A gust of wind foretold winter's deep freeze.

"Roberto's not going to be there, is he?" she asked as they headed for the bakery to buy dessert. A few months ago they couldn't even look at pastries without a shop window between them.

"No. But Papa is cookin' somethin' up. He won't tell me what it is, but somethin's goin' on in that head of his." He held the door open for her, and they entered.

The buttery aroma of baked goods made her mouth water. She browsed the pink-and-green frosted cookies, the fat cream horns, the array of sugar-dusted pastries.

"Butchie, did Papa strike some kind of deal with that family, I mean, marrying me in exchange for something?"

"What deal could Papa have struck up?" Butchie knelt to view the pastries in the display case.

"That's what I can't figure out. They're a prosperous family. What would they want with us?" She fished some money from her purse.

"It's not what they want with us. It's what Roberto wants with you." He stood and looked at her.

"You really think he's in love with me?" She looked away from the pastry display and into his eyes.

"Well, he said it to Papa enough times. He come around on what he said was the first day he seen you."

"Where was that?" she asked.

"At your bank. He went in there one day, saw you, wanted to court you, so he come back and talked to Papa about it."

Her fist closed around her bank notes. "Why didn't he come up to me and ask me himself?"

"You were with McGlory," Butchie said. "He didn't wanna ask you then. So he asked another of the bank workers if they knew who you were. That's how he found where we live."

"Why didn't he ever tell me this?" She turned to the clerk and ordered a dozen cannoli.

"Papa wants you to think he's settin' you up,

arrangin' the marriage, the whole traditional bit, with a kid from a good family. But hey, sis, I guess if you weren't so pretty, Riccadonna wouldn't be after you at all. But don't tell him I told you this." He lowered his voice.

Pastry boxes in hand, they left the bakery. "Then why are you telling me this?"

"'Cause Papa wants you married to him by Christmas. I'm just warnin' you, now. You may just wanna do somethin' to—you know—get out of it." They walked past the doors and windows shut against the cold.

She gasped. "Christmas! That's just over a month away!"

"Yeah, and he's been talkin' to a priest. Father Boccicchio, at the Church of the Transfiguration." He kicked a can to the curb.

"He's *pazzo!*" She stopped dead in her tracks, releasing angry clouds of steam from her mouth. "I am not going to marry this *gavone.*"

"Look." Butchie stopped, clutched her elbow, and leaned against next door's stoop. "I'm tellin' you this for your own good. I know you want to marry the cop. Maybe you just better marry him. The sooner the better."

She couldn't believe this was her brother talking. "Why, Butchie? Why the sudden change of heart?"

"I understand what you're going through right now. I'm in love myself," he revealed, looking straight into her eyes. "With a girl Papa don't like."

"Why don't he like her?" she asked.

"She's Jewish."

Vita stood there, too stunned to even laugh. "You?

And a Jewish girl?"

"Yeah. Marsha Friedman. From Hester Street. And he's havin' fits over it, too. He don't want me with the *matsa Christa*, he says."

Vita's mouth gaped. "He called her a Christ killer right in front of her?"

"Nah, not in front of her. But in front of me, and that's just as bad. Rose seems to be on our side, too. She hocks Papa to leave you alone. To leave us alone, but specially you. She's become a real scooch." He snickered. "You'd think she wanted Roberto for herself, the way she hocks Papa. But she don't want Papa messin' with either of us."

"What do Marsha's parents say?" Vita asked.

He shrugged. "They like me. Their son married a Catholic girl. They don't care."

"Oh, Butchie." She looked up at the clear sky and inhaled the frigid air. "Let's just go up and have supper. It's getting cold out here. I'll think about all this later."

The brother and sister went inside together, and he stepped aside to let her go first.

She kissed Papa and gave him five dollars and the good news. "I'm now working for Mayor Strong as his assistant bookkeeper."

"Hey, he take good care a' you!" He stood and gave her a hug, a rare display of affection. She nearly dropped the pastries all over her tablecloth.

"What was that for?" she blurted out.

"I'm just happy today." He pinched her cheek, Italian style.

She glanced over at the wine jug, a good indication of just how happy he was. But it stood on the shelf.

Rosalia came in with a big box and placed it in

331

front of her. "We don't eat till you open this box, Vita." Her voice carried a note of warning. She nodded at the box, nudging Vita with her elbow. Papa placed a piece of paper in front of her.

Vita glanced at Butchie. He shrugged.

"Open it, Vita, open-a box!" Papa urged, and she pulled the top off.

Inside was all frills and lace and satin. A nightgown? She shuddered with embarrassment.

Rosalia reached across and pulled it out for her. Vita nearly fell face first onto the table. "It's your wedding dress, Vita."

Vita cast an unbelieving glare at Papa.

"For your wedding to Roberto," Rosalia added, this time barely above a whisper. Papa unfolded the piece of paper and shoved it in Vita's face. A marriage license. Before her eyes glazed over, she saw her name and Roberto Riccadonna's and a date, November 28th. It hit her like a sack of silver dollars.

Vita snatched it out of his hand and flung it to the floor. "I'll go to prison first! I'm not going to marry this *asino* on November twenty-eighth or any other time!"

She grabbed her bag and made a dash for the door. Butchie bolted after her. "No, Vita, stay—"

"Forget it, Butchie, I'm not gonna be treated like a slave!"

She ran down the stairs, Butchie at her heels. Papa shouted in Italian for her to come back.

Butchie grabbed her arm at the front door. "I didn't know he did this, Vita, this marriage license thing and the dress. He just don't want you marryin' the cop."

"He's pushing me away, Butchie, that's what he's doing! Married next Sunday? That's crazy!"

Their shoes clicked over the deserted sidewalk. She stopped at the corner to wait for a streetcar, pacing back and forth, expelling puffs of steam with each exasperated breath, peering down the street. "Come on, where is that thing?"

"Vita, whatever you do, he's gonna be mad, so it don't matter what you do," Butchie said.

"Oh, yes it does. I know what I have to do now." A streetcar finally pulled up. Butchie stood on the corner shaking his head, then trotted back up the street as she waved goodbye.

****

The next day couldn't have started out worse if she'd been cursed. The morning greeted her with a hailstorm. She tripped on the sidewalk and skinned her knee through her skirt. And when she got to her office, who did she find there but the last person in the world she wanted to see.

Roberto Riccadonna.

He swaggered up to her.

"Get away from me." She fled to her cubbyhole, her favorite pencils and coffee cup waiting for her like welcoming friends.

He followed her. "I'm working here as Mayor Strong's assistant secretary. I start today. Vita—we're getting married next Sunday. Didn't your father teach you anything about obedience?"

She sank into her chair, wanting to examine her scraped knee, but not daring to show more than an ankle in front of him. So she stared straight ahead, at the calendar. Next Sunday glared at her in red, like a warning written in blood. "Go away, Roberto. I am not marrying you next Sunday or any other day." Her voice rang out louder than she'd wanted.

"What do you plan to do, jump off the Brooklyn Bridge?" His voice reeked of smugness.

She sneered at him. "You don't know me at all." Only one man knew her that well. "Never mind what I'm planning. But I think you'd better leave right now, because I have work to do."

"Look, Vita." He leaned over. "That is no way to talk to me. You watch your mouth or you're going to have problems, you hear it?"

She stood, her eyes boring into those dirt-brown orbs of his. She focused on nothing else; she didn't even see his face. "Get out of here, Roberto, right now, or I'll have you kicked out."

A squeaking sound in the next cubicle told her someone was getting up to investigate. Another bookkeeper, shorter than Roberto, but looking more capable of protecting her, stuck his head into her cubicle. "Is this gentleman bothering you?"

"Yes, but he's no gentleman," she answered.

Roberto gave her a degrading once-over with a cocked brow, straightened his tie, and marched away. She slipped out and headed for the precinct.

Tom wasn't there, so she left him a note. *Meet me in the Breevort café after work. Can't wait to see you. V.*

She wanted him so badly, his absence jarred her like a punch in the gut. Tears froze on her cheeks as she descended the precinct steps. The wind made the garbage swirl like a flock of vultures.

She could avoid Roberto, but she couldn't avoid her future. She would have to find a way to make this work. No one was going to interfere with her and

Tom's future.

****

She nearly tore her skirt rushing to the Brevoort. "My escort will be here any minute," she told the waiter as she ordered a cup of coffee. Her eyes glued to the door, she saw him come in and rushed up to him, arms open. "I don't care who's staring." She gave him a tight embrace.

"Neither do I," he said as she led him to the table. Oh, how she longed to lose herself in his arms and feel his lips against hers.

They sat at the table, and this time she made sure their legs touched. "My father got me a marriage license and a wedding dress and wants me to marry Roberto Sunday—" Her words ran together so fast it was a wonder he understood any of it.

He grasped her hands and stopped them from shaking. "It doesn't matter what he wants. He can't make you do anything."

"But he's my father, Tom." She took a ragged breath. "I want to respect his wishes, yet I don't want him leading my life for me."

"Well, then, maybe you should compromise." A wily grin curled his lips.

"Compromise with Papa?" She shook her head. "He's never heard of the word."

"He wants you married, right?" Tom pressed on.

"Yeah, but Roberto Riccadonna is probably better suited to Rose than he is to me." Her voice dripped with bitterness.

Tom didn't argue. "We both know you're not going to marry Roberto—whatever his name is. So what if you saved him the trouble of finding you another husband and found your own, even sooner than Sunday?" He squeezed her hands.

"How much sooner?" she asked.

"How does tomorrow sound?" His grip on her hands tightened.

She trembled inside and out. "T—tomorrow?"

He nodded. "Why wait? No one can force you to marry anyone else if you're married to me. You can go to work and Roberto won't dare speak to you if you're a married woman. Besides—I'm so in love with you I can't wait another day. So say you'll marry me tomorrow." His eyes locked onto hers. "Please, darling."

His eyes glittered; his voice shook. The hand over hers trembled.

"Yes, I'll marry you tomorrow!" She didn't realize how loud she'd spoken till she saw a few amused heads turn in her direction. A few people clapped.

"We'd better make this a quick dinner—my last as a bachelor." She returned his excited grin as the waiter brought the menus.

"So about this wedding dress," he said as they walked down Fifth Avenue, "uh—you want to go get it?" He sounded embarrassed to bring this up.

"No. I'm not going back there." She cut the air with her hand. "I can't let Papa know this is happening. But there's one person I want at the wedding. If no one else, I want Jadwiga there."

"Of course. You don't mind if Father Callan marries us, do you? He baptized me. He's like part of the family."

"Father Callan?" she asked. "In City Hall?"

"We don't have to get married in City Hall. We can

go right to the chapel there in St. Andrew's."

"But I always wanted to get married in my church." She stopped him and looked into his eyes. "With my angel looking over me."

"Then why can't we?" They resumed walking. She linked her arm in his. "It'll be a simple ceremony, no mass or anything. We can do that at a later date if you really want to, with the wedding gown and the whole fairytale thing. In a nice cozy little corner of the church. Just me, you, and Jadwiga."

"Don't you want a best man to be there?" she asked.

"The only person I ever would have considered for a best man was Mike. And believe me—he'll be there."

****

That evening, as he walked her to Jadwiga's, she craved the taste and feel of her pipe, but she still hadn't told Tom that she smoked.

What she wanted just as badly was a glass of wine, and she didn't have to hide that from him.

Jadwiga threw the door open and hugged them as they bustled in, shivering in the cold. "Jadwiga, before you break out the vodka, we have something to tell you."

"You're getting married—finally!" She guessed, all right.

"I don't know why I even bothered telling you. I should have known you'd know, even without the crystal ball. You just know me too well." She wiggled out of her coat.

"I don't need no crystal ball. Look at your faces, and it ain't from the cold. You're downright rosy." She pinched Vita's cheek and poured them each a shot of vodka. "A toast! *Na zdrowie!*" She knocked hers back. "So do tell—what's the big date?"

"Tomorrow," Vita said.

"Tomorrow?" She blinked. "You've been planning all this and didn't tell me?"

"We didn't plan on anything." Tom lifted Vita's chin with his finger and sent her a kiss. "It was strictly spur of the moment. I took her completely by surprise."

"My father got the license and the wedding dress all ready for me to marry Roberto on Sunday," Vita explained. "So I'm going to beat him at his own game." She added in a bitter tone, "If you want to call it a game."

"Is that right?" Jadwiga sat at her table and poured another horn of vodka. "I think I'd better meet this Papa of yours. My word, he's a fast worker. They could use someone like him down at the post office." She held the glass to the light and took a nip. "So where you gonna live and all that?"

"One of the detectives has rooms on Ninth Street for rent," Tom said.

"Oh, dear God." Vita released a relieved breath. "I didn't even think of where we'd live. I've been so caught up in the shock of getting married."

"I can talk to him first thing tomorrow." He glanced at Vita and smiled. "Right after I get the train tickets for the wedding tour."

"Wedding tour!" Her jaw dropped. "Another thing I hadn't even thought of. Some bride I am! Um, where are we going?" She laughed out loud, realizing how ridiculous she sounded, asking her groom where they were going on their wedding tour.

"It's a surprise." His eyes twinkled. "But it's so

romantic, you'll never want to leave there."

"You can't take a train to Poland, Tom," Jadwiga joked, her eyes dancing over the rim of her glass.

"No, it's in New York. Upcountry. But that's all I'm saying." He made a buttoning gesture over his lips.

"The farthest I've ever been was Mayor Grant's country home. I can't imagine how heavenly it is farther up north." Vita closed her eyes and pictured a romantic mountain hideaway, just the two of them...

"So nobody in your family is attending?" Jadwiga broke her reverie, studying her with a steady eye, and when she gave Vita that look, she knew she'd better tell the truth.

"No. I'm not going to tell any of them. I'd really like to have Butchie there. I know he'd understand. But I just can't let Papa know." She shook her head. A sadness bordering on grief came over her, almost like she'd lost Papa. In a way, she had.

"Why?" Jadwiga asked. "You afraid he'll try to stop it or somethin'?"

"No." She rubbed her eyes, feeling a headache coming on. "He won't understand. No matter what I do, he won't understand. He's set on my marrying this *ciuccio*."

"So you're gonna come home and tell him you just got married." Jadwiga tapped her pipe on the table.

"I'm going to have to."

"Too bad." Jadwiga tightened her lips. "Nobody can talk sense into him? Even his wife?"

"I don't know what's going on with Rose." Vita fiddled with her glass. "She gave me a few funny looks and winks yesterday, but I'm still not sure I trust her."

Jadwiga looked at her watch and cast Vita a sly

glance. "Um—you two, I hate to break this up, but I got some planning to do myself. I gotta get your wedding present together."

"Oh, you don't have to get us anything," Vita protested. "Just your being there tomorrow is the only present I want."

"Yeah, that's what you think. Now git." She shooed them toward the door. "But first—Vita, what are you gonna wear?"

She shrugged. "One of my party dresses, I guess."

"You guess? You?" Jadwiga captured Vita's chin between her fingers. "Our future mayor, maybe president, getting married in an old party dress? Not a chance! I'll have something suitable for a beautiful bride ready for you tomorrow."

"No, I don't want you buying me a wedding dress." She held up her hands. "It would cost a fortune."

"Yeah, and I tell fortunes. So don't worry 'bout it. Now scram." She gave them a little shove. "What time and what church?"

"Meet me at noon at my boardinghouse," Vita answered. "We're not sure what time Father Callan will be available," she answered.

"Noon it is." She looked over at the groom. "Tom, I won't even ask you what you're gonna wear."

"No, and don't try to sew me anything." He gave her arm a playful poke. "Just concentrate on our bride."

****

Tom walked Vita back to her boardinghouse but refused to come in. He backed away, his fingers lingering on hers. "I'll never be able to leave."

"Well, I sure won't get a wink of sleep tonight." She sidled up to him with a goodnight kiss.

She was right. After a bath and a glass of warm milk, she tossed this way and that, kicked the blanket off her hot feet, and counted the seconds till the first sign of light. When she could lie there no longer, she got up in pitch blackness, washed, and packed a few things in her satchel. Then she went downstairs to light a lamp and make coffee. She curled up on the sofa, and when she woke again, it was seven-thirty. She ran up the stairs, tripping over her nightgown. Her heart pounded in anticipation. She tingled all over.

She dressed and paced the parlor like a caged lion, waiting for Jadwiga. Her friend bustled through the door twenty minutes later, loaded down with three department store boxes.

She dropped them on the sofa. "Open 'em. The small one first."

Like a kid at Christmas, Vita tore off the lid. A gorgeous bouquet of violets filled the box. She traced a fingertip over the delicate petals. "Oh, they're beautiful, but you shouldn't have!"

"But I did anyways." Jadwiga pointed to the next box. "Now shut up and open this one."

Vita tore the top off and feasted her eyes on a dainty pair of white shoes and stockings. Her mouth hung open. "I've never had anything like this in my life." She bent over and slipped them on her feet—a perfect fit.

Jadwiga pointed to the third and largest box. "I know you never had nothing like this, either."

Giddy with glee, Vita pulled the top off, shoved aside several layers of tissue paper and gasped. "I don't believe this!" It was the same dress Rosalia had brought out to her last Sunday. Could it be a copy? "What is this?" was all she could think of to say.

"Gift number three. Now—three and a half. Your family knows." She grinned.

Vita's hand flew to her mouth. "No! What did you do?"

"Gift number four. Come on in, Gift Number Four!" The front door opened and Butchie entered, wearing a perfectly fitted brown suit that looked tailor-made for him. She rushed up to him and threw her arms around him.

"Butchie—oh, dear God, Butchie, I didn't want you to know yet—I was afraid you'd come to the church and—"

"I'm good with it." He hugged her and ran his hand up and down her back. "I'm glad she told me. I wouldn't a missed my little sister's wedding. Why didn't you tell me? I'd've never tried to stop it."

"Butchie, I just—I really didn't want—does Papa know?" She swallowed hard.

He nodded, plucked a peppermint from a candy dish on the sideboard and popped it into his mouth. "Yeah. He knows."

"How did he take it?" Her words rushed out. "What'd he say?"

"He just nodded and kept on noddin'." Butchie bobbed his head in imitation of Papa's absentminded nodding.

"He didn't throw anything?"

"Nah." He chomped on the mint. "Ain't nothin' left to throw."

Vita held the gown up. She supposed Papa paid for it with the money she'd given him. "I thought it would be better if we just got married and didn't tell anyone till afterwards. I didn't mean to hurt anyone, Butchie, really. I just thought it was the best thing to do."

"Yeah, well, sometimes it ain't. But after what happened, you know—he just don't get real mad no more. It's hard to explain, but you just gotta see him every day. He changes every day, gets older." Butchie's eyes took on a faraway look.

"Well, I'm glad he's like that now. I'm sorry it took a tragedy like that. I'd love for him to be at the wedding." She sighed with longing.

Butchie popped another mint in his mouth. "Well, he ain't feelin' too good. Stop by after."

Still in shock that Jadwiga had actually done all this, Vita turned to her. "Thank you." She gave her friend a heartfelt hug. "How did Papa act toward you?"

"He was wonderful, Vita," she gushed. "He's one of the sweetest, kindest men I've ever met." Her eyes lit up, her lips spread in a dazzling smile.

Vita turned to Butchie, her eyes nearly crossing in puzzlement. "What came over him? That doesn't sound like Papa." But Butchie nodded.

"He told me he wants to see all of us after the wedding," Jadwiga said. "So I'm gonna make him some *chrusciki.* You think he'd like that, Butch?"

"What's crust—whatcha just said?" He scratched his head.

"It's fried dough with powdered sugar. Kinda like Polish cannoli."

"If it's fried, he'll like it," Vita assured her, still shaking her head in wonder. "Jadwiga, you must've made him swallow some kind of magic potion or something."

Vita turned to Butchie, running her hand over the

spotless soles of her new shoes. "When he said he wants to see us after the wedding, will my husband be included in the 'us'?"

He shrugged. "Bring him. See what he does. Papa will prob'ly offer him some wine."

"Tom doesn't drink wine," she informed him. "He's a whiskey man."

"Maybe he should learn to like it," Butchie said. "Just to get along."

"Yeah, we'll see who gets along." She gave him a dramatic eye roll.

Ted Roosevelt came by and gave her a congratulatory kiss on the hand. "I've been informed that Father Callan will be at the Church of the Transfiguration at two o'clock...and you're to pack a bag for a few days," he added with a flash of his big teeth.

Jadwiga hustled her upstairs. "Now to make you the most gorgeous bride this side of Italy!" She spread the gown on the bed and smoothed it down. "Go have a nice soak in the tub." She handed Vita a bottle of lavender-scented oil. "Present number five. It's not just for the bath, either."

Vita headed down to the bathtub, wondering what she meant by that.

****

When Vita came down the stairs in her bridal gown, Butchie held out his arm for her. Madame Branchard and the neighbors gathered around, oohing and aahing, reaching out to touch her gown.

A shiny white carriage waited at the curb. "Where'd this come from?" she asked as the driver took her hand to help her inside.

Jadwiga walked behind her, holding Vita's voluminous skirts so she wouldn't catch any dirt or droppings in them.

"The coach come prancin' up here 'bout ten minutes ago. The driver said the groom sent him." Butchie tossed her bag to the driver and climbed in, looking around the carriage's interior, running his hands over the velvet seat, the leather trim, the padded ceiling. "Hey, this is real highfalutin. Wonder who McGlory robbed it from?"

"I was going to direct that exact question at you," Vita quipped back as Jadwiga squeezed in next to them.

Gawking neighbors lined the curb as the bridal coach glided down the street toward the church. This day was hers—and she knew she'd never have another one like it as long as she lived.

She entered the church, inhaling sweet incense. Vita's eyes found her angel. There she was, smiling down at her, looking especially cheerful today. "Hello, Mama," Vita greeted her. "I love you."

Jadwiga led her up the side aisle. "Another surprise," she whispered.

They passed the empty pews, Vita's new heels clicking on the stone floor. She saw the outline of a man's head in the front pew, a lone stranger in the empty church. But as they got closer, a familiar form came into view. He stood and turned to face her. She rushed into his open arms, tears blurring her sight.

"Oh, Papa…"

He held her and rocked her for a long time, the beautiful, blue-eyed angel smiling down at them.

The priest approached the altar, Tom at his side, a black suit fitted to his powerful form. Her heart swelled at the sight of her groom. Her breath caught in her throat.

"Come. I give you away." Papa led her to the altar.

She linked her arm through his. As they stepped forward, through the gauzy mist of her veil, she gazed at the love of her life. She strode forward as if an invisible force drew her to him. Candles lined the altar, bathing the church in a golden glow. The sun streamed through the stained glass, throwing jeweled patterns on the flagstones beneath her feet. Tom spoke his vows as if reciting a prayer, his voice deep with emotion, his gaze so earnest, it burned right through to her soul. His impassioned eyes told her she was the most important person in his life. As he lifted her veil, she closed her eyes and tilted her chin to him. As he kissed her, the quiver of his lips melted her heart. When their gazes met for the first time as husband and wife, tears glimmered in his eyes.

It all happened too fast. He whisked her down the aisle, and in the vestibule, they all exchanged hugs, kisses, and tears.

"Come see me after you get back." Papa took Tom's hand and looked up at him. A smile brightened his face.

When her father's eyes met her husband's, a peace she'd never known washed over Vita.

Then she and her new husband climbed into the carriage, and it clip-clopped down the street.

"If we hurry, we'll just make the three-fifteen train." He glanced at his pocket watch.

"Now will you tell me where?" She clasped his arm, giddy with excitement.

"Niagara Falls," he answered.

She gasped. "That must have cost you a fortune! Oh, Tom, we didn't have to do something that extravagant—"

"Next year will be Paris. I promise." Her new husband looked down at her and planted a kiss on her lips.

"I don't think so. I won't want to leave our comfortable brownstone in the Village." She snuggled up to him, still unable to believe that she was now his wife.

"Well, I don't know about the year after that. You might be too busy running for Congress then."

They shared their very first laugh as Mr. and Mrs. Thomas McGlory.

Chapter Twenty-Nine

On their wedding night, she trembled with a delightful mix of trepidation and excitement. She tripped over her nightgown as she preened at the bathroom mirror, squirting perfume on her pulse points. Shaking, she emerged. He sat on the bed, waiting for his bride in the glow of two candles on the nightstands. She tingled in anticipation of the delights ahead as she approached her new husband, a mat of dark curly hair covering his chest. He leaned forward and held his arms out to her, and the sheet fell away and revealed his nakedness underneath. She looked away by instinct and heard him laugh. "It's all right, my darling. I'm your husband now."

She managed a laugh through her trembling as his arms enfolded her.

His lips met hers. He traced a finger down her neck and over each breast, through her chemise, in a slow circular motion. Dancing flames ignited deep within her.

She stroked his chest, her lips upon his earlobe, her tongue flicking it playfully, her breath matching his with increasing intensity.

"You're so beautiful, Vita. Oh, I want you," he whispered between kisses as his body covered hers. Her legs parted, bending to wrap around his waist as he moved to enter her. A sharp pain dissolved into a swirl of surrender as she took him into the depths of her soul.

He pulled back, and she whimpered, intense fire burning inside her. She arched her back, clinging to him. Her breath came in rapid gasps as they moved together, slowly at first, in the rhythm of a graceful piece of music.

A torrent of stars exploded throughout her body, from the tips of her breasts to the delicate flesh in her loins. He plunged into her and she rose to meet him, again and again, until they both cried out in unison, their bodies glistening in the candlelight, one body, one soul, of one earth, soaring to the pinnacles of one heaven.

She cried out again and again, "I love you, I love you..." Oh, how good it felt to say it, how right and natural it felt on her lips, like a luscious delicacy. He echoed her cries until they blended into the depths of the night that swept them into its star-strewn skies.

She woke to find him next to her, and a warm wave of desire shot through her, nestling between her thighs. "Tom, my Tom," she whispered into his ear.

Through his sleep he heard the soft voice, like feathers against his skin. He stirred and caressed her curves, her breasts, her parted thighs, her warm moistness ready for him. He pressed his hard body against her softness, his desire growing more sensitive to the feel of the velvety down as her legs closed around him, squeezing him gently. His mouth descended upon hers, his hands wound through her hair, his tongue probed as he crushed his body to hers. His tongue flicked over her neck, in and out of the shell of her ear. He nibbled her earlobes, murmuring, "You're so beautiful..."

His lips blazed a fiery trail down her neck and between her breasts. He flicked his tongue over the sensitive buds. Her legs wound around his back, pulling him down to her. She arched her hips to meet his as he teased and tormented, then pulled away slowly. He brushed wisps of hair off her cheek.

His mouth left hers and his lips, with agonizing tenderness, traced the hollow of her neck and once more sought her breasts. "Tom," she gasped, but he did not hurry, he did not rush to a shattering climax, prolonging the sweet agony for as long as possible. His hands moved lower to caress the sensitive tops of her thighs, exploring and stroking slowly and gently. She kissed his soft hair, clutching, grabbing it in bunches, feeling its wavy locks slip through her fingers. Her hand sought and grasped him, and she rasped, "Tom, make love to me now, please, I can't wait..." and she held him encircled in her hand, stroking him with her fingertips. He eased himself into her. She cried out again as explosions tore through her, leaving her longing for more. With a ragged moan, he unleashed his desire in a frenzy of passion that sent a galaxy of stars bursting behind her closed lids.

The fierce thrusting calmed into a placid rocking. They continued to move in a sedate rhythm. He grew soft inside her and let his lips linger on her neck, bringing her face to his, meeting her lips with soft kisses. Their mouths nibbled and pecked, in the extended and prolonged relaxation of afterglow.

They lay mingled with the dampness, the warm elixir of their passion. He stroked her hair and planted kisses on her nose, her lips, her cheeks, in a placid conclusion.

Side by side, their heartbeats slowed to a normal pace, arms and legs intertwined, as delicious sleep overtook their senses.

Chapter Thirty

The newlyweds stood at the threshold of their first home. Tom turned the key in the door and swung it open. But he didn't step aside to let her go in first. "Wait!" He held out his arm to block her.

"What?" She turned to him as he dropped their bags. In one swift movement, he swept her off her feet and gathered her into his arms. "Tom, what are you—"

"Carrying you over the threshold. This is something I've always dreamed of—carrying my new bride over the threshold." He stepped into the dark hallway and planted a warm kiss on her lips.

"How 'bout carrying me all the way up our new stairs, then? And straight into our new bedroom?" She nipped at his ear.

A door opened at the top of the stairs. Butchie came charging down.

"Butchie! My God!" Tom set her back on her feet and they stood there, the frozen trio, for an awkward moment.

She clasped her brother's arm. "What's wrong? Is it Papa?"

"Yeah. He's in the hospital. I've been waiting for you here—they told me down at the headquarters you'd be back on the five-fifteen—"

"What happened?" A cold fear gripped at her stomach.

"He's okay, but he kinda collapsed. It happened when Rose told him she wanted a divorce."

She gasped. No, it couldn't be. "She what?"

Butchie edged past them to the bottom of the stairs.

"What's happened here in only five days?" She clutched his arm. "They don't know what's wrong with him?"

"Ulcer or somethin'. Nothin' serious. I mean, he ain't gonna die. They said he'll be out in a coupla days."

"Now, what's with Rose?" she asked, not wanting to know.

He *tsk*'d and shook his head. "I always knew she was a no-good—" He looked at her and caught himself. "She left Papa the day after you got married. You notice she wasn't at the wedding."

"Sure, I noticed," she said. "But I didn't think anything of it. Tell you the truth, I was relieved she didn't show up."

"She ain't been in a church since—" He shrugged, hands raised. "Well, now, she snagged another man."

"Somehow that doesn't surprise me." A calmness slowed her pulse and her breathing. "We all know Rose hasn't been happy married to Papa. I can't presume to judge the woman."

"And you wanna know who she run off with?" A smile spread Butchie's lips.

"Not really." She shook her head. "I'd rather know if there's any wine in the house."

"I'll tell you anyways. I thought you could use a laugh." He paused for a beat. "Roberto Riccadonna."

Her jaw dropped. "Good God, what could he see in her? On second thought, what does she see in *him*?" So there she had her answer.

"They're poifect together." Butchie gave her a big satisfied grin. That added up like the sum at the end of a column of numbers. "I kinda thought they had a thing going but never saw them together alone. If I did, I woulda beat the crap outta him."

"I guess he won't be bothering you anymore." Tom looked at her and smiled. "Save *me* the trouble of beating the crap out of him."

Vita let out a long whistle. "Poor Papa. Poor her."

"Well, the hell with her." Butchie scowled. "And I wouldn't say poor Papa, either. He hasn't been crying into his wine jug."

"No, he won't mourn her loss. That's not Papa's style," Vita assured him.

Butchie waved his hand back and forth. "No, I mean he looks like he might have a cookie on the hook, too. Your friend Yadda-whatever-her-name-is. The Polack dame. She's been up there every day, bringing him wine, soup, some kinda sticky stuff he's been eatin' like a horse."

"Jadwiga?" She looked at Tom, and they exchanged smiles. "Somehow I have a feeling he's going to make a very speedy recovery."

****

She loved their cozy warm apartment, a fireplace in each room, plush rugs on the floors, and paintings of Italy and Ireland on the walls. That was all she wanted in these first blissful weeks of their marriage, but Tom wanted to give her more.

"I like it here right now, Tom," she assured him as they lay together on their soft, sagging but comfortable mattress.

"But I think we're just a wee bit crowded."

She knew what he meant. They'd let Papa move in with them, and he slept in their parlor. It was a small room off the kitchen, and their furniture took up most of the room—their new sofa, end tables, coffee table, and Tom's writing desk. But Papa insisted he liked it in there. Jadwiga kept him occupied, visiting every day, playing cards with him, and listening to all his stories about the old country. Vita saw a new sparkle in Papa's eyes. Now he had a lilt to his voice and an appetite she'd never seen. He was a changed man, all because of Jadwiga's devotion.

He even started getting along with Tom, who took the time to play cards with him in the evenings. But the newlyweds had virtually no privacy. So she spent all her spare time wondering how they could get more space.

Every lunchtime, she strolled around the Village, among the rows of brownstones, gazing at their iron gates, floor-to-ceiling windows, and doors with gleaming brass knockers. Strains of classical piano music drifted out into the street. She peeked into windows at the velveteen furniture, gilt-framed engravings on the walls. Chandeliers hung from the high ceilings. She pictured herself lounging in one of those windowseats, looking back out on the city that she'd grown to love.

One day she walked past an apartment building with a For Sale sign. She inquired and looked around. It was a six-family walk-up of sunny, roomy flats. Each apartment had its own bathroom—complete with a tub. It struck her as homier than anything she'd ever seen on Fifth Avenue.

So she went back to the New York Bank & Trust with Mr. Johnson's wedding gift stock certificate and Papa's wedding gift—two hundred dollars in all.

"Vita! Vita McGlory!" Mr. Johnson clasped her hands as she entered his office.

"Vita McGlory" sounded so wonderful to her, so much more natural than "Violet Greene."

"I see something in your eyes, and it's not just the spark of young love." He offered her a seat.

"Oh, it's that plus something more, Mr. Johnson." She didn't want to sit. "I told you I'd be a customer someday."

They went to see the building, and Mr. Johnson agreed to write her a loan if she had more collateral. She knew Tom owned the house his family lived in. She wondered how badly he really wanted to get out of those small rooms and into their first real home, the first of many. She'd soon find out.

****

"But, Vita, that's all we have. Taking out a lien against it for a rental property is risky. What if these tenants don't pay the rent and we have to give it back?"

She rolled her eyes with a *tsk.* "You think Mr. Johnson would do something like that to us?"

"No, but—who knows?" He paced the parlor.

"Tom, this is our future. This is where it begins. The rents will more than cover the expenses. I have it all figured out. You want to see?" She held up a ledger filled with columns of numbers.

He chuckled. "No. You're the wizard here. Me, I'm just a city cop who's trying to make captain the honest way." He hesitated and glanced around the room, his lips drawn downward. Then he heard Papa and Jadwiga's laughter floating through the wall. He nodded. "Yeah. Liam owes me two favors."

By the end of the week they owned two buildings. When Vita got home the next evening, Papa and Jadwiga were heading for the door, dressed and ready to go out.

"Where are you going?" Vita pulled off her woolen gloves and tossed them on the hall table.

"Furniture shopping." Papa showed her back into the kitchen and handed her an envelope. When she saw what it contained, her eyes almost popped out. Gold coins of all sizes—dozens of them.

"Where did you get these?" She almost feared the answer. She braced herself.

"Well, your former suitor Roberto was good for some-ting. He see you at the bank, the first time he see you, and he fall in love. Then he come to me—'Please, Signor Caputo, lemme court your daughter.' " He mimicked Roberto's high-pitched whine and made both her and Jadwiga laugh out loud. "I wanted you married, but at first I play it hard, to get an edge. So he begged, just what I wanted." He stopped to let out a chuckle. "I know my daughter's beautiful. He plead with me like he begging for bread. I know I have him. I ask him, 'How you gonna support my daughter?' He tell me his family have this music business, they rich, they live in a mansion on Gramercy Park, all a that. So I tell him, 'Put some money in her name. I wanna make sure my daughter is well provided for.' So he give me these coins. One tousand-a dollar."

"A thousand dollars? But Papa—I didn't marry him!" She pushed the envelope back at him. "You have to give it back."

357

"He no want it back. He come see me in the hospital, tell me he want me to keep it. Then he goes and takes Rose." He gave her a wily grin. "Prob'ly felt guilty. I think I make a good deal, no?"

"So you sold Rose."

"Ah, he can have her." He waved his hand. "But he no want the money, so I no give him back the money. You take it. Put me in the flat downstairs from you, I'm happy."

So the money was hers. But guilt didn't nag at her. It wasn't like she'd stolen it from Roberto. She knew Rosalia would make him happier than she ever could. Papa had gotten his money's worth in the long run.

Chapter Thirty-One

"Tom, guess what! I have fabulous news!" Vita burst into his office where he sat behind a mound of paperwork.

He sprang to his feet, grinning. "You're going to have a baby!"

She stopped dead in her tracks. "No." She shook her head. She could be—she wasn't sure if she was or not. But that wasn't her news. "No, it's something about me, not about us." The light went out of his eyes, and he gave her a quick nod. A pang of disappointment for him shot through her. Maybe she shouldn't have surprised him like this. Of course, what else would a newly married man think with his wife bursting in with what she called fabulous news? "I'm sorry, Tom."

He stood, walked around his desk, and draped his arm around her. "Hey, don't be sorry. It was—well, the way you looked, you were so happy and jumping up and down, it was the only thing I thought it could possibly be."

"I'm sorry I let you down. We both want babies, but I never would've guessed you'd thought I was coming here to tell you that. That's something I'll tell you at home, when we're alone," she promised him. "Committeeman Billings retired. So Mayor Strong assigned the post to me." She tried to keep the glee from her voice—after all, he'd hoped for a bundle of

359

joy from her, not another job.

"Committeewoman! Well, that really is fabulous, Vita." He gave her a warm, loving hug.

But she knew he'd have preferred the baby news. Well, not now. Not yet.

"Committeewoman. Yeah! I never thought to call it that. I don't think the city ever had one." She let out an excited squeal.

"I know they've never had one. That's wonderful, darling. I'm very proud of you." He gave her a lingering kiss.

"This is just the next rung in our climb, Tom."

"Just take one rung at a time." He gave her a warning look. "You still don't know how many rungs there are."

She squeezed his hands. "Celebration dinner and a show on the Rialto on your next night off?"

"Sure. Want to invite your father and Jadwiga along?"

"No, I think this should be just us," she said. "Then we can talk about that other thing."

"What other thing?" he asked.

She grinned. "What you thought I was going to announce when I came in here."

"Oh, that you were—" He cupped her cheek. "That's all right." He turned back to his desk, thumbing through some papers. "One rung at a time."

"Well, I thought maybe you'd want to do some more climbing tonight."

****

The following morning she couldn't choke down a piece of dry toast. He went to the drugstore and got some cola syrup, which she managed to get down.

She felt better by the time she got to her office. Then she took a quick swig of the cola syrup from the bottle.

On a hunch, she went to the doctor without telling anyone.

After he examined her, she skipped out of his office, dashed to the precinct and up to Tom, once again buried under paperwork.

"Vita!" He dropped his pen and stood, walking around his desk to her. "What are you doing here?"

"Aren't you going to ask me how I am?"

"Well, you look just fabulous to me." He wrapped his arms around her, warming her.

"I had a checkup."

"For the vomiting and sickness?" He raised her chin with his finger. "That was just nerves, wasn't it? You were fine all day yesterday."

"Well, sort of," she said, her tone coy, batting her eyelashes.

"You didn't tell me. So, what's wrong?" He pulled away to look into her eyes. "What'd the doctor say it was?"

She grinned. "Nothing serious."

"Whew, thank God."

"Just a baby," she added with an airy wave. "I planned to tell you at home, alone, sitting on your lap on the couch, but I couldn't wait."

"Oh, Vita!" He held her at arm's length, and she could have collapsed with laughter, he looked so stunned, his eyes like two marbles about to pop out of his head. "When? How?"

"Well, *when* I can answer, but *how*, you certainly don't need me to tell you!"

He hugged her close but released her as if she were made of hot coal. "No! I can't hug you too tight. I don't want to hurt him—er, her—"

"You won't hurt either of us, I promise." She leapt back into his embrace.

He walked her out and down the steps. The church bell struck one, just as it had that day when she'd first walked down these steps with him, wishing he were holding her arm like they were courting. Now he was.

"Where do you want to go? Anywhere, just name it, the Plaza, Delmonico's, you name it. New York is all yours, Committeewoman McGlory. Mrs. McGlory."

"Home, Tom. I just want to go home."

So he walked her home. Just like they were courting.

Epilogue

November 21, 1896

As I write this, I'm rocking our baby daughter Assunta—"Susan"—in her cradle. I still haven't given up on the dream of buying Vita—and now Susan—a large house, a fancy carriage, and servants. I want them to have all these things.

Vita doesn't agree with me. Working people won't identify with her if she's living on a lofty perch, in fancy clothes, looking unattainable, she says. She came from them and worked her way up but not out. But she allows me my indulgences. I have natty clothes, five watch fobs, and serve the best whiskey to our guests.

About two months ago, she dyed her hair a deep, rich auburn. A few women caught on when she went to some functions with the mayor. Now the neighborhood's women proudly flaunt their new red hair, known as Vita Red, nicknamed for her. Women by the dozens are dying their hair Vita Red with either cheap hennas or more expensive dyes, if they can afford it. Vita Red is all the rage around these parts.

Last night I woke and she wasn't there beside me. I glanced over at the baby asleep in her cradle. I went down to the parlor to find Vita at the desk, hard at work adding up columns of figures. A thin stream of smoke rose from something on the desk. She reached for it and put it to her lips. A small pipe.

"Vita," I called out.

She jumped, turning to me.

"Sorry to startle you. How, uh—" I pointed at the pipe. "How long have you been smoking?"

"Since I met Jadwiga," she answered in that straightforward way of hers.

"You didn't have to hide it from me."

"I just didn't think you'd care for a wife who smoked," she said.

"Well, I wish you wouldn't."

"Want to take a drag?" she asked me.

"No. Keep it. It's yours. You enjoy it? Do it."

She gave me that smile that I love so much. It lights up the entire room. "I don't smoke near the baby."

"When you coming to bed?" I approached her, trying to see what she was working on.

"When I finish this. Just figuring out how much we'll need for a few things I'd like to do. Buy another building, maybe a parking garage, you know, what we talked about."

I went to the desk and opened "my" drawer. She has "her" drawer. And we don't violate each other's privacy. I took something out and unfolded it before her. "Here's a surprise I've been saving for a special occasion. But these days every occasion is special."

"What's this?" she asked.

"A stock certificate."

"Coca-Cola? When did you buy this?"

"Remember that twenty-five dollars I opened that savings account with, when you found my wallet in the music hall and refused the reward?"

"Yeah? Yeah?" She nodded, leaning forward.

She's so impatient sometimes!

"Mr. Johnson told me about this company starting up. He was one of the initial investors. I said, 'What the heck?' and bought into it with that twenty-five dollars. The stock was selling for pennies a share. Now they're worth over five dollars a share."

"From pennies to five dollars?" Her eyes went wide. "And you bought twenty-five dollars' worth?"

"Well, twenty, actually. I had to pay for the marriage license and the wedding tour. But this is it, right before us. Our next rung."

"Oh, Tom!" She sprang up, her pen flew across the room, and we hugged.

"Let's take a stroll up Fifth Avenue tomorrow and see what looks good enough for us."

****

Christmas Day

We sat in our parlor surrounded by our families, presents all opened and dinner eaten. My father and hers were wary of one another at first, but we've managed to bring them together on holidays with food and drink. All kinds. Italian wine. Irish whiskey. Ravioli and colcannon. And a happy home, with one baby and someday many more. Now we had our past, our present, and our future, all within reach. Vita stood and poured us all a glass of Vita Red wine, made by her father in our new wine cellar.

I looked at my beautiful wife and daughter and said, "America will learn to love our children, just as we have grown to love her. Merry Christmas! Salut!"

"Cheers," said Vita as she held up her glass to me.

—From the 1895 journal of Tom McGlory, passed down to me, his great-granddaughter

Author's Note

Hugh J. Grant (1857-1910) was mayor of New York from 1889-1892. A native New Yorker, Grant attended Columbia University Law School. His father, the owner of several west side taverns, helped Grant make connections with many local Irish-American organizations that aided his political career. Backed by Tammany Hall, Grant became a New York Alderman in 1882, sheriff of New York in 1885, and finally mayor in 1889. Inaugurated at only 31 years of age, Grant is remembered as New York City's youngest mayor.

Thomas F. Gilroy (1840-1911) was mayor of New York between Grant and Strong, from 1893-1894. He did not run for reelection.

William Lafayette Strong (1827-1900) was mayor of New York from 1895-1897. A Republican, he was the last mayor before the Consolidation of the City of New York on January 1, 1898.

Theodore Roosevelt stayed out of the mayoral race at his wife's urging. He became president of the board of New York City Police Commissioners in 1895 and reformed the police force, one of the most corrupt in America.

In 1894, the year Vita met Tom, Theodore Roosevelt met Jacob Riis, the *Evening Sun* reporter. Riis had shown the world the terrible living conditions of immigrants with graphic photos in his 1890 book *How the Other Half Lives*, cited in my bibliography.

Bibliography

Barzini, Luigi, *The Italians*, New York, Bantam, 1965

Cateura, Linda, *Growing Up Italian*, New York, Wm Morrow, 1987

Child, Irving, *Italian or American? The Second Generation in Conflict*, New Haven, CT, Yale U Press, 1943

Cordasco, Francesco, *The Italian American Experience*, New York, Arno Press, 1975

DiStasi, Lawrence, *Dream Streets: The Big Book of Italian American Culture*, New York, Harper & Row, 1989

Gambino, Richard, *Blood of My Blood: The Dilemma of the Italian-Americans,* Ontario, Canada, Guernica Editions, 2000

Gardaphe, Fred, Ed., *Italian American Ways: Recipes and Traditions*, New York, Harper & Row, 1989

Giordano, Joseph, Ed., *The Italian American Catalog*, Garden City, NY, Doubleday, 1986

Iorizzo, Luciano & Salvatore Mondello, *The Italian Americans*, New York, Twayne Publishers, 1971

LaGumina, Salvatore John, *The Immigrants Speak: Italian Americans Tell Their Story*, New York, Ctr. for Immigration Studies, 1979

Mondello, Salvatore, *The Italian Immigrant in Urban America, 1880-1920*, Contemp. Periodical Press, NY, Arno Press, 1980

Musmanno, Michael, *The Story of the Italians in America*, Doubleday

Panella, Vincent, *The Other Side: Growing Up Italian in America*, Garden City, NY, Doubleday, 1979

Riis, Jacob, *How the Other Half Lives, Studies Among*

the Tenements of New York, Scribner's Books, 1890

Rolle, Andrew, *The American Italians: Their History & Culture*, Belmont, CA, Wadsworth Publishing, 1972

Tomasi, S.M., *Images: A Pictorial History of Italian Americans*, New York, Ctr. for Migration Studies, 1970

Tricarico, Donald, *The Italians of Greenwich Village*, New York, Ctr. for Immigration Studies, 1984

Novels:

D'Augostino, Guido, *Olives on the Apple Tree*

Fumento, Rocco, *Tree of Reflection*

Puzo, Mario, *The Fortunate Pilgrim*

A word about the author...

Diana Rubino's passion for history and travel has taken her to every locale of her stories, set in Medieval and Renaissance England, Egypt, the Mediterranean, colonial Virginia, New England, and New York. Her urban fantasy romance *Fakin' It* won a Top Pick award from *Romantic Times*. She is a member of Romance Writers of America, the Richard III Society, and the Aaron Burr Association.

She lives on Cape Cod with her husband Chris. In her spare time, Diana bicycles, golfs, plays her piano, and devours books of any genre.

Visit Diana at:
www.dianarubino.com,
www.DianaRubinoAuthor.blogspot.com,
https://www.facebook.com/DianaRubinoAuthor
and on Twitter *@DianaLRubino*.

~*~

**Other books in the New York Saga
at The Wild Rose Press, Inc.**
The End of Camelot (Book Three)
Bootleg Broadway (Book Two)

~*~

**Other books by Diana Rubino
available at The Wild Rose Press, Inc.**
Fakin' It
A Bloody Good Cruise
For Love and Loyalty